나는 나를 응원합니다

세상에 오직 하나밖에 없는 나

나는
나를

응원합니다

글 · 칭고 ─ 그림 · 대불스 ─ 음악 · 나나랜드

퍼블리온
Publion

이 책은 세 커뮤니티의 협업으로 만들었습니다.
글은 칭찬을 통한 가치 성장 '칭고(칭찬받는 고래)'가 담당했고,
각 글에 들어가는 이미지는 NFT 공부하는 '대불스'에서,
NFT 힐링 아트 '나나랜드'에서는 오로지 저희 책만을 위해
음원을 제작해주셨습니다.
내민 손 잡아주셔서 감사하다는 말씀과 더불어
함께 해서 무척 즐거웠다고 꼭 전하고 싶습니다.

이제 본격적으로 어른의 칭찬을 들여다볼 시간입니다.
저희의 글이 낮은 자존감으로 허우적대고 있는
누군가에게 작은 도움이 되길 희망합니다.

나를 칭찬하고, 서로를 칭찬하고,
모두를 칭찬하다

— 칭고

―――――

'다 큰 어른에게도 과연 칭찬이 필요할까?'

이런 질문과 함께 두근거리는 마음으로 커뮤니티 칭고(칭찬받는 고래)를 만들었습니다. 처음엔 반신반의했습니다. 어른이 되어간다는 것은 스스로 칭찬에 둔감진다는 뜻이기도 하니까요. 뭔가를 해낸다 한들 '이 정도는 누구나 다 하는 거 아니야?' 하고 그냥 넘어가기 일쑤입니다. 하지만 칭고 방에서는 그동안 당연시해온 일들을 하나하나 칭찬해보기로 했습니다. 아무리 작고 사사로운 일이라도 매일매일 무조건 나를 칭찬하기 시작했죠.

그럼…… 어떻게 됐을까요?

하루하루가 설렘의 연속이었습니다. 나를 향한 칭찬에 익숙해질수록 일상의 모든 행동이 칭찬받을 만한 일, 설레는 일로 바뀌어갔습니다. 그리고 마침내 그 설렘들이 긍정의 진동으로 변하더니 잠자던 나의 가능성마저 흔들어 깨웠죠. 그제야 확신을 얻었습니다. 어른에게도, 아니 어른이기에 더더욱 칭찬이 필요하다고.

육아와 가사에 지쳐 '나'를 잃어버린 사람들이 하나둘씩 칭고를 찾았습니다. 온갖 스트레스와 삶의 무게에 짓눌려 이미 번아웃 상태가 된 이들도 많았습니다. '나를 칭찬해보세요'라는 말에 처음엔 대부분 머뭇거렸지만, 점점 셀프 칭찬의 놀라운 힘에 눈 뜨기 시작했죠. 내가 나에게 하는 칭찬은 단순한 언어 전달을 넘어 다친 마음을 다독이고, 심지어 용기까지 불러일으켰습니다. 혼자가 아니라 여럿이 모여 나를, 너를, 그리고 우리 모두를 칭찬했더니 시너지 효과마저 생겨났습니다.

이 책에는 칭찬 하나만으로 삶의 변화를 경험한 11명의 이야기가 담겨 있습니다. 나 자신에게 그저 잘했다는 한마디를 해줬을 뿐인데, 그 작은 날갯짓이 어떻게 거센 바람이 되어 한 사람, 한 사람의 삶을 바꿔놓았는지에 관한 설렘의 기록입니다. 우리의 이야기가 여러분에게도 의미 있는 칭찬이 되기를 바랍니다. 그럼 우린 또 이렇게 말할 수 있을 테니까요.

　"우리, 참 잘했어요!"

쉽지만 깊고, 유쾌하면서도
즐거워야 한다

— 대불스

세상을 향한 호기심도, 낯선 분야에 대한 도전 의식도 충분하지만, 어디서부터 어떻게 시작해야 할지 몰라 망설이는 분들을 위해 NFT를 공부하는 커뮤니티 대불스(debulls. '대체 불가능한 스터디'의 약자)를 만들었습니다. 문어 함장과 우주 요원들이 함께 다양한 웹3 세상을 체험하는 여정이 대불스 커뮤니티의 메인 스토리입니다.

"어려운 것을 쉽게, 쉬운 것을 깊게, 깊은 것을 재밌게, 재밌는 것을 진지하게, 진지한 것을 유쾌하게, 그리고 유쾌한 것을 어디까지나 유쾌하게!"

이 말은 일본의 대표적인 극작가 이노우에 하사시의 좌

우명입니다. 그리고 이제는 저의 모토이기도 해서 현재 대불스 운영에도 그대로 적용되고 있습니다.

쉽지만 깊고, 유쾌하면서도 즐거워야 한다는 나름의 가치를 커뮤니티 첫날부터 담아내고 싶어 채팅방에 처음 모인 회원들과 함께 NFT 퀴즈와 게임을 진행하기도 했죠.

학습 자체의 실용성과 유익함도 물론 중요하지만, 저는 무엇보다 회원 개개인이 자신감을 끌어올릴 수 있도록 서로서로 칭찬하고 응원하는 '불스 하트' 문화에 더 큰 비중을 두고 싶습니다. 나를 향한 칭찬, 그리고 너와 우리를 향한 칭찬과 격려가 얼마나 큰 힘을 발휘하는지 깨달았기 때문입니다.

대불스를 관통하는 이 긍정의 에너지는 NFT를 발행하는 손길 하나하나에도 자신감을 실어주었고, 이제는 많은 분이 다양한 활동을 통해 정말 멋진 작품을 발표하면서 당당한 NFT 아티스트, 크리에이터로 성장하고 있습니다.

나 자신을 응원하고, 서로를 응원하는 것이 얼마나 소중하고 귀한 것인지 우리는 대불스 활동을 통해 절감했습니다. 그렇기에 이 책을 만드는 일에도 60여 명의 작가님과 함께 적극적으로 참여할 수 있었죠. 칭찬 에너지의 힘을 믿는 세 개의 커뮤니티가 한마음으로 기획한 이 프로젝트를 시작으로 더 큰 에너지를 좀 더 많은 분과 공유하고자 합니다. 대불스 커뮤니티 식으로 말하면, 여러분 모두에게 우리의 '불스 하트'를 전해드리고 싶습니다.

완벽보다 여유를, 일상에 안주하기보다
설레는 도전을 추구한다

– 나나랜드

"살아 있다는 것 자체가 용감한 행동이다."

로마의 철학자 세네카가 했던 말입니다. 그렇다면 우리는 모두 용감한 사람들입니다. 세네카는 또 이렇게 말했습니다.

"사람에게 가장 좋은 습관은 칭찬이다."

그래서 매일매일 '삶'이라는 용기를 발휘하고 있는 나를, 그리고 우리 모두를 칭찬합니다.

저는 실용음악 아카데미의 대표 겸 입시 레슨 튜터로 25년간 8천 명 넘는 학생들을 가르치며 살아왔습니다. 합격률 100%라는 목표치를 유지하기 위해 스스로 엄한 잣대를

세웠고, 감당하기 힘든 책임감과 압박감을 겪었습니다. 그러면서 가족의 현재와 미래까지도 책임져야 했습니다. 제 사전에 '쉼'이란 없었고, 내 삶에도 '나'는 없었습니다. 하루하루를 완전연소 하듯이 살아온 분들이라면 다 알다시피 사람이 평생 이렇게 살 수는 없겠지요. 저에게도 번아웃이 찾아왔고, 코로나를 시작으로 온갖 악재들이 겹치며 결국 공황장애에 시달리게 되었습니다.

좌절과 고통 속에서 제가 할 수 있는 일이라곤 지쳐 쓰러진 '나'와의 대면뿐이었습니다. 그리고 이렇게까지 살아낸 나를 어루만지기 시작했고, 그때부터 오직 나를 위한 그림, 나만을 위한 음악을 만들기 시작했습니다. 그 과정에서 만나게 된 NFT는 이전과는 전혀 다른 새로운 세상이었고, 사람과 사람이 연결된 성장 커뮤니티였습니다. 저는 이 새로운 세상에서 나를 만나고, 나를 알아가며 조금씩 내면의 숨겨진 창조성을 발견해나갔습니다. 어제보다 조금 더 나아진 나를 칭찬하는 일도 빼먹지 않았습니다.

이제 알 것 같습니다. 나를 칭찬하며 마음을 돌보는 시간이 결국 내 가족과 주변을 지키는 재충전의 시간이라는 것을. 그리고 가족과 주변 모두의 성장을 돕는 일이 결국 나의 성장이 되고 나를 돕는 일이라는 것도 알았습니다.

우리는 모두 연결되어 있고, 그 연결을 지속하는 힘은 바로 칭찬입니다. 세네카의 말처럼, 칭찬이란 참으로 멋진 습관입니다. 오늘을 살아가는 나를, 그리고 우리 모두를 칭찬합니다.

칭찬은 빛이다

1
칭찬은 빛이다

— 엘

무모한, 그래서 더 빛나는 도전

인생의 잿빛 나날들

내가 이 위기를 극복할 수 있을까?

지금까지 잘해왔어, 너 정말 대단해

사람은 누구나 저마다의 빛을 품고 있다

작은 성공, 그리고 빛나는 미래

15년 후, 찬란하고 따뜻하게 빛나는 나의 인터뷰

무모한,
그래서 더 빛나는 도전

―――

가난한 집 아이는 철이 일찍 든다지만, 그것도 사람 나름이 아닐까? 나는 고등학생이 될 때까지 세상이 온통 무지갯빛인 줄만 알던 철부지였으니까. 어릴 때 엄마와 주고받던 대화가 생각난다.

"내 딸은 밥 먹는 모습도 천사네."
"엄마, 난 천사가 아냐. 날개가 없잖아."
"엄마 눈엔 날개가 보여. 아주 예쁜 날개가."

늘 이런 식으로 대화를 나눈 것 같다.
솔직히 나는 밥보다 엄마의 칭찬을 더 많이 먹고 자랐다.

어릴 때부터 그렇게 동화 속 주인공처럼 살아가던 내게 어느 날 불쑥, 현실의 민낯이 보이기 시작했다.

맞아, 난 아빠가 없어.
엄마 혼자 온갖 궂은일을 해가며 나를 키워왔지.
옷 한 벌, 양말 한 켤레를 살 때조차 손이 떨리는 엄마.
그런 엄마가 너무 따뜻해서 세상이 얼마나 차가운지 몰랐던 거야. 뻔하도록 냉엄한 이 현실을 어쩌면 그렇게 모르고 커왔을까?

세상에서 가장 안락하고 행복한 나의 보금자리가 실은 남의 집이고, 우리는 단칸방 하나 소유할 수 없을 만큼 가난하다는 사실을 나는 너무 늦게 알아버렸다.
이게 다 엄마 탓이었다. 아니, 엄마 덕분이었다. 세상의 거센 바람이 행여 내게 불어닥칠까, 10년이 훨씬 넘는 세월을 엄마 혼자 온몸으로 막아온 것이다.

나는 비로소 가난이라는 실체를 인식하기 시작했다.
기댈 곳 하나 없는 싱글맘이 홀로 아이를 키워가며 가난을 벗어나기란 거의 불가능한 세상이란 것도 알았다. 그 즉

시 나에게 꿈이 생겼다. 집 하나 장만해서 엄마랑 알콩달콩
사는 꿈.

　내 머릿속에 하나의 작고 단단한 프레임이 형성되기 시
작한 것도 그때쯤이었다.

　'난 가난한 집 딸이야. 이 가난을 벗어나려면 집부터 사
야 해.'

　10대 후반의 꿈과 소망, 인생의 목표를 모조리 이 프레
임 안에 가둬버린 것이다. 작디작은 꿈, 그러나 벽돌처럼 단
단한 프레임이었다. 이후 고등학교를 졸업하고 대학 4년이
지나는 동안 '집을 사야 가난을 면한다'라는 프레임은 점점
굳어졌다.

　졸업 후 나는 교수님의 추천으로 어느 광고 회사에 취직
했다. 그때부터 일해서 번 돈의 일정 부분을 '집 살 돈'으로
꼬박꼬박 저축하며 열심히 뛰어다녔다. 그렇게 1년간 밑바
닥 막내 생활을 견뎌가던 어느 날, 광고 촬영 현장에서 너무
도 멋진 여성 CEO를 만났다. 그때 그분이 내게 건넨 한마디
가 아직도 기억에 생생하다.

"여자가 광고 바닥에서 살아남기란, 어지간히 특출나지 않고선 거의 불가능한 일이야. 너 스스로 잘할 수 있는 일을 찾아야 해."

　그 한마디가 마치 주술처럼 나를 휘감았다.

　나흘 뒤, 나는 엄청난 모험을 감행했다. 그동안 집을 사려고 알뜰살뜰 모아온 돈 천만 원과 엄마에게서 빌린 천만 원까지 총 2천만 원을 몽땅 쏟아부어 액세서리 사업을 시작한 것이다.

　그때가 스물네 살.

　참 무모한 시절이었고, 세상 무서운 줄 모르는 나이였다.

　사업 경험은커녕 고작 직장 생활 1년이 전부인 애송이가 어떻게 그런 과감한 도전을 시도할 수 있었을까?

　"이제야 내 딸이 날개를 활짝 펴는구나."

　그래, 암만 생각해봐도 엄마 때문인 것 같다.

　어릴 때부터 밤낮으로 가랑비처럼 칭찬 세례를 퍼부어 준 엄마 덕분에 나의 자존감과 용기는 이미 하늘에 닿을 만큼 자라 있었다. 그래, 까짓것, 해보는 거야.

인생의
잿빛 나날들

―――――

나는 밤잠을 아껴가며 일에 파묻혔다.

하루 24시간을 풀가동하느라 몸은 무척 고되었지만, 나 스스로 잘하는 일을 찾은 듯해 기뻤다. 그동안 몰랐던 능력이 내 안에 숨어 있었다는 것도 알았다. 나는 눈코 뜰 새 없이 일했고, 노력한 만큼 수입이 늘며 사업도 빠르게 성장해나갔다.

그로부터 2년 뒤, 나는 마침내 엄마와 함께 살아갈 보금자리를 장만할 수 있었다. 고등학생 때부터 품어온 꿈이 거짓말처럼 이루어진 것이다. 그와 동시에 '집 하나 장만하고 가난에서 벗어나보겠다'라는 나의 오랜 프레임도 깨졌다. 이제 더 큰 꿈을 꿀 시간이다.

행복했다. 인생의 가장 빛나는 나날이 이제 막 시작되는 기분이었다. 그러나 행복의 단맛은 그리 오래가지 않았다. 자신감 넘치게 뛰어다니던 내게 알 수 없는 병이 찾아온 것이다. 상체 일부 마비라는, 딱히 병명조차 없는 해괴한 병이었다.

나는 어쩔 수 없이 직원에게 잠시 사업을 맡기고 병원 치료를 받기 시작했다. 하루, 이틀, 사흘…… 시간은 속절없이 흘렀지만, 병은 좀처럼 낫지 않았다. 그렇게 1년의 절반이 훌쩍 지나가버렸다.

병도 병이지만, 하루하루 내 사업이 무너져내리는 모습을 지켜본다는 것 자체가 끔찍한 고통이었다.

'안 돼, 지켜야 해. 이렇게 포기할 순 없어.'

고심에 고심을 거듭한 끝에 나는 지인에게 동업을 제안하기에 이르렀다. 하지만 그것은, 다시 그때로 돌아갈 수만 있다면 절대로 하지 않았을 최악의 선택이었다. 그동안 이루어놓은 모든 것이 신기루처럼 사라져버리고 말았기 때문이다.

"내 딸, 엄마가 옆에 있는데 걱정할 게 뭐가 있어? 실패도 성공만큼 값진 경험이잖아. 괜찮아, 괜찮아."

엄마 말대로 나는 20대에 성공과 실패를 모두 경험한 셈이었다. 그러나 엄마의 격려와 응원에도 나는 30대 초반이 되도록 과거의 미련에서 헤어나지 못했다. 넘치던 자신감은 온데간데없이 사라지고 오히려 실패에 대한 두려움이 그 자리를 채웠다. 한때 무모하리만큼 과감했던, 그래서 더 빛났던 20대의 열정은 사라진 지 오래였다. 이후로도 나는 이런저런 사업에 도전했지만, 작은 시련에도 쉽게 포기하기를 반복했다.

그렇게 인생의 잿빛 시기가 지나고 서른네 살 무렵에 나는 결혼을 하고 새로운 삶을 시작했다.

"당신, 하고 싶은 게 뭐야?"
남편의 질문에 나는 망설임 없이 대답했다.

"나 쉬고 싶어."

"그럼 쉬어야지."

그동안 사업 실패와 재기를 위한 몸부림으로 지칠 대로 지쳐 있던 내게 남편은 꿀맛 같은 휴식을 선사했다. 그리고 얼마 지나지 않아 아이가 생겼다.

모든 부모에게 그렇듯이 아이는 하늘이 준 선물이었다.

하루하루 배 속에서 커가는 아이의 태동을 느끼며 나는 매일매일 축복 같은 나날을 보냈다. 그제야 나는 '사랑'이라는 단어의 진짜 의미를 알게 되었다. 사랑이란, 나 자신보다 더 귀한 존재를 품는다는 뜻이다. 내가 세상에 태어나 가장 잘한 일, 그것은 아이와의 만남이었다.

내가 이 위기를
극복할 수 있을까?

———

아들이 태어나 네 살이 될 때까지, 나는 엄마로서 더할 나위 없이 행복한 나날을 보냈다. 그러나 그해 10월, 난데없는 시련이 폭풍처럼 몰려왔다. 대출까지 받아 새로 이사한 집이 그만 경매로 넘어가는 바람에 집 안에 온통 빨간딱지가 붙고 말았다. 결혼해서 4년 동안 가족의 미래를 위해 차곡차곡 모아온 희망이 미처 손쓸 겨를도 없이 날아가버린 것이다.

사업에 실패한 남편이 꺼져가는 불씨를 되살리기 위해 필사적으로 몸부림치는 동안 나는 나대로 안정적인 수입원을 마련해야만 했다. 결국 홀로 계신 엄마에게 어린 아들을 맡기고 다시 생활 전선에 뛰어들 수밖에 없었다.

그 뒤로 나는 3년간 불안한 계약직과 아르바이트를 전전해가며 어떻게든 안정적인 직장을 구하기 위해 고군분투했다. 하지만 결혼 후 경력단절이라는 벽을 넘지 못해 번번이 퇴짜 당하기 일쑤였다. 참으로 살얼음판 같은 위태로운 나날이었다. 밤낮을 가리지 않고 죽기 살기로 살아내던 그 시절, 나는 눈물마저 다 말라버린 것 같았다.

'내가 이 위기를 극복할 수 있을까?'

숱한 절망과 불안 속에서 한 방울씩 희망을 쥐어짜며 살아가던 어느 날, 드디어 내게 일자리가 생겼다. 기적 같은 일이었다. 더구나 3년간의 경제적 불안에서 잠시나마 숨을 돌릴 수 있을 만큼 안정적인 직장이었다.

지금까지 잘해왔어
너 정말 대단해

———

　　부지런히 직장 생활을 이어가는 동안, 어느새 5년
이라는 시간이 훌쩍 지나가버렸다. 하루하루를 어떻게 보냈
는지 기억조차 나지 않을 만큼 정신없는 나날들이었다.

　　길을 걷다 문득 쇼윈도에 비친 내 모습을 보면 그저 평
범한 직장인의 모습 그 이상도 이하도 아니었다. 불안했던
시절, 매 순간 최선을 다해 살아내던 나는 어디로 갔을까?
시계추처럼 반복되는 일상에 파묻힌 나에게서 예전의 빛나
던 열정은 찾아볼 수 없었다. 그때의 모든 도전과 설렘을 현
재의 안정된 삶과 바꾸어버린 탓이었다.

　　그런 어느 날, 모처럼 방에서 쉬고 있자니 밖에서 아이

의 목소리가 들려왔다.

"아빠, 엄마는 항상 너무 힘들어 보여."

그 한마디가 비수처럼 내 가슴에 날아와 꽂혔다.

나 자신을 잃어버린 채 정신없이 살아오는 동안 내 몸은 이미 지칠 대로 지쳐 있었다. 병적인 피로가 쌓이고 쌓인 나머지 걸핏하면 몸 구석구석이 쑤시고 아팠다.

미디어에서는 너나 할 것 없이 '쉼'의 중요성을 강조했지만, 내겐 비현실적인 화두였다. 계속되는 경기 침체에 코로나까지 겹친 상황에서 안정적인 수입원을 포기할 수 없었기에 나는 더더욱 나 자신을 채찍질했다. 그런 나의 모습이 아이에게도 불안하게 비친 것이다.

이게 아닌데, 정말 이게 아닌데.

햇살 같은 내 아이 옆에서 나도 언제나 빛나고 싶었는데.

빛나는 나의 아이를 위해 더 나은 미래를 준비하는, 그런 엄마가 되어야 하는데.

하지만 간절한 마음과는 달리 내 건강은 좀처럼 나아지지 않았고, 심지어 우울증까지 더해져 점점 더 깊고 암울한 바닷속으로 가라앉았다.

나는 지푸라기라도 잡는 심정으로 새벽 예배에 참석하기 시작했다. 그리고 애타게 기도하고 또 기도했다.

그런 어느 날, 새벽 예배를 마치고 돌아오는 길에 문득 이런 생각이 들었다.

'나를 사랑하는 것에서부터 다시 시작해야 하지 않을까?'

나를 칭찬하고, 나를 인정하고, 나를 아끼는 일이야말로 나를 다시 빛나게 하는 여정의 시작이라는 생각이 든 것이다. 나는 오른손바닥으로 내 왼쪽 어깨를 톡톡 두드리며 속삭여보았다.

"괜찮아, 괜찮아. 지금까지 정말 잘해왔어. 너 정말 대단해."

갑자기 눈물이 주르륵 흘러내렸다.
잃어버린, 아니 오랫동안 외면해온 나를 처음처럼 다시 만나는 순간이었다.

1
엘

사람은 누구나
저마다의 빛을 품고 있다

———

다음 날 아침에도 나를 들여다보고 안아주고, 긍정의 말로 나를 칭찬해보았다.

"사랑해. 오늘은 어제보다 한 번 더 웃고, 기뻐하며 즐거운 날이 될 거야. 아직은 몸도 마음도 아프지만, 그래도 어제의 나보다 오늘의 내가 더 행복할 테니까."

어릴 때 엄마가 틈만 나면 내게 칭찬 세례를 퍼부어주던 일이 생각난다. 아무리 작고 사소한 행동에도 활짝 웃으며 속삭여준 그 칭찬의 말들을 자양분 삼아 나의 자존감이 쑥쑥 자라났겠지.

그때 엄마가 내게 해준 것처럼, 이제 나 스스로 나에게 칭찬의 말들을 속삭이며 상처받은 영혼을 어루만져주면 어떨까?

그렇게 나와의 소통과 셀프 칭찬으로 계속해서 나 자신을 치유해나갈 생각이었다. 하지만 이 비장한 각오조차 나약한 내 정신과 육체 탓에 작심삼일에 그치고 말았다. 나를 되찾는 일보다 더 급해 보이는 일상적 업무들에 발이 묶인 나머지 내면을 향한 여정이 어이없이 중단된 것이다.

나날이 닥쳐오는 현실의 풍랑 속에서 어떡하면 나의 여정을 지속해나갈 수 있을까? 고민에 고민을 거듭하던 어느 날, 한 가지 묘안이 떠올랐다.

'혼자보다 둘, 셋이 더 낫지 않을까? 여럿이 모여 함께 칭찬한다면 서로에게 더 큰 힘이 되지 않을까?'

살면서 지치고 상처받은 사람이 어디 나 하나뿐이겠는가. 나처럼 힘겨워하는 사람들이 한 공간에 모인다면 어떤 일이 벌어질까?

1
넬

생각이 여기까지 미치자 잠시도 가만있을 수가 없었다. 나는 곧장 행동에 돌입했다. 그리고 마침내 서로를 치유하고 아끼며 성장해갈 수 있는 커뮤니티를 하나 만들었다.

이름은 칭찬받는 고래.

지금은 줄여서 '칭고'라는 애칭으로 통하는 우리의 소중한 커뮤니티가 그렇게 탄생했다.

아무리 작고 사소한 것이라도 칭찬을 받는 순간 우리는 기분이 좋아진다. 각자가 자신을 사랑하는 칭찬 글을 올리고, 춤추는 고래처럼 더 큰 칭찬으로 서로를 응원하자는 뜻에서 시작한 커뮤니티인데 결과는 기대 이상이었다. 하루에 한 번 나를 들여다보고 사랑하는 시간이 하나둘 이어지면서 점점 서로를 칭찬하고 응원하는 글들이 소복소복 쌓여갔다. 그 소중한 글들이 우리에게 얼마나 큰 감동과 힘이 되어주었는지 모른다. 그 첫 만남을 나는 이렇게 기록해두었다.

Dear. 칭찬받을 당신들에게

하늘에 반짝이는 게 별인 줄 알았는데,
반짝이는 건 별이 아니라 우리의 꿈이었어요.

다른 상황에서도 꿈을 향한 우리의 마음이 모이는
따뜻한 칭찬으로 수놓았던 우리 모두를 칭찬해요

칭찬받는 고래를 시작하며
칭찬받을 당신들에게 드립니다.
칭찬받고 칭찬하는 좋은 사람들과 함께해 감사합니다.

From. 엘

커뮤니티를 만들어 칭찬 글을 공유하면서부터 신기한 일이 벌어지기 시작했다. 뭐랄까, 왠지 마음이 너그럽고 한결 여유로워진 느낌? 한마디로 내 주변의 소소한 일들에 새삼 감사한 마음이 들기 시작한 것이다. 솔직히 예전에는 좀처럼 느껴보지 못한 감정이었다. 마음공부에 관한 책이나 영상에서는 항상 감사하는 마음을 가져보라고 하지만, 감사하지도 않은데 억지로 감사한 마음을 갖는다는 게 어디 쉬운 일인가?

그런데 칭찬 커뮤니티를 만들어 글을 올리면서부터 마음 깊은 곳에서 감사한 마음이 샘물처럼 차올랐다.

막 사춘기에 접어든 아이가 뻔한 거짓말을 할 때도 예전에는 꽥꽥, 돌고래 소리를 내며 과민하게 반응했는데 이젠 달랐다. 즉각 반응하기 전에 먼저 아이의 마음부터 읽는 여유가 생긴 것이다. 무슨 말 못 할 이유가 있겠지. 그 이유가 뭘까? 내가 화를 내면 아이는 점점 더 거짓말 뒤에 숨으려고 하겠지? 그래, 지금은 화를 낼 때가 아니라 아이와 공감해야 할 때야……. 이런 식으로 전과는 사뭇 다른 자세를 취하자 아이도 조금씩 변하기 시작했다.

그동안 내 한 몸 건사하기조차 버거워하던 내가 이제는 주변을 찬찬히 둘러볼 수 있을 만큼 마음의 여유가 생겼다는 것, 그 자체만으로도 충분히 감사할 일이었다. 나는 무심코 지나치던 일상의 소소한 풍경에 감사했고, 서로의 응원과 칭찬 글 하나하나에 울고 웃으며 감사했다.

이웃에 누가 사는지도 모르고, 알려고도 하지 않는 이 답답하고 각박한 시대에 서로의 내밀한 마음을 이해하고 이어주며 상대방의 가치를 인정해주는 곳, 칭고는 바로 그런 곳이다. 희미해진, 혹은 꺼져가던 인생의 빛을 다시 켤 수 있다는 것이야말로 함께하는 커뮤니티의 힘이 아닐까.

칭찬은 칭찬에서 그치지 않고, 내 안에 잠들어 있던 가능성과 도전 욕구를 깨우기까지 했다. 지난 7년, 실패가 두려워 도전하지 못하던 시간 동안 나는 너무 작고 초라했다. 하지만 이제 모든 것이 달라지기 시작했다. 서로를 응원하고 칭찬하는 긍정 에너지가 나에게 도전할 힘을 주었고, 그 힘으로 나는 이모티콘 작가라는 새로운 도전을 감행할 수 있게 되었다.

세상을 향한 7년 만의 첫 도전은 나에게 첫 성공이라는 기쁨으로 돌아왔다. 누군가에게는 그리 어려운 일이 아닐지도 모르지만, 나에게는 도전한다는 것 자체가 기적 같은 일이었다. 그리고 그 성공으로 나는 더 많은 일, 더 다양한 분야에 도전할 수 있는 용기가 생겼다. 그래, 나는 꿈꾸는 모든 것에 도전할 수 있다.

사람은 누구나 저마다의 빛을 품고 있다.

준비하고 도전하는 자는 더욱 밝게 빛난다.

작은 성공,
그리고 빛나는 미래

———

　　일단 데뷔는 했어도 달랑 이모티콘 작가라는 타이틀만 한 줄 경력으로 더해졌을 뿐 아직은 세상으로 나아갈 정도는 아니었다. 열심히 작품을 구상하고 작업해서 세상에 내놓았지만, 사람들은 내 작품을 알지 못할뿐더러 내가 꿈꾸고 바라던 것들을 이모티콘에 녹여내는 것도 만만치 않았다.

　　내 안의 빛을 켜자마자 다시 깜빡거리며 꺼질 것 같은 상황이 이어졌다. 하지만 나는 앞으로 나아갈 것이다. 세상이 나라는 빛을 볼 수 있을 때까지. 아니, 내가 세상을 비추는 따뜻한 빛이 될 때까지 절대 꺼지지 않을 것이다. 나약했

1
엘

던 어제의 나, 세상을 피해 작디작은 골방에 나를 가두고 문을 닫아걸었던 나와는 이제 작별이다. 세상과 나의 이야기를 위한 준비를 이제 시작하려 한다.

나는 용기를 내어 〈꿈꾸는 계란 요정 윙윙이〉라는 캐릭터를 세상에 내놓았다. 나의 캐릭터가 많은 사람에게 미소와 힘이 되어주기를 바라는 마음이 간절했다. 하지만 내 안에서 익어가는 따뜻한 이야기들을 세상에 전하는 데 이모티콘만으로는 분명 한계가 있었다. 그래서 찾아낸 것이 바로 NFT(Non-Fungible Token)라는 새로운 세상이었다.

물론 NFT에서 내가 표현하고자 하는 것을 그려내기엔 아직 나의 실력이 부족한 게 사실이다. 괜찮다. 부족하면 채워넣으면 될 일이니까.

세상에 전하고 싶은 따뜻한 빛 이야기를 그려내기 위해 나는 매일매일 준비하고 세상과 소통해가며 처음부터 하나하나 채워나갈 것이다.

나는 매일 아침 5시에 일어나 칭고 커뮤니티의 어제 이야기를 다시 읽으며 오늘 몫의 힘을 얻는다. 그리고 칭찬받을 오늘의 소망과 목표를 세운다. 나의 소망은 언제나 소소하지만 확실하다.

    1. 하루가 다르게 성장하는 내 사랑하는 아이의 얼굴에 오늘도 웃음의 물결이 흘러들기를.

    2. 가족을 위해 오늘도 힘쓰고 애쓰며 굵은 땀을 흘릴 나의 남편이 건강하기를.

    3. 하루하루 기력이 떨어지시는 나의 엄마가 건강하시길.

    세 가지 소망이 나에게는 3년 준비의 출발이자 도착의 기도가 아닐까 생각해본다. 이 기도를 시작으로 나는 더 작은 준비를 시작한다. 부족한 그림과 글쓰기, 인터넷 강좌 듣기, '칭고'들의 콘텐츠 정리하기 등.

    이렇게 나는 소소하지만 따뜻한 나의 빛 이야기를 차곡차곡 쌓아나갔다.

15년 후,
찬란하고 따뜻하게 빛나는 나의 인터뷰

NFT 작품 소개 전문 채널의 진행자 '하오'님과의 인터뷰

진행자   안녕하세요, 여러분! 오늘은 세상에 따뜻한 빛을
           나누어주고 계시는 유명 작가 엘님을 모시고 이
           야기를 나누어보려고 합니다. 안녕하세요, 엘님!
           그동안 잘 지내셨어요?^^

엘   안녕하세요, 하오님! 오랜만에 뵈어요.^^ 하오님
           목소리는 여전히 봄날의 햇살처럼 아름답고 따뜻
           하네요.

진행자   감사합니다! 엘님의 인사말이 저를 행복하게 하

네요. 그럼 먼저 엘님께 첫 질문을 드리겠습니다. 엘님은 항상 따뜻한 빛이라는 주제로 많은 작품을 만들고 세상과 소통하고 계신데요. 먼저 첫 질문으로 작품들이 어떻게 세상에 나오게 되었는지 말씀해주시겠어요?

엘　　30대에 큰 실패를 경험한 뒤부터 저는 실패가 두려워 어떤 일이든 쉽게 포기하고 도망쳤어요. 그렇게 7년 정도 도망 다니다 우연한 기회에 김미경 학장님의 MKYU(열정대학교)에서 새로운 공부를 하게 되었죠. 열정대학교 학생들의 말 그대로 열정 가득한 모습이 저에게는 눈이 부실 정도였죠. 그때 저를 돌아보게 됐어요. 실패가 두려워 미리 포기하고 도망치던 제 모습을 반성하면서 작품을 만들게 되었어요.

진행자　과거에 쉽게 포기하고 도망치던 모습을 바꾸기란 쉽지 않으셨을 텐데, 어떤 계기로 그 부분을 극복하셨는지 말씀해주세요.

엘　　물론 처음부터 쉽게 변화할 수는 없었죠. 칭고 커뮤니티에서 칭고들 모두 제가 힘들 때마다, 그리고 작은 일이라도 성공할 때마다 큰 칭찬으로 저를 응원해주시고 앞으로 나아갈 수 있도록 힘을 주셨어요. 저에게 힘이 되어주신 나의 친구=칭고들 항상 고맙고, 사랑합니다. 그리고 실패에서 첫 성공으로 갈 수 있게 저를 이끌어주신 작가 '토부'님께도 감사하다는 말씀을 전하고 싶네요.

진행자 토부님이라면 〈퓨처스쿨〉 커뮤니티 운영진이자 이모티콘 NFT 작가로 유명하신 분 맞죠?

엘 네, 맞아요. 제가 7년 동안 실패하다 마지막 끈이라도 잡아보자는 심정으로 시작한 일에 성공할 수 있게 도와주신 분이에요.^^

진행자 7년 만의 도전 성공이라……, 말씀만 들어도 마음이 뭉클해지네요.^^ 그럼 두 번째 질문을 드릴게요. 작가님은 NFT 작가로 수많은 작품을 세상에 선보이셨고, 지금도 왕성히 활동 중이신데요. NFT 작가로 데뷔하실 때 어떤 계기나 에피소드가 있나요?

엘 음…… 15년 전만 해도 아직 NFT가 대중적이지 않았던 시기였어요. 그 당시에 전 이모티콘 작가로 막 데뷔했을 때였고, NFT 세상에 대해 잘 알지 못했죠. MKYU에서 열심히 공부하던 중 우연한 기회에 대불스(NFT 스터디 커뮤니티)를 알게 되었어요. 지금은 너무 유명한 곳이지만 그 당시만 해도 작은 커뮤니티였거든요. 전 그곳에서 많은 걸 배우며 작가의 꿈을 키울 수 있었어요. 대한민국의 평범한 아줌마가 작가로 다시 태어날 수 있게 해준 곳이죠.

진행자　작가님은 평범한 대한민국 아줌마셨군요.^^ 그럼 평범한 대한민국 아줌마 작가님께 마지막 질문 드릴게요.

엘　　　^^

진행자　작가님의 작품을 통해 사람들에게 꼭 전하고 싶으신 이야기가 있나요?

엘　　　네. 제 모든 작품에는 나나랜드(NFT 힐링아트 커뮤니티)의 아름다운 음악과 너무나 예쁜 빛나비가 그려져 있어요. 빛은 모일수록 더 밝고 큰 빛을 비

추잖아요. 그 빛들이 모든 사람의 마음속에 아름
다운 음악과 함께 따스하게 스며들면 좋겠어요.

진행자　　말씀 감사합니다. 작가님의 작품을 보면서 여러분
의 마음속에 따뜻한 빛나비가 스며들기를 바라
며 오늘 이야기를 마치겠습니다. 감사합니다!

사람은 누구에게나 따뜻한 빛이 있다.
빛은 모일수록 더 밝은 빛을 발한다.
그 밝은 빛들이 모여
세상의 모든 이들에게 비추어
꿈과 희망의 시작이 되기를……

© 시지나

2

칭찬은 확신이다

— 영글음

BGM MUSIC NFT #15
혼들린 마음이 자신만의 길을 찾아가는 선율로
내면의 확신을 상징합니다.

있어 보이는 길

내가 왜 그랬을까?

뭘 했다고 칭찬을 받아?

그런 걸 다 칭찬한다고?

혼자가 아니었기에

셀프 칭찬을 시작하는 당신에게

있어 보이는
길

A로 갈까, B로 갈까?

나는 뭔가를 선택할 때마다 한참을 망설였다. 가보지 않은 미래는 아무도 알 수 없기에 각각의 길을 갔을 때 펼쳐지는 풍경을 한껏 상상하며 어느 쪽을 선택할지 시간과 공을 많이 들였다. 그러다 겨우 마음을 정했을 때 그 선택 기준은 이것이다.

'남들 눈에 어떻게 보일까?'

솔직히 남들 눈에 멋지게 보이고 싶었다. 프루스트의 시 〈가지 않은 길〉에 나오는 두 갈래 길이 내 앞에 펼쳐졌다면,

나는 뭔가 '있어 보이는 길'을 선택했을 것이다. 알맹이보다 겉껍질이 중요했기에 최종 판단 기준 역시 내가 아닌 타인의 시선이었다.

감성적이고 수학을 싫어하는 내가 고등학교 때 이과를 선택한 것만 봐도 그렇다. 이과야 문과야? 누군가 물었을 때 당당히 이과라고 말하는 게 멋있어 보여서……. 그게 다였다. 당시만 해도 여고에서 공부 잘하는 애들은 다 이과를 선택했으니 나도 그 안에 끼어들면 우등생처럼 보이지 않을까, 그런 얄팍한 기대도 있었으리라.

어릴 때부터 삶의 태도가 이렇게 굳어지면 좀처럼 쉽게 바뀌지 않는다. 대학 졸업 후 나는 전공을 살려 영양사로서 사회에 첫발을 내디뎠다. 그런데 어느 날 가까운 친구가 기자로 활동하고 있다는 소리를 듣자마자 귀가 솔깃해졌다. 기자? 기사 쓰는 사람? 되게 멋있어 보였다. 내가 어떻게 했을까? 얼마 후 회사를 그만두고 잡지사에 들어가 기자가 되었다.

늘 이런 식이었다. 어찌어찌하여 그 이후로 글쓰기에 흥미를 느껴 사보 기자, 홍보팀 직원으로 변신하긴 했지만, 웬

만한 선택의 상황 앞에서는 매번 폼생폼사만 쫓다가 엉뚱한 곳에서 헤매기 일쑤였다.

그런 경험들이 쌓이다 보니 어느 순간부터 내가 선택하고 결정한 일에 대해 점점 확신이 흐려지기 시작했다. 굳은 결심을 하고 결단을 내려도 막상 가보면 생각하던 것과 완전 딴판인 경우가 많았기 때문이다.

'어, 이 길이 아닌 것 같은데? 돌아갈까? 아니야, 너무 멀리 와버렸잖아.'

매번 이런 경우가 무한 반복되었다. 차라리 누군가가 "너는 이 길로 가거라!" 하고 명령을 내려주면 좋겠다는 생각마저 들기도 했다. 그저 따르기만 하면 되니까. 나 같은 사람에겐 정답이 정해져 있어 달달 외우기만 하면 되는 주입식 교육이 어쩐지 딱 맞아 보였다. 다만 삶에는 정답 따위가 없다는 게 문제라면 문제였다.

내가 왜
그랬을까?

우리 집 거실에는 3인용 갈색 가죽 소파가 있다. 구매한 지 6년이 되었는데도 볼 때마다 후회와 안타까움이 스멀스멀 올라온다. 이 소파는 난생처음 내 돈 주고 직접 구매한 것이다. 결혼한 지 13년 만의 일이었다. 한국의 신혼집은 거실 없이 주방만 있었기에 소파 놓을 공간이 없었고, 미국 유학 시절에는 이전 세입자가 남기고 간 것을 헐값에 사서 썼다. 그러다가 영국에서 내 집 마련을 하고 나자 드디어 새 소파를 살 기회가 온 것이다. 얼마나 흥분되고 설레던지!

나는 당시 유행하던 북유럽 스타일로 집을 꾸미고 싶었다. 3인용 소파 하나 들여놓는 것이지만, 우리 돈으로 백만

원 넘게 드는 일이라 신중하게 고르고 싶었다. 게다가 이런 가구는 한 번 사면 웬만해서는 바꿀 일이 없을 테니 선택을 잘해야 했다. 그런데 그때도 마음속에 이런 생각이 자리 잡고 있었다.

'친구들이 우리 집에 와보고 감탄할 만한 소파를 고르고 싶다! 다들 나의 인테리어 감각을 칭찬해주면 좋겠어!'

매일 온라인 숍에 올라온 소파를 보고 또 봤다. 오프라인 매장에도 여러 번 찾아가 색깔과 스타일, 가격을 비교했다. 그렇게 한 달 정도가 흘렀을까? 드디어 내가 원하는 색과 스타일이 정해졌다. 팔걸이 부분이 폭신하고, 앉았을 때 목까지 받쳐줄 수 있는 쿠션이 있어야 하며 원목 다리가 달린 회색 천 재질의 소파. 하지만 이런 소파가 온·오프라인 매장마다 여러 종류라서 어떤 걸 사야 할지 선택하기가 어려웠다. 남편은 알아서 하라며 결정권을 내게 넘겼지만, 이따금 "아이가 있는 집에 천보다는 가죽 소파가 낫지 않나?"라는 말을 슬쩍슬쩍 흘리기도 했다.

문제의 날이 다가왔다. 온 가족이 마트에 들렀다가 나의 권유로 바로 옆에 있는 소파 매장에 들어갔다. 2층짜리 커다란 매장을 보는 순간, 나는 감격에 겨워 몇 바퀴를 맴돌았다. 그때 남편과 딸들이 밝은 갈색 가죽 소파에 앉아보고는 그걸 사면 어떻겠냐고 했다. 회색이 아닌데? 다리도 없는데? 촌스러운데?

아이들은 소파에 앉아 떠날 줄 몰랐다. 남편이 가죽 소파의 장점을 읊어대기 시작했다. 자꾸 나에게 앉아보라고 해서 마지못해 앉았더니…… 편하긴 했다. 언제 왔는지 매장 직원이 우리 옆에 착 달라붙어 "이 소파, 지금 할인 행사 중이에요. 인기 많은 베스트셀러랍니다" 하고 작업을 걸어오기 시작했다. 어머, 안 되는데…… 내가 사고 싶은 건 이게 아닌데……. 아무래도 그날은 귀신에 홀린 게 분명했다. 한 달 이상 고민해서 점찍어둔 나의 스타일이 따로 있는데, 그냥 분위기에 떠밀리고 순간의 멘붕에 흔들린 나머지 "예스!"를 외치고 만 것이다. 정신을 차렸을 때는 이미 비용을 지불하고 배송 날짜까지 확정한 상태였다.

집에 돌아온 뒤부터 마음에 폭풍이 몰아쳤다. '내가 미쳤구나. 이를 어쩌지? 지금이라도 취소할까? 아니야, 그래도 들여놓으면 예쁘지 않을까?' 고민에 고민을 거듭하느라 시간은 흘러버렸고, 결국 소파가 도착하고야 말았다. 쿠션감은 좋았지만 역시 디자인과 색깔이 마음에 들지 않았다. '아, 싫어. 이게 아닌데.'

매일매일 후회했다. 화도 났다. 그런 소파를 사자고 한 딸들에게, 남편에게 화가 났다. 하지만 가장 큰 화풀이 대상은 바로 나였다. 내가 딱 잘라 안 산다고 했으면 남편도 그러자고 했을 것이다. 그런데도 마음에 없는 선택을 해버린 나에게 너무 화가 나고 신경질이 났다.

'그날 나는 왜 마음에도 없는 결정을 했을까?'

선택을 어려워하는 사람들의 내면에는 사실 자기 결정에 대한 책임을 두려워하는 마음이 들어 있다고 한다. 특히 나 같은 사람들에겐 그 책임이 온전히 자신의 몫이라는 사실이 무척 부담스러운 일이다. 이미 북유럽식 소파를 점찍어둔 상태에서 갑자기 튀어나온 갈색 가죽 소파는 분명 나의 답이 아니었다. 그렇다고 원래의 답을 고를 용기도 없어 가족들의 손에 선택권을 맡겨놓고서는 결과물이 마음에 들

지 않는다고 징징거린 것이다. 애도 아니고 이게 뭘가. 도대
체 내 선택에 확신을 가질 방법은 없는 것일까?

뭘 했다고
칭찬을 받아?

처음 셀프 칭찬이라는 말을 듣게 된 건 온라인의 한 커뮤니티에서였다. 자기 자신을 칭찬하자는 말부터 낯설었다. 나를 칭찬하라고?

성인이 되고 두 아이의 엄마가 될 때까지 내가 읽은 칭찬 관련 이야기는 육아서가 전부였다. 자녀에게 칭찬을 많이 해주면 자존감과 용기가 쑥쑥 자란다는 이야기들……. 물론 어느 정도 공감했기에 두 딸에게 '잘한다, 잘한다' 하며 조금은 과장되게 칭찬을 보내주었다. 그런데 '나'를 칭찬하라고? 잘한 것보다 잘못한 게 더 많아서 괴로워 죽겠는데, 이 무슨 해괴망측하고 낯 간지러운 시추에이션이란 말인가.

커뮤니티의 이름은 〈칭찬받는 고래〉였다. 이 방을 이끌어가는 분과의 인연으로 우연히 참석하긴 했지만, 솔직히 처음 든 생각은 '세상엔 별의별 사람들이 다 있구나'였다. 그때까지만 해도 칭찬이란 남이 나한테, 내가 남한테 하는 것이지 내가 나에게 해줄 수 있는 거라고는 한 번도 생각해본 적이 없었다.

하루에 하나씩 셀프 칭찬 글을 올리는 것이 커뮤니티의 규칙이자 챌린지였다. '그래도 인연이 닿은 곳인데 맘 잡고 해봐? 까짓거 나름 얼굴도 두꺼운 편인데 각 잡을 필요도 없이 금세 쓸 수 있지 않을까?'

이 생각이 깨지는 데는 하루도 채 걸리지 않았다. 막상 나 자신을 칭찬하자니 칭찬할 내용이 없었다. 초등학교 때 받은 "참 잘했어요" 도장은 숙제를 잘했을 때 받는 것이었다. 선생님이나 주변 어른에게 칭찬받는 것도 대개는 뭔가를 잘했을 때였다. 가령 시험 점수가 좋거나 피아노 연습을 열심히 했거나 동생에게 양보했을 때처럼. 어릴 때부터 이렇게 '칭찬받을 자격이 주어져야만' 칭찬을 받아온 터라 밑도 끝도 없이 나를 칭찬하라니 막연해질 수밖에.

가벼운 마음으로 책상 앞에 앉았다가 한 줄도 못 쓰고

멍해져 있다 보니 문득 이런 생각이 들었다.

'내가 칭찬받을 자격이 있나?'
'내가 뭘 했다고 칭찬을 받아?'

그런 걸 다
칭찬한다고?

―――――

그런데 세상에는 별의별 사람들이 다 있구나 하는 생각의 실체가 정말로 글이 되어 올라왔다. 커뮤니티에 있는 다른 분들이 적극적으로 칭찬 글을 올리기 시작했으니 말이다. 이들의 칭찬은 소소하게 흘러가는 일상과 맞닿아 있었다. 아이를 혼내지 않고 화를 참았다며 칭찬하고, 라면을 잘 끓였다고 칭찬하고, 오늘 하루를 잘 보냈다고 칭찬하고, 뭐 이런 식이었다. 세상에, 그런 걸 칭찬한다고?

더 놀라운 일이 벌어졌다. 시간이 흐르자 저마다 자신의 변화된 모습을 올리기 시작한 것이다. 그저 자신에게 칭찬 한마디 해줬을 뿐인데 자존감이 올라갔다, 일상이 즐거워졌다, 용기가 생겼다, 화를 내야 할 일에도 마음을 가라앉혔다……. 아주 살짝 바뀐 소소한 변화에도 다들 기뻐하며 감사의 글을 올렸다. 그 과정을 마치 자기 일처럼 공감하며 함께 나누는 이들을 보니 내 마음도 슬슬 움직이기 시작했다.

칭찬은 대개 말로 전달된다. 나에게 "잘했다"라고 말해주면 되는 것이다. '내가 잘한 게 뭐지?' 이런 질문은 잠시 제쳐둬야 한다. '잘했다'라는 말이 꼭 멋지고 바람직한 일을 했을 때만 들을 수 있는 말일까? 뭐든지 내가 내린 선택에 대해서 칭찬해보면 어떨까?

나는 늘 확신 없이 우왕좌왕하던 선택에 "잘했다"를 붙여 보았다. 내가 선택한 것을 스스로 칭찬하자 결정에 확신이 생기기 시작했다. 확신이 들자 자신감도 생겨났다. 늘 이 길이 맞을까, 저 길이 맞을까 고민하느라 갈팡질팡하며 헛되이 보낸 시간, 특히 후회하는 시간이 눈에 띄게 줄어들었다.

뭔가를 꼭 잘해야만 칭찬이 성립되는 건 아니었다.

.

"너 오늘 책을 읽을까 말까 하다가 낮잠 잤지? 잘했어. 쉼도 필요하잖아."

"머리 볼륨매직 파마한 거 잘했어. 좀 안 어울리지만, 지금 아니면 또 언제 해보겠어?"

"집 청소 안 했지? 잘했어. 애들 시키자. 잘했어. 잘했어. 우쭈쭈, 우쭈쭈."

이것은 자기 합리화와는 다른 차원이다. 어차피 벌어진 일, 후회하고 자책하느라 시간 낭비하는 대신 칭찬을 통해 마음의 항로를 긍정적인 방향으로 틀자는 얘기다. 더 나은 선택지가 있었을지도 모르지만, 그때의 결정이 최선이었음을 믿고, 새로운 계획을 세워 다시 앞으로 나아가자는 얘기다.

혼자가
아니었기에

___

혼자서는 못 했을 것이다.

처음에 그 어렵던 셀프 칭찬을 계속해나갈 수 있었던 가장 큰 원동력은 커뮤니티에 있다. 얼떨결에 시작했지만 커뮤니티의 '칭고'들이 자신의 하루를 보듬고 칭찬하는 모습을 보니 나도 할 수 있지 않을까 하는 용기가 생겨난 것이다. 게다가 칭찬이라는 키워드로 뭉친 사람들답게 서로의 행동을 자기 일처럼 칭찬하며 용기를 북돋아주는 그 모습만 해도 다른 모임에서는 쉽게 볼 수 없는 광경이었다.

내가 이 나이에 어디서 이런 칭찬을 들을 수 있을까?

〈칭찬받는 고래〉 방에서는 얼마든지 들을 수 있었다. 하루를 마감하는 시간이 점점 따뜻해지기 시작했다. 다른 분들은 어떤 칭찬으로 오늘을 채웠을까 궁금해지기도 했다. 바쁠 때는 건너뛸 때도 있지만, 언제든 들어가 인사를 남겨도 반갑게 맞이하고 칭찬으로 화답해주는 커뮤니티 친구들이 있다는 사실에 푸근한 소속감마저 생겼다.

여러 활동을 하다 보니 다양한 모임이 생겨났지만, 〈칭찬하는 고래〉 방은 여전히 포근하고 편안하다. 당연히 모두의 마음속에 칭찬이라는 공통분모가 깔려 있기 때문일 것이다.

나를 칭찬하고 너를 칭찬하고, 모두를 칭찬하는 동안 우리에게는 보이지 않는 에너지, 이를테면 그동안 잊고 살았던 자신감이나 자아, 자존감 같은 게 생겨나고 있었다. 혼자였다면 얻지 못했을 이 에너지야말로 칭찬 커뮤니티의 진정한 힘이 아닐까.

셀프 칭찬을 시작하는
당신에게

———

'어떻게 사소한 칭찬 한마디에 사람이 변할 수 있을까?'

커뮤니티 활동을 하는 동안 참 많이 생각해봤다. 그리고 어느 순간, 이것이 단지 칭찬하고 안 하고의 문제가 아니라는 사실을 깨달았다. 〈칭찬받는 고래〉에 모인 사람들은 칭찬 몇 마디 올리는 챌린지에 동참하려고 모인 사람이 아니다. 자신의 삶을 좀 더 나은 쪽으로 이끌고 싶은 사람들, 삶에 치여 잃어버린 자기 자신을 되찾으려는 사람들이다.

나도 마찬가지다. 마흔이 넘었는데도 막상 계획한 대로 펼쳐지지 않는 나의 인생을 조금이나마 바람직하게 만들고 싫어서 문을 두드린 것이다. 우리는 이미 도전하고 변화하려는 마음이 절실한 상태였고, 여러 방법 중에 셀프 칭찬이라는 길을 선택한 것이다. 다시 말해 '칭찬만'이 우리를 바꾼 게 아니라 '칭찬도' 큰 역할을 했다는 뜻이다.

우리는 제각기 다른 커뮤니티에서 책을 나눠 읽고 강의도 들으며 좁았던 자신의 세계를 뚫고 나와 넓은 세상을 만난다. 힘들고 어려운 과정을 잘 헤쳐나가면 또 그것을 자기 칭찬으로 만들어 커뮤니티에 공유한다. 그러면 서로 자극을 받고 잘했다고 칭찬도 하면서 기운을 북돋아준다. 이러한 칭찬의 선순환 시스템이 나의 하루를 더욱 값지고 알차게 만들어주는 것이다. 이렇듯 나도 모르는 새에 1cm씩 높아진 자존감으로 점점 높은 곳을 향해 꿈을 업그레이드해 달려가고 있다.

처음 칭찬을 시작했을 때는 나 자신에게 하는 칭찬조차 남에게 잘 보이고 싶은 마음이 컸다. 저 사람은 칭찬도 잘하네? 저렇게 멋진 성과를 냈으니 당연히 칭찬할 만하지! 이런 말을 듣고 싶었다. 하지만 자기 자신을 칭찬할 때 가장 중요한 건 솔직함이다. 남들은 알 수 없는 나의 진짜 속마음을 들여다볼 수 있어야 한다. 나의 못난 모습조차 인정해야만 진실한 칭찬이 나오고, 그럴 때 하는 칭찬이 쌓이고 쌓여 빛을 발할 테니까.

내 마음속에 강한 인정 욕구가 있고, 남들의 시선에 자주 휘둘리거나 지나치게 신경 쓰는 성격이라는 사실을 이제는 온전히 받아들인다. 고치고 싶지만, 40년 넘게 굳어진 성격이라 쉽게 고쳐지지는 않는다. 다만 나의 이런 면들을 모두 인정하고 받아들이며 '그럼에도 불구하고' 꿋꿋이 나의 기준대로 선택했을 때 자신 있게 칭찬의 말을 덧붙일 수 있다. 설령 타인의 잣대로 내 선택을 재단하더라도 '아, 내가 또 그랬구나!' 하고 알아챌 수 있다면 그것대로 잘한 것이다. 인간이란 죽을 때까지 깨우치며 살아가는 존재 아닌가.

거창하지 않더라도 밤마다 칭찬일기를 써보는 건 어떨까. 감사일기를 쓰는 사람은 많은데 그것과 비슷하게 오늘 하루 나에게 칭찬할 거리를 찾아 기록하도록 권하고 싶다. 아무 일도 없었다고? 온종일 만원 버스에 시달린 게 전부라고? 이때 생각의 전환이 필요하다. 만원 버스, 말만 들어도 숨이 막히고 절로 땀이 흐르는 그 버스를 타고 일터로 향했다는 것은 정말 잘한 일이다. 그만두고 싶은 마음이 굴뚝같은데도 꿋꿋하게 버티고 있는 당신, 내가 볼 땐 정말 장하다. 칭찬 도장 찍어주고 싶다. 참 잘했어요!

춤을 조금만 웃기게 추어도 박수받던 어린 시절을 떠올리면 지금 내가 나를 칭찬하지 못할 이유는 하나도 없다. 나를 칭찬하는 기준은 내가 세우는 것이다. 타인이 아닌 나만의 잣대로 조금만 발상을 전환한다면 하루하루가 칭찬할 일로 가득할 것이다. 긍정의 힘은 이럴 때 나온다. 태어난 것만으로도 충분히 칭찬받을 일인데, 여기에 셀프 칭찬까지 더한다면? 아, 생각만 해도 삶이 한결 말랑말랑해지지 않는가?

그래서 말인데, 6년 전 나에게 이런 칭찬을 전하고 싶다.

"갈색 소파 산 거 잘했어! 가족들이 다 좋아했잖아. 너의 선택을 가족에게 양보한 그 마음, 정말 칭찬해!"

다음 번 소파는 더욱 멋지게 선택해서 나를 칭찬해야지! 소파 가운데가 점점 꺼지고 있어서 조만간 새로 들여와야 할 것 같아 내심 기뻐하고 있다는 건 비밀이다.

© 구은미

3

칭찬은 마중물이다

— 꽃섬전복

BGM MUSIC NFT #10
물과 바람소리, 사람의 소음과 자연의 모든 소리를 담아낸
마중물의 스토리를 힐링사운드로 연결시켜봅니다.

착하게 살아야 하는 이름

나도 말을 잘하고 싶어

칭찬받는 고래와의 만남

그렇게 애쓰면 힘들어요

전복 키우는 사람이 무슨 구글 강의야?

나의 모든 하루를 칭찬해

나인 너, 인선에게

착하게
살아야 하는 이름

어느 해 이른 봄, 첫아기가 태어났을 때 온 가족이 기뻐했다고 한다. 어른들은 아이에게 좋은 이름을 지어주기 위해 고민했다. 할아버지가 어질고 착하게 자라라는 뜻으로 아이 이름을 '인선'이라고 지어주었다. 그게 바로 나다.

이름의 힘은 정말 강하다. 인선이란 이름 때문인지 내겐 어릴 때부터 착하게 살아야 한다는 강박 같은 것이 있었다. 육교 위나 전철 계단, 시장, 거리에서 구걸하는 이들이 눈에 띄면 천 원짜리 한 장이라도 동냥 바구니에 넣어주어야 마음이 편했다. 손수레에 폐지를 잔뜩 싣고 가는 어르신을 보면 뒤에서 밀어드리고, 무거운 짐을 들고 가는 사람이 곤란

해 보일 땐 함께 들어주었다. 약하고 힘없는 사람들을 보고 도 모른 척하며 지나친다는 게 나에겐 더 힘든 일이다.

이런 성격이 형성된 데에는 4대가 함께 모여 살던 대가 족의 환경적 요인도 있을 것이다. 증조할머니, 할머니와 할 아버지, 어머니와 아버지, 나와 여동생, 남동생, 막냇삼촌까 지 9명의 식구가 한집에 살다 보면, 서로 도와야 하고 양보 도 해야 한다. 게다가 나는 유독 효심이 깊은 아버지를 보 며 자랐기에 어른에 대한 공경심이 자연스럽게 싹틀 수 있 었다.

요즘도 아버지는 부모 공경에 관한 글이 있으면 카톡으 로 꼬박꼬박 보내주신다. 그런 아버지에게서 영향을 받아서 일까, 결혼 후에도 나는 농사일에 바쁜 시부모님을 돕기 위 해 매주 시댁을 찾았다. 그러다 보니 어느새 착한 며느리라 는 칭찬까지 듣게 되었다.

스물한 살, 첫 직장에서 남편을 만나 결혼하고 1999년, 첫아이가 네 살이 되던 해에 남편의 고향인 전라남도 해남 으로 내려왔다. 남편과 나는 각자의 일이 있었는데, 시누의

권유로 남편이 먼저 전복 양식업에 뛰어들었다. 남편은 시누 집에서 5년 정도 일을 배운 뒤 혼자 힘으로 전복 양식을 시작했는데, 그 무렵 건강이 안 좋아 잠시 쉬고 있던 나도 남편을 돕기 위해 함께 전복 양식장으로 출근하게 되었다.

나도
말을 잘하고 싶어

전복 양식업을 시작하고 3년쯤 지나자 슬슬 힘들어지기 시작했다. 하지만 워낙 내성적인 데다 소심하기 짝이 없던 나는 누구에게도 힘들다는 말을 속 시원히 털어놓지 못했다. 아무나 할 수 있는 단순한 작업조차 제대로 못하다 보니 자존감은 자존감대로 바닥까지 떨어진 상태였다. 안 해본 일이니까 그렇지, 차근차근 잘 배워가면 되잖아, 하면서 이를 악물고 노력했지만 불가항력이었다. 워낙에 일머리가 없고 동작이 굼뜬 내게 바다는 '노력만으로는 안 되는 일도 있다'라는 교훈을 깨우쳐주었다.

해남에 내려오기 전만 해도 올빼미 생활에 익숙했던 생

체리듬 역시 새벽 4시 알람에 억지로 맞춰야 했다. 육지와 달리 바다는 균형을 잡고 서 있는 것만으로도 몸에 힘이 들어가 피로도가 훨씬 높았다. 고된 일상에 머릿속은 하얗게 지워졌고, 일 끝나면 집으로 돌아와 곧장 쓰러져 잠들기 일쑤였다.

함께 일하던 아주버님이 지나가는 말로 "일이 너무 많아 생각할 시간이 없다"라고 중얼거린 적이 있다. 처음엔 그냥 흘려들었다. 일이 아무리 많아도 생각이란 건 언제 어느 때나 할 수 있는 것 아닌가? 그런데 내가 직접 일을 하면서부터 그 말이 절실히 와닿았다. 생각이 사치처럼 느껴질 정도로 일이 많고 버거웠다.

생각이 없어져 감정이 사라진 걸까? 아니면 일이 힘들어 감정을 나눌 힘조차 없었던 걸까? 지금 사는 동네로 이사 왔을 때만 해도 나는 동네 주민들과 친해지기 위해 함께 차도 마시고 이야기도 나누며 지냈다. 하지만 불규칙한 일상과 매일 '힘들어, 힘들어'를 외치는 나의 안타까운 체력 때문에 이웃들과의 거리마저 소원해졌다.

어쩌면 이웃과 멀어진 데에는 나의 성격 탓도 있을 것이다. 기쁠 때나 우울할 때 간혹 이웃을 만나기도 하는데, 그마저도 시간이 길어진다 싶으면 곧장 지루해지고 피로감이 밀려와 빨리 자리를 뜨고 싶어진다. 더군다나 내가 원하지 않는 자리라면 잠시도 앉아 있기 힘들다. 또 두 사람 이상이 모인 자리에서는 언제, 어느 부분에서 끼어들어야 할지 모르겠고, 조리 있게 말하지 못하는 데다 말하는 속도가 너무 느리거나 혹은 너무 빨라 상대방이 불편해하기 일쑤다.

'나도 말을 잘하고 싶어.'

이것은 나의 오랜 고민이자 간절한 소망이다. 어떻게 하면 말을 잘하게 될까? 고민이 쌓일 대로 쌓인 어느 날, 우연히 알게 된 스피치 강의에 참여하게 되었다.

첫날 자기소개 시간에 나의 고민을 평소와 같은 속도로 이야기했을 때 강사가 이렇게 지적해주었다.

"말을 못 한다기보단 말의 속도가 좀 빠르고 끝맺음이 명확하지 않네요."

평소 내가 고민했던 부분이 그대로 강사에게 전달된 모양이다. 하지만 50년 가까이 몸에 밴 습관이 단 4주 만의 과정으로 고쳐질 수는 없을 것 같았다.

칭찬받는 고래와의
만남

웃음기 하나 없이 하루하루 지쳐가던 내가 안타까웠는지 동네 언니가 유튜브 영상을 추천해주었다. 거짓말 같지만, 그때까지 나는 유튜브라는 걸 제대로 접해본 적이 없었다. 게임 같은 건가? 솔직히 아이들이 그런 자극적인 영상을 보는 것조차 별로 탐탁지 않았던 터라 아예 볼 생각도 하지 않고 살았다.

동네 언니가 추천해준 것은 김창옥 강사의 강연 영상이었다. 처음 그 강연을 듣는 순간, 가슴이 너무 아려왔다. 한마디, 한마디가 귀에 쏙쏙 들어오고 마음을 감싸는 것 같았다.

"삶은 살아보려는 자들을 반드시 도와줍니다."

"10~15% 정도는 이기적으로 살아도 됩니다."

"당신의 마음이 아픈 건 진심이었기 때문입니다."

그렇게 영상들을 보며 마음을 조금씩 추슬러갈 때쯤 〈체인지 그라운드〉라는 채널이 눈에 들어왔다. 빡독(빡세게 독서하기)이라는 이벤트를 진행하고 있었는데, 나는 거기서 파생한 카카오톡 단톡방 중 한 곳에 참여했다. 그렇게 나의 첫 커뮤니티 활동이 시작되었다.

가까운 이웃과의 만남조차 힘들어하는 내가 일면식도 없는 사람들의 모임에 참여할 수 있다는 게 신기했다. 매일 내가 약속한 분량만큼의 페이지를 읽고 인증하는 이 모임은 거리와 공간에 상관없이 사람들이 공통의 관심사로 모일 수 있다는 걸 알게 해준 새로운 경험이었다.

그렇게 독서와 유튜브 등 다양한 콘텐츠들을 통해 나의 내면을 조금씩 채워가던 어느 날, 김미경 학장님의 유튜브 채널을 알게 됐다. TV를 통해 이미 그녀의 강의를 접하면서 멋진 분이라고 생각하던 터라 유튜브 채널에도 쉽게 빠져들었다.

운명이었을까? 사막 같던 내 마음에 한줄기 비가 내리는 것 같았다. 나는 홀린 듯 유튜브를 구독하고 인스타를 만들어 〈김미경과 함께 하는 영어 챌린지〉에 참여하는 등 SNS 세상으로 한 발 더 내디뎠다.

김미경 학장님이 운영하는 MKYU에 입학한 것은 내 인생의 중요한 전환점이자 새로운 출발점이었다. 다람쥐 쳇바퀴 돌듯 살아가던 일상에 지칠 대로 지친 데다 잃어버린 나를 찾고 싶은 마음이 임계점까지 차올랐을 때 딱 맞춰 MKYU의 강의를 듣게 된 것이다. 물론 강의들은 내게 우물 밖 세상을 보게 해주었고, 나의 시야를 폭넓게 확장해주기에 충분했다. 그런데 한편으로 시야가 넓어지면 넓어질수록 현재 나를 둘러싼 현실이 점점 답답하게 느껴졌다.

그러다 만난 커뮤니티 크리에이터 과정.

이 수업의 핵심은 소통이었다. 학생들끼리의 공부 톡방이 꾸려졌고 그곳에서 각자 자신이 꿈꾸는 커뮤니티에 대해서도 의견을 나누었다. 그때 '엘'이라는 분이 '칭찬하는 커뮤니티'를 만들고 싶다는 의견을 내놓았다. 그리고 얼마 후 〈칭찬받는 고래〉라는 방이 만들어졌다. 자신과 삶을 바

3 —
꽃
섬
전
복

로 세우고 싶은 사람은 누구나 참여할 수 있는 방이었다. 내면이 공허하고 약했던 나는 그 취지가 마음에 쏙 들어 당장 그 방의 일원이 되었다.

그렇게 애쓰면
힘들어요

〈칭찬받는 고래〉의 규칙은 간단했다. 먼저 자신에 대한 칭찬 글을 쓴 다음 다른 사람의 칭찬 글에 붙여넣기 해서 올리면 된다. 처음엔 나를 칭찬한다는 게 그다지 어렵게 느껴지지 않았다. 그런데 그게 아니었다. 여태껏 남을 칭찬할 줄만 알았지, 셀프 칭찬은 해본 적이 없다 보니 도대체 어떻게 칭찬해야 할지 막막하기만 했다. 그래서 일단은 톡방에 올라온 글부터 읽기 시작했는데 그래도 어렵긴 마찬가지였다. 칭찬에 서툰 내게 나를 칭찬한다는 것은 정말 쉽지 않았다. 애초에 나를 칭찬하는 법을 배운 적이 없지 않은가. 평범한 일상 속에서 칭찬할 거리를 찾아내야 한다는 숙제가 새삼 무겁게 느껴졌다.

남편은 잘한 일이 있으면 늘 칭찬받고 싶어 하는데, 아쉽게도 난 칭찬에 인색한 편이다. "칭찬 좀 해주면 안 돼? 나 잘했잖아?" 이런 불만을 남편에게서 꽤 자주 듣는다. 보통의 엄마들은 자녀들의 자존감을 키워주기 위해 칭찬을 자주 해준다. 그런데 난 오히려 너무 과한 칭찬은 아이들에게 별 도움이 안 된다고 생각해왔다.

'칭고' 방에 가입한 날, 첫 가입 인사를 남긴 뒤 다른 사람들의 글을 읽으며 '어쩜 다들 칭찬을 이렇게 스스럼없이 잘하지?'라는 의문부터 들었다. 글이나 말, 행동 모두가 경직된 내게는 매일 톡방에 읽지 않은 글이 몇 개인지 보여주는 숫자조차 낯설게 느껴졌다.

인스타그램을 공부하면서 라이브 방송을 해야 한다는 이야기를 듣긴 했지만, 좀처럼 시도하지 못하다가 용기를 내서 전복죽 만들기를 시연한 적이 있다. 그때 한 커뮤니티에서 알게 된 지인이 그 영상을 보고는 "너무 반듯하게 보이려고 하시네요. 그렇게 애쓰면 힘들어요"라고 조언해주었다. '좀 느슨하게 살아도 된다'라는 조언도 들려왔다. 내가 칭찬 글을 올리기 시작한 것은 그 이후의 일이었다.

'일요일이라 푹 쉬고 싶지만, 이 핑계 저 핑계로 미뤄둔 생
선 손질을 끝낸 나를 칭찬해!'

'부지런히 일하고 소통하고 싶고 칭찬하고 싶어 오늘도 칭
고 방에 들어온 나를 칭찬해!'

'시어머니와의 관계를 들어주고 경험담을 얘기하며 마음
을 나눠준 나를 칭찬해!'

이렇게 하루하루 나의 칭찬 글이 차곡차곡 쌓이기 시작
했다.

인원이 많지 않았기에 바로바로 톡 참여는 못 했지만, 그
날그날 '칭고' 방에 올라온 글들을 읽으며(벽 타기) 칭고들의
따뜻함을 느낄 수 있었다. 그렇게 하루하루 지나면서 나는
조금씩 마음을 열고 칭고 방의 일원이 되어갔다.

전복 키우는 사람이
무슨 구글 강의야?

———

셀프 칭찬에 익숙해지면서 나는 조금씩 마음챙김의 시간을 가질 수 있었다. 일찍 자고 일찍 일어난 나를 위해 '내 몸을 생각해준' 나를 칭찬합니다, 힘차게 한 주를 시작하는 나의 첫 발걸음을 칭찬합니다⋯⋯. '이런 것도 칭찬이 될 수 있다고?'라는 생각이 들 정도의 소소한 칭찬을 읽다 보니 그 어떤 것도 칭찬받을 수 있다는 사실을 알게 되었다.

매일매일 스쳐 지나가는 작고 사소한 일들조차 '칭찬 글에 올린다'라는 시선으로 보면 달라진다. 어떤 날은 예전의 나라면 절대 하지 않았을 일들에 도전하고 있는 모습(이모티콘 그리기, 그린플루언서 도전, 새벽 기상 등)을 발견하기도 했다.

나만 외로이 고군분투하는 게 아니라 다들 각자의 자리에서 얼마나 열심히 살고 있는지도 느끼게 되었다. 그동안은 일에 짓눌려 내가 누구인지도 잊고 살았는데, 나를 칭찬하기 위해 나를 되돌아보니 저절로 마음을 살피게 되고 다른 이들의 생각도 읽으며 이 세상에 나만 힘든 게 아니라는 위로도 받게 되었다. 그만큼 함께 하는 분들의 실천에 자극받는 날도 늘어갔다.

늘 힘들다는 핑계로 침대에 누워만 있던 내가 확실히 달라지긴 달라졌다. 자꾸자꾸 새로운 일에 도전하고 싶은 의욕이 생겨 마침내 블로그 카페 방장님께 강의를 한번 해보고 싶다고 요청할 만큼 용기가 생겼으니 말이다. 그렇게 해서 구글 기초 강의를 할 수 있는 기회가 내게 주어졌다. '전복 키우는 사람이 무슨 구글 강의야?'라고 생각할 수도 있을 텐데, 10%만 준비되면 도전하라는 김미경 학장님의 메시지에 힘을 얻어 생활 속에서 사용 가능한 구글 기능들을 모아 강의를 준비했다. 그동안 나는 늘 부족한 사람이라는 생각에 무조건 배우기만 했다. 하지만 '칭고' 방에서 경험한 몇 달이 내게 도전할 수 있는 용기를 주었다.

나의 모든 하루를
칭찬해

모두가 잠든 새벽. 정적을 깨며 울리는 알람 소리.

손가락은 알람을 끄기 위해 더듬거리지만, 몸은 이미 일어나야 한다는 걸 알고 있다. 젖은 솜처럼 무거운 몸을 일으켜 욕실로 향한다. 칙칙, 칙칙 전기밥솥에서 밥 짓는 소리가 요란하다. 보글보글 끓고 있는 된장찌개, 두부조림, 계란말이, 김치와 김이 한 상 가득 차려진 아침밥을 먹고 일터로 향한다.

바다에서 맞이하는 일출.

그리고 노을 지는 수평선의 일몰.

하루의 일과를 마치고 집으로 돌아와 저녁을 먹고 내일을 위해 일찍 잠자리에 든다.

앞의 글에서 우리는 무엇을 칭찬할 수 있을까? '이 글에 무슨 칭찬할 거리가 있어?'라고 생각하는가? 나도 처음엔 그랬다. 칭찬할 줄 몰랐으니까. 하지만 이제는 안다. 단조로워 보이는 하루의 풍경 속에도 얼마나 칭찬할 게 많은지.

첫째, 젖은 솜처럼 무거운 몸을 일으킨 걸 칭찬해.
둘째, 갓 지은 밥에 각종 반찬을 든든히 챙겨 먹은 걸 칭찬해.
셋째, 내일을 위해 일찍 잠자리에 든 걸 칭찬해.

칭고 방에서 나를 칭찬하는 법을 배우지 못했더라면 나 역시 칭찬할 거리를 찾아내지 못했을 것이다. 칭찬이란 뭔가를 잘했을 때 그에 걸맞게 돌아오는 보상이라고만 생각했으니까. 내 몸을 일으켜 세우는 것이, 아침밥을 차려 먹는 것이, 내일을 위해 일찍 자는 것이 칭찬할 만한 가치가 있다는 생각을 전혀 하지 못했을 테니까.

우리는 매일매일 열심히 살아가지만, 노력에 대한 가치를 인정해주는 사람은 많지 않다. 아니, 아예 없다는 표현이 더 맞을 것이다. 하지만 이제 남이 나의 가치를 인정해주기

만을 기다리지 말고 스스로 자신의 가치를 인정해주면 어
떨까? 마지막으로 지금의 나에게 전하는 편지로 이 글을 맺
을까 한다.

나인 너,
인선에게

안녕, 인선아?

내가 나에게 편지를 쓴다는 것이 어색하기도 하고 쑥스럽기도 하네. 반백 년 가까이 너를 쭉 지켜본 사람으로 남은 반백 년은 좀 더 네가 세상을 온전히 느끼며 살아가기를 바라는 마음으로 이 글을 써.

난 네가 남들에게 잘 보이기 위해 너무 애쓰지 않으면 좋겠어. 힘들 땐 힘들다고 투정도 부리고 기쁘고 즐거운 일이 있을 땐 마음껏 웃고 즐겨. 슬픈 일이 있을 땐 펑펑 울어도 돼. 너의 감정을 억누르지 말고 자유롭게 표현해. 표현한다고 해서 너를 비난할 사람은 없어. 사람은 원래 타인에게 별로 관심이 없거든. 각자 자기 살기도 바쁘니까 말이야. 그러니까 다른 사람 눈치 보지 말고 매사에 너의 마음 상태부터 먼저 살피는 거야.

사람들과 만나 대화할 때도 넌 감정이 없는 사람처럼 공감하지 못했었잖아. 뭔가 부족함을 느끼고 그것을 채우기 위해 이곳저곳을 기웃거려보지만, 결국 그 무리에 동화되지 못하고 기름처럼 둥둥 떠 있는 자신을 발견하곤 했지. 난 이제 네가 좀 더 자신감을 가졌으면 해.

자신감을 키우는 가장 좋은 방법이 뭘까? 난 칭찬이라고 생각해. 칭찬을 들으면 기분이 좋아지고 내가 한 일에 뿌듯함을 느끼잖아. 더군다나 칭고 방 커뮤니티에서는 나의 칭찬을 함께 칭찬해주잖아. 칭찬에 칭찬이 더해지니 나의 자존감은 한 단계 더 올라가지. 자존감이 올라가면 용기도 커지는 법이야. 그래서 예전엔 할 수 있을까, 하고 걱정만 하던 일들을 하나하나 실천할 수 있게 될 거야. 예를 들면 혼자 여행 떠나기 같은 거.

매일매일 글을 쓰는 게 얼마나 어려운지 알지? 초등학교 시절 일기장 검사가 얼마나 싫었는지 생각해봐. 글감도 찾아야 하지만, 일단 글을 쓰는 과정 자체가 귀찮아서 한꺼번에 몰아 쓰곤 했잖아. 그래서 결국 너의 글쓰기 실력도 더늘지 못하고 늘 고만고만했지. 그런데 칭고 방에서는 매일매일 일과 중에서 칭찬할 거리를 찾을 수 있으니 소재가 떨어질 리 없잖아. 또 꼬박꼬박 나의 칭찬 글을 쓰고 다른 사람들의 칭찬 글에 댓글을 쓰다 보면 글쓰기가 자연스럽게늘지 않겠어? 지금이야말로 가장 좋은 기회가 될 거야.

용두사미, 작심삼일이 무슨 뜻인지 알지? 내가 왜 이 사자성어를 들먹이는지 잘 알 거야. 처음엔 뭐든지 다 해낼 것처럼 시작부터 해놓고 진행 과정에서 힘이 빠져 마무리는 늘흐지부지, 질질 끄는 그 습관 말이야. 뭐라도 한번 시작하면 끝을 봐야 하는데 번번이 중간에 포기하는 너의 나쁜습관을 생각해봐. 그럴 때마다 넌 의지 하나만으로 다시그 끈을 이어가고 이어가기를 반복하고 있지만 말이야.

그런데 이때 칭찬이 더해지면 새로운 힘을 얻을 수 있지 않을까? 다시 용두사미, 작심삼일이 될지라도 계속해서 시작하고, 또 시작하면 되거든. 우습게도 점이 모여 선이 되듯이

3 | 꽃섬전복

여러 번의 용두사미와 작심삼일이 모이니까 하나의 결과물들이 만들어지긴 하더라.

아무튼 칭찬이란 게 참 신기하지 않아? 약해진 의지를 되살릴 수 있게 만들어주니까 말이야. 이젠 너의 자존감도 세우고 다른 사람에게도 칭찬을 더 많이 해서 그들의 자존감까지 높여주는 사람이 되었으면 해. 잘할 수 있을 거야. 내가 응원할게.

© 백경아

4

칭찬은 추진력이다

— 응원 요정

BGM MUSIC NFT #6
익숙함에서 나와 무지개 저 너머의 세상으로 도전하는
두려움을 이겨낸 용기와 추진력이 느껴지는 곡입니다.

나를 위한 삶은 어디 갔지?

어떻게 내가 나를 칭찬해?

하루를 살았다는 것 자체가 칭찬받을 일

2026년, 스피치 강사가 된 나에게

나를 위한 삶은
어디 갔지?

　　나는 걱정이 참 많은 사람이다.

　　내 걱정도 걱정이지만, 오지랖 넓게 가족이나 친구, 지인들 걱정까지 끌어온다. 남들의 고민을 듣고 나면 마치 내 일 같아 밤잠을 설치기 일쑤였다. 특히 가족들이 힘들어하는 모습을 보면 도저히 외면할 수가 없었다. 오빠가 이혼하고 돌이 갓 지난 조카를 봐달라고 부탁했을 때는 아예 집에 데려와 초등학교 들어가기 전까지 보살펴주기도 했다.

　　나는 3남 4녀 중 여섯째이자 셋째 딸이다. 딱히 책임감이 무거운 위치도 아니고 또 그걸 강요하는 사람도 없는데, 나는 유독 식구들을 챙기며 살아왔다.

어느 날 연로하신 아버지가 치매에 걸려 일상생활이 불편해지자 요양병원에 모시게 되면서부터 엄마 혼자 지내게 되었다. 거동도 불편한 엄마가 혼자 얼마나 힘들고 외로울까 싶어 나는 일주일에 한두 번씩 퇴근길에 들렀다. 일부러 시간을 내어 음식도 만들어드리고 생필품도 떨어지기 전에 넉넉하게 채워놓았다. 날씨가 좋은 날엔 휠체어를 끌고 공원 산책도 시켜드렸다.

회사 업무가 바쁘거나 중요한 약속이 생겨 도저히 시간을 낼 수 없으면 가지 못할 때도 있었다. 엄마는 꼬박꼬박 찾아오는 딸에게 고마워하면서도 가끔 "내가 기다리다 기다리다 이제 안 기다리기로 했다"라며 속마음을 드러냈다. 멀리 살아서 어쩌다 한번 다니러 오는 자식들은 그렇게 반가워하면서 거의 매일같이 들러서 일일이 챙겨주는 딸은 당연하다고 생각하는 걸까? 이런 생각이 들 때면 나도 서운한 마음이 드는 건 어쩔 수 없었다. 그래도 엄마의 마음을 충분히 이해하기에 "오늘 퇴근하면서 들를게"라며 웃으며 넘겼다. 아니 솔직하게 이해하려고 노력했다.

그런 생활을 1년 넘게 하다 보니 문득 이런 생각이 들었다.

'나를 위한 삶은 어디 갔지?'

그때까지 내게 주어진 시간은 대부분 가족에 집중되어 있었다. 내 인생의 주인공이 '나'가 아니라는 사실이 허무하게 느껴졌고, 엄마가 내게 갖는 기대와 서운한 표현들도 점점 참기 힘든 스트레스로 다가오기 시작했다. 그러다 보니 가끔 엄마에게 짜증 섞인 말투가 불쑥불쑥 터져 나왔다.

작년 봄엔 엄마의 핸드폰이 고장 나서 새 것으로 바꿔드렸다. 87세인 엄마는 눈이 침침해서 액정도 보기 힘들고 디지털에도 서툴러 전화를 받는 것도, 거는 것도 어려워했다. 기존에 쓰던 핸드폰과 번호가 일치하게 간편 번호도 등록하고 전화 사용법도 반복해서 알려드렸다.

"엄마, 1번을 길게 꾹 누르면 큰오빠, 2번은 큰언니예요."

그런데 다음날부터 언니, 오빠들의 전화가 내게 빗발치듯 걸려왔다.

"태경아, 엄마 무슨 일 있으시니? 전화해서 아무 말씀도 없다가 그냥 끊으시던데?"

"별일 아니야. 엄마가 아직 새 전화기 사용법에 익숙하지 않아서 그래."

"네가 고생이 많구나. 그래도 어떡하니, 엄마가 제대로 사용할 수 있을 때까지 잘 가르쳐드려야지. 우리도 나이 들면 그렇게 될 수 있어."

"언니! 내가 몇 번을 알려드렸는지 알아?"

내 목소리 톤이 조금 높아지고 말았다. 같은 질문에 똑같은 대답을 반복하던 나는 결국 언니 오빠들에게 '나는 나이 들어도 그렇게 안 될 거야!'라며 짜증을 부렸고, 엄마한테도 자꾸 전화해서 걱정시키지 말고 오는 전화만 받으라며 소리쳤다.

이렇게 감정이 격앙될 때마다 집안 분위기는 나 한 사람 때문에 싸늘해지고, 식구들 마음마저 상하게 하는 상황이 종종 발생하기도 했다.

어떻게 내가
나를 칭찬해?

　　마음이 점점 지쳐가던 어느 날, 친구 S가 이런 말을 했다.

　"30년 가깝게 쉴 새 없이 일만 하다 보니 정말 지친다 지쳐. 더 늦기 전에 나도 버킷리스트를 하나씩 지워나가고 싶어. 내 버킷리스트에 혼자서 여행하기, 전국 맛집 투어, 역사 기행 같은 게 있거든. 한 번도 안 해봐서 막상 해보려고 해도 선뜻 용기가 나지 않아. 그래도 꼭 할 거야. 일도 하고 여행도 하면서 여유롭게 살고 싶어."

　그 말을 듣는 순간, 내 안에서 갑자기 많은 질문이 떠올랐다.

'지금까지 살아오면서 내가 가장 하고 싶었던 건 무엇일까?'

'내가 좋아하는 것은 무엇일까?'

'나에게도 목표가 있을까?'

'나의 꿈은 무엇일까?'

아무것도 없었다. 이런 소소한 질문에도 뚜렷한 답이 나오지 않자 '나는 누굴까?'라는 의문까지 들었다. 맞다. 나는 여태껏 나로 살지 않은 것이다.

버킷리스트를 가진 친구가 부러웠다. 특별한 재능도 없이 평범하게 살아온 지난날들과 내가 부딪쳐야 할 몇 년 후가 겹쳐지면서 조급함이 밀려왔다. 어떻게 해야 할까? 뭔가 방법을 찾아야 했다. 내 시간을 만들어야 했고 '온전한 나'를 찾아야 했다.

일단 남편과 의논해서 엄마를 우리 집으로 모시고 왔다. 남편은 조카가 우리 집에 올 때 그랬듯이 이번에도 내 의견을 존중한다며 흔쾌히 동의해주었다. 내가 힘들어할 때 말 없이 응원해주고 도움을 주는 남편이 늘 고맙다. 요즘 주부들 사이에서 남편을 '남의 편'이라고들 하는데, 내 남편은 오로지 내 편이어서 그저 감사할 따름이다.

엄마에게 화장실이 딸린 안방을 내드렸다.

하루에 몇 시간 정도는 요양보호사가 방문해서 엄마를 돌봐드린다. 식사와 빨래, 방 청소까지 정말 많은 도움을 받고 있다. 이제 숨 좀 돌릴 수 있게 된 것이다. 그동안 다른 형제들이 걱정할까 봐 투정은커녕 힘들지 않은 척, 행복한 척했지만, 솔직히 내 안에는 공허함 같은 게 늘 남아 있었다. 이제 그 공허함을 채우고 싶었다.

엄마와 함께 지내면서 요양보호사의 도움까지 받게 되자 조금 여유가 생겼다. 그때부터 나는 마음잡고 자기계발을 시작했다. 사놓기만 하고 시간 없다는 핑계로 읽지 않고 미뤄둔 책을 한 권씩 읽었다. 예전에 조금 배워본 중국어도 다시 시작하고 싶어 학원에 등록하고 중국어 공부 커뮤니티에도 가입해서 꾸준히 공부했다.

칭찬 커뮤니티와의 인연은 유튜브에서 〈김미경과 함께하는 미라클모닝 514챌린지〉를 접하면서부터 시작되었다.

새벽 5시 기상, 14일간 좋은 습관 만들기……. 챌린지의 취지가 참 매력적으로 느껴졌다. '정말 해낼 수 있을까'란 고민도 해보기 전에 내 손은 링크를 타고 들어가 이미 신청 버튼을 누르고 있었다.

〈칭찬받는 고래〉 방은 514챌린지를 하면서 같은 오픈 카톡방에 있는 분이 만든 커뮤니티다. '칭찬은 고래도 춤추게 한다', '나는 춤추는 고래가 될 것이다', '이제 칭찬받고 함께 성장해요!'라는 설명이 있었는데 그때 의문이 들었다. 칭찬을 받으면 성장한다고? 호기심에 이끌려 대화방에 입장하긴 했지만, 칭찬을 하는 것도 받는 것도 어색하기만 하던 나는 슬그머니 방을 나가고 말았다.

일전에 어느 인터넷 사이트에서 자존감 테스트를 해본 적이 있는데 결과는 '자존감 부족'으로 나왔다. 칭찬을 받으면 자존감이 높아진다는 것까진 알고 있었지만, 나를 칭찬하기가 너무 쑥스럽고 자신이 없었다. 하지만 막상 방을 나오고 나니 오히려 더 궁금해졌다.

매일 나를 들여다보고 칭찬하고 다른 사람을 칭찬해주

면서 성장한다⋯⋯. 정말 그럴까? 망설이고 망설이다 며칠 후 다시 '칭고' 방의 링크를 클릭했다. 칭고들의 열렬한 환영 인사를 받으며 그때부터 나의 자존감 회복 프로젝트가 시작되었다.

하루를 살았다는 것 자체가
칭찬받을 일

챌린지를 시작하면서 나름대로 나 자신과 한 약속
이 하나 있다. '일어날까 말까 망설이지 말고 그냥 일어나자'
라는 약속이다. 뭐가 됐건 일단은 일어나야 시작할 수 있으
니까 말이다.

나처럼 늦게 자는 습관에 익숙해진 사람에게는 가장 힘
든 것이 새벽 기상일 것이다. 그래도 어떻게, 어떻게 약속을
계속 지켜나갔다. 5시에 일어나 챌린지를 끝내고 조금 자는
날도 있었지만, 어쨌든 8개월째 지나고 있는 오늘까지도 새
벽 기상 미션을 잘 실천하고 있다. 칭고 방에서 처음 올린
내 칭찬도 "새벽에 일찍 일어나 인증까지 마친 후 등산 가
는 나를 칭찬합니다"였다.

그런 어느 날, 남편이 늦은 회식을 끝내고 새벽에 귀가했다. 그날 내가 남편에게 한 뜻밖의 행동에 나 스스로 놀라며 칭고 방에 올린 글이 있다.

어제 회식하고 새벽녘에 귀가하여 숙취에 힘들어하는 남편을 위해 북엇국을 끓여서 아침상을 차려주었어요. 들기름에 무와 북어포를 달달 볶다가 쌀뜨물을 부어 푹 끓이고, 콩나물을 넣고 한 번 더 끓인 후 마지막으로 파와 계란을 풀고 새우젓으로 간을 했어요. 압력솥에 갓 지은 찰진 밥과 해장국으로 속을 푼 남편의 얼굴빛은 막 일어났을 때보다 한결 밝아 보였어요. 예전 같으면 잔소리부터 늘어놓았겠죠. 솔직히 만취한 남편을 보자마자 속에서 미운 감정이 욱하고 올라오긴 했지만, 잘 참은 것 같아요. 현명하게 대처한 나를 칭찬합니다.

예전 같으면 미워서 쳐다보지도 않고 묻는 말에 대꾸도 안 하던 내가 아침 일찍 일어나 밥상까지 차려주다니, 정말 스스로 칭찬받을 만했다. 이렇게 매일매일 내가 잘한 일이 뭐가 있을까 생각해보고 아침부터 나의 하루를 돌아보는 일이 이제 루틴이 되었다.

어떤 날은 아무리 머리를 짜내도 칭찬할 거리가 생각나지 않을 때가 있다. 그럴 땐 나를 칭찬하는 시간인 만큼 '나 자신과 연관된 키워드'를 살펴본다.

먼저 주인공인 나, 집에서는 엄마의 딸, 남편의 아내, 아이들의 엄마, 직장에서 내가 맡은 직책 등이 있을 것이다. 이렇게 나눠보면 아침에 눈을 떠서 잠들기 전까지 내가 하는 일들이 역할에 따라 소소하게 많다는 것을 발견할 수 있다.

새벽에 너무 피곤하고 졸려서 일어나기 싫지만, 그래도 몸을 일으켜 나만의 챌린지를 실천하는 성실한 나.

건강을 위해 규칙적으로 운동하는 나.

엄마의 약과 간식거리를 챙기고 목욕도 시켜드리는 나.

가족을 위해 요리하는 나.

아이들에게 친구 같은 엄마가 되기 위해 잔소리 안 하려고 노력하고 이야기 많이 들어주는 공감력 짱인 나.

회사에서 능력을 발휘하는 나.

이 모두가 '나'라는 캐릭터가 아닌가?

이렇게 보면 우리가 매일매일 일상에서 하는 일들이 모두 칭찬받아 마땅한 것들이다. 어떻게 보면 하루를 살았다는 것 자체가 이미 칭찬받을 일인 것이다. 칭고들은 습관적으로 행하는 모든 일상을 너무도 자연스럽게 칭찬하고 있었다. 이젠 나도 아침에 눈을 뜨면서부터 기특하다 칭찬해주고, 가끔 힘들고 지쳐서 우울해질 때면 너무 오래 걸리지 않게 기운 내자며 스스로 위로해주는 나를 발견한다.

항상 나를 돌아보고 칭찬할 일들을 찾다 보니 내가 한 행동이나 말들도 다시 한번 되돌아보게 된다. 예전 같으면 아무 생각 없이 던진 말에 상대방이 상처를 입건 말건 그냥 지나쳤을 일들을 이제는 내가 먼저 사과하고 반성도 할 수 있게 되었다. 그렇게 서로를 칭찬하고 응원해주는 칭고들이 모인 칭찬 커뮤니티라는 공간에서 조금씩 용기를 얻고 자신감도 생기기 시작했다.

셀프 칭찬을 하다 보면 '내가 바라는 나는 어떤 모습일까?'라는 질문과 마주칠 때가 종종 있다. 나는 어릴 때부터 여러 사람 앞에서 당당하게 말 잘하는 사람이 그렇게 부러울 수가 없었다. 예전에는 그저 막연히 부러워하기만 했는데, 셀프 칭찬으로 얻은 용기 덕분에 이젠 도전해보고 싶어졌다. 그래서 온라인 줌을 통해 스피치 수업도 받아보았다.

처음 신청할 때부터 1회차, 2회차 줌 수업을 할 때마다 들어 갈까 말까 계속 망설였을 정도로 진짜 많은 용기와 에너지 가 필요한 과정이었다.

그래도 매 순간 용기 내어 제일 먼저 손 번쩍 들고 큰소 리로 발표도 해보고 큰 소리로 웃는 연습도 해보았다. 상처 받은 나에게 쓴 편지를 읽을 때는 눈물도 흘렸다. 엄두도 못 내던 값진 경험을 해본 내가 대견하고 자랑스러웠다. 스피치 수업이 내 인생의 전환점이 될 듯한 예감에 다음 수업도 대 기자로 등록해놓았다. 단 4회 수업을 받았을 뿐인데 내 목 소리는 몰라보게 커졌고, 도전에 대한 두려움도 사라졌으며 무엇이든 할 수 있으리라는 자신감도 생겼다.

칭찬 커뮤니티에서 나 자신을 칭찬하고 칭고들을 칭찬 해주지 않았다면 어림도 없는 일이었을 것이다. 삶이 버겁 고 힘들 때, 혹은 낯선 사람들과의 관계가 두려울 때마다 칭 찬은 큰 힘이 되어주었다.

2026년,
스피치 강사가 된 나에게

　　이 글은 2026년 어느 날, 스피치 강사라는 나의 간절한 꿈이 실현되어 학생들과 대화하는 장면을 떠올려본 것이다. 과거의 내 모습과 미래의 모습이 정확히 일치하며 오버랩되는 시간이 진짜 현실이 되기를 기대하면서.

　　교실 창밖으로 앙상한 나뭇가지들이 바람에 흔들리고 있다. 실내에 설치된 난로는 덩치만 컸지 40명 넘는 학생들에게 골고루 온기를 나눠주기엔 아무래도 역부족인 듯하다. 특히나 이제 막 시작된 1교시에는 더 그렇다. 모든 것이 얼어붙은 겨울 아침, 검은 뿔테 안경을 쓴 국어 선생님이 여느 때와 마찬가지로 오늘 배울 페이지를 펴고 학생을 지목한다.

"오늘이 며칠이죠? 7일? 7번 김태경, 일어나서 읽어보세요."

"칭찬의 대화란 상대방의 좋은 점을 드러내고 빛내기 위한 대화를 뜻한다. 남을 칭찬하면 자신도 즐겁고 상~대방도 즐거~~워 한다. 또한 칭~찬은 삶의 활~력~소 기능 ~~~~을~~~~~~ 한~~~~~~다~~~."

어, 뭐지? 손과 발만 언 게 아니라 입까지 얼었나? 목소리가 점점 떨리기 시작하더니 자꾸만 어눌해진다. 글을 읽고 있으면서도 머리로는 빨리 다른 아이를 지목해달라고 기도하고 또 기도한다. 심하게 떨고 있는 나를 골탕 먹이려는 듯 선생님은 한참 지켜보더니 '그만!' 하고 다른 학생을 호명한다. 갑작스러운 신체 반응에 내 얼굴은 홍당무가 되고, 친구들 모두 나를 안쓰럽다는 표정으로 쳐다보고 있다. 너무 창피하다.

괴로움에 뒤척이다 잠에서 깨어 시계를 보니 새벽 3시.

또 꿈을 꿨네. 며칠 전부터 계속 같은 꿈이다. 고등학교 1학년 겨울, 수업 시간에 실제로 일어난 이 당혹스러운 경험 때문에 나는 자신감을 잃고, 사람들 앞에 나서기 두려워하는 겁쟁이가 되었다. 여러 사람 앞에서 말해야 하는 순간만 되면 언제나 가슴이 쿵쾅쿵쾅 뛰고 목소리가 떨렸다.

그러나 3년 전부터 칭고 방에서 셀프 칭찬으로 자존감을 회복한 나는 그 오랜 상처들을 모두 극복했을 뿐만 아니라 스피치 학원까지 운영하고 있다. 가끔 기업이나 학교에서 강의 의뢰가 들어오면 출강도 나간다. 나와 비슷한 경험을 하고 상처받은 사람들이 조금씩 자신감을 찾고 변화해가는 모습을 볼 때마다 말로 표현할 수 없는 뿌듯함과 감동이 밀려온다. 그동안 스피치 수업을 하면서 가장 기억에 남는 수강생의 감동 스토리를 소개하고 싶다.

"여러분, 어릴 때의 상처 때문에 힘들어하는 내면의 아이에게 편지를 써보세요. 지금까지 긴 세월 동안 날개 한번 제대로 못 펴고 살아내느라 얼마나 힘들었니? 무엇이 너를 그렇게나 힘들게 했니? 하고 물어봐주고 위로해주고 애썼다고 칭찬도 해주고, 이젠 다 괜찮으니 일어나라고 용기도 주어보세요. 내가 나에게 쓴 편지를 읽어준다는 게 어떻게 보면 무척 소소한 일 같지만, 두고 보세요. 그 순간이 여러분의 상처를 치유하고 자존감을 높이는 아주 훌륭한 경험이 될 수 있을 거예요."

그렇게 약 10분 정도의 시간을 주고 한 사람씩 발표하는 시간을 가졌다. 잠시 후 40대 중반쯤 되는 수강생 한 분이 일어나 편지를 읽기 시작했다.

> 지영아, 너는 어릴 때부터 엄격한 아빠한테 야단을 많이 맞고 자랐지? 그래서 그렇게 다른 사람이 싫어하는 일을 하지 않으려고 항상 조심하고 어른들께 잔소리 듣지 않으려고 눈치도 많이 보며 살았구나. 결혼 후에도 남편이 싫어하는 건 하지 않으려고 노심초사하고, 대인관계도 꽤 힘들었지. 그래도 요즘 커뮤니티에 가입해서 좋은 사람들도 많이 만나고 용기를 얻기 위해 스피치 강의도 신청하고 열정적으로 수업에 참여하고 있어서 나는 요즘 네가 참 좋다. 지영아, 이제부터는 너 하고 싶은 거 다 하면서 무엇이든지 할 수 있다는 희망과 용기를 가져봐. 지영아, 포기하지 말자. 사랑해! 그리고 고마워!

편지를 읽으면서 몇 번이나 목이 메어 읽기를 멈추고 눈물을 훔치던 모습이 눈에 선하다. 어릴 때부터 줄곧 다른 사람들을 살피느라 얼마나 힘들었을까? 가만히 생각해보니 예전의 나를 보는 듯해 너무 마음이 아팠다.

얼마 전 자려고 누웠을 때 새 메일이 도착했다는 알람이 울렸다. 발신인은 바로 울면서 편지를 읽던 그 김지영이라는 분이었다.

선생님, 안녕하세요. 봄학기 강의 들었던 김지영이에요. 선생님께 고맙다는 인사를 꼭 드리고 싶어서 이렇게 메일을 써봅니다. 저는 어려서부터 성인이 될 때까지 수줍음이 참 많았어요. 여러 사람이 모이는 장소에 가야 할 상황이 오면 항상 긴장했고 두려웠죠. 그러다 보니 자연스럽게 저의 울타리도 가족과 직장, 학창 시절의 친구들로 좁혀졌고, 자존감도 많이 낮아져 있었어요.

어느 날 친구의 추천으로 시에서 주관하는 선생님 강의를 들었는데 정말 감동이었어요. 그래서 바로 그날 선생님의 스피치 강의를 신청했고, 정말 너무 간절한 마음이었기에 수업을 열심히 따라갔죠. 또 긍정 확언 문구도 만들었어요.

나는 무엇이든 할 수 있는 용기가 있다.
나는 무엇을 하든 항상 자신감 있게 행동한다.
나는 매일 조금씩 좋아지고 있다.

저는 매일매일 이 긍정 확언을 외치면서 용기와 자신감을 얻는답니다. 오늘은 영어에 관심이 있는 사람들이 함께 모여 공부하는 커뮤니티를 만들고 리더가 되었어요. 아직은 시작이라 작은 모임이지만, 점점 활성화되어 나중엔 재능기부도 하고 수익도 창출하는 멋진 커뮤니티로 만들고 싶어요. 제가 이런 용기를 낸 건 모두 선생님 덕분입니다. 감사한 마음 잊지 않고 선한 영향력 베푸는 리더가 될게요. 편안한 밤 보내세요.

메일을 읽어내려가는 동안 얼마나 벅찼는지 모른다. 밤새 가슴이 콩닥콩닥 뛰는 바람에 잠을 설칠 정도였다. 예전의 나를 보는 이 느낌은 무어라 표현할 수 없을 정도로 감동 그 이상이었다. 이렇게 좋은 일이 있을 때는 당장 '칭고' 방에 들어가서 한 사람을 일으켜준 나를 칭찬해주고, 그렇게 되기까지 열정을 아끼지 않는 나를 자랑한다. 셀프 칭찬이 자연스럽게 내 자랑으로 거듭난다고나 할까?

이렇게 나는 오늘도 칭고 방에서 칭찬하는 방법은 물론 나를 당당하게 드러내고 자랑하는 방법까지 덤으로 배우고 있다.

© 노해정

5
___

칭찬은 펌핑이다

— 시원

BGM MUSIC NFT #27
앞으로 나아가는 선율로 조금 더 힘을 내보자고 손 내밀어주는…
내 안의 나보다 더 큰 나를 만나는 칭찬의 펌핑이 느껴지는 곡입니다.

내 안의 안내요원

이것도 못 해?

당신, 참 긍정적인 사람이네요

때론 링거액 같은 칭찬 한마디가 필요해

내가 나를 칭찬하는 법

내 안의
안내요원

———

　　내 안에는 늘 나와 함께하는 안내요원이 있다. 언제나 같이 자고 같이 깬다. 그리고 온종일 내 곁에 찰싹 달라붙어 끊임없이 참견하고 수다를 떨어대며 하루하루를 함께 살아간다.

　　언제부터였을까? 기억이 시작되는 처음부터 지금까지 모든 순간, 모든 장면이 그랬다. 집에서도 밖에서도, 책을 읽거나 친구를 만나거나 샤워할 때도 온전히 혼자일 때가 없었다.

　　게다가 난 잘하는 게 별로 없어서 늘 혼나기 일쑤다. 늦잠을 자면 늦잠 잤다고 혼나고, 공부하다 졸면 졸았다고 혼난다.

여럿이 모여 내가 모르는 주제로 대화를 나눌 때면 혼자 얼마나 맘이 졸여지고 작아지는지 모른다. 그럴 때면 어김없이 내 안의 안내요원이 버럭 소리를 지른다.

'그것도 몰라?'

사정이 이렇다 보니 나 스스로 나를 감시하고 질책하는 일이 잦아졌다. 아이들이 커가면서 갈등이 생기고 엄마로서 힘들 때도 '난 정말 사랑이 부족해. 엄마 맞아? 자격 미달이야, 정말.' 이렇게 스스로를 비난했다. 이게 다 내 안의 안내요원 때문이다.

그나저나 그 안내요원은 대체 누구일까?

이것도
못 해?

————

　　어릴 때 내가 좋아한 사람은 아버지였다. 그냥 아버지가 멋있고 좋았다. 성실하고 부지런하며 늘 당당한 사람, 그래서 아버지의 말에는 힘이 있었고 또 언제나 옳았다. 가난한 어린 시절을 보내며 누구의 도움도 없이 열정과 의지만으로 삶을 개척해온 분답게 아버지에게는 배울 점이 너무도 많았다.

　　아버지의 소원은 자식들이 공부를 잘해서 다들 좋은 대학에 들어가는 것이었다. 어릴 때 형편이 어려워 교육받지 못한 한을 자식들이 풀어주기를 바란 건데, 섭섭하게도 자식들은 아버지의 기대에 부응하지 못했다. 공부를 인생 최

5
시원

대의 가치로 여기는 아버지의 기준이 너무 높기도 했지만, 어쨌든 아버지의 실망은 이만저만이 아니었다. 하지만 아버지는 좋은 대학을 나와 좋은 직장에 들어가야 안정적으로 돈을 벌 수 있고, 남보다 더 잘 살 수 있다는 나름의 성공 공식을 계속 고수했다.

아버지가 출타 중이던 어느 날 저녁, 난데없이 밖에서 돌이 집 안으로 날아든 적이 있다. 돌은 다행히 싱크대 앞에 떨어졌지만, 그 앞에 누가 서 있었더라면 큰일 날 뻔한 상황이었다. 우리가 놀라고 당황해서 덜덜 떠는 동안 엄마는 아버지에게 전화를 걸었다.

"밖에서 돌이 날아왔어요. 정말 큰일 날 뻔했어요."
그때 수화기 저편에서 아버지의 목소리가 쩌렁쩌렁 들려왔다.

"그러니까 정신을 똑바로 차리고 있어야지!"

정신을 흐리멍덩하게 하고 있으니 그렇게 돌이 날아든 거라는 말도 덧붙였다. 이게 뭔 소린가 싶었다. 멀쩡한 집 안에 돌이 날아온 게 '정신을 안 차려서' 일어난 일이라고? 정신만 똑바로 차리고 있으면 돌이 안 날아왔을 거라고? 정말 어이가 없었다. 늘 옳은 말만 하는 아버지가 왜 그렇게 말했을까?

내가 감기에 걸렸을 때도 아버지는 똑같은 말을 되풀이했다. 정신을 차리지 않아서 감기에 걸린 거라고. 매일 아침 달리기와 동네 골목 쓸기로 성실하게 건강관리를 하는 자신의 기준에서, '정신 똑바로 차리고' 철저히 자기관리를 한다면 감기 따위는 걸리지 않는다는 논리였다.

이제 여든이 넘으신 아버지가 몇 년 전 감기에 걸렸다는 얘기를 들었을 때 나는 아버지 말씀을 그대로 돌려드렸다.

"아버지, 정신을 똑바로 차리고 계셨어야죠! 정신을 똑바로 안 차리고 계시니까 감기 같은 거에나 걸리는 거 아니에요. 정신 똑바로 차리고 계세요."

나도 웃고 아버지도 엄마도 함께 웃었다.
지금 생각해보니 아버지가 우리에게 해주고 싶은 말들

132

5
시
원

을 한 문장에 압축한 것이 바로 '정신 똑바로 차려'였다.

거친 세상 살아가려면 몸도 마음도 강해야 한다, 가진 게 없거나 절망에 부딪힐 때도 마음만 단단히 먹으면 못 이룰 일이 없다, 그러니 언제나 자신감을 지니고 씩씩하게 세상과 맞서야 한다는 응원과 사랑의 메시지가 '정신 똑바로 차려!' 그 한마디에 담겨 있었다.

하지만 어릴 땐 그저 아버지가 너무하다는 생각뿐이었다. 정신만 바짝 차리면 날아올 돌도 안 날아온다는 말을 어떻게 이해하란 말인가. 그런데도 우린 반박 한 번 제대로 하지 못했다. 아버지가 야단을 칠 때면 그저 겁나고 무섭기만 했다.

그렇다고 내가 아버지를 미워한 건 아니다. 기억을 아무리 더듬어보아도 어릴 때 나는 아버지가 마냥 좋았다. 그래서 무조건 아버지 말씀이 다 옳았다. 성적이 기대만큼 나오지 않았을 때 '그래도 약간은 칭찬해주시면 얼마나 좋을까'라고 바라긴 했지만, 결국은 내가 잘못해서 "이것도 못 해?"라는 말을 듣는 거라고, 아버지 말씀이 다 옳다고 생각했다.

그런데 "이것도 못 해?"라는 그 한마디가 살면서 내가 나에게서 가장 많이 듣는 말이 돼버렸다. 나는 왜 이렇게 매사에 나 자신을 탓하기만 했을까? 어릴 때 너무 엄한 환경에서 자라서 그런가?

아니다. 이 글을 쓰는 동안 비로소 알게 된 사실.

내 안에서 쉬지 않고 나를 혼내는 안내요원의 정체가 바로 아버지였다는 것이 이제 확실해졌다. 언제인지 나도 모르게, 내 마음 어딘가에 장착해놓은 칩처럼 안내요원은 삶의 순간순간마다 아버지의 생각과 기준으로 내 생각과 행동을 평가해온 것이다.

당신,
참 긍정적인 사람이네요

1998년쯤 다음 카페에 처음 회원가입을 할 때 나의 첫 아이디는 positive-i(긍정적인 나)였다. 어느 후배가 보더니 '대체 얼마나 부정적이길래?'라고 귀신같이 알아맞히는 바람에 깜짝 놀라기도 했지만, 아무튼 온라인 세상에서의 내 소중한 첫 명함이었다.

어릴 때 욕심 많은 언니의 심통에 가끔 짜증을 내거나 말썽꾸러기 작은오빠에게 괜히 얻어맞아야 하는 것 말고는 큰 어려움이 없었다. 사회에 나와서도 별다른 갈등 없이 인간관계가 그럭저럭 원만한 편이었다. 정작 나를 가장 힘들게 하는 것은 가장 가까운 사람, 바로 남편과의 관계였다. 어려워도 그렇게 어려울 수가 없었다. 결혼하고 아이를 낳고부터 남편과의 의사소통이 점점 힘들어졌다. 뭐가 문제일까? 도무지 해답을 풀어낼 수 없어 맘고생이 정말 심했다.

그리고 아이들…….

어릴 때는 한없이 귀엽고 천사 같은 아이들이었는데, 점점 자라면서 걸핏하면 말도 안 되는 자기주장을 팍팍 내세우며 내 가슴을 뒤집어놓았다. 그동안 내가 잘해주지 못한 것을 나에게 되돌려주는 건지.

한창 어린아이들을 돌봐야 할 때 꼼짝 못 하고 집에만 갇혀 있는 상황에서 남편과의 갈등과 불화는 나를 너무도 힘들게 했다.

마침 그 무렵, 우리 큰애보다 한 살 많은 딸을 둔 옆집 언니를 알게 되었다. 언니와 나는 매일매일 골목에서 아이들 노는 모습을 바라보며 이야기를 나눴다. 하루는 내가 너무 시시한 사람으로 나이 드는 것 같다며 한숨을 내쉬자 언니가 이렇게 말했다.

"너만 모르는구나. 네가 얼마나 괜찮은 사람인지. 머리부터 발끝까지 선함이 그냥 줄줄 흘러. 네가 장사를 하면 손님들이 엄청나게 줄을 설 거야. 넌 정말 따듯해. 게다가 이렇게 훌륭한 아기들을 셋씩이나 키우는 엄마는 세상 어디에도 없을 거야. 네가 이제 서른다섯? 멋진 나이네. 서른 초반까지는 몰라. 아직 애야, 애. 서른다섯 정도는 돼야 이제 인생을 좀 알 나이라고 할 수 있지."

언니의 말에 나는 벌떡 일어나 절을 했다. 뭘 잘 해낸 것도 아닌데, 그저 하루하루 살아서 먹게 된 나이일 뿐인데 왜 그렇게 가슴이 벅찼을까? 딱히 잘한 것도 없이 그냥 있는 그대로인 나 자체를 인정해주는 그 말에 나는 감격하고 말았다. 이어지는 언니의 말도 귀에 쏙쏙 들어왔다.

"간장 달일 때 보면, 처음엔 고린내 같은 게 나. 처음부터 맛있는 냄새가 나진 않거든. 그 역겨운 냄새가 가시고 나야 비로소 우리가 먹을 수 있는 냄새가 나지. 명품 간장처럼 너도 이제 점점 인생을 알아가는 나이가 된 거야."

언니는 그렇게 하루에도 몇 번씩 나를 칭찬하고 응원해주었다. 그런 언니가 우리 집에서 40걸음쯤 거리에 살고 있다는 사실이 내게는 완전 로또 같은 행운이었다. 언니는 반지하에서 살았는데, 그 아담한 부엌이며 나란히 앉아서 이야기 나누던 방석 자리가 마치 아직 덜 자란 나를 키워준 인큐베이터처럼 느껴졌다. 인생의 소중한 자양분을 바로 그 공간에서 얻었으니까.

언니 덕분에 나는 칭찬이 어떻게 사람을 살릴 수 있는지 알게 되었다. 심지어 칭찬은 전파력도 강하다. 언니의 칭찬이 나를 일으켜 세우기도 했지만, 나 역시 다른 사람을 칭찬하기 시작한 것이다. 칭찬받는 사람이 칭찬하는 사람으로 거듭났다고나 할까? 확실히 '칭찬'이라는 시선으로 보게 되자 거의 모든 사람에게서 장점을 찾아낼 수 있었다.

자신만 모르는 자기만의 장점을 내가 짚어내고 응원과 격려를 보내자 주변 사람들의 표정이 점점 환해졌다. 그러는 동안 나는 어느새 긍정적인 사람이라는 이미지까지 얻게 되었다. 시선이 바뀌자 생각이 바뀌고, 생각이 바뀌자 행동이 바뀌면서 삶의 모습이 180도 달라진 셈이다.

"당신, 참 긍정적인 사람이네요."

이런 말을 들을 때마다 참 신기했다. 나의 첫 온라인 명함대로 되었으니 말이다. 그렇지만 나 자신에게 '진짜?'라고 묻는다면 아직 고개가 쉽게 끄덕여지지 않았다. 겉모습은 어느새 바뀌었고, 타인의 좋은 점들은 눈에 잘 보여 거침없이 칭찬해줄 수 있었지만, 내 모습에서는 여전히 칭찬해줄 만한 구석을 찾기 어려웠다. 그래서 타인을 향한 긍정적인 면이 반, 나를 향한 부정적인 면이 반, 다시 말해 밖은 긍정, 안은 부정, 이렇게 긍정과 부정이 반반이었다.

때론 링거액 같은
칭찬 한마디가 필요해

　　나를 칭찬하고 싶어도 칭찬할 게 없어 허탈해하던 차에 〈칭찬받는 고래〉라는 커뮤니티가 눈에 띄었다. 나를 사랑하는 마음으로 먼저 나를 칭찬하자는 취지가 마음에 쏙 들었다.

　'이거 완전 나를 위한 커뮤니티잖아?'

　안 그래도 나를 칭찬해보자는 분명한 목표가 있었기에 나는 초점을 나 자신에게 맞추고 전략적으로 칭찬을 연습하기 시작했다. 우선은 작고 사소한 것들부터 칭찬해볼까?

　역시나 쉬운 일이 아니었다. 예컨대 '4월 방학 특별 줌 미팅 시간 창조자 방에 참여하기'만 해도 일찍 일어나 성공

하면 칭찬받을 일이겠지만, 간혹 늦게 일어나 실패라도 하면 그 즉시 안내요원의 질책이 쏟아졌다.

'어떡할 거야? 다른 사람들은 다 일어났는데 넌 뭐야? 정말 민망해.'

안내요원의 꾸중에 나는 아침부터 기가 죽었다. 돌아보면 '새벽 4시(중국 시간)에 일어나기'를 시작하고 열흘도 채 안 되었을 때니 일어나면 기적이고, 오히려 못 일어나는 게 정상 같은데, 나 스스로에게는 그리도 냉정하고 모질었다.

그래도 포기하지 않고 하루 한 번씩 칭찬 연습을 해 버릇하자 조금씩 변화가 생겨나기 시작했다. 있는 그대로의 나를 온전히 받아들이면서 조금씩 의욕도 살아났다. 마음을 에워싸고 있던 무기력에서 점점 벗어나 스스로 격려하는 일도 전혀 어색하지 않았다.

'내가 할 수 있을까? 글쎄, 잘은 못 하지만, 자꾸자꾸 하다 보면 점점 나아질 거잖아. 아직 익숙하지 않아서 그래. 한 번 더 해보면 돼.'

이런 식으로 나를 편들어주는 긍정의 힘을 내면서부터 그동안 공격 일변도였던 부정적인 마음도 점차 사라지기 시작했다.

솔직히 다그침과 채찍질만이 답이라고 생각하던 때도 있었다. 하지만 나 자신을 칭찬한다는 것은 내가 나를 일으키는 동시에 나 스스로 일어나겠다는 의미였다. 그런 점에서 칭찬이야말로 힘은 적게 들면서 어쩌면 훨씬 더 잘 일어서는 방법이 아닐까?

어떤 칭찬들이 나를 이렇게 북돋아주었나 싶어 지난날의 칭찬 릴레이를 다시 읽어볼 때도 있다. 다시 봐도 정말 흐뭇해지고 마치 달콤한 포도 주스를 한 모금, 한 모금 마시는 것처럼 새삼스레 힘이 난다.

일기로 블로그 쓰기 시작한 나를 칭찬해요. 전 어젯밤 자기 전에 끓여둔 등갈비를 먹을 거예요. 역시 밤에 음식 해두길 잘했어요. 김치 콩나물국이랑요, 잘 먹고 잘 자기요 모두, 미리 음식 해두어 오늘 나를 불 앞에 잠깐만 서 있게 도와준 어젯밤의 나를 칭찬해요, 오늘 @상하이 시원 아트 ㅎㅎ 그림 새 계정 소문내고 다닌 거 칭찬해요. 운 좋게 줌 시간에 번쩍 눈이 뜨여 귀한 아침 잘 맞이했습니다. 기특해요. 어젯밤 아이들과 고스톱 배워서 같이 논 나를 칭찬해요. 7월 챌린지 완주한 거 칭찬해요. 3일차 쩍기상 성공!!! 칭찬해요. 벌떡 일어난 나를 칭찬해요. 깜짝 놀랐어요.

지난 칭찬 글을 읽다 보면 금세 기분이 좋아진다. 글을 쓸 때만 해도 이렇게 좋을지 몰랐는데, 이만큼 좋은 에너지를 내가 나에게 선물해주고 있었구나 싶어 새롭고 반갑다. 정말 잘했다. 하루하루 한 줄 일기를 보는 거 같고, 내 인증이 빠진 날은 그저 아쉽다. 이날 무슨 일이 있었는지 하나도 기억할 수가 없으니 역시 매일 인증을 꼭 해야겠다.

그런데 이 커뮤니티가 신기한 것은 서로에게 해주는 칭찬들이 정말 장난이 아니라는 점이다.

꿀처럼 달고 보약처럼 영양가 있다고 할까? 내 안에서 칭찬거리 찾기, 목표가 분명한 나는 나 자신을 칭찬하는 데 집중했다. 그런데 이게 무슨 일이지? 내가 나를 칭찬하고 나면 그 글에 여러 사람이 나를 마구마구 칭찬해주는 게 아닌가? 다들 내가 올린 이야기를 구석구석 세심하게 살펴가며 다시 한번 더 큰 칭찬으로 돌려주는 것이었다.

처음엔 정말 낯설고 어색했다. 물론 서로를 향한 칭찬과 배려가 이 커뮤니티의 기본 취지라는 건 알고 있었지만, 하루를 마치고 내 칭찬을 하기 위해 들어가 보면 서로에게 주는 칭찬이 너무 과하고 달콤하다는 생각에 뒤로 멈칫 물러나게 될 때도 많았다.

그러다 차츰차츰 '그래, 이런 정도의 칭찬이 필요할 때도 있지'라는 생각이 들기 시작했다. 몸에 기력이 없어 누워 있다가 링거를 맞고 다시 일어난 기억, 마음이 너무 약해졌을 때 '정말 사랑합니다, 축복합니다'라는 링거액 같은 말로 마음을 붙들어준 기억을 떠올리며 '맞다. 맞다. 링거액같이 빠르게 힘을 주는 말이 필요하지' 하고 고개를 끄덕였다.

언젠가부터 칭찬도 좋지만 내 이름이 불리기만 해도 기분이 좋아진다는 걸 알게 됐다. 이름을 불러주면 내가 꽃이라도 된 것처럼, 빗물에 젖어 잎처럼 촉촉해지고 윤기가 흐르는 것처럼 기분이 좋아졌다. 그래서 나도 메시지를 남긴 모든 사람의 이름을 불러 꽃으로 만들어주듯이 일일이 메아리를 해주었다.

내가 나를
칭찬하는 법

첫째, 무조건 "난 이미 충분해!"라고 말한다.

갓 따온 채소처럼 싱싱한 마음으로 일단 "난 괜찮아!"라고 말해본다. 아직 셀프 칭찬에 익숙하지 않은 경우라면 더더욱 자신의 현재 모습 자체를 있는 그대로 다 받아들이고 인정해주는 자세가 필요하다.

칭찬의 위력을 깨닫기까지는 시간이 좀 필요하니까 그전에 먼저 외우고 시작하는 게 빠르다. 믿는 대로 이루어진다고 하지 않았던가? 당신은 존재 자체로 이미 완벽하고 충분하다. 그 사실을 나만 모르고 있을 뿐이다. 이해가 안 되면 일단 먼저, '나는 나에게 만족해. 난 충분해. 난 완벽해'라고 내면을 향해 계속 신호를 보내주자.

음식이 너무 짤 때 설탕을 넣어주듯이 하루를 살다가 내가 부족하다고 느껴지거나 잘하지 못한다고 느껴질 땐 곧바로 생각을 바꿔주자. 예를 들어 새벽 5시 기상을 못 하고 6시에 일어났다면 즉시 이렇게 생각을 전환하는 것이다.

'7시에 일어났더라면 어땠겠어? 6시에라도 일어났으니 얼마나 다행이야? 잘했어, 정말.'

한마디로 더 안 좋은 상황과 비교해서 지금 이만큼도 잘한 거라며 격려하고 응원해준다. 목표치 바로 아래 단계에서 펌프질해주어 가라앉지 않도록 해야 한다. 빵에 이스트를 넣어 부풀게 하는 것처럼, 생선회를 담을 때 우뭇가사리나 천사채를 깔아주는 것처럼, 내려앉으려는 내 마음 아래를 받쳐준다. 또 아래로 내려오는 풍선을 손으로 톡톡 쳐서 계속 올라가게 해주는 것처럼, 나의 실수로 내가 나를 비난해서 상처받고 마음이 가라앉아 누워버리지 않도록 '이 정도도 꽤 잘하고 있는 거야', '이제 점점 더 좋아질 거야' 하고 계속 북돋아준다.

셋째, 무조건 우겨서라도 내가 나의 버팀목이 되어준다.

언제든 내 편이 되어주자. 나를 위해 필요하다면 박박 우거서라도 나 자신의 든든한 버팀목이 되어주는 것이다. 말이 좀 안 된다고 느껴지더라도 철저히 내 편이 돼준다. 그러면 나도 힘이 난다. 나로 살아주느라 애쓰는 내가 고마워서 편들어주는 것이다. 엄마가 만든 건 무조건 맛있다고 우길 때처럼 '누가 뭐래도 너는 오늘 하루도 최고였어!'라고 칭찬해주자.

국물 맛을 내기 어려울 때 넣으면 무조건 맛있어지는 윤종신의 라면 스프*처럼 '무조건 우기기'는 나에게 무한한 힘을 줄 수 있다.

영화 속의 불사신 주인공을 떠올려보자. 관객들은 주인공의 모든 행동을 무조건 응원한다. 그렇기에 그 어떤 적도 주인공을 죽일 수 없고, 어떤 시련이 닥쳐도 주인공은 끝내 이겨낸다. 그 주인공처럼 내 삶의 주인공은 바로 나, 오로지 나일 뿐이다. 그래서 내가 무조건 내 편을 들어주는 것이다.

라면 스프는 틀림없이 맛을 살려준다는 흔들림 없는 믿

---

* 예전에 어느 예능 프로그램에서 윤종신이 찌개 맛을 낼 때마다 일행들 모르게 라면 스프를 넣었는데 그때마다 매번 모두 놀랄 정도로 맛있다고 좋아했다.

음으로 '난 잘하고 있다'라고 믿어주면 맘 깊은 곳에서 뿌듯함이 자라난다.

이런 방법들로 나는 매일매일 나에게 칭찬을 보내며 점차 나만의 방법을 찾게 되었다. 그 누가 해주는 칭찬보다도 내가 날 온전히 받아들이고 인정해주는 칭찬이 제일 뿌듯했다.

셀프 칭찬이 가져다주는 또 하나의 선물이 있다. 처음엔 오로지 나에게만 초점을 맞춰 나 자신에게 '사랑해'라고 말했는데, 시간이 갈수록 내 아이들과 남편에 대해서도 사랑하는 마음이 점점 더 커지는 걸 느낀다. 정말 놀라운 변화 아닌가?

참, 내 안의 안내요원은 요즘 어떨까? 안내요원도 많이 변했다. 그래서 요즘은 지적질보다는 그냥 내가 하는 셀프 칭찬을 가만히 들어준다. 이제는 안내요원이 먼저 내게 힘이 되는 말을 수시로 해준다. 정말 눈물이 올라올 만큼 기쁘다. 이런 날이 오다니.

예전에 김미경 학장님이 자신의 열정에 대해서 이렇게 말한 적이 있다.

"저요? 왜 이렇게 열정이 많냐고요? 전, 저 김미경을 좋아하니까요. 전 김미경을 진짜 좋아해요."

이 말이 내 맘에 콱 박혔다. 맞다. 먼저 자기 자신을 좋아하고 사랑하는 마음이 가장 큰 힘이 되고 의지가 된다.

이제 당신 차례다. 매일매일 자신을 칭찬하고, 그 칭찬의 힘으로 자기 자신을 새롭게, 진정으로 사랑하기를 바란다.

끝으로 나의 셀프 칭찬을 함께 들어주고, 나보다 더 많이 나를 칭찬해준 칭고 여러분, 마음 깊이 감사드려요!

© 김연하

6
칭찬은 존중이다
— 나나

BGM MUSIC NFT #7

오랜 시간 잃어버렸던 나를 다시 만나러 가는 길. 그 여정에서 만난 사람들과 함께하며,
서로에게 아름답게 물들어가는 시간을 연주한 곡입니다.
나나랜드에 즉흥연주로 처음 공유했던 곡이고 첫 번째 디지털 싱글곡으로
미워하던 과거의 나를 다시 사랑하고 존중하게 되는 스토리가 담겨 있습니다.

'나' 없이 시작된 나의 이야기

딸이 아닌 맏이로서의 유년기

쉬는 법을 잃어버린 사람

왜 이제야 알았을까?

지금의 너로 충분해

지금 두렵다면, 좋은 신호다

'나' 없이 시작된
나의 이야기

———

　　글쓰기란 때로 자신의 깊은 마음속 상처를 마주해
야 하는 무척 고통스러운 작업이다. 특히 나 같은 사람에겐.
　　나는 가까운 사람에게도 좀처럼 속마음을 드러내지 못
하고, 내 마음보다는 타인의 마음을 먼저 헤아리느라 정작
자신과의 소통은 늘 뒷전이었다. 행여 남들과의 관계가 불
편해질까 두려운 나머지 언제나 내가 좀 더 배려하고 한 걸
음 물러났다.

　　타인과의 관계는 물론 가족과의 관계에서도 그랬다. 대
화를 통한 소통이 아니라 상대가 원하는 걸 눈치껏 캐치해
서 내가 먼저 해결해주는 식이었다. 그러다 보니 인간관계가

넓어지는 게 점점 부담스러워졌고, 새로운 사람과 가까워지는 것도 나에겐 챙겨야 할 또 하나의 숙제처럼 느껴졌다. 다른 사람에게 언제나 도움이 되어야 하고, 무언가를 먼저 주는 사람이 되어야 한다는 심리적 부담감 때문에 가슴이 늘 답답했다.

"나는 왜 이렇게 마음이 복잡한 사람일까?"

애초에 나의 이야기는 오롯이 나로부터 시작되지 않았다. 가족으로부터, 타인으로부터 시작되었다. 어릴 때부터 떠안게 된 맏이의 임무, 이른 결혼, 임신과 출산, 그리고 부모님이 몸져눕게 되자 다시 떠맡게 된 가장의 역할……. 그야말로 '나'가 아닌 '맏이라는 책임'을 다하기 위해 버텨낸 나날들이었다.

맏이로 태어났다고 해서 누구나 다 그렇지는 않을 텐데, 유독 나에게는 맏이라는 자리가 무겁고 힘겨웠다. 나에게 맏이란 부모님의 기대와 가족의 짐을 혼자 짊어져야 한다는 의미였다. 그렇기에 부모가 기대하는 모습, 주변에서 원하는 모습을 내 모습으로 인식하고, 그 안에 나를 적응시키며 성장기를 보낸 것이다.

동생들이 결혼해서 유학을 떠나고, 공부를 다 마칠 때까지도 나는 여전히 맏이의 역할을 내려놓지 못했다.

'나'가 쏙 빠진 삶에서 다시 나를 찾는 여정을 시작하기 전까지 나는 세 가지 역할에 묶여 있었다. 삶이 고단한 어머니와 병약하신 아버지를 대신해서 가족들을 돌보는 장녀로서의 삶, 친정에 잘하는 만큼 시댁에도 잘해야 한다는 헌신적인 며느리의 삶, 그리고 실용음악 입시 아카데미를 운영하는 입시 레슨 튜터로서 늘 완벽해야 하는 삶…….

나를 돌아볼 여유는커녕 어떻게 살고 싶은지조차 묻지 않았다. 그저 맏이의 책임을 다하는 일이 나에게 가장 중요했고 내가 존재하는 이유라고 받아들였을 뿐.

나는 성격이 내향적이고 마음이 여린 편이지만, 겉으로는 진취적이고 열정 넘치는 완벽주의자의 모습을 애써 유지하며 살아왔다. 입시 합격률 100%라는 타이틀을 가진 25년 차 레슨 튜터이자 실용음악 아카데미 대표로서 리더십을 발휘해야 했고, 오케스트라 편곡과 지휘는 물론 강사 교육팀장의 임무도 완벽하게 소화해내야 했다.

외양은 그럴싸해 보여도 그 이면에는 쉴 새 없이 일해야
만 하는 나의 절박한 상황이 숨어 있다. 물론 내 능력으로
일할 수 있다는 것에 늘 감사한 마음이었지만, 숨 가쁜 일정
에 따른 내면의 고충과 심적 부담을 그 누구에게도 털어놓
지 못한 채 홀로 짊어져야 하는 시간이었다. 누군가와 마음
을 나눌 여유도 없었고, 늘 일정에 떠밀려 정작 나를 들여다
볼 시간조차 없었다. 솔직히 내 공허한 마음을 드러내고 위
로받는 것보다 차라리 겉으로나마 능력 있는 커리어우먼으
로 보이는 게 낫다고 생각했다.

딸이 아닌
맏이로서의 유년기

―――

　　일곱 살 때였던가. 그 시절에도 엄마는 매번 끼니를 거를 만큼 바빴다. 하루는 어린 마음에 엄마가 걱정되어 내가 직접 식사를 챙긴답시고 라면에 찬물을 부은 적이 있다. 라면에 그냥 찬물을 붓기만 하면 저절로 따뜻하게 익을 줄 알았다. 엄마는 찬물에 오래 담가서 불어버린 라면을 삼키며 말없이 눈물을 흘렸다. 그때 엄마의 얼굴에서 두 가지를 보았다.

　　엄마는 행복하지 않다.
　　엄마의 삶은 너무 힘들다.

엄마의 그 슬프고 어두운 감정이 고스란히 느껴지면서 내 안에 한 가지 절대적인 신념이 생겨났다.

'내가 엄마를 지켜야 해.'

어떡하든 엄마의 근심을 조금이라도 덜어야 한다는 생각뿐이었다. 그래서 심지어는 동생의 학부모 상담까지 내가 대신 나갔다. 동생이 수업 준비가 안 되어 부모님을 모셔오라고 했는데, 엄마가 알면 너무 속상해할 거라 내가 대신 나간 것이다. 그때 나는 초등학교 4학년이었다. 동생 담임선생님의 당황해하던 그 표정이 아직도 어렴풋하게 기억에 남아 있다.

나는 애써 모범생이 되려 했고, 매사에 속이 깊고 어른스럽게 행동해야 했으며 때로는 내가 할 수 없는 것들도 해내야 했다. 아무도 내게 그러라고 시킨 적은 없다. 오로지 엄마의 기쁨을 위해, 엄마의 자랑이 되기 위해 나 스스로 선택한 일이었다.

나는 엄마의 고통을 함께 느끼려 했고, 언제나 엄마를 걱정시키면 안 된다는 마음을 품은 채 유년기를 보냈다. 엄마에게 나는 자식이기 전에 아픈 남편을 대신하는 버팀목 같은 존재, 자신으로부터 연결된 연장선이자 분신 같은 존재였다.

결혼해서 가정을 이룬 뒤에도 내 마음속엔 친정엄마의 힘들었던 결혼생활에 대한 보상을 장녀인 내가 해드려야 한다는 심리적 부채가 여전히 남아 있었다.

힘든 날엔 혼자 울컥하기도 했다. 나도 엄마 자식인데, 한 번도 자식으로서 마음을 기대어본 적이 없다는 게 문득 서럽게 다가올 때도 있었다. 하지만 나는 바쁜 엄마 대신 동생들 공부시키고, 사춘기도 없이 동생들을 위해 내 꿈을 양보해가며 부모님이 바라는 맏이의 모습으로 살아가는 것만이 모두를 위한 일이라고 생각했다.

그렇게 가족과 다른 사람을 지나치게 의식하고 배려하는 동안 '나'라는 개인은 점점 사라졌다. 한 번의 실수로 인생이 뒤바뀐다는 부모님의 보수적이고 엄격한 가정 교육은 나의 모든 가능성을 정지시켰다. 맏이가 잘 풀려야 한다는 부모님의 기대에 실수나 실패가 없도록 항상 계획하고, 내가 원하는 방향으로 일을 완성해나가야 한다는 강박 탓에 나는 늘 불안감을 안고 살아왔다. 맞다. 겉과는 달리 내 안에는 늘 불안에 떠는 '또 다른 나'가 있었다. 남들은 물론 나에게조차 들키고 싶지 않아 줄곧 숨겨두기만 했던 또 다른 나.

쉬는 법을
잃어버린 사람

———

　　내면을 돌보지 않은 채 원치 않는 모습으로 살아
가던 내게 뜻밖의 일들이 터지면서 기어코 번아웃이 찾아
왔다.

　　코로나와 함께 모든 일상이 마비된 2020년, 친정아버지
가 혈관 내시경 검사를 받던 중 동맥이 터지는 의료 사고를
당하고 말았다. 아버지는 하루아침에 의식을 잃고 중환자
실로 옮겨져 에크모를 단 채 생사를 넘나들게 되었다. 두 번
의 심정지로 긴급 수술을 받는 동안에도 코로나 때문에 가
족 면회는 불가능한 상황이었다.

"환자의 현재 상태를 가족분들이 직접 보시면 트라우마가 생길 수도 있습니다."

그런 이유로 담당 의사는 일주일 넘도록 중환자실에 홀로 누워 있는 아버지를 볼 수 없게 막았다. 날마다 가족의 목소리를 녹음해 중환자실 간호사의 핸드폰으로 전송하는 것만이 우리가 할 수 있는 전부였다. 속이 타들어갈 만큼 절박하고 불안한 시간이었다.

코로나가 가장 심했던 2020년 초기는 지역 간의 이동도 차단되고, 핸드폰으로 위치가 추적되면서 확진자들이 마녀사냥을 당하는 등 사회 전체가 예민하던 시기였다.

나는 담당 의사를 찾아가 눈물을 펑펑 쏟으며 사정했고, 마침내 직계 가족만 방호복으로 철저히 무장한다는 조건으로 1분이라는 면회 시간을 얻어낼 수 있었다. 나는 아직 체온이 남아 있는 아버지의 손을 꼭 잡아드렸다. 그것이 아버지와의 마지막 순간이었다. 직계 가족이 아닌 사위들은 병실 밖에서 마지막 작별 인사를 나눴다.

사랑하는 사람을 영원히 볼 수 없다는 것만큼 가슴 아

픈 일이 또 있을까? 아버지의 빈자리로 내 삶은 뿌리 뽑힌 나무처럼 내동댕이쳐진 것 같았다. 그런 상황에서도 나는 두 여동생과 친정어머니를 챙겨야 한다는 생각에 제대로 슬 퍼하지도, 맘껏 울지도 못했다. 이후 의료 사고를 입증하는 과정도 너무나 험난했고, 무능력한 나 자신이 너무도 원망 스러웠다.

장녀의 책임을 다하지 못했다는 죄책감, 코로나로 장례 식도 치르지 못한 답답한 현실, 살아생전 당부하신 시신 기 증 과정들이 겹치면서 나는 점점 부정적인 감정에 휩싸여 갔다. 아무리 노력해도 어쩔 수 없는 결과들까지 모두 나의 무능력함으로 돌리며 나 자신에게 끝없이 상처를 내고 있 었다.

아버지의 갑작스러운 사망으로 더욱 깊어진 번아웃과 갱년기의 우울증도 모자라 코로나로 인한 경제적 위기까지 겹쳐 숨조차 제대로 쉴 수가 없었다. 누가 봐도 쉬어야 할 상황이었지만, 나는 쉬고 싶어도 쉬는 법을 잃어버린 사람 이었다. 가만히 있는 시간이 오히려 더 불안했다. 아버지가 돌아가신 당일도 수시 준비가 급한 입시생 레슨을 했다. 한 시간 수업하고 한 시간 울고……, 그렇게 고통스러운 시간을 버텼다.

코로나와 함께 보낸 2년 동안 나는 그렇게 수많은 내적 갈등을 겪으며 그 어느 때보다 길고 어두운 시간을 지나왔다. 뉴스에서 불법 입시 지도에 관한 기사가 뜨고 학원들의 확진 사례가 나올 때마다 모든 일상을 차단하고 살아가는 내 삶이 고통스럽고 억울하게 느껴졌다. 다행히 2020년도, 2021년도 입시생 전원이 수시에 합격하긴 했지만, 나의 유연하지 못한 원칙주의와 코로나 입시를 이끌어가는 과정에서의 스트레스와 긴장감 때문에 기어코 공황장애 증상을 겪게 되었다.

어떤 순간에도 절대 잃어버리면 안 되는 나의 존재 이유를 완전히 상실해버린 것 같았다. 일을 잃어버리게 될까 봐 두려워하기 전에 나를 잃어버리게 될까 봐 두려워했어야 했다. 일을 통해 얻은 결과가 나의 존재 이유를 증명하는 것은 아닌데도 나는 한사코 일의 성과와 나의 가치를 연결하려고 했다.

왜 이제야
알았을까?

번아웃과 공황장애를 거치는 동안 나는 비로소 내 삶에서 가장 우선순위에 올려놔야 할 일이 무엇인지 깨달았다.

'이제, 나를 돌봐야 해.'

가장 중요하면서도 평생 우선순위의 최하위에 버려둔 그 일을 실행하기 위해 2022년 1월 1일, 514챌린지를 시작하게 되었다. 글자 그대로 나에게는 굉장한 도전이었다.

514챌린지를 통해 처음 커뮤니티 활동을 시작하면서 나는 완전히 새로운 세상을 만났다. 하지만 처음엔 내 속에서 심각한 거부 반응이 올라왔다.

6개월 전만 해도 나는 카톡조차 안 쓰는 완벽한 아날로 그인이었다. 평생 가족만을 삶의 중심에 두고, 내 전문 음악 분야 밖의 세상과는 담을 쌓은 채 살았던 만큼 시대의 변화를 읽는 안목도 부족했으며 이렇다 할 커뮤니티 활동도 한 적이 없었다. 20년 전쯤 싸이월드를 끝으로 온라인 세상에는 아예 존재하지 않는 사람이었다.

그런 내게 커뮤니티의 쉼 없는 소통 댓글은 카오스 그 자체였다. 툭하면 몇백 개씩 쌓이는 카톡 메시지도 멀미가 날 만큼 스트레스였고, 일상에 지장이 생길 만큼 많은 시간을 할애하느라 정신이 혼미해졌다. 1,000여 명이 참여하는 커뮤니티 안에서 내 의견과 생각을 드러내며 일일이 끼어드는 것도 심장이 두근거릴 만큼 긴장되는 일이었다. 하지만 나는 점점 낯선 환경에 적응하기 시작했다.

나와 생각이 다른 사람들, 살아온 궤적과 인생 경험이 다른 사람들을 통해 점점 더 많은 것을 알아가는 즐거움도 있었다.

그러면서 점점 내가 살아낸 나날들이 보이기 시작했다. 나의 진짜 모습이 아니라, 가족의 기대와 주어진 환경에 의해 가공된 모습으로 살아오는 동안 나는 한없이 작아져 있었다.

매일 무너지고 다시 일어서는 일이 되풀이되었다. 늘 불안하고 부정적이던 나의 이면, 저 깊은 무의식 차원에 두려움이라는 실체가 있었다는 사실, 그리고 이제 그 어둠의 덩어리를 직시하면서 시시각각 올라오는 감정들을 오롯이 느껴야 하는 시간이 이렇게나 고된 과정일 줄 몰랐다.

514챌린지를 시작하고 5개월 정도 지나서야 서서히 나의 삶 전체를 객관적으로 바라볼 수 있는 마음의 여유가 생기기 시작했다. 잃어버린 나를 찾기 위해, 자신의 성장을 위해 두 번째 스무 살을 시작한 사람들이 함께하는 커뮤니티 안에서 나는 매일매일 하나씩 알아가게 되었다.

나는 언제 행복한가.
나는 어떤 삶을 살고 싶은가.

혼자였다면 보지 못했을 새로운 세상을 보게 되었고, 비로소 내 안의 나를 끄집어내는 일을 시작할 수 있게 되었다. 서로를 응원하고 칭찬하는 사람들 속에서 얻는 긍정적인 성장 에너지가 나를 서서히 변화시켰다.

커뮤니티라는 성장 트랙 위에서 나는 더 깊은 곳의 '나'를 알고 이해하는 시간을 갖게 되었다. 나를 깊이 이해할수록 막연한 불안감이 사라졌고 더 자유로워졌다. 내적 성장에서 출발한 외적 성장이야말로 가장 이상적인 성장의 방향이었고, 모두가 따르는 정답을 쫓던 삶에서 벗어나 나만의 해답을 찾아가는 소중한 시간이었다.

뭔가를 깨닫는 순간, 사람들은 회한과 더불어 이런 질문을 던지곤 한다.

'이걸 왜 이제야 알았을까?'

왜 온갖 고생을 다 치른 뒤에야 알게 되었을까 하는 아쉬움 섞인 질문이다. 나도 같은 질문을 했다.

'왜 그런 시련을 다 겪은 뒤에야 알게 되었을까?'

물론 어리석은 질문이다. 나에게 시련이 없었다면 성장을 꿈꾸는 지금의 나도 없었을 테니까.

내가 겪은 모든 시련은 오늘의 나에게 꼭 필요한 삶의 과정이었다. 남들과 다른 모습이 진짜 내 모습인 줄 모르고, 그저 튀지 않기 위해 남들과 같아지려고 애쓰던 삶도 어쨌든 나의 삶이었다. 나의 희생을 당연하게 여기는 사람들에게 상처받고, 내가 바꿀 수 없는 환경을 탓하며 울음 삼키던 시간도 결국은 나의 삶이었다.

이제 알겠다. 그 세월 동안 나의 진정한 성장을 가로막은 사람은 그 누구도 아닌 나 자신이었다는 사실을. 그리고 나 한 사람을 만족시키는 일이야말로 모두를 만족시키는 일이라는 사실을.

자기 의심에 빠졌다는 것은 자기 확신이 필요한 순간이 왔다는 신호가 아닐까? 나는 스스로에 대한 확신 없이 반복된 삶에 안주한 채 결국 후회스러운 일상을 반복해온 것이다.

익숙한 패턴에서 벗어나려면 새로운 분야에 도전해야 했다. 그래서 디지털 드로잉을 시작했고 마음챙김을 위한 힐링 음악을 작곡하기 시작했다. 피아노를 연주하고 그림에 스토리를 입히는 과정을 반복하면서부터 나와의 소통이 시작되었고, 내 안의 창조성이 깨어나기 시작했다.

감사하게도 나를 찾기 위해 시작한 디지털 드로잉으로 국내 최대 NFT 공모전에 당선되어 상금을 전액 기부할 기회도 생겼다. 게다가 나의 기부가 작은 씨앗이 되어 MKYU에 기업 리더의 선한 가치를 추구하는 앙트러프러너 멤버십 클럽이 만들어졌다. 김미경 학장님이 앙트러프러너 멤버십 0호, 나는 앙트러프러너 멤버십 1호가 되었다. 공부하고 싶어도 여건이 안 되는 이주 여성과 미혼모를 위한 장학금으로 사용한다니 너무나 감격스러웠다.

지금의 너로
충분해

———

　　공모전 당선과 함께 앙트러프러너가 된 계기로 강의 요청까지 들어오기 시작했다. 25년 동안 해온 음악 분야의 재능 기부 강의를 통해 나누며 성장하는 가치를 온몸으로 경험할 수 있다는 것 자체가 나에겐 축복이었다.

　　재능 나눔 강의 홍보를 인스타에 올린 지 몇 시간 만에 선착순 100명이 바로 마감되기도 했다. 그날 강의에 참여한 분들이 나나랜드 힐링아트 커뮤니티의 회원이 되었고, 한 달 만에 200여 명의 뮤즈님과 함께 소통하는 커뮤니티가 되었다.

　　댓글 하나 남기는 것조차 어려워하던 내가 어떻게 여기

까지 오게 됐을까? 두려움과 마주하면서부터일 것이다. 용기를 내어 도전한 작은 시작들이 수많은 인연으로 엮이며 나를 이 자리로 이끌어온 것이다. 돌아보면 모든 일이 정해진 운명처럼 다가온 것 같다.

나는 더더욱 용기를 내어 '그림을 작곡하는 나나'라는 타이틀로 오픈씨(OpenSea, 현재 세계 최대 규모의 NFT 온라인 시장)에서 작품 활동을 시작했고, 음원 NFT 컬렉션은 리스팅한 지 2주 만에 벌써 여섯 작품이 판매되기도 했다.

내가 없던 삶에서 나를 찾겠다고 시작한 514챌린지 커뮤니티 활동인데, 이제 나를 찾는 것을 넘어 새로운 부캐까지 얻게 된 셈이다. NFT 작가 활동을 통한 수익과 이모티콘 작가 활동으로 생긴 수익을 기부하면서 매년 새로운 앙트러프러너 멤버십으로 거듭나겠다는 목표도 생겼다. 본업과 분리된 부캐로 선한 가치를 추구하면서 생긴 수익을 기부하겠다는 꿈이다. 나의 가치도 실현하고 사회적 가치도 실현하는 삶을 살 수 있게 된 것이다.

나의 작품은 단순한 스토리텔링이 아니라 내가 살아낸 하루를 오롯이 담아낸 '스토리 리빙(story living)'이다. 지난 시간 부족했던 내 모습, 오늘을 살아가며 여전히 흔들리는 나와 너, 그러나 포기하지 않고 계속 나아가는 우리의 모습을 그림과 음악에 담아내고 싶다.

이따금 지난 시절, 삶의 물결에 허우적대는 내 모습이 스냅사진처럼 스쳐 지나갈 때도 있다. '나 하나 바뀐다고 뭐가 달라질까?' 하는 내적 갈등을 애써 외면해가며 한사코 긍정 최면을 걸어 나 자신을 채찍질하던 시절이었다. "난 이번에도 잘 해낼 수 있어. 나는 이 문제를 꼭 해결해야만 해." 무한 경쟁에 뒤처지지 않기 위해 어두운 자아는 숨겨버리고, 맹목적인 긍정 확언과 타인으로부터의 인정과 칭찬들로 나를 포장해가며 쉼 없이 나 자신을 밀어붙였다. 나와의 소통이 단절된 채 여기가 어디쯤인지, 내가 어디로 가고 있는지조차 묻지 않고 앞만 보고 달렸다.

나와의 소통을 통해 내면의 트라우마를 극복하지 못했더라면 나는 아직도 여전히 눈 가린 경주마처럼 똑같은 트랙을 내달리고 있지 않았을까?

글을 쓰기 시작하면서 한 발짝 뒤로 물러나 지나온 삶을 객관적으로 바라보게 된 것도 커다란 계기가 되었다. 삶을 해석하는 관점이 바뀌자 똑같은 상황에서도 전혀 다른 선택을 할 수 있게 된 것이다.

세상은 상대적인 가치들이 한 몸처럼 어우러져 돌아간다. 어둠이 있기에 빛이 있듯이 슬픔과 기쁨, 행복과 불행도 저 홀로 존재할 수 없다. 그런 상대성 위에서 갈등하고 수용하고 극복해가며 성장해가는 것이 인간 본연의 모습이라는 사실을 깨닫자 나는 비로소 '늘 행복만을 추구해야 한다'라는 환상에서 벗어날 수 있었다.

나를 아프게 한 사람들을 용서하고, 아무리 노력해도 해결할 수 없는 일들이 존재하는 게 바로 삶이라는 사실도 받아들였다. 누군가를 미워하고 원망하던 마음이야말로 나를 가장 괴롭히는 감정들이었다. 한참을 제자리에 머물며 아픈 마음을 떠나보내고 나서야 나는 다시 편안한 호흡으로 돌아올 수 있었다.

도전하는 것도 용기지만, 제자리에 머물던 나를 온전히 사랑하는 것도 큰 용기일 것이다.

"특별하지 않아도 돼. 지금의 너로 충분해."

부모와 주변의 기대에 부응하기 위해 나 자신을 채근하던 나, 실수와 실패가 두려워 밤잠을 설치던 어린 시절의 나에게 해주고 싶은 말이었다. 스스로 존중하는 마음을 갖게 되니 평범한 일상의 작은 행복들이 더욱 소중해졌다.

오랫동안 나 자신을 엄격하게 몰아세우던 습관 탓일까, 아직은 작고 사소한 일로 나를 칭찬하는 일이 쑥스럽다. 하지만 서로를 칭찬해주는 커뮤니티 안에서 함께 소통하는 것만으로도 내 마음은 따뜻한 온기로 채워졌다. 그런 온기들을 고스란히 음악과 그림에 담아냈고, 그렇게 만들어진 BGM 디지털 싱글 앨범이 어느덧 10집까지 발매되었다.

진심이 통했는지 신기하게도 내 음악을 듣고 서로에게 물들어가는 공감이 느껴진다는 말에 뭉클해지기도 했다. 말로 칭찬을 표현하고 글로도 칭찬을 표현할 수 있지만, 나는 음악으로 칭찬을 담아내고 있었다.

지금 두렵다면,
좋은 신호다

뭔가가 당신을 불쾌하게 한다면 그 안을 들여다봐라. 무언
가 있다는 신호다.
–《타이탄의 도구들》중에서

처음에 Web 3.0 세상은 아날로그인이던 나를 더없이
불편하게 하는 공간이었다. 하지만 나는 익숙한 삶에서 벗
어나고자 용기를 내어 디지털 드로잉을 시작했고, 마침내
힐링 NFT 크리에이트라는 부캐로도 활동하게 되었으며, 심
지어 커뮤니티 리더의 기회까지 얻게 되었다. 나에게 NFT
란 상상력과 용기를 발휘하여 대체 불가능한 나를 만들어
가는 과정이었다. 무엇보다 NFT를 시작하면서 나에게 많은

질문이 생겨나기 시작했다.

'뭘 그리고 싶어?'
'어떤 음악을 작곡하고 싶어?'
'왜 그렇게 표현한 거야?'
'작품 속에 너를 제대로 담았어?'
'지금은 어떤 꿈을 꾸고 있지?'
'세상에 전하고 싶은 메시지가 뭐야?'

끝없이 스스로 묻고 답하는 동안 외부의 조건들에 묶여 있던 마음이 점점 자유로워졌다. 결국 열쇠는 '나'였다. 내가 나를 만나 수용하고 소통하면서 삶이 변하고 나를 둘러싼 세상이 바뀌기 시작한 것이다.

오랫동안 나를 가장 아프게 한 사람은 바로 나였다. '나 상처받았어'라고 말하는 순간 나는 상처받은 사람이 된다. 상처 준 사람 마음까지는 내가 알 수 없지만, 적어도 나에겐 '상처받지 않는 선택'을 할 자유가 있었다. 이 진실을 깨닫기까지 참 힘들었지만, 가장 깊게 성장할 수 있는 시간이기도 했다. 내가 가지 못한 길에 대한 후회와 아쉬움보다 그땐 그 선택이 최선이었고, 그로 인해 충분히 다른 경험을 할 수 있었다. 할 수 없을 것 같은 일에 도전하지 않는다면 내가 원하는 곳에 영원히 이를 수 없다. 기적이라는 것도 용기 내어 첫발을 내디뎌야만 일어나는 일이다.

'내가 잘할 수 있을까?'
'괜한 시간 낭비는 아닐까?'
'실패하면 어떡하지?'

이런 질문들은 우리를 망설이게 할 뿐이다. 진정한 용기란 두렵지 않은 상태가 아니라, 두려워도 도전하는 자세에 있다고 했다. 익숙함에 안주하면 절대 보이지 않는 저 너머의 세상에 호기심을 가져야 한다. 그리고 첫발을 내디뎌야 한다. 나 역시 평생 살아온 것과는 다른 시선으로 살고 싶어서 NFT라는 첫발을 내디뎠기에 여기까지 올 수 있었다. 그런 나를 칭찬한다.

지난 세월, 나에게 부여된 역할에 충실한 사람이 되면 모두가 행복해지는 길이라 여겼던 그 어리석은 마음도 이제는 칭찬해주기로 했다. 그렇게 나라는 개인이 존재하지 않는 삶으로 흔들리는 시간을 보내며 번아웃을 겪었지만, 사실 번아웃도 내가 나약해서가 아니라 열심히 살았던 흔적일 테니까.

후회되는 일, 자책하고 싶은 일들에 대해 뒤늦게나마 칭찬을 보내자 나를 짓누르던 마음의 짐도 훨씬 가벼워졌다. 인생의 성공이란 무엇일까? 지금, 이 순간에 온전히 만족할 수 있다면 그게 성공일 것이다.

이제 누군가를 위해 희생하고 배려해야 한다는 의무감이 아니라 나의 행복을 위해 더 많이 나누고 베푸는 사람이 되고 싶다. 모르면 물어보고 부족하면 배워가면서 점점 더 나은 나를 만들어가고 싶다. 남을 위해서가 아니라 나를 위해서 그렇게 한다면 조금 더 나다운 삶에 가까워지지 않을까.

자신의 진짜 마음을 더 깊이 알고 싶다면 지금 당장 자신과의 소통을 권한다. 새로운 도전이 두려운가? 그렇다면 좋은 신호다. 어쩌면 그것이야말로 내가 하고 싶어서 오랫동안 망설여왔던 '진정 가치 있는 일'일지도 모르니까.

© 공혜린

7

칭찬은 동행이다

— 쩡희

BGM MUSIC NFT #8
느리지만 멈추지 않는 걸음을 응원하는 차분한 멜로디입니다.
제가 청고 방에 들어가서 칭찬이 쑥스러워 음악으로 칭찬을 전하며,
선물로 만들어서 올린 곡입니다.

나만 뒤처지는 건 아닐까?

지금 못 해준 것, 나중에 다 보상해줘야지

두 얼굴의 엄마, 두 얼굴의 아내

칭찬이 아침 루틴이 되면 생기는 일

질리지 않는 칭찬의 맛

나만 뒤처지는 건
아닐까?

'어릴 때 나는 어떤 아이였을까?' 가끔 생각해본다.

일곱 자매의 넷째인 나는 나름 똑똑하고 자기주장도 곧잘 하는 씩씩한 아이였다. 그런가 하면 적당히 꾀도 부리고 예민한 데다 끈기가 부족한 대신 호기심과 공감력이 있고, 단체 생활에서는 협동심이나 책임감을 보이기도 했다. 솔직히 나는 '아들 같은 딸'이고 싶었다. 그래서 전기기술자인 아버지의 공사 현장에 쫄랑쫄랑 참 많이도 따라다녔다. 학교 끝나면 곧장 현장에 달려가 아버지 곁에서 말동무도 하고 심부름도 하면서, '아버지에게 도움이 되는 딸'이라는 자부심도 느끼곤 했다.

놀이터에서 놀고 싶은 날도 있고, 친구의 생일파티에 가고 싶은 날도 있었지만, 나에겐 아버지가 일하는 공사 현장이 우선이었다. 누가 강요하지도 않았는데 나 스스로 나의 역할을 정한 것이다. 주변에서 아버지에게 "딸만 있어 힘들겠다"라고 하면 어린 맘에 "치, 내가 아들 노릇 대신하면 되지, 뭐" 그러면서 더 열심히 아버지를 도왔다. 내가 곁에 있으면 아버지가 덜 외롭고, 덜 힘들어할 거라는 생각에 중학교 2학년 때까지 공사 현상을 잘도 누비고 다녔다.

아버지는 흥이 많은 사람이었다. 노래와 낚시, 캠핑을 좋아했고, 무엇보다 자식 사랑, 아내 사랑이 남달랐다. 덕분에 우리 식구는 1980년대만 해도 흔치 않던 가족 캠핑과 여행을 심심찮게 다녔다.

아버지는 일할 때마다 늘 콧노래 부를 만큼 흥겨웠지만, 추운 날 차가운 전선 줄에 손가락 피부가 쩍쩍 갈라질 때마다 약 바른 손에 장갑을 끼고 잠자리에 들기도 했다. 나는 그런 아버지를 존경했지만, 한편으론 무섭기도 했다.

자수성가한 아버지는 매사에 '평생 공부'와 '정신 상태'를 강조했다. 여자도, 아니 여자일수록 능력이 있어야 한다며, 딸들 대학 졸업시키기 위해 아버지는 정말 열심히 일했다. 엄마는 16년 동안 쉬지 않고 겨울마다 연탄배달을 했다. 아직 중고등학생이던 언니들도 학교 끝나면 열심히 엄마를 도왔다.

아버지는 정도 많고 흥도 많았지만, 부사관으로 전역한 이력답게 시시때때로 우리를 군인 대하듯 하기도 했다. 우리가 무슨 실수라도 하면 "정신 상태가 왜 그 모양이냐?"라며 화를 냈다. 어린 나는 '사람이 실수할 수도 있는 거 아닌가?' 생각하며 유독 실수에 관대하지 못한 아버지가 미웠다. 그래서인지 나 역시 유난히 실수나 실패에 예민해지고, 또 그만큼 두려워하게 되었다. 성인이 된 후에도 나는 실수할 때마다 온종일 스스로 자책하고 후회하며 나 자신을 괴롭혔다. 또 그럴수록 자존감이 떨어지는 건 당연한 일이었다.

'평생 공부'를 입에 달고 살던 아버지는 일흔일곱 살에 갑자기 돌아가시기 전까지도 영어 공부를 놓지 않았다. 젊었을 땐 영어사전이 낡아 겉표지를 전기 테이프로 둘둘 감아 들고 다녔다고 한다.

그런 아버지마저도 지인들에게 두세 번 사기를 당했고,

1997년 IMF 위기 때는 눈물까지 보이기도 했다. 그 당시 엄마 몰래 외삼촌의 보증을 서는 바람에 부도를 맞은 것이다. 집에 압류가 들어오고, 부부가 함께 평생 모은 재산과 노력이 하루아침에 물거품이 되었다.

결혼은 제2의 인생이라고 했던가. 나는 스물일곱 살이 끝나가던 12월에 한 남자를 만났다. 웃는 모습이 유난히 따뜻하고 말과 행동도 온화한 사람이었다. 결혼식을 올렸을 때 내 나이는 스물아홉 살이었고, 직장도 계속 다니고 있었다. 결혼하고 2년 동안 임신이 안 되다가 어쩔 수 없이 퇴사했더니 4개월 만에 아이가 생겼다. 그 뒤로 4년이 흐르면서 나는 어느새 두 형제의 엄마가 되었다.

요즘 말로 '독박육아'의 나날이 계속 이어졌다. 회사가 어려워지면서 남편의 퇴근은 점점 늦어졌고, 나는 어떡하든 아이들을 자연과 만나게 해주고 싶어 도시락을 싸 들고 열심히 밖으로 나갔다. 비가 오면 비를 맞으며 첨벙첨벙, 옷이야 빨면 되니까 맘껏 놀게 했다. 아이들은 자연에서 에너지를 받고 발산해야 한다는 게 내 생각이었다. 덕분에 마음 맞는 엄마들을 만나 지금도 소중한 인연을 맺고 있다.

한편 꾸준히 직장을 다니면서 차곡차곡 승진하는 친구들을 볼 때마다 마음 밑바닥에선 '공부해야 해'라는 생각이 스멀스멀 올라오기도 했다. 그나마 알뜰한 가정주부로서 적은 월급에도 1가구 2주택으로 아이들을 키우고 있다는 자부심에 만족할 따름이었다.

'평생 공부'의 화신과도 같은 아버지는 손자들을 볼 때마다 내게 말했다. "요 두 놈들 키우고 나면 너도 공부 계속해라."

솔직히 아이들이 자라면서 '엄만 모르는 게 많아'라는 소리를 들을까 봐 두려웠고, 스스로가 뒤처지는 것은 더더욱 무섭고 싫었다. 그런데도 나는 하루하루 살기 바쁘다는 이유로 한사코 공부를 외면했다.

지금 못 해준 것,
나중에 다 보상해줘야지

———

　　사람이 무섭다는 말을 뼈저리게 체험한 적이 있다. 같은 층에서 6년 동안 친구처럼 가깝게 지내던 지인에게 돈을 빌려줬는데, 그 사람이 말로만 듣던 야반도주를 해버린 것이다. 아침부터 복도가 시끄러워 나가보니 대여섯 명의 여자가 문을 쾅쾅 두드리고 소리치며 야단법석을 떨고 있었다. 다들 나처럼 돈을 빌려준 사람들이었다. 3억 넘게 사기당한 어느 부부는 서로 친정에도 오갈 정도로 친했다며 분통을 터뜨렸다. 나도 심장이 떨리긴 마찬가지였다.

　　사람의 배신이란 게 이런 거였나, 정말 무서웠다. 그나마 고맙고 힘이 되는 건 남편의 반응이었다. 남편은 힘들어하는 나를 위로하며 차분하게 다음 행동을 준비했다. 즉시 퇴

직급을 중간 정산하여 대출을 처리하고 집을 옮기기로 한 것이다. 계속 그 집에서 살다간 사기당한 기억이 트라우마로 남을 것 같아서였다.

하지만 13년이 흘러도 그때의 충격이 채 가시지 않았는지, 길에서 그 여자와 비슷한 사람만 봐도 심장이 멎는 것 같다. '세상엔 공짜란 절대 없다'라는 교훈을 뼈저리게 느끼며, 아이들에게도 틈만 나면 각인시키고 있다.

남편이 없었다면 어떻게 됐을까? 새삼 남편의 소중함을 알게 됐다. 남편은 빨리 잊으라고 했지만, 지금도 문득문득 생각난다. 여전히 마음이 아프고 떨리는 걸 보면 아직도 그 사건은 현재진행형인 듯하다.

어느 날, 남편이 자기 사업을 해보고 싶다기에 적극적으로 응원해주었다. 젊고 기술도 있고, 아이들도 아직 어리니만에 하나 사업이 뜻대로 안 되더라도 몇 년은 충분히 견딜 수 있다고 생각했다. 이것이 부부가 아닐까? 내 부모가 그랬듯이 우리도 이 사업을 성장 동기로 삼아 함께 도전하고 함께 시련을 이겨나가기로 했다. 언젠가는 그 모든 경험을 추억으로 공유하는 날이 오리라 믿으면서.

남편이 서른아홉 살에 퇴사하고 시작한 사업은 족발 가게였다. 정말 생각지도 못한 도전이었다. 할 줄 아는 요리라곤 고작 라면 하나 끓일 정도인데 족발을?

남편은 3개월 동안 무보수로 일을 배운 다음 마침내 가게를 열었다. 나는 아직 아이들이 어려서 적극적으로 거들 순 없었지만, 그래도 할 수 있는 데까지 도왔다. 매일 아침 농수산 시장에서 장을 봐 오고, 직원 아주머니들 식사 준비까지 해놓은 다음 부랴부랴 아이들 챙기고 새벽엔 남편의 퇴근을 도왔다.

주말도 없이 정말 열심히 했다. 다행히 장사가 잘되어 직원을 다섯 명이나 고용하기도 했다. 한번은 미성년자가 우리 가게에서 술을 마시는 바람에 한 달간 영업정지를 받기도 했다. 직원이 신분증 검사를 하지 않은 게 문제였다. 그런가 하면 오른손잡이인 신랑이 족발을 썰다가 오른쪽 손가락 한 개가 절단되는 사고도 있었다. 그렇게 3년 6개월 동안 하루하루를 정신없이 보냈다.

그런 어느 날, 큰 폭풍이 닥쳐왔다. 수십 년간 묵인하에 장사해온 가게 건물 일부가 불법이 드러나는 바람에 3분의

2를 허물게 된 것이다. 장사가 잘되다 보니 누가 시샘해서 민원을 넣었다는 얘기도 들려왔다.

권리금과 시설 투자비는 물론이고 그 많던 단골손님들까지 하루아침에 다 잃게 된 상황이었다.

이제 어떻게 해야 할까? 그동안 정들었던 족발집 장사를 이대로 접어야 하나? 남편과 나는 늦게까지 머리를 맞대고 궁리했다.

아이들에겐 너무 미안했지만, 아직 어릴 때 고생하자는 마음으로 우리 부부는 다시 시작하기로 했다. 작은 동네에 새로운 족발집을 차리고 직원이나 아르바이트 없이 단둘이서 헤쳐나가기로 한 것이다. 우리 부부는 하루 평균 서너 시간만 자면서 가게 일과 육아를 병행해나갔다. 몸은 점점 피폐해졌지만, 그래도 우리는 고객 숫자가 늘어나는 즐거움 속에서 힘을 얻었다.

다만 아이들을 제대로 돌보지 못하는 현실이 가슴 아팠다. 시간에 쫓겨 제때 밥을 챙겨주지 못한 날이면 냉동조리식품이나 반조리 상태의 음식 따위를 사다 줘야 했다. 예전 같으면 상상도 하지 못할 행동이었다. 게다가 우리 부부가 늦은 밤까지 집에 없다 보니 아이들 수면의 질도 떨어지고, 출출할 땐 저희끼리 몰래 편의점에 가서 간편식을 사 먹기도 했다. 김밥도 전에는 내가 만들어주는 것 말고는 입에도 대지 않던 아이들이었다. 나는 아이들이 살이 찌는 모습을 보고 나서야 그동안 편의점 음식을 자주 사 먹어왔다는 사실을 알게 되었다. 엄마의 부재가 아이들 식생활에서 확연히 드러난 것이다.

두 마리 토끼를 다 잡을 수는 없다는 현실이 우리 부부에게 엄청난 갈등이었지만, 그래도 당장은 뾰족한 수가 없었다. 일단은 먹고사는 게 더 중요했으니까. 솔직히 부모가 열심히 사는 모습을 보면서 아이들이 바르게 자라줄 거라는 막연한 믿음과 자부심도 없지 않았다. 또 장사가 잘되어 가정 경제가 안정되면 그때 가서 얼마든지 아이들에게 못 해준 것들을 보상해줘야지, 하고 내 멋대로 합리화하기도 했다. (아, 이 얼마나 어리석은 생각이었나!)

그렇게 2년쯤 지날 무렵, 또 하나의 날벼락이 떨어졌다. 이번엔 건물주가 우리 가게 자리에서 장사하기로 하는 바람에 어쩔 수 없이 나가야 할 상황이 벌어진 것이다. 하늘이 무너지는 것 같았다. 2년여에 걸친 우리 가족의 희생이 의미 없이 흩어지는 사건이었다.

어쩔 수 없는 상황이라고는 하지만, 두 번의 실패 끝에 우리는 결국 집을 팔고 정리해서 거처를 옮겼다. 신혼 때 살던, 그리고 아이들이 태어난 도시로 되돌아간 것이다.

불행 중 다행으로 남편도 나도 취업이 빨리 되어 소소하게나마 월 소득을 이어갈 수 있었다. 무엇보다 온 가족이 함께 저녁 식사를 할 수 있어 좋았다. 주말도 함께 보내고 작은 일에도 함께 웃을 수 있었다. 아이들은 일요일마다 가족과 함께 지내겠다면서 친구들과의 약속도 잡지 않았다. 초등학교 2학년, 4학년이던 두 아이가 어느새 중 3, 고 2가 되었다. 너무나 잘 자라주고 있는 나의 보물들.

두 얼굴의 엄마,
두 얼굴의 아내

＿＿＿

　　　　오랜 공백 탓인지 직장 생활은 새로움의 연속이었다. 독수리타법에 정보처리 능력은 없고, 엑셀도 전혀 모르는 컴맹 수준이라 자존감이 바닥에 떨어진 기분이었다. 그래서 취업 면접 때 컴퓨터 활용 능력이 없다는 사실을 밝히고, 그에 따라 낮은 급여를 책정받는 것도 받아들였다. 일단 직장 생활을 하면서 차근차근 배워나갈 생각이었다.

　퇴근해서는 오로지 가족을 위해 장을 보고, 다양한 반찬을 매일매일 바꿔가며 푸짐하게 저녁상을 차렸다. 식사가 끝나면 말 그대로 푹 절인 파김치가 되어 식탁 한쪽으로 그릇들을 밀어둔 채 잠시 엎드려 쪽잠을 잔 적도 많았다. 남편과 아이들이 일어나라고 건드리면 짜증도 참 많이 냈다. '내가 왜 이러지' 하면서도 속으론 가족을 위해 헌신하느라 이렇게 힘든 거라고 자위했다. 물론 나의 착각이었지만.

남편은 안쓰럽다며 반찬은 한 가지만 있어도 괜찮다, 없으면 사서 먹는 것도 좋다, 당신 힘든 것보다 그편이 훨씬 낫다며 미안해했지만, 그땐 남편의 마음을 몰랐다. 퇴근하는 엄마를 반기러 나오는 아이들을 안아주기는커녕 방이 왜 이렇게 지저분하냐고 야단부터 치기 일쑤였다. 잔뜩 웅크린 채 동그란 눈만 깜빡거리는 아이들을 보면 또 금세 후회가 밀려오곤 했다. 세상에서 제일 소중한 아이들과 남편에게 계속 잔소리를 퍼붓고 상처만 주는 내 모습이 너무 싫었다. 어릴 때 아버지의 군대식 교육을 그렇게 싫어하던 내가 어느새 그 모습을 고스란히 답습하고 있었다.

일이 그렇게 힘들면 쉬어도 됐을 텐데, 책임감이 무거우면 살짝 내려놓아도 큰일 나는 게 아닐 텐데 왜 그랬을까. 잘해줄 땐 한없이 잘해주다가도 화가 나면 무섭게 돌변하는 두 얼굴의 엄마, 두 얼굴의 아내, 이것이 그 시절의 내 모습이었다. 터져 나오는 감정을 참으려 애쓰고, 때론 조언도 들어가며 노력했지만, 가족이 그런 노력을 몰라주는 것 같아 서운해하기도 했다.

자기 계발은커녕 그냥 이렇게 감정 기복 심하고 자존감 낮은 사람으로 굳어질까 봐 불안했다. '평생 공부'라는 아버지의 선물도 여전히 내 맘을 불편하게 했다.

많은 사람이 그랬듯이 코로나 시기에는 나 역시 유튜브에 푹 빠져 있었다. 알고리즘으로 떠오르는 수많은 정보에 이끌리다 보니 나의 관심사도 점점 넓어졌다. 그렇다고 관련된 책이나 정보를 더 찾아볼 정도는 아니었다. 나는 점점 핸드폰과 밀접한 관계가 되어갔다.

우연히 김미경 학장님의 강의를 보면서 그분의 저서들을 읽어봐야겠다는 생각이 강하게 들었다. 그러나 이번에도 역시 행동으로 이어지진 않았는데, 어느 날 공지가 떴다. '2022년 1월 1일부터 14일까지 미라클모닝 514 챌린지를 시작한다'라는 내용이었다. 이건 또 뭐지?

새벽 5시 기상이라…… 평소보다 한 시간 반 일찍 일어나는 정도니까 그렇게 힘들 것 같진 않았다. 게다가 김미경 학장님과 함께라니, 한번 해볼까? 잠시 고민 끝에 실천해보기로 했다.

인스타그램은커녕 구글 앱도 멀리하던 내가 아이들에게 물어가며 신청서, 구글 폼, 회원가입, 인증서 작성 등을 어찌어찌 완료했다. 괜히 한다고 했나? 그냥 그만둘까? 계속되는 갈등 속에 드디어 챌린지가 시작되었다.

칭찬이 아침 루틴이 되면
생기는 일

─────

2022년 1월 1일.

두근두근, 나는 잠을 설치다가 새벽 4시부터 일어나 기다렸다. 그리고 5시 땡!

세상에, 1만 명 넘는 사람들이 그 시간에 깨어 있었다. 순간 온몸이 짜릿해졌다. 이 놀랍도록 신선한 세계가 너무 좋았다.

가만, 그런데 이거 어떻게 하는 거지? 강의 사진을 캡처하긴 했지만, 구체적으로 내가 뭘 어떻게 해야 하는지 알 수가 없었다. 내가 속한 4번 방의 사이다 방에 물어보니 많은 분이 너무도 친절하게 알려주었다.

내가 인스타그램 첫 인증을 했다! 사진은 잘린 채로 올렸지만, 그래도 내가 해냈다는 성취감이 굉장했다. 2022년이 남다르게 시작되는 기분이었다. 일출 보러 가자고 남편과 미리 약속해둔 터라 함께 집을 나섰다. 그리고 솟아오르는 새해 첫 태양 앞에서 다시 한번 가슴이 벅차올랐다.

오십을 바라보는 나이, 사회에서의 입지가 점점 줄어드는 이 나이에 어떤 공부를 해야 할까. 주변 지인들처럼 사회복지사 자격증이나 요양보호사 자격증을 따야 하나? 이런 고민을 하던 중에 '새로 시작하는 사람. 실력 차이가 아니라 시간 차이다!'라는 말은 나에게 커다란 동기부여가 되었다. 하지만 첫 강의에서부터 너무도 생소한 단어들이 난무하는 것을 보며 충격과 당혹감에 어쩔 줄 몰랐다. 자기 계발이니 평생 공부니 하는 말은 예전부터 아버지가 강조해온 잔소리로만 치부했는데, 그게 아니었다. '생각 조망권, 웹 2.0, 3.0, 인스타, 블로그, 유튜브, 메타버스……' 어쩌다 뉴스에서 얼핏 듣긴 했어도 나에겐 여전히 '외계어'나 다름없는 단어들이 강의 내내 자연스럽게 흘러나왔다.

MKYU에 회원가입은 했지만 일단 거기서 멈췄다. 현재 아이들에게 들어가는 학원비도 학원비려니와 나의 게으름과 귀찮아하는 성향 탓에 아무래도 중도에 포기할 것 같아 망설여졌다. 또 모닝 챌린지가 얼마나 갈까? 온라인상에서 맺어진 인연을 믿을 수 있을까? 이래저래 비용 문제가 발목을 잡는 바람에 결국 무료 강의를 먼저 듣고 난 뒤에 판단하기로 했다.

이 과정에서 나는 알게 모르게 많은 영향을 받게 되었다. 무엇보다 자기 자신을 사랑하는 법, 꾸준하게 공부하면서 '나'를 드러내는 방식에 눈을 뜨기 시작했다.

남편과 아이들에게 너무 미안했고, 이제 용서를 빌고 싶은 마음이 들었다. 나는 그런 마음을 말이 아닌 행동으로 보이려고 노력했다. 맞다, 잠깐이라도 자기만의 시간을 가져야 한다는 말이 정답이었다. 나 자신과 마주한 그 시간을 통해 깊은 반성과 더불어 나는 조금씩 변하기 시작했다. 짜증 내는 횟수가 눈에 띄게 줄어들고, 힘들 땐 식구들에게 도움을 청하기도 했다. 남편이 늘 주장하던 '일요일 아침 외식'도 드디어 실행에 옮겼다. 전반적으로 모든 것이 좋아지는 느낌이었다.

4월 어느 날, 내가 좋아하는 '동행'이란 단어와 함께 어딘가 몽상적이면서도 예쁜 고래 이미지로 꾸며진 방이 눈에 띄었다. 〈칭찬받는 고래〉라는 방이었다. 어떤 방일까? 호기심에 이끌려 오픈 방에 들어가 매일매일 구경했다. 한마디로 '사소한 것까지 아낌없이 칭찬하는 방'이었다.

이런 게 다 칭찬거리가 된다고?

솔직히 잠깐 들어갔다 나오려 했는데, 어느새 나의 아침 루틴이 되어버렸다. 그동안은 강의만 듣고도 나 스스로 '열심히 살고 있다'라고 자족해왔는데, 이젠 '칭찬해요' 한마디와 칭찬 글을 보며 미소 짓는 것으로 하루를 시작한다.

칭고 방에 올라온 여러 칭찬 글들을 보면서 나는 그제야 나 자신을 돌아보았다. 칭찬과는 거리가 먼 내가 과연 할 수 있을까? 여러 날을 고민하고 갈등하다 드디어 용기를 내어 첫 릴레이에 이렇게 올렸다.

'칭찬하기 위해서 내 모습을 보려는 나 자신을 칭찬해요. 무심히 지나쳤던 내 모습에 관심을 가지면서부터 내 주변의 것들에게도 감사를 느껴요.'

이때 엘님이 인스타그램 릴스 글을 올려주고, 나나님은 배경음악까지 멋지게 만들어주었다. 그때의 감동을 어떻게 표현할까. 나에게 이런 일이 생기다니!

질리지 않는
칭찬의 맛

―――――

　　새벽에 일어나 멍하니 아파트 밖을 보기도 하고, 스트레칭도 하면서 하루를 시작한다. 시간을 쪼개어 바쁘게 살던 때보다 오히려 더 여유가 생겨나는 것 같다.

　　칭찬은 동행이다. 새벽에 일어나 발바닥과 종아리를 어루만지며, "장사할 때 잘 지탱해줘서 고마워. 너무 혹사해서 미안해. 지금도 아프지만, 꿋꿋하게 나에게 있어줘서 고마운 널 칭찬해"라고 혼자 중얼중얼한다. 잠든 아이들의 발바닥과 종아리에도 입을 맞추며 소곤거린다. "고마워. 내 아이들을 든든히 지켜줘서."

　　처음엔 그렇게 중얼거리는 내 모습이 우스웠지만, 지금

은 아이들도 때때로 내 손길을 느끼며 꿈틀하면서도 미소 짓는다.

작은 칭찬으로 시작하는 새벽, 내 삶에 속한 이 모든 고맙고 소중한 존재들이 나의 칭찬과 함께 언제까지나 동행할 것이다.

하루는 샤워하고 나오면서 남편에게 화장실 청소를 부탁했다. 그리고 청소하고 나온 남편을 맘껏 칭찬했다. "와, 정말 잘했어요! 너무 깨끗해요. 욕조는 살짝 아쉽지만, 그래도 너무 잘했어요. 욕실을 깨끗이 청소한 당신, 칭찬해요." 엉덩이까지 토닥토닥해가며 이어지는 2단 3단 콤보 칭찬에 남편도, 엿듣던 아이들도 일제히 웃음이 빵 터졌다. 요즘은 아이들도 청소기를 들고 적극적으로 집안일에 가담해준다.

나를 칭찬해보려고 시작한 것이 어느새 긍정의 부메랑이 되어 가족 모두에게 칭찬 세례를 퍼부어준다. 이렇게 칭찬의 힘을 직접 느껴보니 그 파급 효과가 이만저만 큰 게 아니다. 칭찬이란 나를 사랑할 수 있는 작은 첫걸음이면서 동시에 나의 동행 모두에게도 배려와 정이라는 큰 그림을 그릴 수 있게 해준다.

칭찬의 힘은 직장에서도 유감없이 발휘된다.

내가 일하는 회사에 20대 후배 직원이 있는데, 확실히 엄마뻘인 나와는 세대 차이가 날 수밖에 없다. 컴퓨터 다루는 솜씨는 물론이고 검색 능력도 굉장하다. 반면에 나는 여전히 독수리타법에다 인터넷이라곤 쇼핑 도구로만 사용하는 정도이니 후배 눈에 얼마나 답답했을까? 처음 후배에게 배울 때만 해도 '이 친구가 날 무시하나?'라는 생각에 의기소침해지고 자존심도 무척 상했다. 하지만 뭔가를 처음 배울 땐 실력의 차이가 아니라 시간의 차이라는 생각을 하면서부터 칭찬을 아끼지 않았다.

"보라색 윗도리가 피부 톤이랑 참 잘 어울려요."
"매번 알기 쉽게 가르쳐줘서 고마워요."

진심이 담긴 칭찬은 먹어도 질리지 않는 된장찌개 같다.

칭고 방에 올라오는 칭찬 글을 보면서 '나를 사랑하는 방법'은 멀리 있지 않다는 생각이 들었다. 칭찬을 통해 나에게 관심과 애정을 갖고 지그시 관찰해가며 소소하게나마 진심으로 칭찬해주자 내가 변하기 시작했다. 여유도 생기고 무엇보다 나 자신으로 살아갈 수 있는 원동력이 생긴 것이다. 매일매일 마주치는 주변의 골목과 나무, 행인들을 대하는 시선도 많이 변했다. 나는 이제 언제 어디서든 칭찬할 대상을 찾을 수 있다.

확실히 칭찬이란 나와의 영원한 동행이다. 스스로 아무리 부족하게 느껴지더라도 내가 나를 칭찬하며 가는 동안은 언제까지나 함께 간다.

@ga.sol.s

© 이지민

8

칭찬은 치유다

— 라라

BGM MUSIC NFT #9
상처입은 치유자 '힐러'라는 곡입니다.
내 안의 상처 입은 어린 나를 이제 지킬 수 있는 어른이 된 우리들은
이제 나를 넘어 상처 입은 누군가를 다시 일으켜 세우는 힐러이기도 합니다.

나로 살기가 그렇게 어려웠을까?

왜 나만 내 편이 아니었을까?

누구를 위한 완벽주의였을까?

달라지려면 어떻게 해야 할까?

나도 그냥 막 던져봐?

나의 세 가지 비밀 레시피

나로 살기가
그렇게 어려웠을까?

마음은 빙산과 같다.
커다란 얼음덩어리 일부만이
물 위로 노출된 채 떠다닌다.
– 지그문트 프로이트

나는 심리적으로 약간 문제가 있다. 어떤 문제냐 하면, 바로 내 마음속 어린아이를 한사코 외면한다는 것이다. 그런 내가 글쓰기를, 그것도 '내면의 나를 만나는' 글을 쓰려고 하니 심경이 이만저만 복잡한 게 아니다. 써야지, 써야지 하면서도 엄두가 안 난다.

오늘은 정말 끝장을 봐야지, 하며 문까지 꼭 닫고 틀어

박혀 있는데, 갑자기 마음속에서 불안감이 스멀스멀 밀려온다. '시간 있을 때 틈틈이 써두지, 이게 뭔 난리냐'라며 내 이성이 화를 내는 것만 같고…….

원래 내 성향은 꽤 자유로운 편이었다. 그런데 아이들을 키우면서부터 점점 계획형으로 바뀌고, 급기야 어떤 일들이 내 계획대로 되지 않으면 불안감을 넘어 화가 난다. 하지만 오늘만큼은 나의 특별한 결정을 위로해주고 싶다. 아무도 없는 집에서 책을 위해 글을 쓰다니, 비록 잠옷 바람이지만 마음만큼은 이렇게 경건할 수가 없다.

이런 시간이 얼마 만인가. 너무나 소중한 느낌이 든다. 평소 아무도 없는 집에서 나 혼자만의 시간을 누린다는 상상만으로도 짜릿했는데, 오늘 뜻밖에도 그런 시간이 주어진 것이다. 설렘과 불안이 섞이면서 심장이 쿵쿵 뛴다.

오전에 작업실 열고 5시에 퇴근할 때까지, 혼자 있는 시간이 나에겐 아예 없다. 출근 전까지는 남편이, 5시에 집에 오면 아이들이, 그리고 주말에는 온 식구가 집에 있으니 혼자만의 시간이란 게 있을 수 없다.

오후 2시 30분 28초, 29초, 30초……. 째깍째깍 초침 소리와 투둑투둑 빗소리가 크게 들리는 걸 보니 초조한 마음이 점점 더 커지는 모양이다. 어떡하든 결과물을 만들어야 한다는 강박감이 밀려온다. 인간이 온전히 쉴 수 있는 곳은 각자의 내면이라 했던가, 불안과 초조 속에서도 그런 감정에 충실히 나를 던져놓고 나에게서 도망치지 않으려고 애쓰는 중이다.

빙산의 일각에 불과한 나의 표면 의식에서 좀 더 아래로, 좀 더 깊은 심연으로 들어가본다. 내 오랜 과거로부터 형성되어온 억압, 합리화, 불안, 공포, 우울, 분노, 좌절, 열등감, 질투, 집착, 사랑, 슬픔 같은 감정들이 그물처럼 뒤엉켜 나를 에워싼다.

니체의 어느 구절이 기억난다. 자기 안의 심연을 오랫동안 응시하다 보면 어느 순간 그 심연 또한 자기를 들여다본다고.

난 아마도 그게 싫어서 심연 저 밑바닥 끝에서 외롭게 서 있는 나의 어린아이를 외면해온 것 같다. 그곳으로 내려가려고만 하면 가슴이 아프고 금세 눈물이 뚝뚝 떨어진다.

지난날에 대한 절절한 그리움을 위해서라도 그 아이를 안아줘야 하는데, 나 스스로 어떻게 그 아이를 안아줄 수 있을까.

> 당신 자신을 사랑하는 기술은 예술이다.
> – 프리드리히 니체

인생은 물음표가 느낌표로 바뀌는 과정이라고 했다. 나는 임신했을 때 모성이라는 것에 대한 환상이 있었다. 절대적이고 위대한 모성, 엄마가 되면 그런 모성이 한순간 뿅 하고 생기는 줄 알았는데 그게 아니었다. 나는 모성 대신 '그건 환상이었구나!'라는 느낌표만 얻었다. 현실 속 엄마라는 페르소나는 한없이 감정적이고 인성이 부족한, 나약하고 어리석은 모습이었다.

나를 움직이는 것은 내 안의 저 깊은 밑바닥, 눈에 보이지 않는 '또 다른 나'라는 것을 엄마가 되면서 알게 되었다. 아이가 쑥쑥 자라는 동안 내 마음이 내 맘대로 안 될 때마다 나는 속으로 수없이 쓰러지고 무너졌다.

'왜?'라는 물음표가 해결되지 않은 채 다음 날, 또 다음 날이 속절없이 흘러갔다. 그건 마치 먹어도, 먹어도 채워지지 않는 허기처럼 점점 더 나를 힘들게 했다. 마음 깊은 곳에서 복잡한 감정 덩어리들이 괴상한 모습으로 튀어나와 내 아이와 만나게 되고, 때로는 그 괴상한 모습이 내 아이에게서도 보였다.

> 그곳은 다른 사람의 길 아닌가.
> 그래서 어쩐지 걷기 힘들지 않은가.
> 나의 길을 걸어라.
> 그러면 멀리까지 갈 수 있다.
> – 헤르만 헤세

지금 돌아보면 눈에 보이지 않는 그 상처받은 내면 아이를 알아본 것이 너무 감사하다. 내면 아이를 처음 알게 된 것은 스무 살 무렵 헤르만 헤세의 《데미안》을 읽으면서였는데 그때 저장돼 있던 어렵고 알쏭달쏭하던 이야기들이 부모가 되고 나서야 실체적으로 와닿기 시작했다.

나로 사는 것이 그렇게 어려웠을까?

'난 나로 살고 있는데?'라고 생각했던 어린 20대가 왜 그렇게 공허하고 답답했는지 지금은 알 것 같다. 어쩌면 나는 부모라는 책임감을 짊어지고 나서야 비로소 나를 사랑할 준비가 된 게 아닐까? 절대적이고 위대한 모성이라는 것이 나에게 환상일지는 몰라도 하나의 세계를 깨고 나갈 만큼의 동기부여로서는 충분하니까.

　하지만 어제의 나에 비해 오늘의 내가 더 나아지거나 달라진 건 아니었다. 의지가 약한 나는 그래서 더 힘들어지고 포기하고 좌절하고 다시 또 희망을 품었다가 결국에는 이것도 저것도 아닌 애매한 지점에서 이렇게 서성거리고 있다.

왜 나만
내 편이 아니었을까?

────

　　　나의 하루는 늘 그림과 함께 흘러간다. 작업실에서
온종일 그림을 그리거나 디자인 작업을 하고, 또 미술치료
사로 일하는 날은 내담자가 그린 그림을 만난다.

　이따금 아무런 이유 없이 심연 저 아래 어딘가에 서 있
는 나의 어린아이와 만날 때가 있는데, 그럴 때면 슬퍼서 눈
물이 나기도 하고 화가 나기도 한다. 그런 날에는 흘러내리
는 그림을 그린다. 흘러내리는 그림을 그리다 보면 자책하는
마음도, 슬프거나 상처받은 마음도 어디론가 흘러내려가는
느낌이 든다. 물감의 색과 촉감들이 나의 어린아이를 포근
하게 안아주는 것 같다.

그런 시간을 보내고 나면 또 언제 그랬냐는 듯 마음이 어느 정도 말끔해진다. 그림은 내 안의 슬픔과 마주 앉아 소곤소곤 이야기를 나누게 해준다. 누구에게도 말하지 못하는 내 마음을 가장 잘 알고 토닥여주는 느낌…….

곰곰이 생각해보면 어릴 때부터 결과 중심적인 아빠와 경직된 성격의 엄마 밑에서 심리적으로 짓눌려왔다. 두 분 모두 올곧은 교사인 데다 과정보다는 결과로 평가하는 편이었는데, 나는 그 엄한 잣대가 너무 힘들었다. 그 영향 때문일까? 지금은 나도 아이들에게 '이거 해, 이거 하지 마'라고 지시를 하거나 과정보다는 결과로 평가하곤 한다.

오빠와 나, 이렇게 남매인 우리 집은 여느 부모가 그렇듯 온통 첫째인 오빠에게 관심이 집중돼 있었고, 막내인 나는 손이 덜 가는, 그냥 저 혼자 할 일 척척 알아서 잘하는 딸이었다. 실제로 학교 다닐 때 늘 일등을 차지했고, 부모님께 실망을 안긴 적도 별로 없었다. 게다가 나 자신에게도 실패나 좌절이 별로 없었다. 부모님께 혼난 거라곤 초등학교 2학년 때 거짓말하고 피아노 학원에 빠진 일 정도? 그만큼 모범생이고 착한 딸이었다.

아버지는 내가 공무원이 되길 원했다. 공무원 말고 다른 직업은 쳐다보지도 말라고 했다. 하지만 나는 미술 디자인 쪽을 선택했고 아버지는 그런 나를 지지하지 않았다. 엄마도 화를 냈다. 엄마는 따뜻한 성격과는 거리가 멀어서 걱정거리가 생기면 화를 냈다. 솔직히 난 어릴 때부터 미술보다는 음악이 좋았다. 초등학교 때 작곡을 할 만큼 피아노 치는 걸 좋아했고, 당연히 전공으로 삼고 싶었다. 하지만 부모님은 '밥 벌어먹기 힘들다'라는 이유로 반대했다. 또 외고에 가고 싶다고 했을 땐 기숙사 생활이 위험하다며 반대했다.

나는 부모님으로부터 "그래, 한번 해봐. 잘할 수 있을 거야"라는 말을 들어본 기억이 없다. 내가 너무 터무니없는 생각을 해서 그랬을까? 아니, 이런 생각 역시 학습된 자책이 아닐까? 지금 이 글을 쓰면서도 놀랍다. 아직도 나 스스로 검열하고 자책하는 것만 같아서.

어쩌면 나는 일등이라는 무미건조한 결과 대신 그 과정에 대해 더 큰 박수와 인정을 받고 싶었던 게 아닐까.
"정말 자랑스러워. 쉽지 않았을 텐데, 얼마나 힘들었을까? 잠도 제대로 못 자고, 놀고 싶은 것도 꾹 참고……, 그 힘든 걸 혼자 꿋꿋하게 다 이겨내다니, 넌 정말 멋진 딸이야! 결과도 결과지만 포기하지 않고 여기까지 왔다는 게 더 대단해!"

슬프지만, 이런 말은 상상 속에서나 들을 수 있었다. 남들 눈에도 나는 그저 '교사 집안의 공부 잘하는 막내딸'이며 '별 탈 없이 평범하게 살아가는 아이'였다.

20대가 되고 어른의 삶을 살면서부터 기어이 우울증이 찾아왔다. 내가 하는 일의 결과가 좋지 않으면 굉장히 힘들어했고, 스스로 '바보야, 이게 뭐야? 이것밖에 못 해?'라며 후회하고 다그치느라 밤잠을 설치기 일쑤였다.

공부는 물론 일도 사랑도 인간관계도 뭐든지 조금만 삐끗하면 금방 소심해지고 과하게 고민하거나 예민해지면서 결국 나를 미워하고 후회하는……, 나는 그런 사람이었다.

다른 사람에게는 위로도 잘하고, 칭찬이나 조언도 잘해주는 내가, 왜 유독 나에게만 그토록 엄격했을까? 왜 나만 내 편이 아니었을까?

누구를 위한
완벽주의였을까?

　　내가 나를 귀하게 대접해야 남들도 나를 귀하게 대접한다고 했다. 하지만 나는 한 번도 나를 귀하게 대접한 적이 없는 것 같다. 세상에 완벽한 인간이란 없을 텐데, 세상일이 언제나 자기 뜻대로 굴러가는 것도 아닐 텐데 나는 결과가 실망스러울 때마다 늘 자책하고 나 자신을 꾸짖었다. "괜찮아, 넌 최선을 다한 거야"라는 말 대신 언제나 "넌 왜 이것밖에 안 되나"라고.

　　스스로 빈약해진 자존감 탓인지 이상하게도 자꾸만 내가 아닌 타인을 위해 무언가를 더 열심히 하게 되었다. 밥을 차리는 것도 아이들과 남편을 위해서, 아침에 일어나는 것도 아이들을 챙기기 위해서, 책을 읽는 것도 아이들과 남편과의 관계를 위해서, 일을 열심히 하는 것도 부모님께 인정받기 위해서, 그림을 그리는 것도, 무언가를 배우는 것도 내가 아닌 누군가를 위해서였다. 인간은 사회적 동물이라 타인과의 관계 속에서 인정받고 싶은 욕구는 당연하겠지만, 나는 지나치게 애를 썼다. 너무 잘하려고.

대학원 때 발표 시간에 교수님이 내 발표를 다 듣고 나서 해준 말이 있다.

"너무 그렇게 잘하려고 애쓰지 않아도 돼요."

하마터면 펑펑 울 뻔했다. 내 마음이 들킨 것 같아서, 내가 너무 애쓴다는 것이 들킨 것 같아서 순간 쿵, 하고 심장이 가라앉는 느낌이었달까. 도대체 왜, 무엇 때문에, 무엇을 위해 그렇게 애를 썼을까.

나는 발표를 맡으면 우선 완벽하게 하고 싶다는 생각부터 먼저 든다. 발표 내용도 100% 이해해야 한다는 생각에 책을 읽고 관련 문건들을 찾는 등 완벽한 발표 자료를 만들기 위해 무진 애를 쓴다. 그 과정에서 엄청난 스트레스를 받는 건 당연한 일. 아무래도 심리를 들여다보는 내용의 발표

여서 그랬는지 내 안에 쌓여 있던 불안과 스트레스가 교수님 눈에 훤히 보였을 것이다.

아이 셋을 키우면서 나는 어느 한순간도 일을 쉰 적이 없다. 내 마음속엔 언제나 '나는 자아실현을 위해 일한다'라는 생각이 박혀 있었다. 온전히 나를 위해 일한다고 생각했는데 어느 순간, '남들에게서 인정받기 위해' 일해왔다는 사실과 마주쳤다. 친정 가까이에서 공무원이 아닌 남편과 결혼하여 아이들 키우며 잘 사는 모습을 부모님께 보여드리고 인정받고 싶어서 애쓰는 내 모습과 마주하면서 말이다.

부모님은 불쑥불쑥 내가 일하는 작업실까지 찾아와 '돈은 잘 버는지' 물어보았다. 화가 치밀었다. 내가 어떤 일을 하는지도 모르면서, 내가 디자이너로, 미술치료사로, SNS마케터로 어떻게 월, 화, 수, 목, 금, 토, 일을 살아가는지 잘 알지도 못하면서 어쩜 이렇게 돈이라는 결과물로만 판단하려고 하는지 너무나 화가 났다.

솔직히 한 달에 천만 원을 벌어도 나는 만족할 수 없을 것이다. 더 벌어야 인정받을 수 있을 테니까. 그런데 아이러니한 것은, 나 자신조차 내 편이 아니면서 속으론 어린 시절 받아보지 못한 위로와 공감과 칭찬을 절실히 바란다는 점이었다.

꽤 근사한 페르소나의 모습으로 오만함에 사로잡혀 있던 지난날, 매일 한 번이라도 나에게 '괜찮아, 잘했어'라고 해줄걸. 말 그대로 지금 알고 있는 것을 그때도 알았더라면 적어도 지난 10년이 넘는 시간 동안 조금은 덜 힘들었을 텐데.

달라지려면
어떻게 해야 할까?

'온전히 나로 살고 싶어.'

코로나로 인해 가족이 함께 있는 시간이 많아지면서부터 이런 생각이 점점 더 커졌다. 우리 식구는 코로나 시국에 오히려 많은 곳을 다녔다. 사회적으로 여행 자제를 권유하는 분위기였지만, 우린 2주에 한 번꼴로 여행을 다녔다. 어디를 가도 사람이 없었고, 심지어 성산일출봉에서도 우리뿐이었다. 물론 우리에게는 귀하고 소중한 시간이었다. 가족이라는 이름으로 서로에 대해 무조건 잘 안다고 생각했는데, 여행이라는 낯선 시공간 속에서 어쩔 수 없이 서로를 더 깊이 보게 되면서 몰랐던 면들을 새로 발견할 수 있었다.

그리고 나 자신과도 좀 더 가까워졌다.

도란도란 슬픔과 이야기 나누는 시간, 나를 일으켜 세워야 하는 시간, 잘 될 거라고 토닥여주는 시간, 인내의 시간, 앞으로의 계획을 세우는 시간, 나의 부족함을 알게 되는 시간…….

나는 내면의 나를 만나면서 달라지고 싶어졌다. 마음의 심연에서 올라오는 괴상하고 복잡한 감정 덩어리가 내 아이와 만나게 되는 그 지긋지긋한 반복을 이제 멈추고 싶었다. 그 묵은 감정들과 웃으며 이제 안녕, 하고 싶었다.

'달라지려면 어떻게 해야 할까? 온전히 나로 살고 싶은데, 어떻게 하면 진짜 나로 살 수 있지?'

그즈음 나는 밤마다 유튜브에 올라온 영상들을 한참 들여다보았는데, 어느 날 우연히 김미경 학장님의 강의를 만나게 되었다. 그리고 이내 그 강의에 이끌려 MKYU 모닝 쩍쩍이 새벽 5시 기상에 합류하게 되었다. 올빼미 체질이라 보통 새벽 2시는 넘어야 잠을 자는 내게 새벽 5시 기상은 아무래도 무리였지만, 의외로 난 성공했다. 3월, 4월, 5월, 6월……, 그리고 현재까지 새벽 5시에 눈을 떠서 나 자신과의 만남을 지속하고 있다.

나도 그냥
막 던져봐?

"당신에게 새벽 기상은 어떤 의미인가요?"

누가 이렇게 묻는다면 난 즉시 대답할 수 있다.

"후회되는 과거와 불안한 미래로만 향하던 생각을 멈추고, '지금의 나'에게 온전히 몰입할 수 있는 시간이죠."

예민한 성격 탓에 사소한 일에도 밥을 못 먹고 잠도 못자며 내내 자책하고 후회하기 일쑤였는데, 그 소모적인 반복을 멈추고 지금의 나와 제대로 마주 보게 되는 시간이 바로 새벽 5시다.

누구에게나 주어지는 새벽 5시. 나는 전에 없던 선택을 했고, 그 선택으로 매일 0.1%씩 성장하는 느낌을 얻게 되었다. 다른 누구도 아닌 '어제의 나'와 비교하며 오늘 좀 더 뿌듯할 수 있는 시간.

매일 아침 아이들 식사를 챙기고 등교시키기 위해 졸린 눈을 비비며 억지로 일어나던 내 모습이 이제 낯설게 느껴진다. 그리고 새벽 시간에 만나는 쩍쩍이들도 서서히 내 마음속에 들어오게 되었다. (쩍쩍이는 새벽 5시 유튜브 실시간에 김미경 학장님과 만나는 사람들을 일컫는 별칭이다.)

> 친구는 제2의 자신이다.
> – 아리스토텔레스

말 그대로 친구는 나의 또 다른 모습이다. 빨리 가려면 혼자 가고 멀리 가려면 함께 가라는 말이 있듯이 내 마음속에 들어온 쩍쩍이들은 하루하루 나와 함께 멀리 가고 있는 또 다른 내 모습이라는 느낌이 든다. 마치 내 꿈의 동반자인 듯한 느낌?

내가 어떻게 쩍쩍이들의 수많은 커뮤니티 중에서 〈칭찬받는 고래〉에 들어가게 되었는지는 기억나지 않는다. 아마도 어느 정신없는 날, 나도 모르게 휩쓸려 들어가게 되었을 것이다.

이 방의 미션은 '하루에 한 번 나를 칭찬하는 것'이다. 그리고 내가 올린 셀프 칭찬에 다른 사람들의 따뜻한 격려와 지지 댓글이 달리는 곳이기도 하다.

나를 칭찬한다……. 이거 참, 뭔가 새삼스러운 느낌이다. 멋쩍고 쑥스럽지만, 어디 한번 나를 칭찬해볼까? 멋진 그림 그린 거 칭찬해, 맛있는 식사 준비한 거 칭찬해, 최고 매출 찍은 거 칭찬해.

이렇게 쓰면서 나에 대한 칭찬마저 하나같이 결과 중심적이라는 점에 또 한 번 놀랐다. 곧이어 마음이 짠해졌다.

어떤 힘이 나를 이 방으로 데려왔을까? 나의 소소한 일상이 모두 눈부신 칭찬거리라고 꿈틀대는 내 무의식이 데려왔을까, 아니면 나의 모난 내면아이가 이곳으로 나를 데려왔을까?

〈칭찬받는 고래〉 오픈 채팅방에서 나는 대화에 거의 참여하지 않았다. 그저 사람들의 대화 내용을 가만히 지켜보기만 했다. 자신이 없었다. 소소한 나를 칭찬한다는 것이 너무 망설여졌다. 일할 때는 겁 없이 막 저지르고 추진하는 편인데, 정작 나 자신에게 따뜻한 말 한마디 건네주는 데에는 이렇게 서툴고 힘들어하는구나 싶었다.

그러다 한 달쯤 지난 어느 날, 나는 기어이 '칭고' 방에 작별 인사를 남겼다. 그러자 칭고 방 찍찍이들이 일제히 나를 붙잡았다. 나가면 안 돼요, 여기 있어주세요…….

뜻밖의 만류에 차마 나오지 못하고 어정쩡하게 머물게 되었는데, 그때 "라라님을 붙잡은 나를 칭찬해요"라는 메시지가 올라왔다.

'이런 것도 칭찬한다고?'

신선한 충격과 함께 마음의 문이 조금씩 열리기 시작했다. 나도 그냥 막 던져봐?

나의 세 가지
비밀 레시피

나의 첫 번째 비밀 레시피 : "칭찬은 위로다"

눈을 감고 나의 하루를 돌아본다. 소소한 드리마처럼 하루의 풍경이 펼쳐진다. 그 하루에 새들의 지저귐처럼 예쁜 음악을 넣어주고 싶다. 그리고 조각조각 시간을 나누어 매 순간의 나를 자세히 들여다보며 산들바람처럼 소곤거려 주고 싶다. 잘했어, 칭찬해, 괜찮아, 수고했어, 멋져, 최고야.

이 말을 쓰는데 갑자기 눈물이 왈칵 난다. 다른 사람들에게 들을 때는 이런 마음이 아니었는데 왜 눈물이 나는 걸까. 있는 그대로의 나를 따뜻하게 안아준다는 것이 이런 건가. 아무래도 심연 저 밑바닥에 나의 감정 쓰레기통처럼 서 있던 내면아이가 토닥토닥 위로받으며 흘리는 눈물 같다.

나의 두 번째 비밀 레시피 : "칭찬은 나침반이다"

오늘 아침은 비도 오고 유난히 더 자고 싶은 날이었는데 그래도 나를 일으켜 세운 나를 칭찬해. 오늘의 내 모습은 어제의 나와 닮아 있고 내일의 나와 닮아 있을 거라고 했다. 지금의 위치도 소중하지만, 가고자 하는 방향도 중요한 법이니까.

우리는 살면서 시시때때로 많은 고민과 선택에 직면한다. 일어날지 말지, 밥을 먹을지 말지, 운동을 나갈지 말지 등 일상의 사소한 모든 것이 선택의 연속이다. 그리고 중요한 결정을 할 때 지인에게 고민을 털어놓기도 하고 내 결정에 반영하기도 한다. 하지만 사실 모든 고민의 답은 이미 마음속에 있다고 하지 않던가? 그러니 마음이 갈팡질팡 불안하다면, 우선 하던 일을 잠시 멈추고 나 자신을 칭찬해보는 게 어떨까. 내 안에서 답이 나올지도 모르니까.

'고마워, 잘했어, 괜찮아, 잘하고 있어.' 이런 모든 말이 칭찬이고 위로이며 나를 안내해주는 나침반이다. 셀프 칭찬은 자화자찬이 아니다. 뭘 해도 괜찮다는 식의 뻔뻔한 마음이 아니다. 그저 나를 안아주고, 나를 위로해주는 마음이다. 무엇보다 더 나은 내일을 바라보게 해주는 힘이다.

신기한 것은 내가 나를 칭찬해주면서부터 사소하던 일상이 꽤 특별하게 느껴진다는 점이다. 설령 내일 새벽 나를 일으켜 세우지 못하더라도 괜찮다. 그런 날은 그런 날대로 그냥 나를 아껴주면 되니까. 이것은 타인으로부터 인정받기 위해 애쓰는 것이 아니라 내가 나에게 노력하는 마음이다. 이 두 가지가 주는 느낌은 정말 다르다. 서로 결이 다른 노력이다. 나에 대한 노력이 결국 내가 가야 할 방향을 일러주고 있다. 나를 위해 타박타박 걸어갈 수 있는 곳으로.

나의 세 번째 비밀 레시피 : "칭찬은 치유다"

나를 들여다보며 칭찬할 거리를 찾다 보면 점점 나를 알아가는 재미가 쏠쏠해진다. 태어나서 지금까지 쭉 나였는데, 새로운 내가 너무나 많이 보인다. 특히 요즘은 평소 좋아하지 않는 스타일의 그림도 그려보고 있는데, 웬일인지 너무나 재미있다.

20년이 넘는 시간 동안 늘 고만고만하던 그림체가 요즘은 참 좋아졌다. 짧은 시간이지만 모나고 삐뚤빼뚤하던 마음속 내면아이에게 도란도란 칭찬해주니 그 아이가 조금 달라졌달까.

'왜 여태껏 이러지 못했을까' 하는 자책은 하지 않기로 했다. 후회와 자책은 정말 지긋지긋하다. 자꾸 눈물이 난다. 모나고 삐쭉한 나의 내면아이가 너무 좋아서.

얼마 전 나에게 미술치료를 받던 아이와 마주 앉아 자신의 단점에 대한 미술 작업을 하던 중에 그 아이가 말했다.

"선생님, 저는 단점이 다섯 가지가 있는데요. 그래도 괜찮아요. 단점을 잘 고치면 장점이 될 테니까요."

열 살짜리 아이가 나보다 훨씬 낫구나.

아이의 한마디, 한마디가 어른보다 더 큰 울림을 줄 때가 많다. 이미 자신을 알고 있고, 그걸 장점으로 고칠 마음도 있으니 오히려 내가 아이에게 배우고 치유받은 느낌이 든다. 그래, 보이지 않는 마음속 어딘가에 들어 있는 콤플렉스라는 거대한 단점 덩어리가 때때로 이상한 모습을 드러내더라도 괜찮다. 또 다른 나로 발전할 수 있을 테니까.

진정으로 우리 자신인 것만이 치유하는 힘을 갖고 있다.

– 구스타프 융

함께 책을 쓰자는 얘기를 들었을 때, 처음엔 망설였다. 어릴 때부터 책과 글쓰기를 좋아해서 글쓰기 상도 많이 탔고, 출간 제의도 받아봤지만, 지금 하는 일들만으로도 충분하다고 생각했다. 어쩌면 나의 첫 번째 책은 드로잉북일 거라고 생각하고 있었는지도 모르겠다.

그런데 이번 제안이 내키지 않으면서도 마음 한편으로는 조금 욕심이 생겼다. 마음속에서 잠자고 있는, 나도 모르는 내가 있을 것 같아서였을까? 지금 와서 생각해보면 힘들어도 이것을 뛰어넘으면 내가 얼마만큼 성장하게 될까, 하는 기대감이 있었던 것 같다.

나는 거북이처럼 살고 싶다. 얼마 전 막둥이가 나에게 "엄마, 거북이가 왜 오래 사는지 알아요? 심장이 느리게 뛰기 때문이래요"라고 말했다. 쿵!

나는 저혈압이지만 심장이 갑자기 빨리 뛸 때가 종종 있기 때문이었을까? 막둥이의 말이 꽤 큰 충격과 여운을 주었다. 빠르게 바뀌고 새로워지는 메타버스 디지털 세상에 맞추다 보니 나도 모르게 심장이 두근두근 빨리 뛸 때가 많아졌다.

난 여전히 아날로그가 좋다. 시대에 뒤떨어지는 소리지만, 나는 디지털이 아날로그를 완벽하게 이길 수는 없다고 확신한다. 코로나가 생기면서 세상의 많은 것이 디지털 온라인 세계로 진입했고, 물론 나도 그곳에 있다. 또 디스코드와 NFT를 하고 있고 메타버스 가상공간에서 이번 77주년 광복절 그림 전시회도 오픈했지만, 나는 여전히 느릿한 아날로그가 좋다. 왜냐하면, 우리 삶은 아날로그니까. 디지털 세상은 우리 삶을 풍요롭게 해주는 공간일 뿐, 그 자체가 삶이 될 수는 없으니까. 아무리 메타버스 안에서 즐거워도 직접 만나는 것보다는 덜 즐겁다는 걸 우리 모두 알고 있다. 오프라인의 강력한 힘을.

온라인 커뮤니티를 통해서 나를 만나고, 책도 쓰면서 오프라인의 강력한 힘이라니. 결국 내가 나로 살아가는 것은 아날로그에서 가능하다. 아날로그에서 더 느리게 살고 싶다. 천천히 차근차근 나를 들여다보면서.

© 이선숙

9

칭찬은 사랑이다

— 미인요정

BGM MUSIC NFT #28
사랑의 설렘이 담긴 몽글몽글한 사운드의 곡으로
스무 살의 몽글몽글한 시간도 떠올려보고 사랑하는 아이를 바라보는
엄마의 따뜻한 시선도 떠올리며 만든 사랑이 담긴 곡입니다.

너무 힘들어하지 마라

이렇게 사는 게 맞나?

더 늦기 전에 돌파구를 찾아야 해

새벽 5시, 모닝 쨱쨱!

칭찬이란 서로의 샘물을 채워가는 것

영원히 돌아오지 않을 '지금'이기에

나를 칭찬한다는 것

너무
힘들어하지 마라

———

　　1997년 IMF가 터졌을 때 나는 고등학교 1학년이
었다. 아버지의 청춘을 바친 회사도 결국은 문을 닫고 말았
다. 망연자실한 아버지를 보며 엄마가 말했다.

　"이렇게 마냥 손 놓고 있을 수만은 없잖아요. 우리 같이
힘내요."

　위기를 극복하기 위해 부모님은 이 일 저 일 가리지 않
고 쉴 새 없이 일했다. 집안의 장녀이지만, 아직 학생이었던
나로서는 용돈을 아껴가며 공부하는 것 외에는 도와드릴
방법이 없었다.

　나는 목표하던 교대가 아닌 지방 국립대학에 진학했다.

그리고 졸업할 때까지 꼬박 4년 동안 쉬지 않고 아르바이트를 해야 했다.

졸업을 앞두고 취업 준비를 위해 아르바이트를 그만두자 몸이 그렇게 편할 수가 없었다. 하지만 휴식도 잠시, 몸이 편하니 온갖 생각이 꼬리에 꼬리를 물고 몰려왔다.

'나는 앞으로 어떻게 살아야 하나, 어떤 일을 하며 살아갈까?'

재학 중에는 공부와 아르바이트를 병행하며 그저 눈앞에 주어진 일만 해나가느라 앞으로의 인생을 생각할 겨를이 없었다. 그런데 이젠 구체적인 진로와 삶의 방향을 선택해야 하는 상황이었다.

나는 마치 안개 속에서 헤매는 심정이었다. 힘들어하는 내 모습을 보며 엄마가 그랬다.

"사춘기도 그냥 넘긴 놈이 오춘기라도 온 거냐? 하다 보면 때가 오겠지. 너무 힘들어하지 마라."

물론 그 말이 내게 위로가 될 리 없었다. 삶의 무게가 마치 거대한 바위처럼 가슴을 짓눌러 숨조차 제대로 쉬지 못했을 때였으니까.

나는 일단 학교를 휴학하고 서울로 올라가 일 년쯤 외삼촌의 회사에서 사회생활을 익혔다. 그리고 학교를 졸업한 뒤에는 전문적인 일을 하기 위해 자격증 공부를 하며 직장을 다니던 중 한 살 터울인 사촌 언니의 소개로 한 남자를 만났다.

인테리어 관련 일을 해가며 열정적으로 살아가는 그의 모습이 인상적이었다. 우리는 서로에게 호감을 느끼게 되었고, 일 년가량 교제한 끝에 이듬해 가을 결혼식을 올렸다. 그때 내 나이가 스물일곱 살이었다. 친구 중에서는 가장 이른 결혼이었다.

이렇게
사는 게 맞나?

결혼하고 바로 첫아이를 낳았다. 그리고 연이은 출산으로 어느새 세 아이의 엄마가 되었다. 아이 셋을 키워본 엄마라면 다들 절감하듯이 하루하루가 어떻게 지났는지 모를 만큼 정신없는 나날의 연속이었다. 아이들은 너무 예쁘고 사랑스럽지만, 하루가 저물고 지쳐 쓰러져 잠들 때마다 왠지 모를 허탈감이 몰려왔다.

'나 지금 뭐 하고 있지? 이렇게 사는 게 맞나?'

어제가 오늘 같고, 내일도 오늘과 다르지 않을 것 같은 반복되는 하루하루……. 마냥 행복하고 즐겁지만은 않았다. 그런 내 모습을 보고 친정엄마가 또 한마디 했다.

"다들 그러고 산다. 엄마도 그랬다. 세월 가면 그런 못난 마음들도 이겨낼 수 있는 강단이 생긴다. 그래도 몸이 약하게 태어난 내 딸이 아이 셋을 키우는 엄마가 된 걸 보니 참 대견하다."

이번엔 엄마의 말이 조금 위로가 되었다.

막내가 세 살 되던 해 가을, 아버지가 병으로 우리 곁을 떠나셨다. 이렇게 빨리, 이렇게 갑자기 떠나실 줄 몰랐기에 우리 모두 충격과 슬픔에 어쩔 줄 몰랐다. 결혼기념일 때마다 잊지 않고 샴페인과 케이크를 챙기시던 아버지의 미소가 생각날 때마다 가슴이 아팠다. 일찍 결혼해서 남편과 세 아이를 챙기며 바쁘다는 핑계로 자주 찾아뵙지 못한 후회가 뒤늦게 밀려왔다.

하지만 삶은 계속되었고, 현실은 변하지 않았다. 다시 일상으로 돌아와 바쁘고 정신없이 살아가는 동안 슬픔도 그리움도 조금씩 무뎌져갔다. 물론 세 아이의 엄마로서 계속 주저앉아 있을 수도 없는 일이었다. 어쨌든 나는 다시 일어서야만 했다.

어느 날 거울 앞에서 펑퍼짐한 바지에 늘어난 티셔츠를 입고 있는 나 자신을 보았다. '저게 나라고?'

너무 초라해 보였다. 어쩌면 멋지고 화려한 옷을 차려입었다 해도 딱히 갈 곳이 없는 내가 더 안타까웠는지도 모른다.

아이가 아직 어렸을 적엔 집에서 살림을 잘하는 것만이 내가 할 수 있는 전부였다. 그래서 아이들에게 내가 줄 수 있는 사랑을 듬뿍 주며 정성껏 키울 수 있었다. 아이들이 커 가는 모습은 늘 뿌듯했지만, 솔직히 육아와 살림에만 신경 쓰다 보니 나를 돌아볼 여유가 거의 없었다. 그나마 막내가 유치원에 들어가면서부터 시간과 마음에 어느 정도 여유가 생겼고, 그제야 뒷전에 밀쳐두었던 나를 돌아보게 되었다.

'나는 어떤 사람인가.'

어릴 때는 꿈이 선생님인 적도 있지만, 사실 현모양처가 되고 싶다는 말을 자주 했다. 위인전 속의 수많은 위인 중에서도 신사임당이 제일 마음에 들었고, 막연히 그런 인물이 되고 싶었다.

결혼하고 아이를 키우면서도 좋은 아내, 좋은 엄마가 되고 싶다는 생각은 늘 마음 깊이 깔려 있었다. 특히 아이들이 믿고 따를 수 있는 엄마, 누구보다 든든한 배경이 되어주고 싶었다. 엄마가 먼저 가서 길을 닦아 놓을 테니 따라오라고 말할 수 있는 그런 엄마가 되고 싶었다. 그런데 문득 되돌아보니, 어느새 이렇다 할 경력 하나 없는 나 자신이 눈에 들어온 것이다.

이런 내 마음을 남편에게 털어놓자 남편도 혼자 생각해둔 게 있다면서 자기 구상을 이야기했다. 목수인 남편이 전국 곳곳을 다니다 보니 인테리어에 대한 트렌드가 보이기 시작했다며 우리가 사는 곳에 인테리어디자인 매장을 열어보면 어떨까 하고 생각해왔다는 것이다. 나는 그 자리에서 찬성했다.

우리는 몇몇 가게를 알아보고, 그동안 모아둔 돈에 대출을 얹어 타 업체와 차별화된 매장을 꾸며 사업을 시작했다. 이때부터 나도 회계업무나 문서작성 등 나름의 역할을 해나갔다. 그런데 일을 하다 보니 업무량이 조금씩 늘었고, 자연스럽게 업무량과 범위도 늘기 시작했다.

더 늦기 전에
돌파구를 찾아야 해

────

　　시간이 흐르면서 전화상담과 마감재 선택, 그리고 선택된 마감재를 주문하는 일이며 마케팅 업무까지 내가 도맡아서 하게 되었다. 특히 마케팅 업무 부분은 인테리어 업체 특성상 제품을 파는 것이 아니라 디자인을 파는 것이기에 SNS에 업체를 홍보하는 것이 필수였다. 하지만 홍보 업체를 통하면 비용이 많이 들었기 때문에 나로서는 블로그나 인스타에 글과 사진을 올려 홍보하는 방식을 선택할 수밖에 없었다.

　　'어떻게 하면 많이 노출시킬 수 있을까?'
　　SNS에 관한 공부를 시작할 때만 해도 너무 어렵고 힘들었지만, 시간이 지나자 조금씩 익숙해지고 틀도 잡혀갔다. 현장에서 남편이 완성한 결과물들을 블로그나 인스타에 계속 올리며 꾸준히 소통하다 보니 SNS를 보고 찾아오는 고객들도 점차 늘었다. 공사가 끝난 뒤 만족해하는 고객들의 반응에 뿌듯했고, 또 그 고객들이 퍼뜨린 입소문으로 새로운 일이 들어오니 힘들어도 힘든 줄 모르고 일했다.

스스로 노력해서 얻은 대가가 너무 값지고 귀하다는 생각이 들었다. 할 수 있을까, 없을까 망설이던 일도 일단 뛰어들어 최선을 다하면 해낼 수 있다는 사실을 새삼 깨닫게 되었다. 그렇게 부부가 힘을 합쳐 밤낮으로 일하다 보니 사업도 점차 안정되어갔다.

계속 이렇게만 굴러간다면 얼마나 좋을까……. 그러나 뜻밖의 시련이 닥치고 말았다. 코로나가 터진 것이다.

세계를 휩쓴 코로나 폭풍이 인테리어 업계에도, 그리고 우리 부부의 작은 매장에도 여지없이 몰아쳤다. 상상도 못했던 재앙에 모두가 힘들어했듯이 우리 부부의 경제 사정도 하강 곡선을 긋기 시작했다. 엎친 데 덮친 격으로 막내아들이 학교에서 코로나에 걸려 집에 왔다. 그리고 아들을 간호

하다 나까지 감염되고, 급기야 온 식구가 코로나 환자가 되는 바람에 한 달 동안 가족 전체의 삶이 정지되고 말았다.

경험해본 사람은 다 알겠지만, 이 병이 참 희한한 게 심한 감기처럼 아프다가 후유증이 오래가는 이상한 병이었다. 사람에 따라 증상이 다양했지만, 나는 유난히 머리가 멍하고 입맛도 없는 데다 잠이 계속 쏟아지는 증상이 꽤 오래갔다. 일상생활 자체가 점점 힘들어지면서 무기력증까지 겹쳐지는 것 같았다.

'계속 이러다간 큰일 나겠다'라는 생각이 들었다. 무기력증이 위험한 것은 그것을 이겨낼 의지조차 사라진다는 점이다. 이러다가 도저히 손쓸 수 없는 상황이 되면 그땐 정말 답이 없을 것 같았다. 더 늦기 전에 돌파구를 찾아야 했다.

새벽 5시,
모닝 짹짹!

———

　　그렇게 돌파구를 찾다 만나게 된 것이 바로 514챌
린지였다. 514챌린지는 그동안 내가 꾸준히 해오던 독서 모
임을 통해 알게 되었는데, 그 독서 모임의 리더분이 가끔 김
미경 선생님의 강의를 이야기할 때마다 내 마음에 깊은 울
림이 있었다. 그나저나 내가 새벽 5시에 꼬박꼬박 일어날
수 있을까?

　　514챌린지는 매달 1일부터 14일까지 매일 새벽 5시에
일어나 김미경 선생님의 강의를 듣고 나만의 챌린지를 시도
하는 것이다. 나는 일단 514챌린지를 신청하고 새벽 5시 알
람을 맞추었다. 처음엔 정말 일어나기 힘들었지만, 도대체

어떤 내용으로 강의가 진행될까 하는 설렘에 이끌려 결국 눈을 비벼 뜨고 유튜브에 접속했다. 그런데 세상에! 그 시각에 이미 만 명에 달하는 사람들이 강의를 듣고 있었다.

새벽 5시에 모닝 짹짹을 외치며 쉴 새 없이 올라오는 실시간 댓글들을 보며 나는 입을 다물지 못했다. 정말 대단한 사람들 아닌가? 그동안 내가 깊은 잠에 빠져 있던 이 시간에 이렇게 많은 사람이 저마다의 열정을 뿜어내고 있었다니! 들어와 보지 않았으면 영영 몰랐을 세상이었다. 평소 김미경 선생님의 유튜브나 책들을 통해 그분 특유의 폭발적인 에너지는 잘 알고 있었지만, 함께 강의를 듣는 사람들의 열정과 에너지도 절대 만만치 않았다.

내가 514챌린지를 시작한 날은 4월 10일이었다. 그런데 마침 그날은 1월 1일부터 챌린지를 시작한 사람들에게 100일이 되는 날이었다. 나는 여기에 또 놀랐다. 이 힘든 걸 1월부터 쉬지 않고 쭉 해왔다고? 그동안 난 새벽에 일어나는 사람들은 뭔가 특별한 의지가 있는 줄 알았는데, 꼭 그런 것도 아니었다. 나와 비슷한 고민, 나와 비슷한 어려움을 지닌 사람들이 벌써 100일 전부터 그렇게 하고 있었다.

난 다짐했다. 그래, 내가 해야 할 건 바로 이거야!

다음 날에도 나는 정확히 새벽 5시에 일어나 강의를 들었다. 성공의 크기와 가치에 대한 그날의 강의를 들으며 오랫동안 느껴온 내면의 갈증이 해소되는 느낌이었다. 그리고 그다음 날에도 나는 어김없이 새벽 5시에 일어났다. 그러는 동안 514챌린지에서만 통하는 새로운 용어들도 알게 되었다. 김미경 선생님에 대한 호칭은 '학장님'이고, 514챌린지에 참여하는 이들을 '짹짹이'라 부른다는 것, 그리고 펜트하우스에서 만나자며 서로를 응원한다는 것도 알았다. '펜트하우스'란 매달 14일 동안 나를 돌아보고 공부하는 과정에서 생각의 조망권이 달라지는 것을 의미했다.

그렇게 14일째 되는 날, 강의를 들으며 나 스스로 마음가짐이 사뭇 달라졌음을 느꼈다. 그동안 나를 짓눌러온 무기력증은 어느새 사라지고, 그 빈자리에 새로운 열정이 들어차고 있었다. 나 스스로 대견했고, 이제 뭐든지 해낼 수 있을 것만 같았다. 나보다 일찍 시작한 선배 짹짹이들이 내뿜는 엄청난 열정이 이제 나에게도 전이된 것이다.

칭찬이란
서로의 샘물을 채워가는 것

MKYU에서 514챌린지를 신청하면 커뮤니티라 불리는 오픈 채팅방과 연결이 된다. 한 커뮤니티에 각양각색의 사람이 천여 명쯤 모여 있고, 그 속에 또 다른 커뮤니티들이 있어 책 읽기를 인증하거나 손글씨를 쓰며 개인적인 관심사를 나눌 수 있다.

여러 카톡방 중에 나의 호기심을 자극하는 이름이 눈에 들어왔다.

'칭찬받는 고래'

뭘까? 호기심에 이끌려 참여하기를 눌러 들어가보았다.

처음엔 '나를 칭찬하는 방'이라는 소개 글이 약간 당황스러웠다. 무엇보다 내가 나를 칭찬한다는 말부터 어색했다. 보통은 내가 다른 사람을, 혹은 다른 사람이 나를 칭찬하는 것 아닌가? 내가 나를 어떻게, 왜 칭찬하는 걸까? 이상해서 그냥 나가려고 했다. 하지만 〈칭찬받는 고래〉 카톡방에 있는 사람들이 그런 내 맘을 알았는지 4월부터 514챌린지를 시작했다는 내 소개 글에 난데없이 뜨거운 응원을 보내왔다. 무리하지 말고 조금씩 해나가다 보면 익숙해질 거예요. 힘내세요!

뜻밖의 반가운 반응 때문에 좀 더 머물러보기로 했다.

처음엔 너무 어색해서 다른 사람들이 어떻게 하는지 지켜보기만 했다. 아이를 혼내지 않아서, 친정엄마를 보살펴드려서, 아침에 일어나 식구들 밥을 챙겨줘서 나를 칭찬한다는 내용이었다. '이런 건 나도 늘 하는 일 아닌가?' 그럼 나도 얼마든지 나의 시시콜콜한 일상사를 칭찬할 수 있을 것 같았다. 하지만 역시 나 자신을 칭찬한다는 것 자체가 내 성격상 쉽지 않았다. 아무래도 칭찬이란 건 누가 봐도 칭찬받을 만한 일을 했을 때만 하는 거라는 생각에 며칠간 그저 지켜보기만 했다. 그런데 보면 볼수록 이 방을 감싸고 흐르는 따스함과 서로에 대한 응원의 마음이 진솔하게 다가왔다.

어느 날, 용기를 내어 셀프 칭찬을 해보기로 했다. 나의 어떤 점을 칭찬할 수 있을까? 곰곰이 생각하다 그동안 아침 시간 북 미팅에 꾸준히 참여해온 나를 칭찬하기로 했다. 그런데 글을 올리자마자 '와, 정말 대단해요!'라는 댓글과 함께 응원 메시지들이 줄줄이 달리기 시작했다. 나는 얼떨떨해졌다. 이렇게 칭찬받을 일이었나? 난 지금도 그때 그 느낌을 잊을 수 없다. 이름도 얼굴도 모르는 사람들에게 칭찬과 응원을 받을 때의 그 감격이란 정말이지 경험해보지 않으면 절대 알 수 없을 것이다.

모든 것이 처음에만 어려운 법이다. 셀프 칭찬을 한번 해본 뒤로 점점 용기가 났다. 그래서 아이들에게 따뜻한 말을 해준 것, 남편에게 힘내라고 맛있는 음식을 차려준 것, 심지어 아침 일찍 일어나는 것까지 칭찬하게 되었다. 평소에 그냥 지나치던 일들, 내 일상의 온갖 자잘한 행동들을 모두 칭찬하게 된 것이다. 또 그때마다 여러 사람이 나를 칭찬하고 응원해주었다. 그리고 나 역시 다른 이들의 셀프 칭찬에 열렬한 응원과 격려를 보냈다. 진심은 통한다고 나의 응원에 사람들은 감동했고, 그 감동을 이어받아 또 다른 칭찬과 응원들이 이어졌다.

마치 마음의 샘물처럼, 사람들이 내게 칭찬이라는 물을 부어주어 나의 샘이 가득 차게 되자 이번엔 내가 다른 사람의 샘에 물을 부어주는 선순환이 계속되었다.

영원히 돌아오지 않을
'지금'이기에

─────

    이 글을 쓰면서 짧게나마 지난 삶을 되돌아보며 미소 짓기도 하고 눈시울이 촉촉해지기도 했다. 그리고 내가 아직 꿈을 잃지 않았다는 것, 그 꿈을 현실화하고 싶다는 것도 알았다.

    누구나 그렇듯이 삶 속에 늘 행복하고 즐거운 일들만 있는 건 아니다. 너무 지치고 힘들어서 무기력해질 때도 있지만, 그래도 지나온 뒤에 돌아보면 그마저도 추억이 된다. 별거 아닌 일들이 모여 별거가 되는 것이 삶이며 그 누구도 아닌 나의 스토리라는 사실을 새삼 깨닫는다. 이 사실을 예전에 알았더라면 내가 나를 조금은 더 너그럽고 애틋하게 대

해주지 않았을까? 영원히 돌아오지 않을 '지금'이기에 회한
과 질책보다는 칭찬과 응원으로 따뜻하게 어루만져주지 않
았을까?

나는 소심하면서도 게으른 완벽주의자다. 남들 앞에 서
면 떨려서 생각도 제대로 못 하고 말도 어눌해진다. 그런 내
가 너무 싫었다. 하지만 이젠 그런 내 모습 역시 나 자신이
라는 것을 온전히 받아들이고 싶다. 창고 방을 만나면서 나
는 이렇게나 많이 달라졌다.

못나건 잘나건 세상에 하나뿐인 나를 인정하고 칭찬하
면서부터 그동안 약점이라고만 여겨왔던 나의 면면들이 조
금씩 반전을 일으키는 것 같다. 소심해서 머뭇거리던 일들
에 대해 용기를 낼 수 있게 되었고, 지쳐 쓰러질 것 같은데
도 숨 고르기를 하며 다음을 약속할 수 있게 되었다. 중대
한 도전 앞에서도 실패를 두려워하며 아등바등하지 않고,
결국 해낼 거라는 믿음 하나로 묵묵히 걸어가는 쪽으로 초
점을 바꾸고 있다.

나를
칭찬한다는 것

나를 칭찬한다는 것은 나를 사랑하는 일이다.

언제 어디서든 나를 지지해주는 사람이 있다고 상상해보자. 내가 어떤 실수를 하거나 좌절할 때도, 혹은 슬프거나 우울할 때도 늘 내 편이 되어 나를 사랑하고 지지해주는 사람이 있다면 어떨까? 온 세상이 날 버리고 외면해도 끝까지 내 곁에서 "언제까지나 너를 사랑해. 너라서 영원히 사랑해"라며 끝까지 지켜줄 수 있는 사람이 있다면?

누구에게나 영원히 자신을 사랑해줄 '단 한 사람'이 있다. 다만 자신에게 그런 존재가 있다는 것을 매 순간 느끼며 사는 것과 느끼지 못하며 사는 것에 차이가 있을 뿐이다. 어떤 경우에도 나를 지지하고 사랑해줄 그 사람은, 다른 누구도 아닌 바로 '나 자신'이다.

내가 나로 살아간다는 것은 어쩌면 '나를 사랑하는 나'와의 아름다운 동행이 아닐까? 시련 앞에서 내가 처한 상황을 탓하고 싶을 때마다 '마음가짐을 달리해봐. 네가 어떻게 바라보고, 어떤 자세를 선택하느냐에 따라 상황은 얼마든지 달라질 수 있어'라며 토닥여줄 수 있는 나. 지금까지 잘해왔고, 앞으로도 잘할 거라며 다독여줄 수 있는 나. 그런 '나'를 불러내고 싶을 땐 간단한 주문을 외우면 된다. 그 주문이란 '사소한 칭찬'이 아닐까?

나를 칭찬한다는 것은 나를 믿어주는 일이다.

얼마 전 드라마에서 '추앙'이라는 표현을 만났다. 평소에 잘 쓰지 않는 단어라 생경했다. 여주인공이 남주인공에게 "나를 추앙해"라고 하자 "어떤 게 추앙하는 거냐"라고 되물으니 "나를 응원해주면 돼"라고 말하는 장면이었다.

추앙한다, 추앙한다……. 그 대사를 되뇌며 정말 추앙한다는 게 뭘까 곰곰이 생각해봤다. 추앙, 그건 믿음 속에서 피어나는 게 아닐까? 사랑하는 감정이 있더라도 그 밑바탕에 믿음이 깔려 있지 않다면 추앙할 수 없을 것이다.

나를 칭찬하면 나를 사랑하게 되고, 그 바탕 위에서 나에 대한 굳건한 믿음이 형성된다. 그러니까 나를, 나 자신을 추앙하면 된다. 그러면 물 흐르듯이 당연하게 나를 응원하게 된다. 나를 응원하니 삶의 물음표에 내가 답하고 조금 더 나은 방향으로 나를 옮겨가게 된다.

나를 칭찬한다는 것은 내가 원하는 바를 꿈꾸는 것이다. 우리는 매일매일 소중하고 아름다운 것들과 만난다. 아침에 떠오르는 찬란한 태양, 풀벌레 소리, 아이들의 웃음소리, 해 질 녘 하늘의 노을빛……. 누구나 매일매일 누릴 수 있는 것들이다.

힘들고 지칠 때면 잠시 걸음을 멈추고, 나를 다독이며 '매일매일 누릴 수 있는 것들'을 돌아본다. 그렇게 쉬어가며 다시 나를 일으켜 세우고 오늘을 충실히 살아가는 것이다. 그리고 또 다른 '오늘'이 될 내일, 내가 원하는 꿈에 한 발 더 다가갈 그 날을 기대하는 것이다.

나무에 물을 주듯이 매일매일 나에게 용기라는 이름의 물을 주자. 나에게 물을 주는 일은 쉽다면 쉬운 일이고 어렵게 생각하면 어려운 일이다. 하지만 살아가는 일은 그리 만만하고 쉬운 일이 아니기에 내가 나에게 용기를 주지 않으면 너무 힘겹지 않은가? 나 스스로 잘한다고, 잘하고 있으니 앞으로도 잘해보자고 용기를 주자. 때로 힘들고 지쳐 주저앉아도 괜찮다. 쓰러진 게 아니라 잠시 쉬어가는 거라고, 내가 묻고 내가 답하며 용기를 내면 된다. 꿈을 향해 이렇게 스스로 용기를 주며 한 걸음씩 나아가다 보면 언젠가는 이루어지지 않을까?

　　이 글을 쓰며 처음으로 내 인생을 풀어서 펼쳐보았다. 사는 일이 늘 두렵고 힘들었는데, 그래도 나름 잘 살아왔다는 생각이 든다. 물론 그때 그랬더라면, 하는 순간도 있지만, 이미 지나간 시간을 돌이킬 수는 없을 테니 이제 지나간 날들이 아닌 오늘, 바로 '지금'에 충실할 따름이다. 그리고 나와 비슷한 이들에게 용기를 주고 싶다. 사람 사는 거 다 비슷하다고. 나를 사랑하고 나를 믿어주며 내가 원하는 방향으로 꿈꾸며 살아가보자고 이야기하고 싶다.

© 이미경

10

칭찬은 비타민이다

— 트루북스

BGM MUSIC NFT #3
나를 돌아보는 여유와 힐링의 시간으로 일상을 이야기하는 멜로디로
내면의 좋은 에너지를 전하는 비타민처럼 밝은 곡입니다.

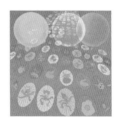

이러다간 디지털 폐인이 될지도 몰라

새벽 5시, 그들은 깨어 있었다

정작 '나'는 누가 응원해줬지?

칭찬하면 여유가 생긴다

칭찬은 꿈의 자양분이다

내가 나를 응원하는 시스템

비타민처럼 에너지가 솟는 칭찬

세상 모든 것이 칭찬받아 마땅하다

이러다간
디지털 폐인이 될지도 몰라

2019년 2월 이후 우리의 일상에서 코로나를 빼고 이야기할 수 있을까? 잠깐일 것 같던 사회적 격리로 인해 봄맞이 꽃구경은커녕 여유로워야 할 식당이나 카페에서도 잔뜩 긴장한 채 우리 모두 창살 없는 감옥에 갇힌 삶을 살아야 했다.

외출이 허락되지 않아 종일 꼼짝할 수 없는 날이면 어김없이 스마트폰과 하루를 보내야 했다. 지나간 드라마 다시보기, 지나간 예능 프로그램 다시 보기……, 어떤 날은 새벽 3시까지 드라마에 빠져 있기도 했다. 일상이 바삐 돌아가던 때는 유용한 소통 수단이던 스마트폰이 점점 시간 파괴자,

시간 도둑이 되어가고 있었다.

그렇게 어제와 똑같은 오늘이 끝없이 반복되면서 나는 점점 디지털의 노예가 되어갔다. 유튜브 알고리즘을 타고 여기저기 누르다 보면 시간은 어느새 점심, 저녁이 훌쩍 지나 자정을 향하기 일쑤였다. 나의 다리를 묶어둔 건 코로나였지만, 나의 정신과 나의 하루하루를 붙잡은 건 스마트폰이었다. 멍한 머리와 충혈된 눈……, 나는 지쳐가고 있었다.

이러다간 정말 폐인이 되겠다 싶어 지난겨울, 영어 공부를 시작하기로 했다. 영어를 공부해야겠다는 생각은 늘 머릿속에 있었지만, 외국여행을 간다거나 토익 토플 시험을 치겠다는 목표 같은 건 딱히 없었다. 단지 나태하고 무미건조한 삶의 패턴을 바꾸고 싶어 영어를 선택한 것이다.

나는 일단 '케이크'라는 앱을 깔았다. '케이크'는 영어 관련 앱인데 문제를 맞힐 때마다 별을 받을 수 있었다. 나는 열심히 자판을 눌러가며 별을 모아나갔다.

케이크 앱으로 나름 영어 공부를 하다 보니 자신감이 조금씩 생기면서 '뭐라도 해야겠다'라는 의욕이 솟아났다.

그리하여 나만의 챌린지를 시작하게 되었다.

챌린지는 매일매일 케이크에 인증하고, 카페에서 활발하게 활동하여 노트에 적는 방식이었다. 나의 활동명은 랄라였다. 랄라, 랄라 신나게 영어 공부를 하겠다는 의미로 붙인 이름이다. 나는 제법 활발하게 공부하며 리워드도 꼬박꼬박 받았다. 욕심이 생겨 노트에 매일매일의 표현도 쌓아갔다. 그러다가 뭐에 이끌렸는지 인스타그램에 노트 사진을 올리기 시작했다.

새벽 5시,
그들은 깨어 있었다

나는 매일매일 인스타그램에 인증을 올렸다. 어떤 날은 글도 쓰고 어떤 날은 댓글과 '좋아요', '하트'도 누르고 받으면서 상대방이 먼저 손 내밀어주는 선팔도 받아봤다.

그즈음 '페르소나'라는 분을 알게 되었다. 그녀는 내게 하트를 아낌없이 보내주고 매일매일 나의 챌린지에 '파이팅 하세요', '해피한 하루', '꺅' 같은 응원 댓글을 달아주었다. 진솔한 마음이 한껏 묻어 있는 응원과 칭찬들……. 그때부터 내 인스타그램 명은 '트루북스'가 되었다.

이름이 불린다는 건 정말 에너지가 한가득 충전되는 기분이다. 그녀의 인스타 피드를 찬찬히 읽어보면 '나를 찾는다, 나를 일으킨다, 나를 응원한다'와 같은 긍정의 메시지들이 빼곡했다. 게다가 그녀는 새벽 기상 챌린지와 영어로 확언 필사까지 하고 있었다. 공부는 물론 브랜딩도 열심히 하는 멋진 사람이었다.

그리고 실시간 업데이트되는 SNS 속엔 '미라클모닝 새벽 기상'이란 피드들이 쏟아졌다. 이렇게 많은 사람이 새벽 5시에 일어난다고? 그렇게 일찍 일어나서 도대체 뭘 할까? 나에게 새벽 5시는 아직 꿈속에 있을 시간이었다. 그때까지 나는 7시에 일어나 허둥지둥 애들 깨우고, 학교 보내는 것이 하루의 시작이었다.

'그런데 5시라고? 새벽 5시면 정말 모두 잠든 밤 같은 시간인데.'

하지만 인스타그램 세상 속엔 내가 경험하지 못한 새벽의 일상이 있었다. 운동, 성경 읽기, 영어 공부, 독서…… 내가 모르는 시간, 내가 잃어버린 시간에 그들은 벌써 일어나 자신을 위해 가장 알찬 활동을 하고 있었다.

무엇이 이토록 그들을 열광하게 할까? 새벽 기상, 모닝 챌린지, 514챌린지, 이건 또 뭐지? 처음으로 호기심이 생기는 순간이었다.

정작 '나'는
누가 응원해줬지?

―――

　　나의 변화를 이야기하자면 엘님을 빠뜨릴 수 없다. 페르소나님과 매일매일 댓글로 소통하던 중, 엘님의 피드가 눈에 들어왔는데, 피드가 유난히 깔끔하고 예뻤다. 인스타그램 특성상 어떻게 엘님을 팔로우했는지 모르겠지만, 그때 이런 멘트를 보내온 것으로 기억한다.

　'먼저 손 내밀어주셔서 감사합니다.'

　그 뒤 문장은 기억이 나지 않지만, 댓글로 봐서 내가 먼저 팔로우했나 보다. 그날부터 잔잔한 엘님의 피드에 하트를 꼬박꼬박 보내고 응원 메시지를 받았다.

　그러던 중 또다시 '새벽 기상'이 궁금해졌다. 새벽 5시?

미라클모닝? 과연 가능할까? 밤늦도록 유튜브에 인스타에 12시를 훌쩍 넘기는 올빼미 스타일인데 과연 내가 할 수 있을까?

"나 5시에 깨워줄 수 있어?"

남편에게 물었다.

"얼마든지. 일어나기만 한다면야."

아, 내가 정말 할 수 있을까? 아니, 꼭 해야 하나? 시도라도 한번 해볼까?

망설임 끝에 일단 워밍업 삼아 6시 기상부터 시도해보기로 했다.

그때가 3월의 끝자락이었나? 4월엔 뭔가 하나라도 해내리란 기대로 챌린지를 신청하고 카톡방 배정도 받았다. 챌린지를 시작한다고 하니 엘님도 페르소나님도 자기 일처럼 기뻐해주었다.

아, 정말 드디어 시작인가! 경건한 마음과 함께 3월의 마지막 밤이 저물고 있었다.

두근두근 4월 1일, 새벽 5시 기상 챌린지가 시작되었다.

1일 차, '누군가를 응원하는 방법'

그런데 가만, 지금까지 나는 누굴 응원했지? 결혼 전엔 친구를 응원하고 아이를 낳고는 '잘한다, 내 새끼', '이쁜 내 새끼' 하며 아이를 응원하고, 직장에 다닐 땐 동료들을 응원했다. 하지만 정작 나는 누가 응원해주었나? 당연한 도리에 대한 칭찬이나 성과에 대한 의례적 칭찬 말고 오롯이 나를 위한 칭찬은 빠져 있었다.

어릴 땐 그나마 귀엽다고, 노래 잘한다고 칭찬받았지만, 나이 들고 나서는 딱히 칭찬받을 일이 없었다. 요리? 밥해 줄 사람은 엄마뿐이니 아이들은 '맛있어'라고 칭찬해주긴 하는데 솔직히 엎드려 절받기 아닌가? 솔직히 이런 칭찬은 가볍게 흘려듣기 일쑤다. 물론 이것도 엄마에 대한 아이들의 배려와 응원인 건 맞지만.

매일매일 새로운 주제로 챌린지가 이어졌고, 나는 꼬박꼬박 노트에 기록해가며 인스타그램에 열심히 인증 글을 남겼다. 챌린지가 진행되는 동안 '나를 들어올려라', '내가 바뀌어야 한다', '내 마음의 소리를 들어라' 등 알면서도 실천하지 못하던 미션이 매일매일 쏟아졌다. 그렇게 정신없이 첫 번째 챌린지가 끝이 났다.

챌린지가 끝난 뒤 엘님의 피드에 〈칭찬받는 고래〉가 나타났다.《칭찬은 고래도 춤추게 한다》라는 책이 떠올랐다.

나를 칭찬해요. 우리를 칭찬해요. 온 세상 사람들이 매일매일 칭찬하는 그 날까지 〈칭찬받는 고래〉가 쏘아 올린 선한 영향력 '칭고 방'을 소개합니다.

〈칭찬받는 고래〉 오픈 카톡방? 이건 뭐지? 들어가볼까?

그래, 궁금은 하네. 디지털에 취약한 나는 떨리는 마음으로 오픈 카톡방 비번을 눌렀고, 그렇게 칭고들과 친구 사이가 되었다. 오픈 카톡방에 들어가니 칭찬봇이 나를 반겨주었다. 이 아이는 또 누구지? 인스타 아이디로 변경해주세요? 인스타 아이디는 왜?

뭐가 뭔지 모른 채 나는 카톡방 아이디를 '트루북스'로 변경했다.

칭찬하면
여유가 생긴다

'엘님 덕분에 미라클모닝을 알게 됐고 챌린지를 완주한 나를 칭찬해요.'

'저의 꼬임에 넘어가 챌린지를 시작하고 멋지게 변화하고 계신 트루북스님을 응원하고 칭찬합니다.'

'꼬임, 달콤한 유혹, 안 하면 하게 하라, 오지 않으면 오게 하라…… 이렇게 불굴의 열정으로 저를 일어나게 만드신 엘님을 칭찬합니다.'

챌린지가 끝난 날, 엘님이 릴스 선물을 보내왔다.

'밥상은 차려드렸으니 맛있게 드시는 건 본인 몫이 어요.'

밥상이라고? 칭찬 릴스를 밥상에 비유하다니, 속으로 웃음이 터져 나왔다. 두 번째 미션으로 리그램 이벤트를 하라는데 이건 또 뭐지? 조금 버벅거렸지만, 다행히 미니 챌린지에서 배운 가락으로 리그램에 성공했다. '잘한다, 잘한다!' 칭찬의 힘으로 나는 성장하고 있었다.

칭고 방 릴레이는 '나'를 칭찬하는 것에서부터 시작된다. 나를 칭찬하다 보면 먼저 내 마음에 여유가 생기고, 나중엔 다른 사람들을 돌아볼 여유까지 생겨난다. 매일매일 내가 하는 말들이 나와 내 주변을 변화시킨다는 말처럼 칭찬은 정말 나를 긍정적으로 변화시키고 있었다.

쉼이란 뭘까? 아무것도 하지 않는 것? 무리 속에 들어 있던 나를 잠시 빼내는 것? 복잡한 관계와 상황의 물결 속에서 빠져나와 물가에 가만히 앉아 있는 것?

이리 치이고 저리 치여 자존감이 떨어지고 지쳐버린 나를 발견할 때마다 나는 자꾸만 땅속으로 숨어들고 싶었다. 하지만 세상은 아무 때나 쉼을 허락할 만큼 너그럽진 않다. 그래서 평소에 마음 근육을 다져놔야 한다. 마치 가장 가까운 곳에 늘 있는 파랑새처럼 마음 깊이 희망을 품고 있어야 한다. 희망을 품고 있는 그 보금자리가 바로 나의 안식처이기 때문에.

칭고 방을 만나기 전만 해도 나는 사회적으로 블러 처리된 사람이었다. 밖에선 허허실실하다가 집에 와선 우울감에 빠지는 사람, 딱히 인간관계랄 것도 없어 업무적인 대화 말고는 이렇다 할 소통도 필요 없는 사람이었다.

그런 내게 칭고 방이라는 세계가 비집고 들어온 것이다. 무슨 얘길 해도 *끄덕끄덕* 맞장구쳐주는 곳, 힘들 때나 기쁠 때나 자랑하고 싶을 때 언제든지 머물 수 있는, 말 그대로 비빌 언덕이 생긴 거다.

커뮤니티의 힘이란 이런 건가! 칭고 방은 서로 얼굴을 몰라도 무조건 반가운 곳이다. 내 삶의 안식처 칭고 방이 있어 참 든든하다.

칭찬은
꿈의 자양분이다

내가 드디어 동행 요정이 되었다. 다른 오픈 카톡 방에선 부방장이라고 하지만, 칭고 방에선 요정이라 부른다. 내가 동행 요정이 된 건 칭고 방에 들어오는 분들께 '환영합니다'와 '따뜻한 동행'이라는 이모티콘을 보내면서였다. 물론 누군가 들어오면 냉큼 찾아가 꼼꼼히 가이드도 잘해주었다. 그리고 얼마 후 엘님과 칭고들의 응원으로 동행 요정이 된 것이다. 이제 핑크빛 왕관까지 씌워졌으니 더 열심히 해야겠다는 생각이 샘솟는다.

칭고들의 칭찬 덕분에 용기가 생긴 걸까? 미니 챌린지 때 배운 실력으로 별거 아닌 글그램을 올려봤다. 벗꽃 사진에 두 줄 남짓 글을 올렸는데 여기저기서 칭찬이 쏟아졌다. 정말 별거 아니라 생각했는데 막상 칭찬을 듣다 보니 자신감이 더 커졌다. 그때부터 글그램이 말을 걸 때나 갑자기 미친 듯이 생각이 떠오를 때마다 내 맘대로 노트에 기록했다. 노트 메모 기능은 우리 집 디지털 튜터인 중학생 딸에게서 배운 것이다. 요즘 중딩, 정말 대단하다.

하루에 한 개씩 앱의 활용법을 배우는 미니 챌린지의 리더 리부트란님이 언젠가 그랬다. 우리는 돈 주고 배우는 것을 아이들은 그냥 아는 거라고. 맞다. 우리 세대와 중딩의 차이는 주춤주춤하느냐 과감히 눌러보느냐다.

어쨌든 노트 기능을 익힌 뒤로 내 글이 확실히 풍성해졌다. 매일매일 칭찬받고 칭찬을 하다 보니 칭찬의 나비효과, 칭찬의 선한 영향력으로 나는 점점 변화하고 성장했다. 이를테면 '하고 싶은 것'이 생긴 거다. 사람들은 하고 싶고 되고 싶은 것을 꿈이라 부른다. 나에게도 그런 꿈이 생겼다. 언젠가 다른 이들에게 감동을 줄 수 있는 글을 쓰고 싶다는 꿈. 비록 지금은 땅속에서 간신히 눈을 떠 뿌리털을 한 가닥 꺼내고 새싹 하나 틔운 정도지만, 그래도 가슴속에서 몽글몽글 피어나고 있다. '시인 트루북스'라는 꿈이.

내가 나를
응원하는 시스템

————

어느 날부턴가 미라클모닝 514 챌린지가 끝나면 그날그날 요약하면서 강의에 나만의 색깔을 입혀 글그램 트루북스로 발행하기 시작했다. 그리고 용기를 내어 칭고 방에 먼저 요약 글과 글그램을 올렸다. 역시나 칭고들의 응원 세례가 쏟아졌다. 나는 좀 더 용기를 내어 소규모의 카톡방에서부터 내 글을 올리기 시작했다. 좋은 글이라며 하트와 엄지척이 쌓이면서 점점 규모가 큰 오픈 카톡방에도 글을 올렸다. 그런 날은 몇 번이나 그 카톡방으로 손이 갔고, 하트나 엄지척이 쌓여 있는 날은 종일 기분이 좋았다. 공감 댓글에도 힘이 났다.

'책 내시면 1호 팬 될게요.'

'책 내셔도 되겠어요.'

'직업이 시인이세요?'

이렇게 하루하루 올린 글이 쌓일 때마다 언니에게 보냈더니 또 칭찬과 응원이 날아왔다.

"와, 잘하고 있네! 조금만 더 힘을 내보자. 시집을 내려면 100편 정도는 쌓여야겠지?"

시집이라는 소리만 들어도 가슴이 떨린다. 인스타그램에 문인이라고 소개 글을 달아놔서인지 진짜 시인과도 인스타 친구가 되었다.

'고운 밤 되세요.'

'행복한 밤 되세요.'

이미 세 권의 시집을 출간한 그분은 매번 나에게 따뜻한 댓글을 남겨주었다. 주로 절절하고 애틋한 이별을 노래하는 시인인데, 읽을 때마다 눈물이 또르르 흘러내린다. 연인과 아픈 이별을 하신 건가? 왜 이렇게 가슴 절절한 이별 시만 쓰실까? 아니, 그걸 꼭 경험해야만 아나?

그렇게 시인님과 소통하던 어느 날, 나는 무슨 맘에서인지 그분께 내 자작 시를 보냈다. 두근두근, 무슨 대회 출품도 아닌데 괜스레 떨렸다. 시인님은 글이 따뜻하다며 응원 글을 보내왔다.

나에게 칭찬은 내가 나를 응원하는 시스템이다.

눈 뜨기 정말 힘든 날에도 나를 일으켜주는 힘은 결국 나에 대한 믿음과 응원이었다.

나는 글을 쓰며 나를 응원하고 칭찬한다. 챌린지 기간엔 강의를 듣고 1시간 남짓 글을 쓴다. 글을 써놓고는 글그램 사진과 캘리그래피를 맞춰본다. 모든 게 딱딱 들어맞는 날도 있지만, 도통 맘에 들지 않는 날도 있다. 이럴 땐 오늘 하루 쉴까? 하루 정도는 괜찮잖아? 하는 얄팍한 속삭임이 들려오기도 한다. 그래도 난 계속 써 내려간다. 혹시라도 나의 글을 기다리는 독자를 위해, 혹은 숨어서 하트는 안 누르고 눈팅만 열심히 하고 계신 잠재적 독자를 위해 나는 계속 글을 쓴다. 나의 글쓰기는 점점 아침 루틴이 되어갔다.

비타민처럼
에너지가 솟는 칭찬

'방학 때는 좀 쉴까?' 이런 생각을 하고 있던 어느 날, 모르는 분에게서 1:1 톡이 도착했다.

"챌린지 이후 기간에도 좋은 글 부탁드려도 될까요?"

어찌 내 맘을 아시고 이렇게 딱 맞춰 보내주실까. 처음 엔 답을 하지 않고 1:1 톡으로 다음 시를 보냈다.

하루하루

열심히 살아가다 가도

일이 뜻대로 되지 않고

삶이 해답을 주지 않을 땐 포기하고 싶을 때가 있다.

여기서 멈출까? 여기서 포기할까?

'포기'라는 말이 마음속에 문을 두드리는 순간

그 순간이 바로

진정 나를 일으켜야 하는 시간이다.

일이 술술 풀릴 때는

앞만 보고 달리지만

때론 잠시 멈춰서

돌아보는 시간도 필요하다.

나는 무엇을 하고 있는가?

나는 왜 여기에 서 있나!

묻고 답하고 묻고 답하고

끊임없이 일으키다 보면

삶이 내게 해답을 준다.

그래 바로 그거야. 잘했어!

포기하지 않았다는 건

성장했다는 증거야.

넌 스스로 해답을 찾은 거야.

넌 할 수 있어.

너를 믿어봐.

넌 해낼 거야.

넌 최고로 빛나는 보석이니까!

그러자 이런 대답이 돌아왔다.

"저도 그래요. 늘 포기하고 다시 사는 삶의 연속이지요.
그래도 끈을 놓지 않으려고요."

아침부터 어찌나 뭉클하던지. 내 글에 '좋아요'와 하트,
엄지척을 날려주며 공감한다는 댓글을 보면서 생각했다. 지
금 당장 뭐가 되진 않겠지만, 오늘도 나는 내 가슴속에 이렇
게 작은 씨앗 하나를 심었다고. 그리고 주문처럼 되뇐다.
"잘했어. 잘하고 있어. 잘할 거야."
내일도 해는 뜰 것이고 선물처럼 아침이 올 것이다. 그러
면 언제나처럼 어제의 나에게 '고마워' 인사하고, 빛나는 아
침을 맞을 수 있음에 감사하며 주어진 하루를 잘 살아낼 것
이다.

나에게 칭찬은 비타민이다. 먹으면 힘이 생기고 에너지
가 솟구친다. 셀프 칭찬을 하면서 느낀 점 한 가지, 나를 일
으켜 세우는 게 오로지 나만의 힘은 아니라는 것. 내 옆에
서, 내 뒤에서 묵묵히 나를 지켜봐주는 누군가가 늘 있었다.
나를 응원하고 지켜봐주는 사람들, 이젠 내가 그들의 힘이

되어줄 차례다. '또 다른 나'와도 같은 그들을 응원하고 칭찬하고 소통하며 나의 '때'를 기다릴 것이다.

'때'라는 게 뭘까? 밥 먹을 때, 놀 때, 공부할 때, 그건 어떤 일을 하기 위한 적당한 시간이라는 것이다. 그렇다면 나의 때는 왔을까? 오고 있을까? 지나갔을까? 나는 나의 때가 오고 있다고 생각하기로 했다. 그래야 꿈틀꿈틀 씨앗처럼 희망이 살아나니까. 씨앗은 내 안에 들어 있는, 지금보다 더 큰 미래다. 그 씨앗이 목마르지 않게, 힘들지 않게 적당히 물을 주고 양분을 주며 잘 가꾸어야 한다. 그렇게 나를 계속 키워간다면, 언젠가는 가지를 쭉쭉 뻗을 수 있을 것이다. 꽃이 피고 열매가 열릴 것이다.

다시 나의 꿈을 적어본다. 그리고 나를 반짝반짝 빛나게 해줄 그 이름을 불러본다. "시인 트루북스"라고.
언제가 될진 모르지만, 스페이셜에서 작품을 발표하고 전자책을 발행하고 싶다. Web 2.0도 시작한 지 얼마 안 되었지만, 스텝 바이 스텝으로 도전해야겠다. 물론 나의 꿈은 시인이며 내 이름 걸고 시집을 내는 것이다. 어릴 적 막연히 꿈꾸던 작가의 꿈은 지금도 여전히 진행 중이다.

꿈에 날개가 있는 게 아니라 꿈을 입 밖으로 내는 순간 날개가 활짝 펼쳐지며 사람을 둥실둥실 떠오르게 한다. 칭찬과 응원으로 오늘도 나는 성장한다. 오늘도 나는 꿈을 꾸고 내일도 나는 꿈을 꿀 것이다.

세상 모든 것이
칭찬받아 마땅하다

　　셀프 칭찬이 처음이거나 평소 칭찬에 인색한 사람이라면 칭찬 자체가 어색하고 낯간지러워 힘들어할 수도 있다. 그럴 땐 일상을 들여다보자.

　오늘은 잘 일어났는지, 오늘 누군가를 배려하고 응원했는지, 혹시 지금이라도 칭찬해주고 싶은 사람은 없는지……. 나를 칭찬하는 건 힘들지만 누군가를 꼭 칭찬하려고 마음먹으면 그 찾기 힘든 칭찬거리가 보인다. 이럴 때 미러링을 해보자.

　'맞아, 나도 저러는데. 나도 저랬는데!'

　속으로 이렇게 맞장구를 쳐보자. 그리고 일단 자판이든

펜이든 들고 '잘했어. 잘하고 있어. 잘할 거야' 주문을 적어보자. 칭찬? 처음이 어렵지, 하다 보면 쉽다. 칭찬이 어렵다는 생각을 아예 버리고 일단 꺼내보자. 내 마음의 소리를.

칭찬의 대상이 꼭 사람이어야만 할 까닭은 없다. 가끔은 주변의 사물들에도 칭찬을 건네보자. 나를 포근하게 감싸는 이불, 더운 날 땀을 식혀주는 선풍기, 시원한 과일과 채소를 보관해주는 냉장고……. 우리와 일상을 함께하는 고마운 것들이 얼마나 많은지 깜짝 놀라게 된다.

어느 주말, 칭고 방에서 감자밭을 칭찬한 적이 있다. 미니 챌린지 기간이었는데, 그날은 주말이라 푹 자고 일어났다고 했더니 응원요정님이 '미니 챌린지도 주말엔 쉬는군요'라고 보내왔다. 나는 이렇게 댓글을 올렸다.

'원래는 안 쉬는데 리더님 감자 캐러 가셨어요. 맞다, 리더님 시댁 감자밭을 칭찬해야겠어요. 덕분에 저도 다른 분들도 밀린 잠을 챙겼으니 감자밭에 고마운 제 맘을 담아 칭찬합니다.'

일단 그렇게 칭찬하고 났더니 한 번도 본 적 없는 감자밭이 갑자기 정겨워졌다. 사물에 대한 칭찬 릴레이가 시작된 건 그때부터였다.

'나를 기다려준 지하철 빈자리를 칭찬합니다.'
'소통할 수 있게 해준 핸드폰을 칭찬합니다.'
'사연 있는 감자밭을 칭찬해요.'
'오늘, 지금까지 열 일하고 있는 세탁기와 건조기를 칭찬합니다.'

그렇다. 칭찬은 이런 거다. 누구나 쉽게 할 수 있고, 칭찬하는 순간 행복해지는, 마치 연금술 같은 행위다. 칭찬이 일상이 되면 얼마나 좋을까? 칭찬은 중2병도 이긴다. 예전에 어느 강의에서 교육 코칭 전문가가 이런 말을 한 적이 있다.

'자녀에게 하루에 3가지씩 칭찬하라.'

그때 학부모들이 이구동성으로 '칭찬을 세 가지나 할 게 있어야 하죠?'라고 반문하자 강사는 딱 잘라 이렇게 말했다.

"칭찬할 거리가 없다면 그 입 다물라."

그러면서 100일 동안 3가지씩 칭찬하면 아이가 바뀐다고 했다. 그 한마디가 지금도 귓가에 맴돈다. 감자밭에도, 지하철 빈자리며 핸드폰, 세탁기, 건조기에도 칭찬할 거리가 넘치는데 하물며 내 아이에게 없을까? 고마운 마음으로 돌아보면 세상 모든 것이 칭찬받아 마땅한 것들이다. 칭찬은 모든 것을 바꾼다. 칭찬은 고래도 춤추게 한다. 내친김에 고래들을 찾아 응원하고 칭찬해주어야겠다. 어떤 고래를 먼저 칭찬해줄까?

© 정은희

11

칭찬은 꿈의 완성품이다 — 미소라떼

BGM MUSIC NFT #29
따스한 꿈을 그리고 따뜻한 시선을 가진 사람들의 마음을 보듬고
손잡아주는 꿈을 응원하는 곡입니다.

내 삶에 칭찬은 존재하지 않았다

엄마의 기쁨 나무, 아들에게

나를 되찾아가는 여정

칭찬 레시피는 내 꿈의 완성품

내 삶에
칭찬은 존재하지 않았다

———

　　따스한 햇볕이 내려앉은 마당 한 모퉁이에서 지긋
한 눈빛으로 한 꼬마를 지켜보는 순둥이 강아지가 있었다.
여자아이는 순둥이와 눈높이를 맞추려고 양손에 슬리퍼를
낀 채 납작 엎드렸다.

　　이 천진난만한 일곱 살 여자아이가 바로 나다. 딸 부잣
집의 다섯 딸 중 막내인 나는 늘 귀여움과 내리사랑을 독차
지한 덕분에 그저 세상의 선한 면만 보며 자랐다.

　　까슬까슬한 수염이 아팠지만, 아버지는 언제나 "이쁜 우
리 막내딸!" 하고 볼을 비벼댔다. 엄마는 대가족 살림이 녹
록지 않은 듯, 들킬세라 한숨을 길게 내뿜다가도 고운 손길

로 나의 긴 머리카락을 빗겨주었다. 어린 내게 엄마는 세상에서 가장 곱고 섬세한 분이었다.

해마다 어린이날이 되면 언니들은 자그마한 나의 체구에 줄자를 대어가며 의상실의 양장 맞춤옷을 입혀주었다. 그리고 늘 내 손에 솜사탕을 쥐여주고 어린이대공원에서 마냥 행복해하는 나를 사진에 담으며 흐뭇한 미소를 지었다.

천진난만하던 여자아이는 어느덧 성인이 되어 한 남자를 배우자로 맞이했다. 그리고 이때부터 세상은 이전과 사뭇 다른 빛을 띠기 시작했다. 온통 사랑과 칭찬뿐이던 나의 삶과 칭찬에 인색하고 엄격한 가정에서 자란 배우자의 삶은 함께 어울리기엔 너무도 결이 달랐다. 틀린 것이 아니라 다른 것이라며 스스로 인정하려 애썼지만, 그래도 힘든 건 어쩔 수 없었다.

남편은 절제된 감정과 무언의 무게감이 가정을 지켜나가는 올바른 가장의 모습이라 여길 만큼 보수적이었다. 그래서 나는 더더욱 나를 희생하고, 감정을 수면 아래로 감춰야 했다. 가정의 온전한 평화를 위해선 인내가 곧 미덕이었으니까.

　내 삶에 칭찬은 존재하지 않았다. 이런 생활은 한동안 이어졌고, 긴긴 칭찬의 부재는 결국 '자신감의 상실과 자존감의 추락'으로 나타났다. 내 삶의 시점도 일인칭이 아닌 이인칭이 되면서 악순환의 연결고리는 점점 견고해졌다.

　겉보기엔 마냥 선량해 보여도 나 스스로 생각의 틀을 깨지 못하니 돌아도, 돌아도 늘 제자리에 웅크리고 있는 나약한 모습일 뿐이었다. 이렇게 힘든 시간을 보내던 중 다행스럽게도 나 자신을 가까스로 일으켜 세운 힘이 생겼다. 내가 엄마가 된 것이다.

　결혼 2년 차에 세상에서 가장 멋진 아들을, 그리고 나를 쏙 빼닮은 어여쁜 딸을 얻었다. 점점 잃어가던 '나'라는 존재는 역시나 자연스레 사라졌지만, 대신에 엄마라는 새로운 존재로 거듭났으니 그저 행복할 따름이었다. 엄마가 된 나의 가슴속엔 아이들에게 퍼부어줄 사랑과 칭찬이 가득 준비되어 있었다.

　나는 두 아이에게 사랑과 격려, 그리고 칭찬을 아끼지

않았다. 고맙게도 아이들은 건강하게 잘 자라주었고, 모난 구석 없이 학창 시절을 잘 이겨내어 누구나 원하는 대학 군으로 진학했다. 돌이켜보면 한없이 격려해주고 바라봐주며 힘들 때마다 사랑 가득한 칭찬을 보내준 것이 정답이었을 것이다.

그러나 고통과 시련이 없는 삶이란 게 어디 있을까? 나 역시 죽을 만큼 힘든 시간이 있었다. 큰아이가 자라면서 뒤늦게 '선천성 혈관종'이 발견되었을 때 심장이 내려앉는 충격을 경험했다. 내가 받아야 하는 벌을 고스란히 아이가 받게 된 것만 같아 가슴이 찢어질 듯 괴로웠다. 지방 종합병원에서 악성으로 보인다고 큰 병원행을 권고받았을 때는 정말 세상이 무너지는 듯했다.

나는 아이와 함께 기필코 이 시련을 이겨내리라 다짐했다. 그리고 그 방법 중 하나로 칭찬을 통한 자신감과 긍정의 마음을 택했다. 다행히 아이의 병은 음성으로 판정받아 지금 이렇게 미소를 지을 수 있게 되었다. 그 해답은 다음 한 통의 편지글로 대신한다.

엄마의 기쁨 나무,
아들에게

2007년 11월 손편지

며칠 전 우리 가족 모두 지리산 법계사에 오를 때 본 그 아름답고 고운 색깔들 기억나니? 붉게 물든 단풍잎 사이사이로 배어 나오던 가을 햇살이 네 머리 위로 가만히 내려앉은 모습에 엄마는 깜짝 놀랐단다. 엄마 앞에 번뜩이는 왕관을 쓰고, 붉은 가운을 입은 왕자가 떡하니 서 있었기 때문이지.

그래, 바로 우리 아들이 엄마에게는 이 세상 가장 멋지고 당당한 왕자님이야. 11월 4일 케이크 위에 꽂힌 열 개의 촛

불을 힘찬 입김으로 '후우' 하고 불어 보이는 너의 따뜻한 손을 살며시 잡으며 엄마는 잠시 지난 기억 속에 담겼단다. 그때였지.

"엄마 나 소원이 있어!"

평소와는 다르게 울먹이는 표정으로 내뱉는 너의 한마디에 엄마는 잔뜩 긴장했어. 갑자기 핑 도는 눈물과 함께 윗옷을 걷어 올리며 네가 한 말.

"내 몸에 있는 이게 제발 없어지면 좋겠어!"

그때 엄마는 우리 아들이 몸집도 성장해가고 있구나, 생각하면서도 사실은 많이 당황했어. 너의 가슴과 등에 자리 잡은 '선천성 정맥 기형'. 아직은 어리다는 생각만으로 너의 마음을 읽어주지 못해 너무 미안했단다. 너는 남들에게 보여주기 싫어 이제 목욕탕도 안 가려고 하는데, 그저 엄마 피로 풀자고 찜질방 같이 가자며 억지 부려 너무 미안했어.

네가 소원을 말하고 불과 이틀 뒤에야 그 일이 벌어진 거야, 넌 이미 몸에 이상 증세가 느껴져서 그렇게 말한 걸까? 오한과 40도의 고열을 오가는, 난생처음 겪는 아픔을! 아니, 네 또래 아이들은 겪어보지 못한 아픔이 너에게 찾아왔지. 그런 널 보면서도 엄마가 아무것도 해줄 수 없다는 게 정말 힘들었단다.

엄마가 할 수 있는 거라곤 일주일 동안 한 시간 남짓 자면서 발가벗긴 너의 몸을 얼음 수건으로 닦아 내리는 일뿐이었어. 밤새 주무르고 열을 식히면서 파르르 질린 채 오한으로 이를 딱딱 부딪치는 너를 안고 같이 울 수밖에 없었단다.

엄마는 너에게 어떤 일에도 당당하고 강해야 한다고 했지만, 어쩔 수 없이 엄마 눈에도 눈물이 고였지. 그때 엄마의 마음을 꼭 잡아준 사람은 바로 너야.

"엄마 나 참을 수 있어! 엄마도 팔 많이 아프지? 내일 사무실에 가서 일해야 하는데 잠 오면 어떡할래? 이제 괜찮은 것 같아. 나 이겨낼게."

바짝 말라 버린 입술로 힘을 모아가며 쉬지도 않고 말하는 너의 숨결에 엄마는 세상을 다 얻은 것 같았단다.

있잖아, 고통이란 건 누구에게나 감당할 수 있을 만큼만 주어진단다. 그러니까 지금 너의 아픔을 이겨낼 힘이 네 안에 있다는 뜻이야. 그 아픔을 잘 다스리고 이겨낸다면 자기 삶의 진정한 주인 노릇을 할 수 있게 되겠지. 그런 멋진 주인에게는 어떤 어려움과 고통도 벗이 될 수 있고, 자신에게 도움을 주는 약이 될 수도 있을 거야.

그리고 이 세상에는 남보다 백 가지를 더 가지고 있어도 가장 중요한 한 가지가 없어서 불행한 사람도 많단다. 넌 그 한 가지를 이미 갖고 있어. 그래서 아무리 힘든 일도 이겨낼 수 있을 거야. 그 한 가지가 뭔지 알지? 바로 사랑이야. 엄마에 대한 너의 사랑, 그리고 너에 대한 엄마의 사랑.

이 한 가지를 가졌기에 넌 지금까지 그 아픔을 다 이겨낼 수 있었고, 또 앞으로 어떤 어려움도 거뜬히 다스릴 수 있을 거야. 그리고 너의 몸에 자리 잡은 그 혈관종도 사랑하자꾸나. 널 아프게 했지만, 먼 훗날 언젠가 분명히 너의 마음을 어루만져주고 강하게 이끌어준 친구로 기억될 거라 여겨지는구나.

며칠 후면 우리 가족 모두 또 서울 가는 날이야. 이제는 왠지 기다려지고 신난다. 정기 검사를 위해 병원에 가는 길이지만 KTX 안에서 끝말잇기도 하고, 묵찌빠 놀이도 하며 꿀밤 맞기 또 해야지.

내 아들, 엄마 가슴이 왜 이렇게 따뜻한지 아니? 그 무엇과도 바꿀 수 없는 소중한 보물을 안고 있기 때문이야. 너라는 보물 말이야. 우리, 사랑과 꿈과 용기를 잃지 말고 오늘 하루를 또 멋지게 살아보자꾸나. 사랑해.

나를 되찾아가는
여정

나는 내가 어릴 적 받던 칭찬을 고스란히 내 아이들에게 돌려주려고 노력했고, 어느새 아이들에게도 자유롭고 튼튼한 날개가 돋아나 있었다. 부모의 둥지를 떠나 햇살 가득한 넓은 세상으로 훨훨 날려 보내도 될 만큼 큰 날개였다. 각자의 삶을 향한 아이들의 날갯짓이 곧 나의 절대적인 소명이라 여겼기에 너무 행복했고, 또 뿌듯했으며 마치 긴 원고를 탈고한 기분이었다.

문제는 그다음부터였다. 아이들이 둥지를 떠나고 난 뒤의 나날들을 나는 미처 준비하지 못했다. 오롯이 아이들에게만 집중해온 그 시간과 공간 속에 이제는 빈 껍데기만 건

조하게 남아 있었다. 24시간이란 톱니바퀴를 쉴 새 없이 돌렸지만, 나라는 존재는 그저 허울뿐이었다. 그동안 나를 지탱해온 마지막 자존감의 흔적마저 텅 비어버린 것 같은 마음이었다.

아침에 눈 뜨면 기계적으로 일어나 출근하는 직장인, 영혼 없는 모습으로 퇴근하면 '오늘 저녁은 뭐 먹을까?' 나의 입맛보다 가장이 선호하는 메뉴로 밥상을 차리는 가정주부……. 나의 정체성에 대해서 한 번이라도 제대로 생각해본 적이 있나? 나 자신에게 사랑은커녕 관심 한 번 주지 않았다는 사실이 갑자기 의식의 수면 위로 떠올랐다.

나는 왜 나 자신을 투명 인간으로 치부한 채 그렇게 방치해왔을까? 나를 위로해주기는커녕 어째서 내가 뭘 하고 싶은지 생각할 기회조차 주지 않았을까? 다른 이들에게는 칭찬하고 온정을 베풀면서도 정작 50여 년을 살아오는 동안 나에게 스스로 칭찬해준 적이 없다는 사실에 마음이 휑하게 느껴졌다. 칭찬이란 남이 나에게, 내가 남에게 하는 것이고, 그렇게 나와 타인이라는 상호 관계에서만이 가능하다는 고정관념이 나에게도 있었다.

나를 찾고 싶다는 간절함과 절박함에 갈증을 느끼던 어느 날, 드디어 유일한 방법을 찾았다. 나의 내면에 집중할 수 있는 수단은 바로 '그림'이었다. 물론 그림 그리는 재능을 타고나지는 않았다. 그러나 하얀 도화지에 붓과 색연필, 펜을 가지고 선 하나하나에 색감을 곱게 물들여가는 순간만큼은 그렇게 평온할 수 없었다. 그렇게 그림을 그리기 시작한 것이 '잃어버린 나'를 되찾는 출발점이었다.

행복했다. 매일매일 그림을 완성해가는 나에게 처음으로 칭찬을 하기 시작했고, 여기에 용기를 얻어 본격적으로 꿈을 향해 나아가기로 했다. 항상 밝고 따스한 미소로 소중한 사람들과 함께하자는 뜻으로 지은 닉네임 '미소라떼'로서의 새 삶을 살아가기로.

본격적인 출발을 다짐하는 의미에서 우선 구체적인 실행 미션을 찾았다. 나에게 새벽 시간을 선사하는 것이었다.

중년이 되기까지 셀 수 없이 맞이했던 새벽! 솔직히 그냥 눈을 떠서 맞이하면 그만이었고, 선택의 여지 없이 누구에게나 주어진 공평한 시간이라고만 여기며 의미 없이 흘려보낸 그 새벽을 나만의 시간으로 만들자. 그래, 그 시간을

오롯이 나에게 집중할 수 있는 보석 같은 시간으로 바꾸어
보자!

　2021년 10월 25일, 나는 아무것에도, 누구에게도 방해
받지 않는 새벽에 일어나 제일 먼저 나를, 그리고 함께하는
사람들을 떠올리며 감사하는 마음을 담아 편지를 쓰기 시
작했다.
　그러다가 그해 연말 무렵, 유튜브에서 2022년 새해 첫날
부터 시작되는 '김미경과 함께하는 미라클모닝 514챌린지'
소개 영상을 우연히 보게 되었다. 순간 '이거구나!' 하고 머
릿속에 환한 빛줄기 하나가 내려왔다.
　나는 조금도 망설이지 않고 MKYU 열정 대학에 입학했
다. 그리고 '오늘부터 다시 스무 살입니다(도서명)'가 되기로
나 자신과 약속했다. 그때부터 공부를 통한 새로운 삶이 전
개되기 시작했다.

　확실하게 말할 수 있는 건, 살아오면서 가장 잘한 일 중
하나가 바로 'MKYU 입학'이라는 것이다. 꾸준히 공부해가
며 나를 일으켜 세우고, 또 그렇게 성장해가는 기쁨이 이렇
게 클 줄은 미처 몰랐다. 정말 새로운 세상이고, 놀라운 경

11
미
소
라
떼

314

험이었다.

무에서 유를 창조하는 힘! 나를 인정하고 자신 있게 걸음을 내디디며 한 번도 드러내지 못한 내면의 잠재된 꿈을 찾아 떠날 수 있게 해준 그 힘은 바로 '칭찬'이었다. 그야말로 이제껏 몰랐던 나를 발견하고, 매 순간 전율과 행복이 느껴지는 시간이었다.

칭찬의 힘이 나에게 얼마나 멋진 선물을 주고, 얼마나 값진 성장을 가능하게 해줬는지 그 발자취를 소개해본다.

1. 웹 3.0 가상공간에서 그림 그리는 나

새벽 기상과 함께 시작된 공부 과정에는 정말 생각지도 못한 세상이 펼쳐지고 있었다. 모든 것이 낯설어서 예전 같으면 나와 상관없는 일이라며 외면하고 지나쳤을 것이다. 다행히 그 생소한 세계를 거부하지 않고 고스란히 흡수하며 무조건 도전한 나 자신을 칭찬한다.

모든 것이 낯선 가운데 메타버스(이프랜드)에서 아바타로 소통하고 학습과 강의도 할 수 있는 콘텐츠가 마음에 쏙 들어왔다. 아무래도 내가 추구하는 것들에 다가가는 좋은 수단이 될 것 같아 이프랜즈 밋업 5주 과정 수업을 선택하여 적극적으로 배워나갔다.

드디어 2022년 4월 17일, 내가 처음 칭찬하게 된 나의 그림 '보태니컬 아트로 작가 되다'를 소개하며 첫 발표를 열었다. 정말 떨리고 머리가 온통 하얘지는 것 같았지만, 지인과 친구들의 응원을 받으며 잘 마무리했다. 이루 말할 수 없을 만큼 벅찬 성취감과 함께 내게 큰 희망을 안겨준 경험이었다.

나를 드러내지 않으면 아무도 알 수 없다며 나의 IP를 만들라던 김미경 학장님의 말씀이 옳았다. 이 일을 계기로 비로소 나의 존재감이 세상에 드러난 것이다. 칭찬이 고래뿐만 아니라 나까지 춤추게 만든 셈이다.

2. '버킷리스트 공개 확언' 및 '나 소개하기' 발표

그 무렵 나는 MKYU 교양과목 가운데 하나인 디지털 튜터 자격증(시니어의 '디지털 문맹' 탈출을 위해 일상생활에 필요한 스마트폰 등 활용법을 안내하는 새로운 직업) 과정을 수강하고 있었다.

시험 실전을 위해 선택한 스터디 방에서 2월부터 참여

하던 중, 부 수업으로 버킷리스트를 작성해보는 시간이 주어졌다. 그동안 머릿속에만 넣어둔 채 구차한 핑계를 대가며 실천하지 못하고 있었는데, 이번에 통째로 끄집어내어 하나하나 실행할 수 있는 To Do List를 기록했다. 매일 할 일을 적은 다음, 1개월 후, 6개월 후, 또 1년 뒤, 2년 뒤, 그리고 최종적으로 도달하게 될 나의 꿈터를 명시하고 확언했다. 나 자신과의 약속이자 정성을 다해 꾸준히 걷고자 하는 다짐이 그 확언에 모두 담겨 있었다.

곧이어 스터디그룹 리더가 나의 버킷리스트를 수업 시간에 발표해보라고 제의해왔다. 나에게 온라인 영상(Zoom)으로 많은 사람 앞에서 발표하는 기회가 주어진 것이다.

그 결과 기대 이상의 큰 박수와 격려, 그리고 버거울 만큼 많은 칭찬이 돌아왔다. 나의 정신적 성장판이 활짝 열리는 순간이었다. 그로부터 사흘 뒤, 스터디그룹에서 또 다른 제의가 들어왔다. 버킷리스트 발표에 대한 호응도가 너무 좋으니 수업 정규 프로그램 중 하나인 일명 '나 소개하기' 시간에 발표해달라는 요청이었다. 원래는 강사님들이 자신을 소개하는 시간인데, 내가 수강생으로서는 처음으로 발표하는 영광을 얻게 된 것이다.

시작은 분명 힘들었지만, 이렇게 하나둘 경험이 쌓여갈수록 자신감도 축적되었다. 이런 선순환이 이어져 나는 '디지털 튜터' 자격시험에도 우수한 성적으로 당당히 합격했다.

3. 《오늘 나의 인생 책》 첫 전자책 발간

버킷리스트 중의 하나인 전자책 발간은 MKYU 챌린지 '하루의 루틴, 명상 글쓰기'에 참여하면서부터 도전하기 시작했다. 정말 쉽지 않은 시간이었다. 직장을 비롯하여 이런저런 본연의 일을 다 마친 뒤에야 글을 쓸 수 있는 시간이 주어졌기 때문에 집중도가 떨어졌고, 무엇보다 소망과 현실 사이의 괴리감이 크게 느껴져 포기하고픈 순간도 많았다. 하지만 이미 나 자신과 약속했고, 또 내가 좋아서 하는 일이라 매일매일 조금씩 이겨나간 끝에 마침내 생애 첫 전자책인 《오늘 나의 인생 책》이 발간되었다. 예전엔 언제나 '불가능한 일'로만 보이던 일들을 하나둘씩 실현해가는 나의 성장에 나 스스로 아낌없이 칭찬을 보낸다.

4. NFT 디지털 아티스트의 꿈을 이루다

그림과 관련해서 나는 다가올 미래에 발맞추기 위해 'NFT 아티스트'의 꿈을 갖고 있었다. 그래서 나름 NFT에 대해 열심히 공부했고, 디지털 드로잉과 그 문화에 대한 지식도 흡수했다. 그 과정에서 로고 공모전과 여러 프로젝트에 참여하고 수상하는 등 많은 경험을 쌓아나갔다.

직장인과 가정주부로 살던 지난 시간은 그렇게 힘들었는데, 꿈을 키워가는 그 시간은 나 스스로 놀랄 만큼 에너지와 열정이 뿜어져 나왔다. 모자라는 24시간을 쪼개고 쪼개어 살아가는 내가 너무 대견하고 자랑스러웠다. 매일매일 어제와 다른 오늘의 나에게 칭찬 세례를 퍼붓는 일도 잊지 않았다.

그리고 마침내 NFT 신인 작가에 '미소라떼'라는 이름을 올리는 가슴 벅찬 순간이 왔다. 또 하나의 꿈이 이루어진 것이다.

이후 각종 이벤트나 공모전에 열정을 다해 참여하면서 나는 세상의 어느 한 영역에서만큼은 꼭 필요한 사람으로서 존재감을 드러내기 시작했다.

칭찬 레시피는
내 꿈의 완성품

———

　　나에게 칭찬이란 꿈을 이룰 수 있게 만들어준 에너지이고, 성장과 용기를 주는 최고의 벗이다. 만약 스스로에 대한 칭찬이 없었더라면 나의 성장 가능성은 지금까지 계속 멈춰 있었을 것이고, 변화 없는 위치에 안주하며 다람쥐 쳇바퀴 돌듯 살았을 것이 분명하다. 아무것도 못 할 것 같던 내가 이렇게 성장해서 자신감과 행복을 누릴 수 있게 된 것은 언제나 나를 칭찬하는 또 다른 벗이 용기와 응원으로 늘 곁에 있어줬기 때문일 것이다.

　　칭찬은 삶의 성패를 결정할 정도로 강력할 뿐만 아니라 돈으로도 살 수 없는 멋진 경험을 안겨준다. 칭찬은 또한 주

320

어진 매 순간이 얼마나 소중한지 깨닫게 해주고, 어둠 속에서도 늘 가야 할 방향을 알려주는 등불 역할을 해준다.

칭찬을 통해 나는 분명 달라졌고, 이룰 수 없을 것 같은 꿈들을 이루었다. 그리고 내가 기대하는 미래의 그림 역시 아름다울 것이다. 그 그림을 멋지게 완성하기 위해 오늘도 나는 희망의 빛으로 성취의 선들을 하나하나 정성껏 그려가고 있다.

5년 뒤 나는 좀 더 성숙하게 무르익어 있을 것이고, 아직 꿈을 향한 도약의 기회를 잡지 못한 많은 분과 함께 열정을 공유하는 드림 카페의 주인이 되어 있을 것이다. 그 공간에서 내가 걸어온 수많은 성장의 발걸음들을 아낌없이 공유하고 소통하게 될 것이다. 생각만으로도 설레는 이 행복한 상상을 실현하기 위해 미리 초대장을 적어본다.

드림 카페 오픈 초대장

안녕하세요? 드림 공방 카페지기 미소라떼입니다.
저는 NFT 아티스트, 전자책 작가이며 디지털 튜터 자격증도 있고요, 따뜻한 감성을 지닌 사람이며, 앞으로 여러분께 선한 영향력을 나누어드리고자 합니다.

사실 저는 정말 평범하고 재능도 없는 사람이었습니다. 하지만 지금은 자랑스럽게 나 자신을 사랑하고, 꿈을 찾아 계속 성장하는 사람이 되었어요. 저처럼 평범한 사람도 '칭찬'으로 나를 보듬어주고 꾸준히 꿈을 찾기 위해 노력한다면 언젠가는 변화된 삶을 살아갈 거라는 메시지를 전달하려고 해요.

과거의 나를 들여다보고, 현재를 가장 소중한 선물로 여기며 미래의 나를 꿈꾸는 멋진 여행! 어떠세요, 함께 손잡고 떠나보시지 않겠습니까? 저와 함께 하고 싶다면 언제든지 드림 공방을 방문해주세요. 드림 카페의 주인으로서 여러분이 꿈을 실현할 때까지 뜨겁게 응원하고 칭찬하겠다고 약속합니다.

드림 카페에서는 다음과 같은 아름다운 시간을 보내게 될 거예요. 생존하기 위해서 사는 것이 아니라 나답게 사는 시간, 나를 위해 사는 시간, 열정과 사랑을 찾는 시간, 신명 나는 마인드 셋 레시피를 공유하고 배우는 시간……. 그리고 늘 우리와 함께하는 소중한 이들에게 잊고 있었던 감사의 마음도 함께 나누려 합니다.

그림을 좋아하는 분, 글쓰기를 사랑하는 분, 소외된 계층으로 배움의 기회를 놓치신 분들이라면 주저하지 마시고 언제든지 오셔서 꿈을 찾는 방법을 함께 나누어요. 그리고 마지막으로 드림 카페에 오실 때는 꼭 지참하실 준비물이 있습니다. 나에게 아낌없이 보내줄 '칭찬'을 마음속에 꼭 담아 오세요.

꿈이란 없는 것이 아닙니다. 다만 찾으려고 하지 않을 뿐이죠. 여러분은 분명 자신의 꿈을 찾게 될 거예요. 자, 이제 일어나세요! 그리고 용기와 희망을 품고 함께 걸어요! 감사합니다.

– 드림 공방 카페지기 미소라떼 드림

나는
나를

응원합니다

저자 소개

1. 엘(정채윤)
   작고 아름다운 빛을 그리는 빛나비 작가

2. 영글음(안송이)
   여성이 행복하면 온 인류가 행복할 거라 믿는 에세이스트

3. 꽃섬전복(나인선)
   삶을 칭찬으로 물들이고 싶은 인선

4. 응원요정(김태경)
   가슴 설레는 삶을 즐기는 태경

5. 시원(홍현주)
   칭찬으로 날 격려하며 성장 중인 그림일기 작가

6. 나나(나정숙)
   음악을 그리고 힐링을 연주하는 NFT 작곡가

7. 쩡희(김정희)
   칭찬의 세상에 같이 동행하실래요

8. 라라(김라라)
   일상의 아름다움을 그리는 무궁화 작가

9. 미인요정(정지민)
   나를 믿고 꿈꾸며 나아가는 미인요정

10. 트루북스(박화선)
    내 꿈은 진행중 꿈을 그리는 작가

11. 미소라떼(조정희)
    용기와 희망을 전하고픈 NFT 작가

나는
나를

응원합니다

컬렉션 소개

《나는 나를 응원합니다》 컬렉션은 칭고, 대불스, 나나랜드 세 개 커뮤니티와 퍼블리온 출판사가 함께 미혼모, 경력 단절 여성 관련 기관을 지원하기 위해 만든 선한 협업프로젝트입니다.

11명의 공동저자 에세이와 60여 명의 NFT 작가, 그리고 나나랜드의 힐링 음악이 함께 어우러져, 나 자신을 응원하고 자존감을 찾아가는 이야기를 담았습니다.

출판된 책과 이 컬렉션을 보고 듣는 이들이 따뜻한 마음을 오롯이 느끼길 원합니다.

《나는 나를 응원합니다》 컬렉션에 참여한 NFT ARTIST의 그림과 음원 NFT를 오픈씨(OpenSea)에서 만나보세요.

NFT ARTIST

강민경	신지숙
강이청	오유미
공혜린	이미홍
권민경	이선숙
김민경	이수경
김연진	이수민
김유경	이수진
김윤수	이숙향
김은숙	이영주
김정혜	이은빛
김지원	이인순
김지은	이정란
김채형	이정윤
김효신	이지민
남보람	이현주
노해정	이혜연
문신임	임설아
박문주	임정희
박미선	장지안
박수연	장현주
박여옥	정은희
배수연	정혜선
변언화	조우현
서인정	존스피
손희경	진은선
송선희	최유경
송원실	최은영
시지나	황현미
신사훈	황희

나는 나를 응원합니다

1판 1쇄 발행 2022년 12월 25일

글	칭고
그림	대불스
음악	나나랜드
펴낸이	박선영
편집	이효선
마케팅	김서연
디자인	씨오디
발행처	퍼블리온
출판등록	2020년 2월 26일 제2021-000048호
주소	서울시 영등포구 양평로 157, 408호 (양평동 5가)
전화	02-3144-1191
팩스	02-3144-1192
전자우편	info@publion.co.kr
ISBN	979-11-91587-31-9 03810

※ 책값은 뒤표지에 있습니다.

WORD
POWER
made easy

영어판

윌북

월북 홈페이지 **willbookspub.com** 자료실에서
mp3 파일을 다운받을 수 있습니다.

일러두기

60년 전통의 베스트셀러 〈WORD POWER made easy〉의 원문이 실린 영어판입니다. 부록 영어판에는 한국어 완역판에서 원서의 영문이 제공되지 않은 부분을 모두 수록하였습니다. 영어판과 한국어 완역판으로 〈WORD POWER made easy〉 원서 전문을 보실 수 있습니다. 본문 ORIGIN 시작 부분 상단에 표기된 쪽수는 한국어 완역판의 쪽수를 가리킵니다.

Table of Contents

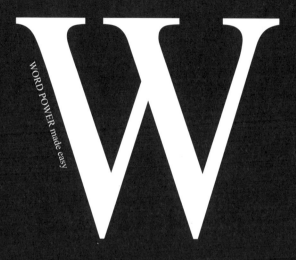

WORD POWER made easy

W

CHAPTER
1

HOW TO TALK ABOUT PERSONALITY TYPES

Words that describe all kinds and sorts of people, including terms for self-interest, reactions to the world, attitudes to others, skill and awkwardness, marital states, hatred of man, of woman, and of marriage. How one session of pleasant work can add more words to your vocabulary than the average adult learns in an entire year; why it is necessary to develop a comfortable time schedule and then stick to it.

ORIGIN

Every word in the English language has a history—and these ten are no exception. In this section you will learn a good deal more about the words you have been working with; in addition, you will make excursions into many other words allied either in meaning, form, or history to our basic ten.

⊜ the ego

Egoist and egotist are built on the same Latin root—the pronoun ego, meaning I. I is the greatest concern in the egoist's mind, the most overused word in the egotist's vocabulary. (Keep the words differentiated in your own mind by thinking of the t in talk, and the additional t in egotist.) Ego itself has been taken over from Latin as an important English word and is commonly used to denote one's concept of oneself, as in, "What do you think your constant criticisms do to my ego?" Ego has also a special meaning in psychology—but for the moment you have enough problems without going into that.

If you are an egocentric(ee´-gō-SEN´-trik), you consider yourself the center of the universe—you are an extreme form of the egoist. And if you are an egomaniac(ee´-gō-MAY´-nee-ak), you carry egoism to such an extreme that your needs, desires, and interests have become a morbid obsession, a mania. The egoist or egotist is obnoxious, the egocentric is intolerable, and the egomaniac is dangerous and slightly mad.

Egocentric is both a noun ("What an egocentric her new roommate is!") and an adjective ("He is the most egocentric person I have ever met!").

To derive the adjective form of egomaniac, add -al, a common adjective suffix. Say the adjective aloud:

egomaniacal   ee´-gō-mə-NĪ´-ə-kəl

⊕ others

In Latin, the word for other is alter, and a number of valuable English words are built on this root.

Altruism(AL´-trōō-iz-əm), the philosophy practiced by altruists, comes from one of the variant spellings of Latin alter, other. Altruistic(al-trōō-IS´-tik) actions look toward the benefit of others. If you alternate(AWL´-tər-nayt´), you skip one and take the other, so to speak, as when you play golf on alternate(AWL´-tər-nət) Saturdays.

An alternate(AWL´-tər-nət) in a debate, contest, or convention is the other person who will take over if the original choice is unable to attend. And if you have no alternative(awl-TUR´-nə-tiv), you have no other choice.

You see how easy it is to understand the meanings of these words once you realize that they all come from the same source. And keeping in mind that alter means other, you can quickly understand words like alter ego, altercation, and alteration.

An alteration(awl´-tə-RAY´-shən) is of course a change—a making into something other. When you alter(AWL´-tər) your plans, you make other plans.

An altercation(awl´-tər-KAY´-shən) is a verbal dispute. When you have an altercation with someone, you have a violent disagreement, a "fight" with words. And why? Because you have other ideas, plans, or opinions than those of the person on the other side of the argument. Altercation, by the way, is stronger than quarrel or dispute—the sentiment is more heated, the disagreement is likely to be angry or even hot-tempered, there may be recourse, if the disputants are human, to profanity or obscenity. You have altercations, in short, over pretty important issues, and the word implies that you get quite excited.

Alter ego(AWL´-tər EE´-gō), which combines alter, other, with ego, I, self, generally refers to someone with whom you are similarly, and are, in temperament, almost mirror images of each other. Any such friend is your other I, your other self, your alter ego.

ORIGIN

● depends how you turn

Introvert, extrovert, and ambivert are built on the Latin verb verto, to turn. If your thoughts are constantly turned inward(intro-), you are an introvert; outward(extro-), an extrovert; and in both directions(ambi-), an ambivert. The prefix ambi-, both, is also found in ambidextrous(am´-bə-DEKS´-trəs), able to use both hands with equal skill. The noun is ambide xterity(am´-bə-deks-TAIR´-ə-tee).

Dexterous(DEKS´-tə-rəs) means skillful, the noun dexterity (deks-TAIR´-ə-tee) is skill. The ending -ous is a common adjective suffix(famous, dangerous, perilous, etc.); -ity is a common noun suffix(vanity, quality, simplicity, etc.).

(Spelling caution: Note that the letter following the t- in ambidextrous is -r, but that in dexterous the next letter is -e.)

Dexter is actually the Latin word for right hand—in the ambidextrous person, both hands are right hands, so to speak.

The right hand is traditionally the more skillful one; it is only within recent decades that we have come to accept that "lefties" or "southpaws" are just as normal as anyone else—and the term left-handed is still used as a synonym of awkward.

The Latin word for the left hand is sinister. This same word, in English, means threatening, evil, or dangerous, a further commentary on our early suspiciousness of left-handed persons. There may still be some parents who insist on forcing left-handed children to change (though left-handedness is inherited, and as much an integral part of its possessor as eye color or nose shape), with various unfortunate results to the child—sometimes stuttering or an inability to read with normal skill.

The French word for the left hand is gauche, and, as you would suspect, when we took this word over into English we invested it with an uncomplimentary meaning. Call someone gauche(GŌSH) and you imply clumsiness, generally social rather than physical. (We're right back to our age-old misconception that left-handed people are less skillful than right-handed ones.) A gauche remark is tactless; a gauche offer of sympathy is so bumbling as to be embarrassing; gaucherie(GŌ´-shə-ree) is an awkward, clumsy, tactless, embarrassing way of saying things or of handling situations. The gauche person is totally without finesse.

And the French word for the right hand is droit, which we have used in building our English word adroit(ə-DROYT´). Needless to say, adroit, like dexterous, means skillful, but especially in the exercise of the mental facilities. Like gauche, adroit, or its noun adroitness, usually is used figuratively. The adroit person is quick-witted, can get out of difficult spots cleverly, can handle situations ingeniously. Adroitness is, then, quite the opposite of gaucherie.

⊛ love, hate, and marriage

Misanthrope, misogynist, and misogamist are built on the Greek root misein, to hate. The misanthrope hates mankind(Greek anthropos, mankind); the misogynist hates women(Greek gyne, woman); the misogamist hates marriage(Greek gamos, marriage).

Anthropos, mankind, is also found in anthropology(an-thrə-POL´-ə-jee), the study of the development of the human race; and in philanthropist(fə-LAN´-thrə-pist), one who loves mankind and shows such love by making substantial financial contributions to charitable organizations or by donating time and energy to helping those in need.

The root gyne, woman, is also found in gynecologist(gīn-ə-KOL´-ə-jist or jin-ə-KOL´-ə-jist), the medical specialist who treats female disorders. And the root gamos, marriage, occurs also in monogamy(mə-NOG´-ə-mee), bigamy(BIG´-ə-mee), and polygamy (pə-LIG´-ə-mee). (As we will discover later, monos means one, bi- means two, polys means many.)

So monogamy is the custom of only one marriage (at a time).

Bigamy, by etymology, is two marriages—in actuality, the unlawful act of contracting another marriage without divorcing one's current legal spouse.

And polygamy, by derivation many marriages, and therefore etymologically denoting plural marriage for either males or females, in current usage generally refers to the custom practiced in earlier times by the Mormons, and before them by King Solomon, in which the man has as many wives as he can afford financially and/or emotionally. The correct, but rarely used, term for this custom is polygyny(pə-LIJ´-ə-nee)—polys, many, plus gyne, woman.

What if a woman has two or more husbands, a form of marriage practiced in the Himalaya Mountains of Tibet? That custom is called polyandry(pol-ee-AN´-dree), from polys plus Greek andros, male.

☻ making friends with suffixes

English words have various forms, using certain suffixes for nouns referring to persons, other suffixes for practices, attitudes, philosophies, etc, and still others for adjectives.

Consider:

Person	Practice, etc.	Adjective
1. misanthrope *or* misanthropist	misanthropy	misanthropic
2. misogynist	misogyny	misogynous *or* misogynistic
3. gynecologist	gynecology	gynecological
4. monogamist	monogamy	monogamous
5. bigamist	bigamy	bigamous
6. polygamist	polygamy	polygamous
7. polygynist	polygyny	polygynous
8. polyandrist	polyandry	polyandrous
9. philanthropist	philanthropy	philanthropic
10. anthropologist	anthropology	anthropological

You will note, then, that -ist is a common suffix for a person; -y for a practice, attitude, etc.; and -ic or -ous for an adjective.

● living alone and liking it

Ascetic is from the Greek word asketes, monk or hermit.

A monk lives a lonely life—not for him the pleasures of the fleshpots, the laughter and merriment of convivial gatherings, the dissipation of high living. Rather, days of contemplation, study, and rough toil, nights on a hard bed in a simple cell, and the kind of self-denial that leads to a purification of the soul.

That person is an ascetic who leads an existence, voluntarily of course, that compares in austerity, simplicity, and rigorous hardship with the life of a monk.

The practice is asceticism(ə-SET´-ə-siz-əm), the adjective ascetic.

ADVICE

STICK TO YOUR TIME SCHEDULE!

In three sessions, you have become acquainted with scores of new, vital, exciting words. You understand the ideas behind these words, their various forms and spellings, their pronunciation, their derivation, how they can be used, and exactly what they mean. I do not wish to press a point unduly, but it is possible that you have learned more new words in the short time it took you to cover this chapter than the average adult learns in an entire year. This realization should make you feel both gratified and excited.

Funny thin about time. Aside from the fact that we all, rich or poor, sick or well, have the same amount of time, exactly twenty-four hours every day (that is looking at time from a static point of view), it is also true that we can always find time for the things we enjoy doing, almost never for the things we find unpleasant (and that is looking at time from the dynamic point of view). I am not merely being philosophical—I am sure you will agree with this concept if you give it a little thought.

If you have enjoyed learning new words, accepting new challenges, gaining new understanding, and discovering the thrill of successful accomplishment, then make sure to stay with the time schedule you have set up for yourself.

A crucial factor in successful, ongoing learning is routine.

Develop a comfortable time routine, persevere against all distractions, and you will learn anything you sincerely want to learn.

So, to give yourself an edge, write here the day and hour you plan to return to your work:

DAY : _____

DATE : _____

TIME : _____

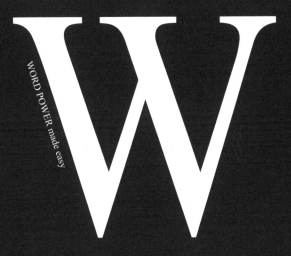

CHAPTER
2

HOW TO TALK ABOUT DOCTORS

Words that relate to medical specialists and specialties. Terms for experts in disorders of the female organs; childhood diseases; skin ailments; skeletal deformities; heart ailments; disorders of the nerves, mind, and personality. How self-discipline and persistence will ultimately lead to complete mastery over words.

ORIGIN

☻ inside you

Internist and internal derive from the same Latin root, internus, inside. The internist is a specialist in internal medicine, in the exploration of your insides. This physician determines the state of your internal organs in order to discover what's happening within your body to cause the troubles you're complaining of.

Do not confuse the internist with the intern (also spelled interne), who is a medical graduate serving an apprenticeship inside a hospital.

☻ doctors for women

The word gynecologist is built on Greek gyne, woman, plus logos, science; etymologically, gynecology is the science (in actual use, the medical science) of women. Adjective: gynecological(gīn[or jin or jīn]-ə-kə-LOJ′-ə-kəl).

Obstetrician derives from Latin obstetrix, midwife, which in turn has its source in a Latin verb meaning to stand—midwives stand in front of the woman in labor to aid in delivery of the infant.

The suffix -ician, as in obstetrician, physician, musician, magician, electrician, etc., means expert.

Obstetrics(ob-STET′-riks) has only within the last 150 years become a respectable specialty. No further back than 1834, Professor William P. Dewees assumed the first chair of obstetrics at the University of Pennsylvania and had to brave considerable medical contempt and ridicule as a result—the delivery of children was then considered beneath the dignity of the medical profession.

Adjective: obstetric(ob-STET´-rik) or obstetrical(ob-STET´-rə-kəl).

♋ children

Pediatrician is a combination of Greek paidos, child; iatreia, medical healing; and -ician, expert.

Pediatrics(pee-dee-AT´-riks), then, is by etymology the medical healing of a child. Adjective: pediatric(pee-dee-AT´-rik).

(The ped- you see in words like pedestal, pedal, and pedestrian is from the Latin pedis, foot, and despite the identical spelling in English has no relationship to Greek paidos.)

Pedagogy(PED´-ə-gō-jee), which combines paidos with agogos, leading, is, etymologically, the leading of children. And to what do you lead them? To learning, to development, to growth, to maturity. From the moment of birth, infants are led by adults—they are taught, first by parents and then by teachers, to be self-sufficient, to fit into the culture in which they are born. Hence, pedagogy, which by derivation means the leading of a child, refers actually to the principles and methods of teaching. College students majoring in education take certain standard pedagogy courses—the history of education; educational psychology; the psychology of adolescents; principles of teaching; etc. Adjective: pedagogical(ped-ə-GOJ´-ə-kəl).

A pedagogue(PED´-ə-gog) is versed in pedagogy. But pedagogue has an unhappy history. From its original, neutral meaning of teacher, it has deteriorated to the point where it refers, today, to a narrow-minded, strait-laced, old-fashioned, dogmatic teacher. It is a word of contempt and should be used with caution.

Like pedagogue, demagogue(DEM´-ə-gog) has also deteriorated in meaning. By derivation a leader(agogos) of the people(demos), a demagogue today is actually one who attempts, in essence, to mislead the people, a politician who foments discontent among the masses, rousing them to fever pitch by wild oratory, in an attempt to be voted into office.

Once elected, demagogues use political power to further their own personal ambitions or fortunes.

Many "leaders" of the past and present, in countries around the world, have been accused of demagoguery(dem-ə-GOG´-ə-ree). Adjective: demagogic(dem-ə-GOJ´-ik).

● skin-deep

The dermatologist, whose specialty is dermatology(dur-mə-TOL´-ə-jee), is so named from Greek derma, skin. Adjective: dermatological (dur´-mə-tə-LOJ´-ə-kəl).

See the syllables derma in any English word and you will know there is some reference to skin—for example, a hypodermic (hī-pə-DUR´-mik) needle penetrates under (Greek, hypos) the skin; the epidermis(ep-ə-DUR´-mis) is the outermost layer of skin; a taxidermist(TAKS´-ə-dur-mist), whose business is taxidermy (TAKS´-ə-dur-mee), prepares, stuffs, and mounts the skins of animals; a pachyderm(PAK´-ə-durm) is an animal with an unusually thick skin, like an elephant, hippopotamus, or rhinoceros; and dermatitis(dur-mə-TĪ´-tis) is the general name for any skin inflammation, irritation, or infection.

☻ the eyes have it

Ophthalmologist—note the ph preceding th—is from Greek ophthalmos, eye, plus logos, science or study. The specialty is ophthalm ology(off″-thal-MOL′-ə-jee), the adjective ophthalmological(off″-thal-mə-LOJ′-ə-kəl).

An earlier title for this physician, still occasionally used, is oculist (OK′-yə-list), from Latin oculus, eye, a root on which the following English words are also built:

1. ocular(OK′-yə-lər)—an adjective that refers to the eye
2. monocle(MON′-ə-kəl)—a lens for one(monos) eye, sported by characters in old movies as a symbol of the British so-called upper class
3. binogulars(bə-NOK′-yə-lərz)—field glasses that increase the range of two(bi-) eyes
4. And, strangely enough, inoculate(in-OK′-yə-layt′), a word commonly misspelled with two n's. When you are inoculated against a disease, an "eye," puncture, or hole is made in your skin, through which serum is injected.

Do not confuse the ophthalmologist or oculist, a medical specialist, with two other practitioners who deal with the eye—the optometrist(op-TOM′-ə-trist) and optician(op-TISH′-ən).

Optometrists are not physicians, and do not perform surgery or administer drugs; they measure vision, test for glaucoma, and prescribe and fit glasses.

Opticians fill an optometrist's or ophthalmologist's prescription, grinding lenses according to specification; they do not examine patients.

Optometrist combines Greek opsis, optikos, sight or vision, with metron, measurement—the optometrist, by etymology, is one who measures vision. The specialty is optometry(op-TOM´-ə-tree).

Optician is built on opsis, optikos, plus -ician, expert. The specialty is optics(OP´-tiks).

Adjectives: optometric(op-tə-MET´-rik) or optometrical(op-tə-MET´-rə-kəl), optical(OP´-tə-kəl).

⟨Word Power⟩ p.77

❀

ORIGIN

➥ the straighteners

The orthopedist is so called from the Greek roots orthos, straight or correct, and paidos, child. The orthopedist, by etymology, straightens children. The term was coined in 1741 by the author of a textbook on the prevention of childhood diseases—at that time the correction of spinal curvature in children was a main concern of practitioners of orthopedics(awr-thə-PEE´-diks).

Today the specialty treats deformities, injuries, and diseases of the bones and joints (of adults as well as children, of course), often by surgical procedures.

Adjective: orthopedic(awr-thə-PEE´-dik).

Orthodontia(awr-thə-DON´-shə), the straightening of teeth, is built on orthos plus odontos, tooth. The orthodontist(awr-thə-DON´-tist) specializes in improving your "bite," retracting "buck teeth," and by means of braces and other techniques seeing to it that every molar, incisor, bicuspid, etc. is exactly where it belongs in your mouth.

Adjective: orthodontic(awr-thə-DON´-tik).

☜ the heart

Cardiologist combines Greek kardia, heart, and logos, science.

The specialty is cardiology(kahr-dee-OL´-ə-jee), the adjective cardiol ogical(kahr´-dee-ə-LOJ´-ə-kəl).

So a cardiac(KAHR´-dee-ak) condition refers to some malfunctioning of the heart; a cardiogram(KAHR´-dee-ə-gram´) is an electrically produced record of the heartbeat. The instrument that produces this record is called a cardiograph(KAHR´-dee-ə-graf˘).

☜ the nervous system

Neurologist derives from Greek neuron, nerve, plus logos, science.

Specialty: neurology(nŏŏr-OL´-ə-jee); adjective: neurological(nŏŏr-ə-LOJ´-ə-kəl).

Neuralgia(nŏŏr-AL´-ja) is acute pain along the nerves and their branches; the word comes from neuron plus algos, pain.

Neuritis(nŏŏr-Ī´-tis), is inflammation of the nerves.

Neurosis(nŏŏr-Ō´-sis), combining neuron with -osis, a suffix meaning abnormal or diseased condition, is not, despite its etymology, a disorder of the nerves, but rather, as descried by the late Eric Berne, a psychiatrist, ". . . an illness characterized by excessive use of energy for unproductive purposes so that personality development is hindered or stopped. A man who spends most of his time worrying about his health, counting his money, plotting revenge, or washing his hands, can hope for little emotional growth."

Neurotic(nŏŏr-OT´-ik) is both the adjective form and the term for a person suffering from neurosis.

⊜ the mind

A neurosis is not a form of mental unbalance. A full-blown mental disorder is called a psychosis(sī-KŌ´-sis), a word built on Greek psyche, spirit, soul, or mind, plus -osis.

A true psychotic(sī-KOT´-ik) has lost contact with reality—at least with reality as most of us perceive it, though no doubt psychotic (note that this word, like neurotic, is both a noun and an adjective) people have their own form of reality.

Built on psyche plus iatreia, medical healing, a psychiatrist by etymology is a mind-healer. The specialty is psychiatry(sī- or sə-KĪ´-ə-tree);the adjective is psychiatric(sī-kee-AT´-rik).

Pediatrics, as you know, is also built on iatreia, as is podiatry(pə-DĪ´-ə-tree), discussed in the next chapter, and geriatrics(jair´-ee-AT´-riks), the specialty dealing with the particular medical needs of the elderly. (This word combines iatreia with Greek geras, old age.)

The specialist is a geriatrician(jair´-ee-ə-TRISH´-ən), the adjective is geriatric(jair´-ee-AT´-rik).

A D V I C E

TWO KEYS TO SUCCESS:
SELF-DISCIPLINE AND PERSISTENCE

You can achieve a superior vocabulary in a phenomenally short time—given self-discipline and persistence.

The greatest aid in building self-discipline is, as I have said, a matter of devising a practical and comfortable schedule for yourself and then keeping to that schedule.

Make sure to complete at least one session each time you pick up the book, and always decide exactly when you will continue with your work before you put the book down.

There may be periods of difficulty—then is the time to exert the greatest self-discipline, the most determined persistence.

For every page that you study will help you attain a mastery over words; every day that you work will add to your skill in understanding and using words.

RANDOM NOTES ON MODERN USAGE

English grammar is confusing enough as it is—what makes it doubly confounding is that it is slowly but continually changing.

This means that some of the strict rules you memorized so painfully in your high school or college English courses may no longer be completely valid.

Following such outmoded principles, you may think you are speaking "perfect" English, and instead you may sound stuffy and pedantic.

The problem boils down to this: If grammatical usage is gradually becoming more liberal, where does educated, unaffected, informal speech end? And where does illiterate, ungrammatical speech begin?

The following notes on current trends in modern usage are intended to help you come to a decision about certain controversial expressions. As you read each sentence, pay particular attention to the italicized word or words. Does the usage square with your own language patterns? Would you be willing to phrase your thought in just terms? Decide whether the sentence is right or wrong, then compare your conclusion with the opinion given in the explanatory paragraphs that follow the test.

1. If you drink too many vodka martinis,   RIGHT   WRONG
   you will surely get sick.

2. Have you got a dollar?	RIGHT	WRONG
3. No one loves you except I.	RIGHT	WRONG
4. Please lay down.	RIGHT	WRONG
5. Who do you love?	RIGHT	WRONG
6. Neither of these cars are worth the money.	RIGHT	WRONG
7. The judge sentenced the murderer to be hung.	RIGHT	WRONG
8. Mother, can I go out to play?	RIGHT	WRONG
9. Take two spoonsful of this medicine every three hours.	RIGHT	WRONG
10. Your words seem to infer that Jack is a liar.	RIGHT	WRONG
11. I will be happy to go to the concert with you.	RIGHT	WRONG
12. It is me.	RIGHT	WRONG
13. Go slow.	RIGHT	WRONG
14. Peggy and Karen are alumni of the same high school.	RIGHT	WRONG
15. I would like to ask you a question.	RIGHT	WRONG

1. If you drink too many vodka martinis, you will surely get sick.

RIGHT. The puristic objection is that get has only one meaning—namely, obtain. However, as any modern dictionary will attest, get has scores of different meanings, one of the most respectable of which is become. You can get tired, get dizzy, get drunk, or get sick—and your choice of words will offend no one but a pedant.

2. Have you got a dollar?

RIGHT. If purists get a little pale at the sound of "get sick," they turn chalk white when they hear have got as a substitute for have. But the fact is that have got is an established American form of expression.

Jacques Barzun, noted author and literary critic, says: "Have you got is good idiomatic English—I use it in speech without thinking about it and would write it if colloquialism seemed appropriate to the passage."

3. No ones loves you except I.

WRONG. In educated speech, me follows the preposition except. This problem is troublesome because, to the unsophisticated, the sentence sounds as if it can be completed to "No one loves you, except I do," but current educated usage adheres to the technical rule that a preposition requires an objective pronoun (me).

4. Please lay down.

WRONG. Liberal as grammar has become, there is still no sanction for using lay with the meaning of recline. Lay means to place, as in "Lay your hand on mine." Lie is the correct choice.

5. Who do you love?

RIGHT. "The English language shows some disposition to get rid of whom altogether, and unquestionably it would be a better language with whom gone." So wrote Janet Rankin Aiken, of Colombia University, way back in 1936. Today, many decades later, the "disposition" has become a full-fledged force.

The rules for who and whom are complicated, and few educated speakers have the time, patience, or expertise to bother with them. Use the democratic who in your everyday speech whenever it sounds right.

6. Neither of these cars are worth the money.

WRONG. The temptation to use are in this sentence is, I admit, practically irresistible. However, "neither of" means "neither one of" and is, therefore, is the preferable verb.

7. The judge sentenced the murderer to be hung.

WRONG. A distinction is made, in educated speech, between hung and hanged. A picture is hung, but a person is hanged—that is, if such action is intended to bring about an untimely demise.

8. Mother, can I go out to play?

RIGHT. If you insist that your child say may, and nothing but may, when asking for permission, you may be considered puristic. Can is not discourteous, incorrect, or vulgar—and the newest editions of the authoritative dictionaries fully sanction the use of can in requesting rights, privileges, or permission.

9. Take two spoonsful of this medicine every three hours.

WRONG. There is a strange affection, on the part of some people, for spoonsful and cupsful, even though spoonsful and cupsful do not exist as acceptable words. The plurals are spoonfuls and cupfuls.

I am taking for granted, of course, that you are using one spoon and filling it twice. If, for secret reasons of your own, you prefer to take your medicine in two separate spoons, you may then properly speak of "two spoons full (not spoonsful) of medicine."

10. Your words seem to infer that Jack is a liar.

WRONG. Infer does not mean hint or suggest. Imply is the proper word; to infer is to draw a conclusion from another's words.

11. I will be happy to go to the concert with you.

RIGHT. In informal speech, you need no longer worry about the technical and unrealistic distinctions between shall and will. The theory of modern grammarians is that shall-will differences were simply invented out of whole cloth by the textbook writers of the 1800s. As the editor of the scholarly Modern Language Forum at the University of California has stated, "The artificial distinction between shall and will to designate futurity is a superstition that has neither a basis in historical grammar nor the sound sanction of universal usage."

12. It is me.

RIGHT. This "violation" of grammatical "law" has been completely sanctioned by current usage. When the late Winston Churchill made a nationwide radio address from New Haven, Connecticut, many, many years ago, his opening sentence was: "This is me, Winston Churchill." I imagine that the purists who were listening fell into a deep state of shock at these words, but of course Churchill was simply using the kind of down-to-earth English that had long since become standard in informal educated speech.

13. Go slow.

RIGHT. "Go slow" is not, and never has been, incorrect English—every authority concedes that slow is an adverb as well as an adjective. Rex Stout, well-known writer of mystery novels and creator of Detective Nero Wolfe, remarked: "Not only do I use and approve of the idiom Go slow, but if I find myself with people who do not, I leave quick."

14. Peggy and Karen are alumni of the same high school.

WRONG. As peggy and Karen are obviously women, we call them alumnae(ə-LUM´-nee); only male graduates are alumni(ə-LUM´-nī).

15. I would like to ask you a question.

RIGHT. In current American usage, would may be used with I, though old-fashioned rules demand I should.

Indeed, in modern speech, should is almost entirely restricted to expressing probability, duty, or responsibility.

As in the case of the charitable-looking dowager who was approached by a seedy character seeking a handout.

"Madam," he whined, "I haven't eaten in five days."

"My good man," the matron answered with great concern, "you should force yourself!"

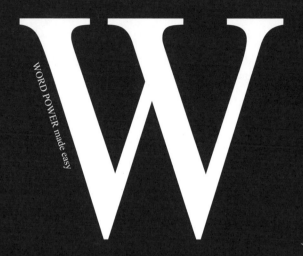

W

CHAPTER
3

HOW TO TALK ABOUT VARIOUS PRACTITIONERS

Words that describe a variety of professions, including those dealing with the human mind; teeth; vision; feet; handwriting; aging; etc. How you are becoming more and more conscious of the new words you meet in your reading.

ORIGIN

◉ the mental life

Psychologist is built upon the same Greek root as psychiatrist—psyche, spirit, soul, or mind. In psychiatrist, the combining form is iatreia, medical healing. In psychologist, the combining form is logos, science or study; a psychologist, by etymology, is one who studies the mind. The field is psychology(sī-KOL´-ə-jee), the adjective psychological (sī´-kə-LOJ´-ə-kəl).

Psyche(SĪ´-kee) is also an English word in its own right—it designates the mental life, the spiritual or non-physical aspect of one's existence. The adjective psychic(SĪ´-kik) refers to phenomena or qualities that cannot be explained in purely physical terms. People may be called psychic if they seem to possess a sixth sense, a special gift of mind reading, or any mysterious aptitudes that cannot be accounted for logically. A person's disturbance is psychic if it is emotional or mental, rather than physical.

Psyche combine with the Greek pathos, suffering or disease, to form psychopathic(sī-kə-PATH´-ik), an adjective that describes someone suffering from a severe mental or emotional disorder. The noun is psychopathy(sī´-KOP´-ə-thee).*

The root psyche combines with Greek soma, body, to form psycho somatic(sī´-kō-sə-MAT´-ik), an adjective that delineates the powerful influence that the mind, especially the unconscious, has on bodily diseases. Thus, a person who fears the consequence of being present at a certain meeting will suddenly develop a bad cold or backache, or even be injured in a traffic accident, so that his appearance at this meeting is made impossible. It's a real cold, it's far from an imaginary backache, and of course one cannot in any sense doubt the reality of the automobile that injured him. Yet, according to the psychosomatic theory of medicine, his unconscious made him susceptible to the cold germs, caused the backache, or forced him into the path of the car.

A psychosomatic disorder actually exists insofar as symptoms are concerned (headache, excessive urination, pains, paralysis, heart palpitations), yet there is no organic cause within the body. The cause is within the psyche, the mind. Dr. Flanders Dunbar, in Mind and Body, gives a clear and exciting account of the interrelationship between emotions and diseases.

Psychoanalysis(sī´-kō-ə-NAL´-ə-sis) relies on the technique of deeply, exhaustively probing into the unconscious, a technique developed by Sigmund Freud. In oversimplified terms, the general principle of psychoanalysis is to guide the patient to an awareness of the deep-seated, unconscious causes of anxieties, fears, conflicts, and tension. Once found, exposed to the light of day, and thoroughly understood, claim the psychoanalyst, these causes may vanish like a light snow that is exposed to strong sunlight.

Consider an example: You have asthma, let us say, and your doctor can find no physical basis for your ailment. So you are referred to a psychoanalyst (or psychiatrist or clinical psychologist who practices psychoanalytically oriented therapy).

With your therapist you explore your past life, dig into your unconscious, and discover, let us say for the sake of argument, that your mother or father always used to set for you impossibly high goals. No matter what you accomplished in school, it was not good enough—in your mother's or father's opinion (and such opinions were always made painfully clear to you), you could do better if you were not so lazy. As a child you built up certain resentments and anxieties because you seemed unable to please your parent—and (this will sound farfetched, but it is perfectly possible) as a result you became asthmatic. How else were you going to get the parental love, the approbation, the attention you needed and that you felt you were not receiving?

In your sessions with your therapist, you discover that your asthma is emotionally, rather than organically, based—your ailment is psychogenic(sī′-kō-JEN′-ik), of psychic origin, or (the terms are used more or less interchangeably although they differ somewhat in definition) psychosomatic, resulting from the interaction of mind and body. (Psychogenic is built on psyche plus Greek genesis, birth or origin.)

And your treatment? No drugs, no surgery—these may help the body, not the emotions. Instead, you "work out" (this is the term used in psychoanalytic[sī-kō-an′-ə-LIT′-ik] parlance) early trauma in talk, in remembering, in exploring, in interpreting, in reliving childhood experiences. And if your asthma is indeed psychogenic (or psychosomatic), therapy will very likely help you; your attacks may cease, either gradually or suddenly.

Freudian therapy is less popular today than formerly; many newer therapies—Gestalt, bioenergetics, transactional analysis, to name only a few—claim to produce quicker results.

In any case, psychotherapy(sī-kō-THAIR′-ə-pee) of one sort or another is the indicated treatment for psychogenic (or psychosomatic) disorders, or for any personality disturbances. The practitioner is a psych otherapist(sī-kō-THAIR´-ə-pist) or therapist, for short; the adjective is ps ychotherapeutic(sī-kō-thair´-ə-PYŌŌ´-tik).

* Psychopathy is usually characterized by antisocial and extremely egocentric behavior. A psychopath(SĪ´-kə-path´), sometimes called a psychopathic personality, appears to be lacking an inner moral censor, and often commits criminal acts, without anxiety or guilt, in order to obtain immediate gratification of desires. Such a person may be utterly lacking in sexual restraint, or addicted to hard drugs. Some psychologists prefer the label sociopath(SŌ´-shee-ə-path´ or SŌ´-see-ə-path´) for this type of personality to indicate the absence of a social conscience.

⟨Word Power⟩ p.105

ORIGIN

☻ the whole tooth

Orthodontist is built on orthos, straight, correct, plus odontos, tooth.

A pedodontist(pee´-dō-DON´-tist) specializes in the care of children's teeth—the title is constructed from paidos, child, plus odontos. The specialty: pedodontia(pee´-dō-DON´-sha); the adjective: pedodontic(pee´-dō-DON´-tik).

A periodontist(pair´-ee-ō-DON´-tist) is a gum specialist—the term combines odontos with the prefix peri-, around, surrounding. (As a quick glance in the mirror will tell you, the gums surround the teeth, more or less.)

Can you figure out the word for the specialty? _____.

For the adjective? _____.

An endodontist(en´-dō-DON´-tist) specializes in work on the pulp of the tooth and in root-canal therapy—the prefix in this term is endo-, from Greek endon, inner, within.

Try your hand again at constructing words. What is the specialty? _____. And the adjective? _____.

The prefix ex-, out, combines with odontos to form exodontist(eks´-ō-DON´-tist). What do you suppose, therefore, is the work in which this practitioner specializes? _____. And the term for the specialty? _____. For the adjective? _____.

☻ measurement

The optometrist, by etymology, measures vision—the term is built on opsis, optikos, view, vision, plus metron, measurement.

Metron is the root in many other words:

1. thermometer(thər-MOM´-ə-tər)—an instrument to measure heat (Greek therme, heat).

2. barometer(bə-ROM´-ə-tər)—an instrument to measure atmospheric pressure (Greek baros, weight); the adjective is barometric (bair´-ə-MET´-rik).

3. spygmomanometer(sfig´-mō-mə-NOM´-ə-tər)—a device for measuring blood pressure (Greek sphygmos, pulse).

4. metric system—a decimal system of weights and measures, long used in other countries and now gradually being adopted in the United States.

☻ bones, feet, and hands

Osteopath combines Greek osteon, bone, with pathos, suffering, disease. Osteopathy(os´-tee-OP´-ǝ-thee), you will recall, was originally based on the theory that disease is caused by pressure of the bones on blood vessels and nerves. An osteopathic(os´-tee-ǝ-PATH´-ik) physician is not a bone specialist, despite the misleading etymology—and should not be confused with the orthopedist, who is.

The podiatrist (Greek pous, podos, foot, plus iatreia, medical healing) practices podiatry(pǝ-DĪ´-ǝ-tree). The adjective is podiatric(pō´-dee-AT´-rik).

The root pous, podos is found also in:

1. octopus(OK´-tǝ-pǝs), the eight-armed (or, as the etymology has it, eight-footed) sea creature(Greek okto, eight).

2. platypus(PLAT´-ǝ-pǝs), the strange water mammal with a duck's bill, webbed feet, and a beaver-like tail that reproduces by laying eggs(Greek platys, broad, flat—hence, by etymology, a flatfoot!).

3. podium(PŌ´-dee-ǝm), a speaker's platform, etymologically a place for the feet. (The suffix -ium often signifies "place where," as in gymnasium, stadium, auditorium, etc.)

4. tripod(TRĪ´-pod), a three-legged (or "footed") stand for a camera or other device(tri-, three).

5. chiropodist(kǝ-ROP´-ǝ-dist), earlier title for a podiatrist, and still often used. The specialty is chiropody(kǝ-ROP´-ǝ-dee).

Chiropody combines podos with Greek cheir, hand, spelled chiro- in English words. The term was coined in the days before labor-saving machinery and push-button devices, when people worked with their hands and developed calluses on their upper extremities as well as on their feet. Today most of us earn a livelihood in more sedentary occupations, and so we may develop calluses on less visible portions of our anatomy.

Chiropractors heal with their hands—the specialty is chiropractic(kī-rō-PRAK´-tik).

Cheir(chiro-), hand, is the root in chirography(kī-ROG´-rə-fee). Recalling the graph- in graphologist, can you figure out by etymology what chirography is? _____.

An expert in writing by hand, or in penmanship (a lost art in these days of electronic word-processing), would be a chirographer(kī-ROG´-rə-fər); the adjective is chirographic(kī´-rō-GRAF´-ik).

If the suffix -mancy comes from a Greek word meaning foretelling or prediction, can you decide what chiromancy(KĪ´-rō-man´-see) must be? _____. The person who practices chiromancy is a chiromancer (KĪ´-rō-man´-sər); the adjective is chiromantic(kī´-rō-MAN´-tik).

⟨Word Power⟩ p.114

ORIGIN

⊕ writing and writers

The Greek verb graphein, to write, is the source of a great many English words.

We know that the graphologist analyzes handwriting, the term combining graphein with logos, science, study. The specialty is graphology(grə-FOL´-ə-jee), the adjective graphological(graf˝-ə-LOJ´-ə-kəl).

Chirographer is built on graphein plus cheir(chiro-), hand.

Though chirography may be a lost art, calligraphy(kə-LIG´-rə-fee) is enjoying a revival. For centuries before the advent of printing, calligraphy, or penmanship as an artistic expression, was practiced by monks.

A calligrapher(kə-LIG´-rə-fər) is called upon to design and write announcements, place cards, etc., as a touch of elegance. The adjective is calligraphic(kal´-ə-GRAF´-ik). Calligraphy combines graphein with Greek kallos*, beauty, and so, by etymology, means beautiful writing.

If a word exists for artistic handwriting, there must be one for the opposite—bad, scrawly, or illegible handwriting. And indeed there is— cacography(ke-KOG´-rə-fee), combining graphein with Greek kakos, bad, harsh.

By analogy with the forms of calligraphy, can you write the word for:

One who uses bad or illegible handwriting? _____. Pertaining to, or marked by, bad handwriting (adjective)?_____.

Graphein is found in other English words:

1. cardiograph—etymologically a "heart writer" (kardia, heart).

2. photograph—etymologically, "written by light" (Greek photos, light).

3. phonograph—etymologically, a "sound writer" (Greek phone, sound).

4. telegraph—etymologically a "distance writer" (Greek tele-, distance).

5. biography—etymologically "life writing" (Greek, bios, life).

---

* An entrancing word that also derives from kallos is callipygian(kal´-ə-PIJ´-ee-ən), an adjective describing a shapely or attractive rear end, or a person so endowed—the combining root is pyge, buttocks.

⊗ aging and the old

We know that a geriatrician specializes in the medical care of the elderly. The Greek word geras, old age, has a derived form, geron, old man, the root in gerontologist. The specialty is gerontology(jair´-ən-TOL´-ə-jee), the adjective is gerontological(jair´-ən-tə-LOJ´-ə-kəl).

The Latin word for old is senex, the base on which senile, senescent, senior, and senate are built.

1. senile(SEE´-nīl)—showing signs of the physical and/or mental deterioration that generally marks very old age. The noun is senility(sə-NIL´-ə-tee).

2. senescent(sə-NES´-ənt)—aging, growing old. (Note the same suffix in this word as in adolescent, growing into an adult, convalescent, growing healthy again, and obsolescent, growing or becoming obsolete.) The noun is senescence(sə-NES´-əns).

3. senior(SEEN´-yər)—older. Noun: seniority(seen-YAWR´-ə-tee).

4. senate(SEN´-ət)—originally a council of older, and presumably wiser, citizens.

BECOMING WORD-CONSCIOUS

Perhaps, if you have been working as assiduously with this book as I have repeatedly counseled, you have noticed an interesting phenomenon.

This phenomenon is as follows: You read a magazine article and suddenly you see one or more of the words you have recently learned. Or you open a book and there again are some of the words you have been working with. In short, all your reading seems to call to your attention the very words you've been studying.

Why? Have I, with uncanny foresight, picked words which have suddenly and inexplicably become popular among writers? Obviously, that's nonsense.

The change is in you. You have now begun to be alert to words, you have developed what is known in psychology as a "mind-set" toward certain words. Therefore, whenever these words occur in your reading you take special notice of them.

The same words occurred before—and just as plentifully—but since they presented little communication to you, you reacted to them with an unseeing eye, with an ungrasping mind. You were figuratively, and almost literally, blind to them.

Do you remember when you bought, or contemplated buying, a new car? Let's say it was a Toyota. Suddenly you began to see Toyotas all around you—you had a Toyota "mind-set."

It is thus with anything new in your life. Development of a "mind-set" means that the new experience has become very real, very important, almost vital.

If you have become suddenly alert to the new words you have been learning, you're well along toward your goal of building a superior vocabulary. You are beginning to live in a new and different intellectual atmosphere—nothing less!

On the other hand, if the phenomenon I have been describing has not yet occurred, do not despair. It will. I am alerting you to its possibilities—recognize it and welcome it when it happens.

HOW GRAMMAR CHANGES

If you think that grammar is an exact science, get ready for a shock. Grammar is a science, all right—but it is most inexact. There are no inflexible laws, no absolutely hard and fast rules, no unchanging principles. Correctness varies with the times and depends much more on geography, on social class, and on collective human caprice than on the restrictions found in textbooks.

In mathematics, which is an exact science, five and five make ten the country over—in the North, in the South, in the West; in Los Angeles and Coral Gables and New york. There are no two opinions on the matter— we are dealing, so far as we know, with a universaland indisputable fact.

In grammar, however, since the facts are highly susceptible to change, we have to keep an eye peeled for trends. What are educated people saying these days? Which expressions are generally used and accepted on educated levels, which others are more ore less restricted to the less educated levels of speech? The answers to these questions indicate the trend of usage in the United States, and if such trends come in conflict with academic rules, then the rules are no longer of any great importance.

Grammar follows the speech habits of the majority of educated people—not the other way around. That is the important point to keep in mind.

The following notes on current trends in modern usage are intended to help you come to a decision about certain controversial expressions. As you read each sentence, pay particular attention to the italicized word or words. Does the usage square with your own language patterns? Would you be willing to phrase your thought in just such terms? Decide whether the sentence is right or wrong, then compare your conclusion with the opinions given following the test.

TEST YOUR SELF

1. Let's keep this between you and *I*.	RIGHT WRONG
2. I'm your best friend, *ain't I*?	RIGHT WRONG
3. Five and five *is* ten.	RIGHT WRONG
4. I never *saw* a man get so mad.	RIGHT WRONG
5. Every one of his sisters *are* unmarried.	RIGHT WRONG
6. He visited an *optometrist* for an eye operation.	RIGHT WRONG
7. Do you *prophecy* another world war?	RIGHT WRONG
8. *Leave* us not mention it.	RIGHT WRONG
9. If you expect *to eventually succeed*, you must keep trying.	RIGHT WRONG

1. Let's keep this between you and I.

WRONG. Children are so frequently corrected by parents and teachers when they say *me* that they cannot be blamed if they begin to think that this simple syllable is probably a naughty word. Dialogues such as the following are certainly typical of many households.

"Mother, can *me and Johnnie* go out and play?"

"No, dear, not until you say it correctly. You mean 'May Johnnie and

I go out to play?"

"Who wants a jelly apple?"

"Me!"

"Then use the proper word."

(The child becomes a little confused at this point—there seem to be so many "proper" and "improper" words.)

"Me, please!"

"No, dear, not me."

"Oh, I, please?"

(This sounds terrible to a child's ear. It completely violates his sense of language, but he does want the jelly apple, so he grudgingly conforms.)

"Who broke my best vase?"

"It wasn't me!"

"Is that good English, Johnnie?"

"Okay, it wasn't I. But honest, Mom, it wasn't me—I didn't even touch it!"

And so, if the child is strong enough to survive such constant corrections, he decides that whenever there is room for doubt, it is safer to say I.

Some adults, conditioned in childhood by the kind of misguided censorship detailed here, are likely to believe that "between you and I" is the more elegant form of expression, but most educated speakers, obeying the rule that a preposition governs the objective pronoun, say "between you and me."

2. I'm your best friend, ain't I?

WRONG. As linguistic scholars have frequently pointed out, it is unfortunate that ain't I? is unpopular in educated speech, for the phrase fills a long-felt need. Am I not? is too prissy for down-to-earth people; amn't I? is ridiculous; and aren't I, though popular in England, has never really caught on in America. With a sentence like the one under discussion you are practically in a linguistic trap—there is no way out unless you are willing to choose between appearing illiterate, sounding prissy, or feeling ridiculous.

"What is the matter with ain't I? for am I not?" language scholar Wallace Rice once wrote. "Nothing whatever, save that a number of minor grammarians object to it. Ain't I? has a pleasant sound once the ears are unstopped of prejudice." Mr. Rice has a valid point there, yet educated people avoid ain't I? as if it were catching. In all honesty, therefore, I must say to you: don't use ain't I?, except humorously. What is a safe substitute? Apparently none exists, so I suggest that you manage, by some linguistic calisthenics, to avoid having to make a choice. Otherwise you may find yourself in the position of being damned if you do and damned if you don't.

3. Five and five is ten.

RIGHT. But don't jump to the conclusion that "five and five are ten" is wrong—both verbs are equally acceptable in this or any similar construction. If you prefer to think of "five-and-five" as a single mathematical concept, say is. If you find it more reasonable to consider "five and five" a plural idea, say are. The teachers I've polled on this point are about evenly divided in preference, and so, I imagine, are the rest of us. Use whichever verb has the greater appeal to your sense of logic.

4. I never saw a man get so mad.

RIGHT. When I questioned a number of authors and editors about their opinion of the acceptability of mad as a synonym for angry, the typical reaction was: "Yes, I say mad, but I always feel a little guilty when I do."

Most people do say mad when they are sure there is no English teacher listening; it's a good sharp word, everybody understands exactly what it means, and it's a lot stronger than angry, though not quite as violent as furious or enraged. In short, mad has a special implication offered by no other word in English language; as a consequence, educated people use it as the occasion demands and it is perfectly correct. So correct, in fact, that every authoritative dictionary lists it as a completely acceptable usage. If you feel guilty when you say mad, even though you don't mean insane, it's time you stopped plaguing your conscience with trivialities.

5. Every one of his sisters are unmarried.

WRONG. Are is perhaps the more logical word, since the sentence implies that he has more than one sister and they are all unmarried. In educated speech, however, the tendency is to make the verb agree with the subject, even if logic is violated in the process—and the better choice here would be is, agreeing with the singular subject, every one.

6. He visited an optometrist for an eye operation.

WRONG. If the gentleman in question did indeed need an operation, he went to the wrong doctor. In most states, optometrists are forbidden by law to perform surgery or administer drugs—they may only prescribe and fit glasses. And they are not medical doctors. The M. D. who specializes in the treatment of eye diseases, and who may operate when necessary, is an ophthalmologist.

7. Do you prophecy another world war?

WRONG. Use prophecy only when you mean prediction, a noun. When you mean predict, a verb, as in this sentence, use prophesy. This distinction is simple and foolproof. Therefore we properly say: "His prophecy(prediction) turned out to be true," but "He really seems able to prophesy(predict) political trends." There is a distinction also in the pronunciation of these two words. Prophecy is pronounced PROF´-ə-see; prophesy is pronounced PROF´-ə-sī´.

8. Leave us not mention it.

WRONG. On the less sophisticated levels of American speech, leave is a popular substitute for let. On educated levels, the following distinction is carefully observed: let means allow; leave means depart. (There are a few idiomatic exceptions to this rule, but they present no problem.) "Let me go" is preferable to "Leave me go" even on the most informal of occasions, and a sentence like "Leave us not mention it" is not considered standard English.

9. If you expect to eventually succeed, you must keep trying.

RIGHT. We have here, in case you're puzzled, an example of that notorious bugbear of academic grammar, the "split infinitive." (An infinitive is a verb preceded by to: to succeed, to fail, to remember.)

Splitting an infinitive is not at all difficult—you need only insert a word between the to and the verb: to eventually succeed, to completely fail, to quickly remember.

Now that you know how to split an infinitive, the important question is, is it legal to do so? I am happy to be able to report to you that it is not only legal, it is also ethical, moral, and sometimes more effective than to not split it. Benjamin Franklin, Washington Irving, Nathaniel Hawthorne, Theodore Roosevelt, and Woodrow Wilson, among may others, were unconscionable infinitive splitters. And modern writers are equally partial to the construction.

To bring this report up to the minute, I asked a number of editors about their attitude toward the split infinitive. Here are two typical reactions.

An editor at Doubleday and Company: "The restriction against the split infinitive is, to my mind, the most artificial of all grammatical rules. I find that most educated people split infinitives regularly in their speech, and only eliminate them from their writing when they rewrite and polish their material."

An editor at Reader's Digest: "I want to defend the split infinitive. The construction adds to the strength of the sentence—it's compact and clear, This is to loudly say that I split an infinitive whenever I can catch one."

And here, finally, is the opinion of humorist James Thurber, as quoted by Rudolf Flesch in The Art of Plain Talk: "Would has somehow got around that the split infinitive is always wrong. This is of a piece with the outworn notion that it is always wrong to strike a lady."

I think the evidence is conclusive enough—it is perfectly correct to consciously split an infinitive whenever such an act increases the strength or clarity of your sentence.

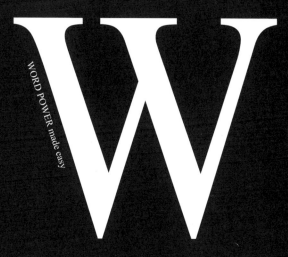

WORD POWER made easy

W

CHAPTER
4

HOW TO TALK ABOUT SCIENCE AND SCIENTISTS

Words that describe students of human development, of the heavens, of the earth, of plant and animal life, of insect forms, of words and language, of social organization. Books on psychology that will add immeasurably both to your store of new words and ideas, and also to your understanding of yourself and of other people.

ORIGIN

☺ people and the stars

Anthropologist is constructed from roots we are familiar with—
anthropos, mankind, and logos, science, study.

The science is anthropology(an′-thrə-POL′-ə-jee). Can you write the
adjective form of this word? _____. (Can you pronounce it?)

Astronomer is built on Greek astron, star, and nomos, arrangement,
law, or order. The astronomer is interested in the arrangement of stars
and other celestial bodies. The science is astronomy(ə-STRON′-ə-mee),
the adjective is astronomical(as′-trə-NOM′-ə-kəl), a word often used in
a non-heavenly sense, as in "the astronomical size of the national debt."
Astronomy deals in such enormous distances (the sun, for example, is
93,000,000 miles from the earth, and light from stars travels toward
the earth at 186,000 miles per second) that the adjective astronomical
is applied to any tremendously large figure. Astron, star, combines
with logos to form astrology(ə-STROL′-ə-jee), which assesses the
influence of planets and stars on human events. The practitioner
is an astrologer(ə-STROL′-ə-jər). Can you form the adjective?
_____.

By etymology, an astronaut(AS′-trə-not′) is a sailor among the
stars(Greek nautes, sailor). This person is termed with somewhat less
exaggeration a cosmonaut(KOZ′-mə-not′) by the Russians(Greek
kosmos, universe). Nautical(NOT′-ə-kəl), relating to sailors, sailing,
ships, or navigation, derives also from nautes, and nautes in turn is from

Greek naus, ship—a root used in nausea (etymologically, ship-sickness or seasickness!).

Aster(AS´-tər) is a star shaped flower. Asterisk(AS´-tə-risk), a star-shaped symbol(*), is generally used in writing or printing to direct the reader to look for a footnote. Astrophysics(as´-trə-FIZ´-iks) is that branch of physics dealing with heavenly bodies.

Disaster(də-ZAS´-tər) and disastrous(də-ZAS´-trəs) also come from astron, star. In ancient times it was believed that the stars ruled human destiny; any misfortune or calamity, therefore, happened to someone because the stars were in opposition. (Dis-, a prefix of many meanings, in this word signifies against.) Nomos, arrangement, law, or order, is found in two other interesting English words.

For example, if you can make your own laws for yourself, if you needn't answer to anyone else for what you do, in short, if you are independent, then you enjoy autonomy(aw-TON´-ə-mee), a word that combines nomos, law, with autos, self. Autonomy, then, is self-law, self-government. The fifty states in our nation are fairly autonomous (aw-TON´-ə-məs), but not completely so. On the other hand, in most colleges each separate department is pretty much autonomous. And of course, one of the big reasons for the revolution of 1776 was that America wanted autonomy, rather than control by England.

You know the instrument that beginners at the piano use to guide their timing? A pendulum swings back and forth, making an audible click at each swing, and in that way governs or orders the measure (or timing) of the player. Hence it is called a metronome(MET´-rə-nōm´), a word that combines nomos with metron, measurement.

☻ the earth and its life

Geologist derives from Greek ge(geo-), earth. The science is geology (jee-OL´-ə-jee). Can you write the adjective? _____.

Geometry(jee-OM´-ə-tree)—ge plus metron—by etymology "measurement of the earth," is that branch of mathematics treating of the measurement and properties of solid and plane figures, such as angles, triangles, squares, spheres, prisms, etc. (The etymology of the word shows that this ancient science was originally concerned with the measurement of land and spaces on the earth.)

The mathematician is a geometrician(jee´-ə-mə-TRISH´-ən), the adjective is geometric(jee´-ə-MET´-rik).

Geography(jee-OG´-rə-fee) is writing about (graphein, to write), or mapping the earth. A practitioner of the science is a geographer (jee-OG´-rə-fər), the adjective is geographic(jee-ə-GRAF´-ik).

(The name George is also derived form ge(geo-), earth, plus ergon, work—the first George was an earth-worker or farmer.)

Biologist combines bios, life, with logos, science, study. The science is biology(bī-OL´-ə-jee). The adjective? _____.

Bios, life, is also found in biography(bī-OG´-rə-fee), writing about someone's life; autobiography(aw´-tə-bī-OG´-rə-fee), the story of one's life written by oneself; and biopsy(BĪ´-op-see), a medical examination, or view (opsis, optikos, view, vision), generally through a microscope, of living tissue, frequently performed when cancer is suspected. A small part of the tissue is cut from the affected area and under the microscope its cells can e investigated for evidence of malignancy. A biopsy is contrasted with an autopsy(AW´-top-see), which is a medical examination of a corpse in order to discover the cause of death. Th autos in autopsy means, as you know, self—in an autopsy, etymologically speaking, the surgeon or pathologist determines, by actual view or sight rather than by theorizing (i.e., "by viewing or seeing for oneself"), what brought the corpse to its present grievous state.

Botanist is from Greek botane, plant. The field is botany(BOT´-ə-nee); the adjective is botanical(bə-TAN´-ə-kəl).

Zoologist is from Greek zoion, animal. The science is zoology. The adjective? _____. The combination of the two o's tempts many people to pronounce the first three letters of these words in one syllable, thus: zoo. However, the two o's should be separated, as in co-operate, even though no hyphen is used in the spelling to indicate such separation. Say zō-OL´-ə-jist, zō-OL´-ə-jee, zō-ə-LOJ´-ə-kəl. Zoo, a park for animals, is a shortened form of zoological gardens, and is, of course, pronounced in one syllable.

The zodiac(ZŌ´-dee-ak) is a diagram, used in astrology, of the paths of the sun, moon, and planets; it contains, in part, Latin names for various animals—scorpio, scorpion; leo, lion; cancer, crab; taurus, bull; aries, ram; and pisces, fish. Hence its derivation from zoion, animal.

The adjective is zodiacal(zō-DĪ´-ə-kəl).

⟨Word Power⟩ p.143

❀

ORIGIN

∞ cutting in and out

Flies, bees, beetles, wasps, and other insects are segmented creatures—head, thorax, and abdomen. Where these parts join, there appears to the imaginative eye a "cutting in" of the body.

Hence the branch of zoology dealing with insects is aptly named entomology, from Greek en-, in, plus tome, a cutting. The adjective is entomological(en´-tə-mə-LOJ´-ə-kəl).

(The word insect makes the same point—it is built on Latin in- in, plus sectus, a form of the verb meaning to cut.)

The prefix ec-, from Greek ek-, means out. (The Latin prefix, you will recall, is ex-.) Combine ec- with tome to derive the words for surgical procedures in which parts are "cut out," or removed: tonsillectomy(the tonsils), appendectomy(the appendix), mastectomy(the breast), hysterectomy(the uterus), prostatectomy(the prostate), etc.

Combine ec- with Greek kentron, center(the Latin root, as we have discovered, is centrum), to derive eccentric(ək-SEN´-trik)—out of the center, hence deviating from the normal in behavior, attitudes, etc., or unconventional, odd, strange. The noun is eccentricity(ek´-sən-TRIS´-ə-tee).

☻ more cuts

The Greek prefix a- makes a root negative; the atom(AT´-əm) was so named at a time when it was considered the smallest possible particle of an element, that is, one that could not be cut any further. (We have long since split the atom, of course, with results, as in most technological advances, both good and evil.) The adjective is atomic(ə-TOM´-ik).

The Greek prefix ana- has a number of meanings, one of which is up, as in anatomy(ə-NAT´-ə-mee), originally the cutting up of a plant or animal to determine its structure, later the bodily structure itself. The adjective is anatomical(an´-ə-TOM´-ə-kəl).

Originally any book that was part of a larger work of many volumes was called a tome(TŌM)—etymologically, a part cut from the whole. Today, a tome designates, often disparagingly, an exceptionally large book, or one that is heavy and dull in content.

The Greek prefix dicha-, in two, combines with tome to construct dichotomy(dī-KOT′-ə-mee), a splitting in two, a technical word used in astronomy, biology, botany, and the science of logic. It is also employed as a non-technical term, as when we refer to the dichotomy in the life of a man who is a government clerk all day and a night-school teacher after working hours, so that his life is, in a sense, split into two parts. The verb is dichotomize(dī-KOT′-ə-mīz′); the adjective is dichotomous(dī-KOT′-ə-məs).

Dichotomous thinking is the sort that divides everything into two parts—good and bad; white and black; Democrats and Republicans; etc. An unknown wit has made this classic statement about dichotomous thinking: "There are two kinds of people: those who divide everything into two parts, and those who do not."

Imagine a book, a complicated or massive report, or some other elaborate document—now figuratively cut on or through it so that you can get to its essence, the very heart of the idea contained in it. What you have is an epitome(ə-PIT′-ə-mee), a condensation of the whole. (From epi-, on, upon, plus tome.)

An epitome may refer to a summary, condensation, or abridgment of language, as in "Let me have an epitome of the book," or "Give me the epitome of his speech."

More commonly, epitome and the verb epitomize(ə-PIT′-ə-mīz′) are used in sentences like "She is the epitome of kindness," or "That one act epitomizes her philosophy of life." If you cut everything else away to get to the essential part, that part is a representative cross-section of the whole. So a woman who is the epitome of kindness stands for all people who are kind; and an act that epitomizes a philosophy of life represents, by itself, the complete philosophy.

⊜ love and words

Logos, we know, means science or study; it may also mean word or speech, as it does in philology(fə-LOL´-ə-jee), etymologically the love of words (from Greek philein, to love, plus logos), or what is more commonly called linguistics(ling-GWIS´-tiks), the science of language, a term derived from Latin lingua, tongue. Can you write, and pronounce, the adjective form of philology? _____.

⊜ more love

Philanthropy(fə-LAN´-thrə-pee) is by etymology the love of mankind—one who devotes oneself to philanthropy is a philanthropist(fə-LAN´-thrə-pist); the adjective is philanthropic(fil-ən-THROP´-ik).

The verb philander(fə-LAN´-dər), to "play around" sexually, be promiscuous, or have extramarital relations, combines philein with andros, male. (Philandering, despite its derivation, is not of course exclusively the male province. The word is, in fact, derived from the proper name conventionally given to male lovers in plays and romances of the 1500s and 1600s.) One who engages in the interesting activities catalogued above is a philanderer(fə-LAN´-dər-ər).

By etymology, philosophy is the love of wisdom(Greek sophos, wise); Philadelphia is the City of Brotherly Live(Greek adelphos, brother); philharmonic is the love of music or harmony(Greek harmonia, harmony); and a philter, a rarely used word, is a love potion. Today we call whatever arouses sexual desire an aphrodisiac(af´-rə-DIZ´-ee-ak´), from Aphrodite, the Greek goddess of love and beauty.

Aphrodisiac is an adjective as well as a noun, but a longer adjective form, aphrodisiacal(af´-rə-də-ZI´-ə-kəl), is also used. A bibliophile(BIB´-lee-ə-fīl´) is one who loves books as collectibles, admiring their binding, typography, illustrations, rarity, etc.—in short, a book collector. The combining root is Greek biblion, book. An Anglophile(ANG´-glə-fīl´) admires and is fond of the British people, customs, culture, etc. The combining root is Latin Anglus, English.

☻ words and how they affect people

The semanticist is professionally involved in semantics(sə-MAN´-tiks). The adjective is semantic(sə-MAN´-tik) or semantical(sə-MAN´-tə-kəl).

Semantics, like orthopedics, pediatrics, and obstetrics, is a singular noun despite the -s ending. Semantics is, not are, an exciting study. However, this rule applies only when we refer to the word as a science or area of study. In the following sentence, semantics is used as a plural: "The semantics of your thinking are all wrong."

☻ how people live

The profession of the sociologist is sociology(sō´-shee-OL´-ə-jee or sō-see-OL´-ə-jee). Can you write, and pronounce, the adjective?

_____.

Sociology is built on Latin socius, companion*, plus logos, science, study. Socius is the source of such common words as associate, social, socialize, society, sociable, and antisocial; as well as asocial (ay-SŌ´-shəl), which combines the negative prefix a- with socius.

The antisocial person actively dislikes people, and often behaves in ways that are detrimental or destructive to society or the social order(anti-, against).

On the other hand, someone who is asocial is withdrawn and self-centered, avoids contact with others, and feels completely indifferent to the interests or welfare of society. The asocial person doesn't want to "get involved."

---

* Companion itself has an interesting etymology—Latin com-, with, plus panis, bread. If you are social, you enjoy breaking bread with companions. Pantry also comes from panis, though far more than bread is stored there.

WHERE TO GET NEW IDEAS

People with superior vocabularies, I have submitted, are the people with ideas. The words they know are verbal symbols of the ideas they are familiar with—reduce one and you must reduce the other, for ideas cannot exist without verbalization. Freud once had an idea—and had to coin a whole new vocabulary to make his idea clear to the world. Those who are familiar with Freud's theories know all the words that explain them—the unconscious, the ego, the id, the superego, rationalization, Oedipus complex, and so on. Splitting the atom was once a new idea—anyone familiar with it knew something about fission, isotope, radioactive, cyclotron, etc.

Remember this: your vocabulary indicates the alertness and range of your mind. The words you know show the extent of your understanding of what's going on in the world. The size of your vocabulary varies directly with the degree to which you are growing intellectually.

You have covered so far in this book several hundred words. Having learned these words, you have begun to think of an equal number of new ideas. A new word is not just another pattern of syllables with which to clutter up your mind—a new word is a new idea to help you think, to help you understand the thoughts of others, to help you express your own thoughts, to help you live a richer intellectual life.

Realizing these facts, you may become impatient. You will begin to doubt that a book like this can cover all the ideas that an alert and intellectually mature adult wishes to be acquainted with. Your doubt is well-founded.

One of the chief purposes of this book is to get you started, to give you enough of a push so that you will begin to gather momentum, to stimulate you enough so that you will want to start gathering your own ideas.

Where can you gather them? From good books on new topics. How can you gather them? By reading on a wide range of new subjects. Reference has repeatedly been made to psychology, psychiatry, and psychoanalysis in these pages. If your curiosity has been piqued by these references, here is a good place to start. In these fields there is a tremendous and exciting literature—and you can read as widely and as deeply as you wish.

What I would like to do is offer a few suggestions as to where you might profitably begin—how far you go will depend on your own interest. I suggest, first, half a dozen older books(older, but still immensely valuable and completely valid) available at any large public library.

The Human Mind, by Karl A . Menninger
Mind and Body, by Flanders Dunbar
The Mind in Action, by Eric Berne
Understandable Psychiatry, by Leland E . Hinsie

A General Introduction to Psychoanalysis, by Sigmund Freud

Emotional Problems of Living, by O. Spurgeon English and Gerald H. J. Pearson

Next, I suggest books on some of the newer approaches in psychology. These are available in inexpensive paperback editions as well as at your local library.

I Ain't Well—But I Sure Am Better, by Jess Lair, Ph.D.

The Disowned Self, by Nathaniel Brandon

A Primer of Behavioral Psychology, by Adelaide Bry

I'm OK—You're OK, by Thomas A. Harris, M.D.

Freedom to Be and Man the Manipulator, by Everett L. Shostrum

Games People Play, by Eric Berne, M.D.

Love and Orgasm, Pleasure and The Language of the Body, by Alexander Lowen, M.D.

The Transparent Self, by Sydney M. Jourard

Don't Say Yes When You Want to Say No, by Herbert Fensterheim & Jean Baer

Gestalt Therapy Verbatim, by Frederick S. Perls

Born to Win, by Muriel James & Dorothy Jongeward

Joy and Here Comes Everybody, by William C. Schutz

The Fifty-Minute Hour, by Robert Lindner

HOW TO AVOID BEING A PURIST

Life, as you no doubt realize, is complicated enough these days. Yet puristic textbooks and English teachers with puristic ideas are striving to make it still more complicated. Their contribution to the complexity of modern living is the repeated claim that many of the natural, carefree, and popular expressions that most of us use every day are "bad English," "incorrect grammar," "vulgar," or "illiterate."

In truth, many of the former restrictions and "thou shalt nots" of academic grammar are now outmoded—most educated speakers quite simply ignore them.

Students in my grammar classes at Rio Hondo College are somewhat nonplused when they discover that correctness is not determined by textbook rules and cannot be enforced by schoolteacher edict. They invariably ask: "Aren't you going to draw the line somewhere?"

It is neither necessary nor possible for any one person to "draw the line." That is done—and quite effectively—by the people themselves, by the millions of educated people throughout the nation.

Of course certain expressions may be considered "incorrect" or "illiterate" or "bad grammar"—not because they violate puristic rules, but only because they are rarely if ever used by educated speakers.

Correctness, in short, is determined by current educated usage.

The following notes on current trends in modern usage are intended to help you come to a decision about certain controversial expressions. As you read each sentence, pay particular attention to the italicized word or words. Does the usage square with your own language patterns? Would you be willing to phrase your thought in just such terms? Decide whether the sentence is "right" or "wrong," then compare your conclusions with the opinions given after the test.

TEST YOUR SELF

1. Let's not walk any *further* right now.	RIGHT WRONG
2. Some people admit that their *principle* goal in life is to become wealthy.	RIGHT WRONG
3. What a nice thing to say!	RIGHT WRONG
4. He's *pretty* sick today.	RIGHT WRONG
5. I feel *awfully* sick.	RIGHT WRONG
6. Are you going to invite Doris and *I* to your party?	RIGHT WRONG

1. Let's not walk any further right now.

RIGHT. In the nineteenth century, when professional grammarians attempted to Latinize English grammar, an artificial distinction was drawn between farther and further, to wit: farther refers to space, further means to a greater extent or additional. Today, as a result, many teachers who are still under the forbidding influence of nineteenth-century restrictions insist that it is incorrect to use one word for the other.

To check on current attitudes toward this distinction, I sent the test sentence above to a number of dictionary editors, authors, and professors of English, requesting their opinion of the acceptability of further in reference to actual distance. Sixty out of eighty-seven professors, over two thirds of those responding, accepted the usage without qualification. Of twelve dictionary editors, eleven accepted further, and in the case of the authors, thirteen out of twenty-three accepted the word as used. A professor of English at Cornell University remarked: "I know of no justification for any present-day distinction between further and farther"; and a consulting editor of the Funk and Wagnalls dictionary said, "There is nothing controversial here. As applied to spatial distance, further and farther have long been interchangeable."

Perhaps the comment of a noted author and columnist is most to the point: "I like both further and farther, as I have never been able to tell which is or why one is any farther or further than the other."

2. Some people admit that their principle goal in life is to become wealthy.

WRONG. In speech, you can get principal and principle confused as often as you like, and no one will ever know the difference—both words are pronounced identically. In writing, however, your spelling will give you away.

There is a simple memory trick that will help you if you get into trouble with these two words. Rule and principle both end in -le—and a principle is a rule. On the other hand, principal contains an a, and so does main—and principal means main. Get these points straight and your confusion is over.

Heads of schools are called principals, because they are the main person in that institution of learning. The money you have in the bank is your principal, your main financial assets. And the stars of a play are principals—the main actors.

Thus, "Some people admit that their principal(main) goal in life is to become wealthy," but "Such a principle(rule) is not guaranteed to lead to happiness."

3. What a nice thing to say!

RIGHT. Purists object to the popular use of nice as a synonym for pleasant, agreeable, or delightful. They wish to restrict the word to its older and more erudite meaning of exact or subtle. You will be happy to hear that they aren't getting anywhere.

When I polled a group of well-known authors on the acceptability in everyday speech of the popular meaning of nice, their opinions were unanimous; not a single dissenting voice, out of the twenty-three authors who answered, was raised against the usage. One writer responded: "It has been right for about 150 years. . ."

Editors of magazines and newspapers questioned on the same point were just a shade more conservative. Sixty out of sixty-nine accepted the usage. One editor commented: "I think we do not have to be nice about nice any longer. No one can eradicate it from popular speech as a synonym for pleasant, or enjoyable, or kind, or courteous. It is a workhorse of the vocabulary, and properly so."

The only valid objection to the word is that it is overworked by some people, but this shows a weakness in vocabulary rather than in grammar.

As in the famous story of the editor who said to her secretary: "There are two words I wish you would stop using so much. One is 'nice' and the other is 'lousy.'"

"Okay," said the secretary, who was eager to please. "What are they?"

4. He's pretty sick today.

RIGHT. One of the purist's pet targets of attack is the word pretty as used in the sentence under discussion. Yet all modern dictionaries accept such use of pretty, and a survey made by a professor at the University of Wisconsin showed that the usage is established English.

5. I feel awfully sick.

RIGHT. Dictionaries accept this usage in informal speech and the University of Wisconsin survey showed that it is established English.

The great popularity of awfully in educated speech is no doubt due to the strong and unique emphasis that the word gives to an adjective—substitute very, quite, extremely, or severely and you considerably weaken the force.

On the other hand, it is somewhat less than cultivated to say "I feel awful sick," and the wisdom of using awfully to intensify a pleasant concept ("What an awfully pretty child,"; "That book is awfully interesting") is perhaps still debatable, tough getting less and less so as the years go on.

6. Are you going to invite Doris and I to your party?

WRONG. Some people are almost irresistibly drawn to the pronoun I in constructions like this one. However, not only does such use of I violate a valid and useful grammatical principle, but, more important, it is rarely heard in educated speech. The meaning of the sentence is equally clear no matter which form of the pronoun is employed, of course, but the use of I, the less popular choice, may stigmatize the speaker as uneducated.

Consider it this way: You would normally say, "Are you going to invite me to your party?" It would be wiser, therefore, to say, "Are you going to invite Doris and me to your party?"

W

CHAPTER
5

HOW TO TALK ABOUT LIARS AND LYING

Words that accurately label different types of liars and lying. Terms that relate to fame, artistry, reform, heredity, time, place, suffering, etc. Four lasting benefits you have begun to acquire from your work in vocabulary building.

ORIGIN

☻ well-known

"Widely but unfavorably known" is the common definition for notorious. Just as a notorious liar is well-known for unreliable statements, so a notorious gambler, a notorious thief, or a notorious killer has achieved a wide reputation for some form of antisocial behavior. The noun is notoriety(nō-tə-RĪ´-ə-tee).

The derivation is from Latin notus, known, from which we also get noted. It is an interesting characteristic of some words that a change of syllables can alter the emotional impact. Thus, an admirer of certain business executives will speak of them as "noted industrialists"; these same people's enemies will call them "notorious exploiters." Similarly, if we admire a man's or a woman's unworldliness, we refer to it by the complimentary term childlike; but if are annoyed by the trait, we describe it, derogatively, as childish. Change "-like" to "-ish" and our emotional tone undergoes a complete reversal.

☻ plenty of room at the top

The top of a mountain is called, as you know, the summit, a word derived from Latin summus, highest, which also gives us the mathematical term sum, as in addition. A consummate artist has reached the very highest point of perfection; and to consummate(KON´-sə-mayt´) a marriage, a business deal, or a contract is, etymologically, to bring it to the highest point; that is, to put the final touches to it, to bring it to completion. [Note how differently consummate(kən-SUM′-ət), the adjective, is pronounced from the verb to consummate(KON′-sə-mayt′)].

Nouns are formed from adjectives by the addition of the noun suffix -ness: sweet—sweetness; simple—simpleness; envious—enviousness; etc. Many adjectives, however, have alternate noun forms, and the adjective consummate is one of them. To make a noun out of consummate, add either -ness or -acy; consummateness(kən-SUM′-ət-nəs) or consummacy(kən-SUM′-ə-see).

Verbs ending in -ate invariably tack on the noun suffix -ion to form nouns: create—creation; evaluate—evaluation; etc.

Can you write the noun form of the verb to consummate? _____.

● no help

Call people incorrigible(in-KAWR′-ə-jə-bəl) if they do anything to excess, and if all efforts to correct or reform them are to no avail. Thus, one can be an incorrigible idealist, an incorrigible criminal, an incorrigible optimist, or an incorrigible philanderer. The word derives from Latin corrigo, to correct or set straight, plus the negative prefix in-. (This prefix, depending on the root it precedes, may be negative, may intensify the root, as in invaluable, or may mean in.) The noun is incorrigibility(in-kawr′-ə-jə-BIL′-ə-tee) or, alternatively, incorrigibleness.

● veterans

Inveterate, from Latin vetus, old,* generally indicates disapproval.

Inveterate gamblers have grown old in the habit, etymologically speaking; inveterate drinkers have been imbibing for so long that they, too, have formed old, well-established habits; and inveterate liars have been lying for so long, and their habits are by now so deep-rooted, that one can scarcely remember (the word implies) when they ever told the truth.

The noun is inveteracy(in-VET´-ər-ə-see) or inveterateness.

A veteran(VET´-ə-rən), as of the Armed Forces, grew older serving the country; otherwise a veteran is an old hand at the game (and therefore skillful). The word is both a noun and an adjective: a veteran at (or in) swimming, tennis, police work, business, negotiations, diplomacy—or a veteran actor, teacher, diplomat, political reformer.

* Latin senex, source of senile and senescent, also, you will recall, means old. In inveterate, in- means in; it is not the negative prefix found in incorrigible.

⊜ birth

Greek genesis, birth or origin, a root we discovered in discussing psychogenic, is the source of a great many English words.

Genetics(jə-NET´-iks) is the science that treats of the transmission of hereditary characteristics from parents to offspring. The scientist specializing in the field is a geneticist(jə-NET´-ə-sist). the adjective is genetic(jə-NET´-ik). The particle in the chromosome of the germ cell containing a hereditary characteristic is a gene(JEEN).

Genealogy(jeen´-ee-AL´-ə-jee) is the study of family trees or ancestral origins (logos, study). The practitioner is a genealogist(jeen´-ee -AL´-ə-jist). Can you form the adjective? _____.

The genital(GEN´-ə-təl). or sexual, organs are involved in the process of conception and birth. The genesis(JEN´-ə-sis) of anything—a plan, idea, thought, career, etc.—is its beginning, birth, or origin, and Genesis, the first book of the Old Testament, describes the creation, or birth, of the universe. Congenital is constructed by combining the prefix con-, with or together, and the root genesis, birth.

So a congenital defect, deformity, condition, etc. occurs during the nine-month birth process (or period of gestation, to become technical). Hereditary(hə-RED´-ə-tair´-ee) characteristics, on the other hand, are acquired at the moment of conception. Thus, eye color, nose shape, hair texture, and other such qualities are hereditary; they are determined by the genes in the germ cells of the mother and father. But a thalidomide baby resulted from the use of the drug by a pregnant woman, so the deformities were congenital. Congenital is used both literally and figuratively. Literally, the word generally refers to some medical deformity or abnormality occurring during gestation. Figuratively, it widely exaggerates, for effect, the very early existence of some quality: congenital liar, congenital fear of the dark, etc.

〈Word Power〉p.179

ORIGIN

● of time and place

A chronic liar lies constantly, again and again and again; a chronic invalid is ill time after time, frequently, repeatedly. The derivation of the word is Greek chronos, time. The noun form is chronicity (krə-NIS´-ə-tee).

An anachronism(ə-NAK´-rə-niz-əm) is someone or something

out of time, out of date, belonging to a different era, either earlier or late. (The prefix ana- like a-, is negative.) The adjective is anachronous(ə-NAK´-rə-nəs) or anachronistic(ə-nak´-rə-NIS´-tik).

Wander along Fifty-ninth Street and Central Park in Manhattan some Sunday. You will see horse-drawn carriages with top-hatted coachmen—a vestige of the 1800s. Surrounded by twentieth-century motorcars and modern skyscrapers, these romantic vehicles of a bygone era are anachronous.

Read a novel in which a scene is supposedly taking place in the nineteenth century and see one of the characters turning on a TV set. An anachronoism! Your friend talks, thinks, dresses, and acts as if he were living in the time of Shakespeare. Another anachronism! Science fiction is deliberately anachronous—it deals with phenomena, gadgetry, accomplishments far off (possibly) in the future.

An anachronism is out of time; something out of place is incongruous(in-KONG´-grōō-əs), a word combining the negative prefix in-, the prefix con-, with or together, and a Latin verb meaning to agree or correspond. Thus, it is incongruous to wear a sweater and slacks to a formal wedding; it is anachronous to wear the wasp waist, conspicuous bustle or powdered wig of the eighteenth century. The noun form of incongruous is incongruity(in-kəng-GRŌŌ´-ə-tee).

Chronological(kron-ə-LOJ´-ə-kəl), in correct time order, comes from chronos. To tell a story chronologically is to relate the events in the time order of their occurrence. Chronology(krə-NOL´-ə-jee) is the science of time order and the accurate dating of events (logos, science)—the expert in this field is a chronologist(krə-NOL´-ə-jist)—or a list of events in the time order in which they have occurred or will occur.

A chronometer(krə-NOM´-ə-tər), combining chronos with metron, measurement, is a highly accurate timepiece, especially one used on ships. Chronometry(krə-NOM´-ə-tree) is the measurement of time—the adjective is chronometric(kron´-ə-MET´-rik).

Add the prefix syn-, together, plus the verb suffix -ize, to chronos, and you have constructed synchronize(SIN´-krə-nīz´), etymologically to time together, or to move, happen, or cause to happen, at the same time or rate. If you and your friend synchronize your watches, you set them at the same time. If you synchronize the activity of your arms and legs, as in swimming, you move them at the same time or rate. The adjective is synchronous(SIN´-krə-nəs); the noun form of the verb synchronize is synchronization(sin´-krə-nə-ZAY´-shən).

⊜ disease, suffering, feeling

Pathological is diseased (a pathological condition)—this meaning of the word ignores the root logos, science, study. pathology(pə-THOL´-ə-jee) is the science or study of disease—its nature, cause, cure, etc. However, another meaning of the noun ignores logos, and pathology may be any morbid, diseased, or abnormal physical condition or conditions; in short, simply disease, as in "This case involves so many kind of pathology that several different specialists are working on it."

A pathologist(pə-THOL´-ə-jist) is an expert who examines tissue, often by autopsy or biopsy, to diagnose disease and interpret the abnormalities in such tissue that may be caused by specific diseases.

Pathos occurs in some English words with the additional meaning of feeling. If you feel or suffer with someone, you are sympathetic (sim-pə-THET´-ik)—sym- is a respelling before letter p of the Greek prefix syn-, with or together. The noun is sympathy(SIM´-pə-thee), the verb sympathize(SIM´-pə-thīz). Husbands, for example, so the story goes, may have sympathetic labor pains when their wives are about to deliver.

The prefix anti-, you will recall, means against. If you experience antipathy(an-TIP´-ə-thee) to people or things, you feel against them—you feel strong dislike or hostility. The adjective is antipathetic(an´-tə-pə -THET´-ik), as in "an antipathetic reaction to an authority figure."

But you may have no feeling at all—just indifference, lack of any interest, emotion, or response, complete listlessness, especially when some reaction is normal or expected. Then you are apathetic (ap-ə-THET´-ik); a-, as you know, is a negative prefix. The noun is apathy (AP´-ə-thee), as in voter apathy, student apathy, etc.

On the other hand, you may be so sensitive or perceptive that you not only share the feelings of another, but you also identify with those feelings, in fact experience them yourself as if momentarily you were that other person. What you have, then, is empathy(EM´-pə-thee); you empathize(EM´-pə-thīz´), you are empathetic(em-pə-THET´-ik), or, to use an alternate adjective, empathic(em-PATH´-ik). Em- is a respelling before the letter p of the Greek prefix en-, in.

Someone is pathetic(pə-THET´-ik) who is obviously suffering—such a person may arouse sympathy or pity (or perhaps antipathy?) in you. A pathetic story is about suffering and, again, is likely to arouse sadness, sorrow, or pity. Some interesting research was done many years ago by Dr. J. B. Rhine and his associates at Duke University on extrasensory perception; you will find an interesting account of Rhine's work in his book The Reach of the Mind. What makes it possible for two people separated by miles of space to communicate with each other without resource to messenger, telephone, telegraph, or postal service? It can be done, say the believers in telepathy(tə-LEP´-ə-thee), also called mental telepathy, though they do not yet admit to knowing how. How can one person read the mind of another? Simple—by being telepathic(tel´-ə-PATH´-ik), but no one can explain the chemistry or biology of it. Telepathy is built by combining pathos, feeling, with the prefix tele-, distance, the same prefix we found in telephone, telegraph, telescope.

Telepathic(tel´-ə-PATH´-ik) communication occurs when people can feel each other's thoughts from a distance, when they have ESP.

⟨Word Power⟩ p.187

⚛ ORIGIN

∞ knowing

Psychopaths commit antisocial and unconscionable acts—they are not troubled by conscience, guilt, remorse, etc. over what they have done.

Unconscionable and conscience are related in derivation—the first word from Latin scio, to know, the second from Latin sciens, knowing, and both using the prefix con-, with, together. Etymologycally, then, your conscience is your knowledge with a moral sense of right and wrong; if you are unconscionable, your conscience is not(un-) working, or you have no conscience. The noun form is unconscionableness or unconscion ability(un-kon´-shə-nə-BIL´-ə-tee).

Conscious, also from con- plus scio, is knowledge or awareness of one's emotions or sensations, or of what's happening around one. Science, from *sciens*, is systematized knowledge as opposed, for example, to belief, faith, intuition, or guesswork. Add Latin *omnis*, all, to *sciens*, to construct omniscient(om-NISH´-ənt), all-knowing, possessed of infinite knowledge. The noun is omniscience(om-NISH´-əns).

Add the prefix pre-, before, to *sciens*, to construct prescient(PREE´-shənt)—knowing about events before they occur, i.e., psychic, or possessed of unusual powers of prediction. The noun is prescience (PREE´-shəns).

And, finally, and the negative prefix ne- to *sciens* to produce nescient(NESH´-ənt), not knowing, or ignorant. Can you, by analogy with the previous two words, write the noun form of nescient? _____.

☻ fool some of the people . . .

Glib is from an old English root that means slippery. Glib liars or glib talkers are smooth and slippery; they have ready answers, fluent tongues, a persuasive air—but, such is the implication of the word, they fool only the most nescient, for their smoothness lacks sincerity and conviction.

The noun is glibness.

☻ herds and flocks

Egregious(remember the pronunciation? ə-GREE´-jəs) is from Latin *grex, gregis*, herd or flock. An egregious lie, act, crime, mistake, etc. is so exceptionally vicious that it conspicuously stands out (e-, a shortened form of the prefix ex-, out) from the herd or flock of other bad things. The noun is egregiousness(ə-GREE´-jəs-nəs).

A person who enjoys companionship, who, etymologically, likes to be with the herd, who reaches out for friends and is happiest when surrounded by people—such a person is gregarious(grə-GAIR′-ee-əs). Extroverts are of course gregarious—they prefer human contact, conversation, laughter, interrelationships, to solitude. The suffix -ness, as you know, can be added to an adjective to construct a noun form. Write the noun for gregarious: _____.

Add the prefix con-, with, together, to grex, gregis, to get the verb congregate(KONG′-grə-gayt′); add the prefix se-, apart, to build the verb segregate(SEG′-rə-gayt′); add the prefix ad-, to, toward(ad-changes to ag- before a root starting with g-), to construct the verb aggregate(AG-rə-gayt′). Let's see what we have. When people gather together in a herd or flock, they (write the verb) _____. The noun is congregation(cong′-grə-GAY′-shən), one of the meanings of which is a religious "flock." Put people or things apart from the herd, and you (write the verb) _____ them. Can you construct the noun by adding the suitable noun suffix? _____. Bring individual items to or toward the herd or flock, and you (write the verb) _____ them. What is the noun form of this verb? _____.

The verb aggregate also means to come together to or toward the herd, that is, to gather into a mass or whole, or by extension, to total or amount to. So aggregate, another noun form, pronounced AG′-rə-gət, is a group or mass of individuals considered as a whole, a heard, or a flock, as in the phrase "people in the aggregate . . ."

FOUR LASTING BENEFITS

You know by now that it is easy to build your vocabulary if you work diligently and intelligently. Diligence is important—to come to the book occasionally is to learn new words and ideas in an aimless fashion, rather than in the continuous way that characterizes the natural, uninterrupted, intellectual growth of a child. (You will recall that children are top experts in increasing their vocabularies.) And an intelligent approach is crucial—new words can be completely understood and permanently remembered only as symbols of vital ideas, never if memorized in long lists of isolated forms.

If you have worked diligently and intelligently, you have done much more than merely learned a few hundred new words. Actually, I needn't tell you what else you've accomplished, since, if you really have accomplished it, you can feel it for yourself; but it may be useful if I verbalize the feelings you may have.

In addition to learning the meanings, pronunciation, background, and use of 300-350 valuable words, you have:

1. Begun to sense a change in your intellectual atmosphere. (You have begun to do your thinking with many of the words, with many of the ideas behind the words. You have begun to use the words in your speech and writing, and have become alert to their appearance in your reading.)

2. Begun to develop a new interest in words as expressions of ideas.

3. Begun to be aware of the new words you hear and that you see in your reading.

4. Begun to gain a new feeling for the relationship between words. (For you realize that many words are built on roots from other languages and are related to other words which derive from the same roots.)

Now, suppose we pause to see how successful your learning has been.

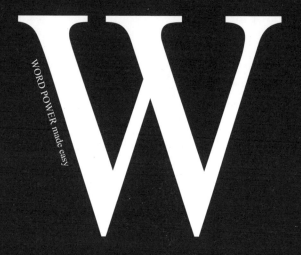

W

WORD POWER made easy

CHAPTER
6

HOW TO TALK ABOUT ACTIONS

Verbs that accurately describe important human activities. Excursions into expressive terms for good and evil, doing, saying, wishing, and pleasing. Further proof that you can learn, in a few weeks or less, more new words than the average adult learns in an entire year.

ORIGIN

☻ equality

If you play golf, you know that each course or hole has a certain par, the number of strokes allowed according to the results achieved by expert players. Your own accomplished on the course will be at par, above par, or below par.

Similarly, some days you may feel up to par, other days below par.

Par is from a Latin word meaning equal. You may try, when you play golf, to equal the expert score; and some days you may, or may not, feel equal to your usual self.

When we speak of parity payments to farmers, we refer to payments that show an equality to earnings for some agreed-upon year.

So when you disparage, you lower someone's par, or feeling of equality, (dis- as you know, may be a negative prefix). The noun is disp aragement(dis-PAIR′-əj-mənt), the adjective disparaging(dis-PAIR′-əj-ing), as in "Why do you always make disparaging remarks about me?"

Parity(PAIR′-ə-tee) as a noun means equality; disparity(dis-PAIR′-ə-tee) means a lack of equality, or a difference. We may speak, for example, of the disparity between someone's promise and performance; or of the disparity between the rate of vocabulary growth of a child and of an adult. The adjective disparate(DIS′-pə-rət) indicates essential or complete difference or inequality, as in "Our philosophies are so disparate that we can never come to any agreement on action."

The word compare and all its forms (comparable, comparative, etc.)

derive from par, equal. Two things are compared when they have certain equal or similar qualities, (con-, com-, together, with).

Pair and peer are also from par. Things (shoes, socks, gloves, etc.) in pairs are equal or similar; your peers are those equal to you, as in age, position, rank, or ability. Hence the expression "to be judged by a jury of one's peers." (British peers, however, such is the contradiction of language, were nobles.)

⊜ how to say yes and no

Equivocate is built on another Latin word meaning equal—aequus(the spelling in English is always equ-)—plus vox, vocis, voice.

When you equivocate(ə-KWIV′-ə-kayt′), you seem to be saying both yes and no with equal voice. An equivocal(ə-KWIV′-ə-kəl) answer, therefore, is by design vague, indefinite, and susceptible of contradictory interpretations, quite the opposite of an unequivocal(un′-ə-KWIV′-ə-kəl) response, which says YES! or NO!, and no kidding. Professional politicians are masters of equivocation(ə-kwiv′-ə-KAY′-shən)—they are, on most vital issues, mug-wumps; they sit on a fence with their mugs on one side and their wumps on the other. You will often hear candidates for office say, publicly, that they unequivocally promise, if elected, to . . . ; and then they start equivocating for all they are worth, like people who say, "Let me be perfectly frank with you"—and then promptly and glibly lie through their teeth.

⊜ statements of various kinds

Do not confuse equivocal with ambiguous(am′-BIG′-yoo-əs). An equivocal statement is purposely, deliberately (and with malice aforethought) couched in language that will be deceptive; an ambiguous statement is accidentally couched in such language. Equivocal is, in short, purposely ambiguous.

You will recall that ambi-, which we last met in ambivert and ambidextrous, is a root meaning both; anything ambiguous may have both one meaning and another meaning. If you say, "That sentence is the height of ambiguity," you mean that you find it vague because it admits of both affirmative and negative interpretations, or because it may mean two different things. Ambiguity is pronounced am´-bə-GYOO-ə-tee.

Another type of statement or word contains the possibility of two interpretations—one of them suggestive, risqué, or sexy. Such a statement or word is a double entendre. This is from the French and translates literally as double meaning. Give the word as close a french pronunciation as you can—DOOB´-ləhn-TAHN´-drə. (The n's are nasalized, the r somewhat throaty, and the final syllable is barely audible.)

⟨Word Power⟩ p.220

ORIGIN

☯ more on equality

The root aequus, spelled equ- in English words, is a building block of:

1. equity(EK´-wə-tee)—justice, fairness; i.e., equal treatment. (By extension, stocks in the financial markets are equities, and the

value of your home or other property over and above the amount of the mortgage you owe is your equity in it.) The adjective is equitable(EK´-wə-tə-bəl).

2. inequity(in-EK´-wə-tee)—injustice, unfairness(equity plus the negative prefix in-). Adjective: inequitable(in-EK´-wə-tə-bəl).

3. iniquity(in-IK´-wə-tee)—by one of those delightful surprises and caprices characteristic of language, the change of a single letter (e to i), extends the meaning of a word far beyond its derivation and original denotation. Injustice and unfairness are sinful and wicked, especially if you naively believe that life is fair. So a "den of iniquity" is a place where vice flourishes; an iniquity is a sin or vice, or an egregiously immoral act; and iniquity is wickedness, sinfulness. Adjective: iniquitous(in-IK´-wə-təs).

4. equinox(EE´-kwə-noks´)—etymologically, "equal night," a combination of aequus and nox, noctis, night. The equinox, when day and night are of equal length, occurs twice a year: about March 21, and again about September 21 or 22. (The adjective is equinoctial—ee´-kwə-NOK´-shəl.) Nocturnal(nok-TURN´-əl), derived from nox, noctis, describes people, animals, or plants that are active or flourish at night rather than during daylight hours. Cats and owls are nocturnal, as is the moonflower, whose blossoms open at night; not to mention "night people," whose biorhythms are such that they function better after the sun goes down, and who like to stay up late and sleep well into midmorning. A nocturne(NOK´-turn) is a musical composition of dreamy character (i.e., night music), or a painting of a night scene.

5. equanimity(ee´-kwə-NIM´-ə-tee or ek´-wə-NIM´-ə-tee)— etymologically aequus plus animus, mind, hence "equal mind."

Maintain your equanimity, your evenness of temper, your composure, your coolness or calmness, when everyone around you is getting excited or hysterical, and you will probably be considered an admirable person, though one might wonder what price you pay for such emotional control.

6. Equability(ee´-kwə-BIL´-ə-tee or ek´-wə-BIL´-ə-tee)—a close synonym of equanimity. A person of equable(EE´-kwə-bəl or EK´-wə-bəl) temperament is characteristically calm, serene, unflappable, even-tempered.

7. equilibrium(ee´-kwə-LIB´-ree-əm)—by derivation aequus plus libra, balance, weight, pound, hence "equal balance." Libra(LĪ-brə) is the seventh sign of the zodiac, represented by a pair of scales. Now you know, in case the question has been bothering you, why the abbreviation for the word pound is lb. and why the symbol for the British pound, the monetary unit, is £. Equilibrium is a state of physical balance, especially between opposing forces. When you are very drunk you may have difficulty keeping your equilibrium—the force of gravity is stronger than your ability to stay upright. An equilibrist(ə-KWIL´-ə-brist), as you might guess, is a professional tightrope walker—a performer successfully defying the law of gravity (when sober) by balancing on a thin overhead wire.

The equator divides the earth into equal halves, and words like equation, equivalent, equidistant, equiangular, and equilateral (from Latin latus, lateris, side) are self-explanatory.

☻ not to be confused with horses

Equestrian(ə-KWES´-tree-ən) is someone on a horse (as pedestrian is someone on foot); an equestrienne(ə-kwes´-tree-EN´) is a woman on a horse (if you must make the distinction); and equine(EE´-kwīn) is like a horse, as in appearance or characteristics, or descriptive of horses.

Equestrian is also an adjective referring to horseback riding, as an equestrian statue; and equine is also a noun, i.e., a horse.

So the equ- in these words, from Latin equus, horse, is not to be confused with the equ- in the words of the previous section—that equ- is from aequus, equal. (Remember, also, not to confuse the ped- in pedestrian, from Latin pedis, foot, with the ped- in pediatrician, from Greek paidos, child.)

☻ hear voices?

Equivocal, you will recall, combines aequus with vox, vocis, voice; and vox, vocis combines with fero, to bear or carry, to form vociferous(vō-SIF´-ər-əs), etymologically "carrying (much) voice," hence loud, noisy, clamorous, as vociferous demands (not at all quiet or subtle), or the vociferous play of young children ("Please! Try to be quiet so Dad can get his work done!"), though unfortunately TV addiction has abnormally eliminated child noises, at least during the program breaks between commercials.

If you are vocal(VŌ´-kəl), you express yourself readily and freely by voice; vocal sounds are voiced; vocal music is sung; and you know what your vocal cords are for.

To vocalize(VŌ´-kə-līz´) is to give voice to ("Vocalize your anger, don't hold it in!"), or to sing the vocals (or voice parts) of music. (Can you write the noun form of the verb vocalize? _____.) A vocalist(VŌ´-kə-list) is a singer. And Magnavox(vox plus magnus, large) is the trade name for a brand of radios and TV sets.

〈Word Power〉 p.228

ORIGIN

☻ how to tickle

Titillate comes from a Latin verb meaning to tickle, and may be used both literally and figuratively. That is (literally), you can titillate by gentle touches in strategic places; you are then causing an actual (and always very pleasant) physical sensation. Or you can (figuratively) titillate people, or their minds, fancies, palates (and this is the more common use of the word), by charm, brilliance, wit, promises, or in any other way your imagination can conceive. Titillation(tit´-ə-LAY´-shən) has the added meaning of light sexual stimulation. (Note that both noun and verb are spelled with a double l, not a double t.)

☻ how to flatter

A compliment is a pleasant and courteous expression of praise; flattery is stronger than a compliment and often considered insincere. Adulation(aj´-ə-LAY´-shən) is flattery and worship carried to an excessive, ridiculous degree. There are often public figures (entertainers, musicians, government officials, etc.) who receive widespread adulation, but those not in the public eye can also be adulated, as a teacher by students, a wife by husband (and vice versa), a doctor by patients, and so on. (The derivation is from a Latin Verb meaning to fawn upon.)

The adjective adulatory(aj´-ə-lə-TAWR´-ee) ends in -ory, a suffix we are meeting for the first time in these pages. (Other adjective suffixes: -al, -ic, -ical, -ous.)

⊜ ways of writing

Proscribe, to forbid, is commonly used for medical, religious, or legal prohibitions.

A doctor proscribes a food, drug, or activity that might prove harmful to the patient. The church proscribes, or announces a proscription(prō-SKRIP´-shən) against, such activities as may harm its parishioners. The law proscribes behavior detrimental to the public welfare.

Generally, one might concede, proscribed activities are the most pleasant ones—as Alexander Woolcott once remarked, if something is pleasurable, it's sure to be either immoral, illegal, or fattening.

The derivation is the prefix pro-, before, plus scribo, scriptus, to write. In ancient Roman times, a man's name was written on a public bulletin board if he had committed some crime for which his property or life was to be forfeited; Roman citizens in good standing would thereby know to avoid him. In a similar sense, the doctor writes down those foods or activities that are likely to commit crimes against the patient's health—in that way the patient knows to avoid them.

Scribo, scriptus is the building block of scores of common English word; scribe, scribble, prescribe, describe, subscribe, script, the Scriptures, manuscript, typescript, etc. Describe uses the prefix de-, down—to describe is, etymologically, "to write down" about.

Manuscript, combining manus, hand (as in manual labor), with scriptus, is something handwritten—the word was coined before the invention of the typewriter. The Scriptures are holy writings. To subscribe (as to a magazine) is to write one's name under an order or contract (sub-, under, as in subway, subsurface, etc.); to subscribe to a philosophy or a principle is figuratively to write one's name under the statement of such philosophy or principle. To inscribe is to write in or into(a book, for example, or metal or stone). A postscript is something written after(Latin post, after) the main part is finished.

Note how -scribe verbs change to nouns and adjectives:

VERB	NOUN	ADJECTIVE
prescribe	prescription	prescriptive
subscribe	subscription	subscriptive

Can you follow the pattern?

describe	_____	_____
inscribe	_____	_____
proscribe	_____	_____

☻ it's obvious

You are familiar with the word via, by way of, which is from the Latin word for road. (The Via Appia was one of the famous highways of ancient Roman times.) When something is obvious, etymologically it is right there in the middle of the road where no one can fail to see it— hence, easily seen, not hidden, conspicuous. And if you meet an obstacle in the road and dispose of it forthwith, you are doing what obviate says. Thus, if you review your work daily in some college subject, frenzied "cramming" at the end of the semester will be obviated. A large and steady income obviates fears of financial insecurity; leaving for work early will obviate worry about being late. To obviate, then, is to make unnecessary, to do away with, to prevent by taking effective measures or steps against (an occurrence, a feeling, a requirement, etc.). The noun is obviation(ob´-vee-AY´-shən).

Surprisingly, via, road, is the root in the English word trivial(tri-, three). Where three roads intersect, you are likely to find busy traffic, lots of people, in short a fairly public place, so you are not going to talk of important or confidential matters, lest you be overheard. You will, instead, talk of trivial(TRIV´-ee-əl) things—whatever is unimportant, without great significance; you will confine your conversation to trivialities(triv´-ee-AL´-ə-teez) or to trivia (also a plural noun, pronounced TRIV´-ee-ə), insignificant trifles.

☺ war

Militate derives from militis, one of the forms of the Latin noun meaning soldier or fighting man. If something militates against you, it fights against you, i.e., works to your disadvantage. This, your timidity may militate against your keeping your friends. (Militate is always followed by the preposition against and, like obviate, never takes a personal subject—you don't militate against anyone, but some habit, action, tendency, etc. militates against someone or something.)

The adjective militant(MIL´-ə-tənt) comes from the same root. A militant reformer is one who fights for reforms; a militant campaign is one waged aggressively and with determination. The noun is militancy(MIL´-ə-tən-see), and militant is also a noun for the person— "Sally is a militant in the Women's Liberation movement."

Military and militia also have their origin in militis.

🞊 first the bad news

Built on Latin malus, bad, evil, to malign is to speak evil about, to defame, to slander. Malign is also an adjective meaning bad, harmful, evil, hateful, as in "the malign influence of his unconscious will to fail." Another adjective form is malignant(mə-LIG´-nənt), as in "a malignant glance," i.e., one showing deep hatred, or "a malignant growth," i.e., one that is cancerous (bad).

The noun of malignant is malignancy(mə-LIG´-nən-see), which, medically, is a cancerous growth, or, generally, the condition, state, or attitude of harmfulness, hatefulness, evil intent, etc. The noun form of the adjective malign is malignity(mə-LIG´-nə-tee).

Observe how we can construct English words by combining malus with other Latin roots.

Add the root dico, dictus, to say or tell, to form malediction(mal´-ə-DIK´-shən), a curse, i.e., an evil saying. Adjective: maledictory(mal´-ə-DIK´-tə-ree).

Add the root volo, to wish, to will, or to be willing, and we can construct the adjective malevolent(mə-LEV´-ə-lənt), wishing evil or harm—a malevolent glance, attitude, feeling, etc. The noun is malevolence(mə-LEV´-ə-ləns).

Add the root facio, factus, to do or make (also, spelled, in English words, fec-, fic-, factus, or, as a verb ending, -fy), to form the adjective maleficent(mə-LEF´-ə-sənt), doing harm or evil, or causing hurt—maleficent acts, deeds, behavior. Can you figure out, and pronounce, the noun form of maleficent? _____.

A malefactor(MAL´-ə-fak´-tər) is a wrongdoer, an evildoer, a criminal—a malefactor commits a malefaction(mal´-ə-FAK´-shən), a crime, an evil deed.

French is a "Romance" language, that is, a language based on Roman or Latin (as are, also, Spanish, Portuguese, Italian, and Romanian), and so Latin malus became French mal, bad, the source of maladroit(mal´-ə-DROYT´), clumsy, bungling, awkward, unskillful, etymologically, having a "bad right hand." The noun is maladroitness. Also from French mal: malaise(mə-LAYZ´), an indefinite feeling of bodily discomfort, as in a mild illness, or as a symptom preceeding an illness; etymologically, "bad ease," just as disease(dis-ease) is "lack of ease."

Other common words that you are familiar with also spring from Latin malus: malicious, malice, malady; and the same malus functions as a prefix in words like maladjusted, malcontent, malpractice, malnutrition, etc., all with the connotation of badness.

⟨Word Power⟩ p.239

ORIGIN

😑 so now what's the good news?

Malus is bad; bonus is good. The adverb from the Latin adjective bonus is bene, and bene is the root found in words contrast with the mal-terms we studied in the previous session.

So benign(bə-NĪN´) and benignant(bə-NIG´-nənt) are kindly, good-natured, not harmful, as in benign neglect, a benign judge, a benign tumor (not cancerous), a benignant attitude to malefactors and scoundrels. The corresponding nouns are benignity(bə-NIG´-nə-tee) and benignancy(bə-NIG´-nən-see).

A malediction is a curse; a benediction(ben´-ə-DIK´-shən) is a blessing, a "saying good." The adjective is benedictory(ben´-ə-DIK´-tə-ree).

In contrast to maleficent is beneficent(bə-NEF´-ə-sənt), doing good. The noun? _____.

In contrast to malefactor is benefactor(BEN´-ə-fak´-tər), one who does good things for another, as by giving help, providing financial gifts or aid, or coming to the rescue when someone is in need. If you insist on making sexual distinctions, a woman who so operates is a benefactress(BEN´-ə-fak´-trəs). And, of course, the person receiving the benefaction(ben´-ə-FAK´-shən), the recipient of money, help, etc., is a beneficiary(ben´-ə-FISH´-ər-ee or ben-ə-FISH´-ee-air-ee). Benefit and beneficial are other common words built on the combination of bene and a form of facio, to do or make.

So let others be malevolent toward you—confuse them by being benevolent(bə-NEV´-ə-lənt)—wish them well. (Turn the other cheek? Why not?) The noun? _____.

The adjective bonus, good, is found in English bonus, extra payment, theoretically—but not necessarily—for some good act; in bonbon, a candy(a "good-good," using the French version of the Latin adjective); and in bona fide(BŌ´-nə FĪD´ or BŌ´-nə FĪ´-dee), etymologically, "in good faith," hence valid, without pretense, deception, or fraudulent intent—as a bona fide offer, a bona fide effort to negotiate differences, etc. Fides is Latin for faith or trust, as in fidelity(fə-DEL´-ə-tee), faithfulness; Fido, a stereotypical name for a dog, one's faithful friend;

infidel(IN´-fə-dəl), one who does not have the right faith or religion (depending on who is using the term), or one who has no religion (Latin in-, not); and infidelity(in´-fə-DEL´-ə-tee), unfaithfulness, especially to the marriage vows.

∞ say, do, and wish

Benediction and malediction derive from dico, dictus, to say, tell. Dictate, dictator, dictation, dictatorial(dik´-tə-TAWR´-ee-əl)—words that signify telling others what to do("Do as I say!")—are built on dico, as is predict, to tell beforehand, i.e., to say that something will occur before it actually does (pre-, before, as in prescient).

The brand name Dictaphone combines dico with phone, sound; contradict, to say against, or to make an opposite statement ("Don't contradict me!"; "That contradicts what I know") combines dico with contra-, against, opposite; and addiction, etymologically "a saying to or toward," or the compulsion to say "yes" to a habit, combines dico with ad-, to, toward.

Facio, factus, to do or make (as in malefactor, benefactor), has, as noted, variant spelling in English words: fec-, fic-, or, as a verb ending, -fy.

Thus factory is a place where things are made(-ory, place where); a fact is something done (i.e., something that ocurs, or exists, or is, therefore, true); fiction, something made up or invented; manufacture, to make by hand (manus, hand, as in manuscript, manual), a word coined before the invention of machinery; artificial, made by human art rather than occurring in nature, as artificial flowers, etc.; and clarify, simplify, liquefy, magnify (to make clear, simple, liquid, larger) among hundreds of other -fy verbs.

Volo, to wish, to will, to be willing (as in malevolent, benevolent), occurs in voluntary, involuntary, volunteer, words too familiar to need definition, and each quite obviously expressing wish or willingness. Less common, and from the same root, is volition(vō-LISH´-ən), the act or power of willing or wishing, as in "of her own volition," i.e., voluntarily, or "against her volition."

☻ if you please!

Placate is built on the root plac- which derives from two related Latin verbs meaning, 1) to please, and 2) to appease, soothe, or pacify.

If you succeed in placating an angry colleague, you turn that person's hostile attitude into one that is friendly or favorable. The noun is placation(play-KAY´-shən), the adjective either placative(PLAK´-ə-tiv or PLAY´-kə-tiv) or placatory(PLAK´-ə-taw-ree or PLAY´-kə-taw-ree). A more placatory attitude to those you have offended may help you regain their friendship; when husband and wife, or lovers, quarrel, one of them finally makes a placative gesture if the war no longer fulfills his or her neurotic needs—one of them eventually will wake up some bright morning in a placatory mood.

But then, such is life, he other one may at that point be implacable(im-PLAK´-ə-bəl or im-PLAY´-kə-bəl)—im- is a respelling of in-, not, before the letter p. One who can be soothed, whose hostility can be changed to friendliness, is placable(PLAK´-ə-bəl or PLAY´-kə-bəl).

Implacable has taken on the added meaning of unyielding to entreaty or pity; hence, harsh, relentless, as "The governor was implacable in his refusal to grant clemency."

The noun form of implacable is implacability(im-plak´-ə-BIL´-ə-tee or im-play′-kə-BIL′-ə-tee). Can you write (and pronounce) the noun derived from placable? _____.

If you are placid(PLAS′-id), you are calm, easygoing, serene, undisturbed—etymologically, you are pleased with things as they are. Waters of a lake or sea, or the emotional atmosphere of a place, can also be placid. The noun is placidity(plə-SID′-ə-tee).

If you are complacent(kəm-PLAY′-sənt), you are pleased with yourself(com-, from con-, with, together); you may, in fact, such is one common connotation of the word, be smug, too pleased with your position or narrow accomplishments, too easily self-satisfied, and the hour of reckoning may be closer than you realize. (Humans, as you know, are delighted to be critical of the contentment of others.)

The noun is complacence(kəm-PLAY′-səns) or complacency(kəm-PLAY′-sən-see).

☻ how to give—and forgive

To condone is to forgive, overlook, pardon, or be uncritical of (an offense, or of an antisocial or illegal act). You yourself might or might not indulge in such behavior or commit such an offense, but you feel no urge to protest, or to demand censure or punishment for someone else who does. You may condone cheating on one's income tax, shoplifting from a big, impersonal supermarket, or exceeding the speed limit, though you personally observe the law with scrupulousness. (Not everyone, however, is so charitable or forgiving.) The noun is condonation(kon′-dō-NAY′-shən).

Condone is built on Latin dono, to give, the root found in donor, one who gives; donate, to give; and donation, a gift.

ADVICE

THE THRILL OF RECOGNITION

You have been adding, over the past twenty-three sessions, hundreds of words to your vocabulary; you have been learning hundreds of prefixes, roots, and suffixes that make it possible for you to figure out the meaning of many unfamiliar words you may come across in your reading.

As time goes on and you notice more and more of the words you have studied whenever you read, or whenever you listen to lectures, the radio, or TV, the thrill of recognition plus the immediate comprehension of complex ideas will provide a dividend of incalculable value.

You will hear these words in conversation, and you will begin to use them yourself, unself-consciously, whenever something you want to say is best expressed by one of the words that exactly verbalizes your thinking. Another priceless dividend!

So keep on! You are involved in a dividend-paying activity that will eventually make you intellectually rich.

HOW TO SPEAK NATURALLY

Consider this statement by Louis Bromfield, a noted author: "If I, as a novelist, wrote dialogue for my characters which was meticulously grammatical, the result would be the creation of a speech which rendered the characters pompous and unreal."

And this one by Jasques Barzun, former literary critic for Harper's: "Speech, after all, is in some measure an expression of character, and flexibility in its use is a good way to tell your friends from the robots."

Consider also this puckish remark by the late Clarence Darrow: "Even if you do learn to speak correct English, who are you going to speak it to?"

These are typical reactions of professional people to the old restrictions of formal English grammar. Do the actual teachers of English feel the same way? Again, some typical statements:

"Experts and authorities do not make decisions and rules, by logic or otherwise, about correctness," said E. A. Cross, then Professor of English at the Greeley, Colorado, College of Education. "All they can do is observe the customs of cultivated and educated people and report their findings."

"Grammar is only an analysis after the facts, a post-mortem on usage," said Stephen Leacock in How To Write. "Usage comes first and usage must rule."

One way to discover current trends in usage is to poll a cross section of people who use the language professionally, inquiring as to their opinion of the acceptability, in everyday speech, of certain specific and controversial expressions. A questionnaire I prepared recently was answered by eighty-two such people—thirty-one authors, seven book reviewers, thirty-three editors, and eleven professors of English. The results, some of which will be detailed below, may possibly prove startling to you if you have been conditioned to believe, as most of us have, that correct English is rigid, unchangeable, and exclusively dependent on grammatical rules.

TEST YOURSELF

1. Californians boast of the healthy climate of their state.	RIGHT	WRONG
2. Her new novel is not as good as her first one.	RIGHT	WRONG
3. We can't hardly believe it.	RIGHT	WRONG
4. This is her.	RIGHT	WRONG
5. Who are you waiting for?	RIGHT	WRONG
6. Please take care of whomever is waiting.	RIGHT	WRONG
7. Whom would you like to be if you weren't yourself?	RIGHT	WRONG
8. My wife has been robbed.	RIGHT	WRONG
9. Is this desert fattening?	RIGHT	WRONG

1. Californians boast of the healthy climate of their state.

RIGHT. There is distinction, says formal grammar, between healthy and healthful. A person can be healthy—I am still quoting the rule—if he possesses good health. But climate must be healthful, since it is conducive to health. This distinction is sometimes observed in writing but rarely in everyday speech, as you have probably noticed. Even the dictionaries have stopped splitting hairs—they permit you to say healthy no matter which of the two meanings you intend.

"Healthy climate" was accepted as current educated usage by twenty-six of the thirty-three editors who answered the questionnaire, six of the seven book reviewers, nine of the eleven professors of English, and twenty of the thirty-one authors. The earlier distinction, in short, is rapidly becoming obsolete.

2. Her new novel is not as good as her first one.

RIGHT. If you have studied formal grammar, you will recall that after a negative verb the "proper" word is so, not as. Is this rule observed by educated speakers? Hardly ever.

In reference to the sentence under discussion, author Thomas W. Duncan remarked: "I always say—and write—as, much to the distress of my publisher's copyreader. But the fellow is a wretched purist."

The tally on this use of as showed seventy-four for, only eight against.

3. We can't hardly believe it.

WRONG. Of the eighty-two professional people who answered my questionnaire, seventy-six rejected this sentence; it is evident that can't hardly is far from acceptable in educated speech. Preferred usage: We can hardly believe it.

4. This is her.

WRONG. This substitution of her where the rule requires she was rejected by fifty-seven of my eighty-two respondents. Paradoxically enough, although "It's me" and "This is me" are fully established in educated speech, "This is her" still seems to be condemned by the majority of cultivated speakers. Nevertheless, the average person, I imagine, may feel a bit uncomfortable saying "This is she"—it sounds almost too sophisticated.

This is more than an academic problem. If the voice at the other end of a telephone conversation makes the opening move with "I'd like to speak to Jane Doe [your name, for argument's sake]," you are, unfortunately, on the horns of a very real dilemma. "This is she" may sound prissy— "This is her" may give the impression that you're uneducated. Other choices are equally doubtful. "Taking!" is suspiciously businesslike if the call comes to your home, and "I am Jane Doe!" may make you feel like the opening line of a high school tableau. The need for a decision arises several times in a busy day—and, I am sorry to report, the English language is just deficient enough not to be of much help. I wonder how it would be if you just grunted affably?

5. Who are you waiting for?

RIGHT. Formal grammar not only requires whom but demands that the word order be changed to: "For whom are you waiting?" (Just try taking with such formality on everyday occasions and see how long you'll keep your friends.)

Who is the normal, popular form as the first word of a sentence, no matter what the grammatical construction; and an opinion by Kyle Crichton, a well-known magazine editor, is typical of the way many educated people feel. Mr. Crichton says: "The most loathsome word (to me at least) in the English language is whom. You can always tell a half-educated buffoon by the care he takes in working the word in. When he starts it, I know I am faced with a pompous illiterate who is not going to have me long as company."

The score for acceptance of the sentence as it stands (with who) was sixty-six out of eighty-two. If, like most unpedantic speakers, you prefer who to whom for informal occasions, or if you feel as strongly about whom as Mr. Crichon does, you will be happy to hear that modern trends in English are all on your side.

6. Please take care of whomever is waiting.

WRONG. Whomever is awkward and a little silly in this sentence and brings to mind Franklin P. Adams' famous remark on grammar: "'Whom are you?' asked Cyril, for he had been to night school." It is also contrary to grammatical rule. People who are willing to be sufficiently insufferable to use whomever in this construction have been tempted into error by the adjacent word of. They believe that since they are following a preposition with an objective pronoun they are speaking impeccable grammar. In actuality, however, whomever is not the object of the preposition of but the subject of the verb is waiting. Preferable form: Please take care of whoever is waiting.

7. Whom would you like to be if you weren't yourself?

WRONG. Here is another and typical example of the damage which an excessive reverence for whom can do to an innocent person's speech. Judged by grammatical rule, whom is incorrect in this sentence (the verb to be requires who); judged by normal speech patterns, it is absurd. This use of whom probably comes from an abortive attempt to sound elegant.

8. My wife has been robbed.

RIGHT —if something your wife owns was taken by means of thievery. However, if your wife herself was kidnapped, or in some way talked into leaving you, she was stolen, not robbed. To rob is to abscond with the contents of something—to steal is to walk off with the thing itself. Needless to say, both forms of activity are highly antisocial and equally illegal.

9. Is this desert fattening?

WRONG. The dessert that is fattening is spelled with two s's. With one s, it's a desert, like the Sahara. Remember the two s's in dessert by thinking how much you'd like two portions, if only your waistline permitted.

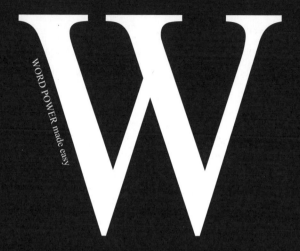

WORD POWER made easy

W

CHAPTER
7

HOW TO TALK ABOUT VARIOUS SPEECH HABITS

Words that explore in depth all degrees and kinds of talk and silence. More
books that will increase your alertness to new ideas and new words.

ORIGIN

☜ about keeping one's mouth shut

If you let your mind play over some of the taciturn people you know, you will realize that their abnormal disinclination to conversation makes them seem morose, sullen, and unfriendly. Cal Coolidge's taciturnity was world-famous, and no one, I am sure, ever conceived of him as cheerful, overfriendly, or particularly sociable. There are doubtless many possible causes of such verbal rejection of the world: perhaps lack of self-assurance, feelings of inadequacy or hostility, excessive seriousness or introspection, or just plain having nothing to say. Maybe, in Coolidge's case, he was saving up his words—after he did not "choose to run" in 1928, he wrote a daily column for the New York Herald Tribune at a rumored price of two dollars a word—and, according to most critics (probably all Democrats), he had seemed wiser when he kept silent. Coolidge hailed from New England, and taciturnity(tas-ə-TURN´-ə-tee) in that part of the country, so some people say, is considered a virtue. Who knows, the cause may be geographical and climatic, rather than psychological.

Taciturn is from a Latin verb taceo, to be silent, and is one of those words whose full meaning cannot be expressed by any other combination of syllables. It has many synonyms, among them silent, uncommunicative, reticent, reserved, secretive, close-lipped, and close-mouthed; but no other word indicates the permanent, habitual, and temperamental disinclination to talk implied by taciturn.

😊 better left unsaid

Tacit(TAS´-it) derives from taceo.

Here is a man dying of cancer. He suspects what his disease is, and everyone else, of course, knows. Yet he never mentions the dread word, and no one who visits him ever breathes a syllable of it in his hearing. It is tacitly understood by all concerned that the word will remain forever unspoken. (Such a situation today, however, may or may not be typical—there appears to be a growing tendency among physicians and family to be open and honest with people who are dying.)

Consider another situation:

An executive is engaging in extracurricular activities with her secretary. Yet during office time they are as formal and distant as any two human beings can well be. Neither of them ever said to the other, "Now, look here, we may be lovers after five o'clock, but between nine and five we must preserve the utmost decorum, okay?" Such speech, such a verbal arrangement, is considered unnecessary—so we may say that the two have a tacit agreement (i.e., nothing was ever actually said) to maintain a complete employer-employee relationship during office hours.

Anything tacit, then, is unspoken, unsaid, not verbalized. We speak of a tacit agreement, arrangement, acceptance, rejection, assent, refusal, etc. A person is never called tacit.

The noun is tacitness(TAS´-it-nəs). (Bear in mind that you can transform any adjective into a noun by adding -ness, though in many cases there may be a more sophisticated, or more common, noun form.)

Changing the a of the root taceo to i, and adding the prefix re-, again, and the adjective suffix -ent, we can construct the English word reticent(RET´-ə-sənt).

Someone is reticent who prefers to keep silent, whether out of shyness, embarrassment, or fear of revealing what should not be revealed. (The idea of "againness" in the prefix has been lost in the current meaning of the word.)

We have frequently made nouns out of -ent adjectives. Write two possible noun forms of reticent: _____, or, less commonly,

_____.

☻ talk, talk, talk!

Loquacious people love to talk. This adjective is not necessarily a put-down, but the implication, when you so characterize such people, is that you wish they would pause for breath once in a while so that you can get your licks in. The noun is loquacity(lō-KWAS´-ə-tee), or, of course, loquaciousness.

The word derives from Latin loquor, to speak, a root found also in:

1. soliloquy(sə-LIL´-ə-kwee)—a speech to oneself (loquor plus solus, alone), or, etymologically, a speech when alone.

   We often talk to ourselves, but usually silently, the words going through our minds but not actually passing our lips. The term soliloquy is commonly applied to utterances made in a play by characters who are speaking their thoughts aloud so the audience won't have to guess. The soliloquist(sə-LIL´-ə-kwist) may be alone; or other members of the cast may be present on stage, but of course they don't hear what's being said, because they're not supposed to know. Eugene O'Neill made novel uses of soliloquies in Mourning Becomes Electra—the characters made honest disclosures of their feelings and thoughts to the audience, but kept the other players in the dark. The verb is to soliloquize (sə-LIL´-ə-kwīz´).

2. A ventriloquist(ven-TRIL´-ə-kwist) is one who can throw his voice. A listener thinks the sound is coming from some source other than the person speaking. The combining root is Latin venter, ventris, belly; etymologically, ventriloquism(ven-TRIL´-ə-kwiz-əm) is the art of "speaking from the belly." The adjective is ventriloquistic (ven-tril´-ə-KWIS´-tik). Can you figure out how the verb will end? Write the verb: _____.

3. Colloquial(kə-LŌ´-kwee-əl) combines loquor, to speak, with the prefix con-. (Con- is spelled col- before a root starting with l; cor- before a root starting with r; com- before a root starting with m, p, or b.) When people speak together they are engaging in conversation—and their language is usually more informal and less rigidly grammatical than what you might expect in writing or in public addresses. Colloquial patterns are perfectly correct—they are simply informal, and suitable to everyday conversation.

A colloquialism(kə-LŌ´-kwee-ə-liz-əm), therefore, is a conversational-style expression, like "He hasn't got any" or "Who are you going with?" as contrasted to the formal or literary "He has none" or "With whom are you going? Colloquial English is the English you and I talk on everyday occasions—it is not slangy, vulgar, or illiterate.

4. A circumlocution(sur-kəm-lō-KYOO´-shən) is, etymologically, a "talking around" (circum-, around). Any way of expressing an idea that is roundabout or indirect is circumlocutory(sur´-kəm-LOK´-yə-tawr´-ee)—you are now familiar with the common adjective suffix -ory.

ORIGIN

● a Spartan virtue

In ancient Sparta, originally known as Laconia, the citizens were long-suffering, hard-bitten, stoical, and military-minded, and were even more noted for their economy of speech than Vermonters, if that is possible. Legend has it that when Philip of Macedonia was storming the gates of Sparta (or Laconia), he sent a message to the besieged king saying, "If we capture your city we will burn it to the ground." A one-word answer came back: "If." It was now probably Philip's turn to be speechless, though history does not record his reaction.

It is from the name Laconia that we derive our word laconic—pithy, concise, economical in the use of words almost to the point of curtness; precisely the opposite of verbose.

Like the man who was waiting at a lunch counter for a ham sandwich. When it was ready, the clerk inquired politely, "Will you eat it here, or take it with you?" "Both," was the laconic reply.

Or like the woman who was watching a lush imbibing dry martinis at a Third Avenue bar in New York City. The drunk downed the contents of each cocktail glass at one gulp, daintily nibbled and swallowed the bowl, then finally turned the glass over and ate the base. The stem he threw into a corner. This amazing gustatory feat went on for half an hour, until a dozen stems were lying shattered in the corner, and the drunk had chewed and swallowed enough bowls and bases to start a glass factory.

He suddenly turned to the lady and asked belligerently, "I suppose you think I'm cuckoo, don't you?" "Sure—the stem is the best part," was the laconic answer.

(It was doubtless this same gentleman, in his accustomed state of intoxication, who found himself painfully weaving his way along Wilshire Boulevard in Beverly Hills, California—he had somehow gotten on a TWA jetliner instead of the subway—when he realized, almost too late, that he was going to bump into a smartly dressed young woman who had just stepped out of her Mercedes-Benz to go window-shopping along the avenue. He quickly veered left, but by some unexplainable magnetic attraction the woman veered in the same direction, again making collision apparently inevitable. With an adroit maneuver, the drunk swung to the right—the lady, by now thoroughly disoriented, did the same. Finally both jammed on the brakes and came to a dead stop, face to face, and not six inches apart; and as the alcoholic fumes assailed the young lady's nostrils, she sneered at the reeking, swaying man, as much in frustration as in contempt: "Oh! How gauche!" "Fine!" was his happy response. "How goesh with you?" This answer, however, is not laconic, merely confused.)

We have learned that -ness, -ity, and -ism are suffixes that transform adjectives into nouns—and all three can be used with laconic:

. . .with characteristic laconicness(lə-KON´-ək-nəs)

. . .her usual laconicity(lak´-ə-NIS´-ə-tee)

. . .his habitual laconism(LAK´-ə-niz-əm)

. . .with, for him, unusual laconicism(lə-KON´-ə-siz-əm)

A laconism is also the expression itself that is pithy and concise, as the famous report from a naval commander in World War II: "Saw sub, sank same."

✿ brilliant

Cogent is a term of admiration. A cogent argument is well put, convincing, hardly short of brilliant. Cogency(KŌ´-jən-see) shows a keen mind, an ability to think clearly and logically. The word derives from the Latin verb cogo, to drive together, compel, force. A cogent argument compels acceptance because of its logic, its persuasiveness, its appeal to one's sense of reason.

✿ back to talk

You will recall that loquor, to speak, is he source of loquacity, soliloquy, ventriloquism, colloquialism, circumlocution. This root is also the base on which eloquent(EL´-ə-kwənt), magniloquent(mag-NIL´-ə-kwənt), and grandiloquent(gran-DIL´-ə-kwənt) are built.

The eloquent person speaks out(e-, from ex-, out), is vividly expressive, fluent, forceful, or persuasive in language ("the prosecutor's eloquent plea to the jury"). The word is partially synonymous with cogent, but cogent implies irresistible logical reasoning and intellectual keenness, while eloquent suggests artistic expression, strong emotional appeal, the skillful use of language to move and arouse a listener.

Magniloquent (magnus, large) and grandiloquent (grandis, grand) are virtually identical in meaning. Magniloquence or grandiloquence is the use of high-flown, grandiose, even pompous language; of large and impressive words; of lofty, flowery, or overelegant phraseology. Home is a place of residence; wife is helpmate, helpmeet, or better half; women are the fair sex; children are offspring or progeny; a doctor is a member of the medical fraternity; people are the species Homo sapiens, etc., etc.

Loquacious, verbose, voluble, and garrulous people are all talkative;

but each type, you will recall, has a special quality.

If you are loquacious, you talk a lot because you like to talk and doubtless have a lot to say. If you are verbose, you smother your idea with excess words, with such an overabundance of words that your listener either drops into a state of helpless confusion or falls asleep. If you are voluble, you speak rapidly, fluently, glibly, without hesitation, stutter, or stammer; you are vocal, verbal, and highly articulate. If you are garrulous, you talk constantly, and usually aimlessly and meaninglessly, about trifles. We often hear the word used in "a garrulous old man" or "a garrulous old women," since in very advanced age the mind may wander and lose the ability to discriminate between the important and the unimportant, between the interesting and the dull.

Verbose is from Latin verbum, word—the verbose person is wordy.

Voluble comes from Latin volvo, volutus, to roll—words effortlessly roll off the voluble speaker's tongue.

And garrulous derives from Latin garrio, to chatter—a garrulous talker chatters away like a monkey.

The suffix -ness can be added to all these adjectives to form nouns. Alternate noun forms end in -ity:

verbosity	(vər-BOS´-ə-tee)
volubility	(vol´-yə-BIL´-ə-tee)
garrulity	(gə-ROOL´-ə-tee)

⊛ at large

We discovered magnus, large, big, great, in discussing Magnavox (etymologically, "big voice"), and find it again in magniloquent (etymologically, "talking big"). The root occurs in a number of other words:

1. Magnanimous(mag-NAN´-ə-məs)—big-hearted, generous, forgiving(etymologically, "great-minded"). (Magnus plus animus, mind.)

2. Magnate(MAG´-nayt)—a person of great power or influence, a big wheel, as a business magnate.

3. Magnify—to make larger, or make seem larger (magnus plus -fy from facio, to make), as in "magnify your problems."

4. Magnificent—magnus plus fic-, from facio.

5. Magnitude—magnus plus the common noun suffix -tude, as in fortitude, multitude, gratitude, etc.

6. Magnum (as of champagne or wine)—a large bottle, generally two fifths of a gallon.

7. Magnum opus(MAG´-nəm Ō´-pəs)—etymologically, a "big work"; actually, the greatest work, or masterpiece, of an artist, writer, or composer. Opus is the Latin word for work; the plural of opus is used in the English word opera, etymologically, "a number of works," actually a musical drama containing overture, singing, and other forms of music, i.e., many musical works. The verb form opero, to work, occurs in operate, co-operate, operator, etc.

☯ words, words, words!

Latin verbum is word. A verb is the important word in a sentence; verbatim(vər-BAY´-tim) is word-for-word (a verbatim report).

Verbal(VUR´-bəl), ending in the adjective suffix -al, may refer either to a verb, or to words in general (a verbal fight); or it may mean, loosely, oral or spoken, rather than written (verbal agreement or contract); or, describing people ("she is quite verbal"), it may refer to a ready ability to put feelings or thoughts into words.

Working from verbal, can you add a common verb suffix to form a word meaning to put into words? _____.

Verbiage(VUR´-bee-əj) has two meanings: an excess of words ("Such verbiage!"); or a style or manner of using words (medical verbiage, military verbiage).

☻ roll on, and on!

Volvo, volutus, to roll, the source of voluble, is the root on which many important English words are based.

Revolve(rə-VOLV´)—roll again (and again), or keep turning round. Wheels revolve, the earth revolves around the sun, the cylinder of a revolver revolves. (The prefix is re-, back or again.)

The noun is revolution(rev´-ə-LOO´-shən), which can be one such complete rolling, or, by logical extension, a radical change of any sort (TV was responsible for a revolution in the entertainment industry), especially political (the American, or French Revolution). The adjective revolutionary(rev´-ə-LOO-shən-air´-ee) introduces us to a new adjective suffix, -ary, as in contrary, disciplinary, stationary, imaginary, etc. (But -ary is sometimes also a noun suffix, as in dictionary, commentary, etc.)

Add different prefixes to volvo to construct two more English words:

1. involve—etymologically, "roll in" ("I didn't want to get involved!"). Noun: involvement.

2. evolve(ə-VOLV´)—etymologically, "roll out" (e-, out); hence to unfold, or gradually develop ("The final plan evolved from some informal discussions"; "The political party evolved from a group

of interested citizens who met frequently to protest government actions")

By analogy with the forms derived from revolve, can you construct the noun and adjective of evolve? Noun: _____. Adjective:

_____.

⟨Word Power⟩ p.282

⊛

ORIGIN

☻ front and back—and uncles

The ventriloquist appears to talk from the belly (venter, venris plus loquor) rather than through the lips (or such was the strange perception of the person who first used the word).

Venter, ventris, belly, is the root on which ventral(VEN´-trəl) and ventricle are built.

The ventral side of an animal, for example, is the front or anterior side—the belly side.

A ventricle(VEN´-trə-kəl) is a hollow organ or cavity, or, logically enough, belly, as one of the two chambers of the heart, or one of the four chambers of the brain. The ventricles of the heart are the lower chambers, and receive blood from the auricles, or upper chambers. The auricle(AW´-rə-kəl), so named because it is somewhat ear-shaped (Latin auris, ear), receives blood from the veins; the auricles send the blood into the ventricles, which in turn pump the blood into the arteries. (It's all very complicated, but fortunately it works.)

The adjective form of ventricle is ventricular(ven-TRIK´-yə-lər), which may refer to a ventricle, or may mean having a belly-like bulge.

Now that you see how ventricular is formed from ventricle, can you figure out the adjective of auricle? _____. How about the adjective of vehicle? _____. Of circle? _____.

No doubt you wrote auricular(aw-RIK´-yə-lər), vehicular, and circular, and have discovered that nouns ending in -cle from adjectives ending in -cular.

So you can now be the first person on your block to figure out the adjective derived from:

clavicle: _____.

cuticle: _____.

vesicle: _____.

testicle: _____.

uncle: _____.

The answers of course are clavicular, cuticular, vesicular, testicular—and for uncle you have every right to shout "No fair!" (But where is it written that life is fair?)

The Latin word for uncle (actually, uncle on the mother's side) is avunculus, from which we get avuncular(ə-VUNG´-kyə-lər), referring to an uncle. Now what about an uncle? Well, traditional or stereotypical uncles are generally kindly, permissive, indulgent, protective—and often give helpful advice. So anyone who exhibits one or more of such traits to another (usually younger) person is avuncular or acts is an avuncular capacity.

So, at long last, to get back to ventral. If there's a front of belly side, anatomically, there must be a reverse—a back side. This is the dorsal(DAWR′-səl) side, from Latin dorsum, the root on which the verb endorse(en-DAWRS′) is built. If you endorse a check, you sign it on the back side; if you endorse a plan, an idea, etc., you back it, you express your approval or support. The noun is endorsement(en-DAWRS′-mənt).

● the noise and the fury

Vociferous derives from Latin vox, vocis, voice, plus fero, to bear or carry. A vociferous rejoinder carries a lot of voice—i.e., it is vehement, loud, noisy, clamorous, shouting. The noun is vociferousness(vō-SIF′-ə-rəs-nəs); the verb is to vociferate(vō-SIF′-ə-rayt′). Can you form the noun derived from the verb? _____.

● to sleep or not to sleep—that is the question

The root fero is found also in somniferous(som-NIF′-ə-rəs), carrying, bearing, or bringing sleep. So a somniferous lecture is so dull and boring that it is sleep-inducing.

Fero is combined with somnus, sleep, in somniferous. (The suffix -ous indicates what part of speech? _____.)

Tack on the negative prefix in- to somnus to construct insomnia(in-SOM′-nee-ə), the abnormal inability to fall asleep when sleep is required or desired. The unfortunate victim of this disability is an insomniac(in-SOM′-nee-ak), the adjective is insomnious(in-SOM′-nee-əs). (So, -ous, in case you could not answer the question in the preceding paragraph, is an adjective suffix.)

Add a different adjective suffix to somnus to derive somnolent(SOM′-nə-lənt), sleepy, drowsy. Can you construct the noun form of somnolent?

_____ or _____.

Combine somnus with ambulo, to walk, and you have somnambulism (som-NAM´-byə-liz-əm), walking in one's sleep. With your increasing skill in using etymology to form words, write the term for the person who is a sleepwalker. _____. Now add to the word you wrote a two-letter adjective suffix we have learned, to form the adjective:

_____.

∞ a walkaway

An ambulatory(AM´-byə-lə-taw´-ree) patient, as in a hospital or convalescent home, is finally well enough to get out of bed and walk around. A perambulator(pə-RAM´-byə-lay´-tər). a word used more in England than in the United States, and often shortened to pram, is a baby carriage, a vehicle for walking an infant through the streets (per-, through). To perambulate(pə-RAM´-byə-layt´) is, etymologically, "to walk through"; hence, to stroll around. Can you write the noun form of this verb? _____.

To amble(AM´-bəl) is to walk aimlessly; an ambulance is so called because originally it was composed of two stretcher-bearers who walked off the battlefield with a wounded solder; and a preamble(PREE´-am-bəl) is, by etymology, something that "walks before" (pre-, before, beforehand), hence an introduction or introductory statement, as the preamble to the U. S. Constitution ("We the people . . ."), a preamble to the speech, etc; or any event that is introductory or preliminary to another, as in "An increase in inflationary factors in the economy is often a preamble to a drop in the stock market."

∞ back to sleep

Somnus is one Latin word for sleep—sopor is another. A soporific (sop´-ə-RIF´-ik) lecture, speaker, style of delivery, etc. will put the audience to sleep (fic- from facio, to make), and a soporific is a sleeping pill.

∞ noun suffixes

You know that -ness can be added to any adjective to construct the noun form. Write the noun derived from inarticulate: _____. Inarticulate is a combination of the negative prefix in- and Latin articulus, a joint. The inarticulate person has trouble joining words together coherently. If you are quite articulate(ahr-TIK´-yə-lət), on the other hand, you join your words together easily, you are verbal, vocal, possibly even voluble. The verb to articulate(ahr-TIK´-yə-layt´) is to join (words), i.e., to express your vocal sounds—as in "Please articulate more clearly." Can you write the noun derived from the verb articulate? _____.

Another, and very common, noun suffix attached to adjectives is, as you have discovered, -ity. So the noun form of banal is either banalness, or, more commonly, banality(bə-NAL´-ə-tee).

Bear in mind, then, that -ness and -ity are common noun suffixes attached to adjectives, and -ion (or -ation) is a noun suffix frequently affixed to verbs (to articulate—articulation; to vocalize—vocalization; to perambulate—perambulation).

ADVICE

BECOMING ALERT TO NEW IDEAS

Some chapters back I suggested that since words are symbols of ideas, one of the most effective means of building your vocabulary is to read books that deal with new ideas. Along that line, I further suggested that the fields of psychology, psychiatry, and psychoanalysis would be good starting points, and I mentioned a number of exciting books to work with.

Needless to say, you will not wish to neglect other fields, and so I want to recommend, at this point, highly readable books in additional subjects. All these books will increase your familiarity with the world of ideas—all of them, therefore, will help you build a superior vocabulary.

SEMANTICS

Language in Thought and Action, by S. I. Hayakawa

People in Quandaries, by Wendell Johnson

EDUCATION AND LEARNING

How to Survive in Your Native Land, by James Herndon

Education and the Endangered Individual, by Brian V. Hill

How Children Fail and What Do I Do Monday?, by John Holt

Teaching Human Beings, by Jeffrey Schrank

Education and Ecstasy, by George B. Leonard

Human Teaching for Human Learning, by George Isaac Brown

SEX, LOVE, MARRIAGE

Couple Therapy, by Gerald Walker Smith and Alice I. Phillips

Your Fear of Love, by Marshall Bryant Hodge

Sexual Suicide, by George F. Gilder

Intimacy, by Gina Allen and Clement G. Martin, M.D.

How to Live with Another Person, by David Viscott, M.D.

Pairing, by George R. Bach and Ronald M. Deutsch

The Intimate Enemy, by George R. Bach and Peter Wyden

The Rape of the Ape, by Allan Sherman (Humor)

The Hite Report, by Shere Hite

Sex in Human Loving, by Eric Berne, M.D.

WOMEN, FEMINISM, ETC.

Rebirth of Feminism, by Judith Hole and Ellen Levine

The Way of All Women, by M. Esther Harding

Knowing Woman, by Irene Claremont de Castillejo

Sexist Justice, by Karen De Crow

Our Bodies, Our Selves, by The Boston Women's Health Book Collective

CHILDREN, CHILD-RAISING, ETC.

Between Parent and Child and Between Parent and Teenager, by Dr. Haim Ginott

Children Who Hate, by Fritz Redl and David Wineman

Parent Effectiveness Training, by Dr. Thomas Gordon

How to Parent, by Dr. Fitzhugh Dodson

Escape from Childhood, by John Holt

One Little Boy, by Dorothy W. Baruch

HEALTH

Save Your Life Diet Book, by David Reuben, M.D.

Folk Medicine, by D. C. Jarvis, M.D.

Get Well Naturally, by Linda Clark

Let's Eat Right to Keep Fit, by Adelle Davis

PHILOSOPHY

The Way of Zen and What Does It Matter?, by Alan W. Watts

Love's Body, by Norman O. Brown

BUSINESS, ECONOMICS, FINANCE

The Affluent Society, by John Kenneth Galbraith

Parkinson's Law, by C. Northcote Parkinson

The Peter Principle, by Laurence J. Peter

Up the Organization, by Robert Townsend

SOCIOLOGY

Passages, by Gail Sheehy

Future Shock, by Alvin Toffler

Hard Times, by Studs Terkel

Roots, by Alex Haley

DEATH AND DYING

Life After Life, by Raymond A. Moody, Jr., M.D.

On Death and Dying, by Elizabeth Kubler Ross

All but one or two of these stimulating and informative books are available in inexpensive paperback editions—most of them can be found in any large public library. Any one of them will provide an evening of entertainment and excitement far more rewarding than watching TV, will possibly open for you new areas of knowledge and understanding, and will undoubtedly contain so many of the words you have learned in this book that you will again and again experience the delicious shock of recognition that I spoke of in an earlier chapter.

Additionally, you may encounter words you have never seen before that are built on roots you are familiar with—and you will then realize how simple it is to figure out the probable meaning of even the most esoteric term once you have become an expert in roots, prefixes, and suffixes.

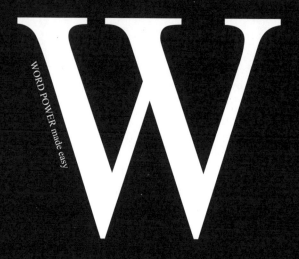

WORD POWER made easy

CHAPTER
8

HOW TO INSULT YOUR ENEMIES

Terms for describing a disciplinarian, toady, dabbler, provocative woman, flag-waver, possessor of a one-track mind, free-thinker, sufferer from imaginary ailments, etc. Excursions into words relating to father and mother, murder of all sorts, sexual desires, and various manias and phobias. Magazines that will help you build your vocabulary.

ORIGIN

⊛ the French drillmaster

Jean Martinet was the Inspector General of Infantry during the reign of King Louis XIV—and a stricter, more fanatic drillmaster France had never seen. It was from this time that the French Army's reputation for discipline dated, and it is from the name of this Frenchman that we derive our English word martinet. The word is always used in a derogatory sense and generally shows resentment and anger on the part of the user. The secretary who calls his boss a martinet, the wife who applies the epithet to her husband, the worker who thus refers to the foreman—these speakers all show their contempt for the excessive, inhuman discipline to which they are asked to submit.

Since martinet comes from a man's name (in the Brief Intermission which follows we shall discover that a number of picturesque English words are similarly derived), there are no related forms built on the same root. There is an adjective martinetish(mahr-tə-NET′-ish) and another noun form, martinetism, but these are used only rarely.

⊛ a Greek "fig-shower"

Sycophant comes to us from the Greeks. According to Shipley's Dictionary of Word Origins:

When a fellow wants to get a good mark, he may polish up an apple and place it on teacher's desk; his classmates call such a lad an apple-shiner. Less complimentary localities use the term bootlicker. The

Greeks had a name for it: fig-shower. Sycophant is from Gr. sykon, fig, [and] phanein, to show. This was the fellow the informed the officers in charge when (1) the figs in the sacred groves were being taken, or (2) when the Smyrna fig-dealers were dodging the tariff.

Thus, a sycophant may appear to be a sort of "stool pigeon," since the latter curries the favor of police officials by "peaching" on his fellow criminals. Sycophants may use this means of ingratiating themselves with influential citizens of the community; or they may use flattery, servile attentions, or any other form of insinuating themselves into someone's good graces. A sycophant practices sycophancy(SIK´-ə-fən-see), and has a sycophantic(sik´-ə-FAN´-tik) attitude. All three forms of the word are highly uncomplimentary—use them with care.

Material may be so delicate or fine in texture that anything behind it will show through. The Greek prefix dia- means through; and phanein, as you now know, means to show—hence such material is called diaphanous(dī-AF´-ə-nəs). Do not use the adjective in reference to all material that is transparent (for example, you would not call glass diaphanous, even though you can see right through it), but only material that is silky, gauzy, filmy, and, in addition, transparent or practically transparent. The word is often applied to female garments—nightgowns, negligees, etc.

☯ just for one's own amusement

Dilettante is from the Italian verb dilettare, to delight. The dilettante paints, writes, composes, plays a musical instrument, or engage in scientific experiments purely for amusement—not to make money, become famous, or satisfy a deep creative urge (the latter, I presume, being the justifications for the time that professional artists, writers, composers, musicians, poets, and scientists spend at their chosen work). A dilettantish(dil-ə-TAN´-tish) attitude is superficial, unprofessional; dilettantism(dil-ə-TAN´-tiz-əm) is superficial, part-time dabbling in the type of activity that usually engages the full time and energy of the professional artist or scientist.

Do not confuse the dilettante, who has a certain amount of native talent or ability, with the tyro(TĪ´-rō), who is the inexperienced beginner in some art, but who may be full of ambition, drive, and energy. To call a person a tyro is to imply that he is just starting in some artistic, scientific, or professional field—he's not much good yet because he has not had time to develop his skill, if any. The dilettante usually has some skill but isn't doing much with it. On the other hand, anyone who has developed consummate skill in an artistic field, generally allied to music, is called a virtuoso(vur´-choo-Ō´-sō)—like Heifetz or Menuhin on the violin, Horowitz or Rubinstein on the piano. Pluralize virtuoso in the normal way—virtuosos; or if you wish to sound more sophisticated, give it the continental form—virtuosi(vur´-choo-Ō´-see). Similarly, the plural of dilettante is either dilettantes or dilettanti(dil´-ə-TAN´-tee).

The i ending for a plural is the Italian form and is common in musical circles. For example, libretto, the story (or book) of an opera, may be pluralized to libretti; concerto, a form of musical composition, is pluralized concerti. However, the Anglicized librettos and concertos are perfectly correct also. Libretto is pronounced lə-BRET´-ō; libretti is lə-BRET´-ee; concerto is kən-CHUR´-tō; and concerti is kən-CHUR´-tee. Suit your plural form, I would suggest, to the sophistication of your audience.

● "masculine" women

Virago comes, oddly enough, from the Latin word for man, vir. Perhaps the derivation is not so odd after all; a virago, far from being stereotypically feminine (i.e., timid, delicate, low-spoken, etc.), is stereotypically masculine in personality—coarse, aggressive, loud-mouthed. Termagant(TUR′-mə-gənt) and harridan(HAIR′-ə-dən) are words with essentially the same uncomplimentary meaning as virago. To call a brawling woman a virago, a termagant, and a harridan is admittedly repetitious, but is successful in relieving one's feelings.

● the old man

Nicolas Chauvin, soldier of the French Empire, so vociferously and unceasingly aired his veneration of Napoleon Bonaparte that he became the laughingstock of all Europe. Thereafter, an exaggerated and blatant patriot was known as a chauvinist—and still is today. Chauvinism(SHŌ′-və-niz-əm), by natural extension, applies to blatant veneration of, or boastfulness about, any other affiliation besides one's country. To be patriotic is to be normally proud of, and devoted to, one's country—to be chauvinistic(shō′-və-NIS′-tik) is to exaggerate such pride and devotion to an obnoxious degree.

We might digress here to investigate an etymological side road down which the word patriotic beckons. Patriotic is built on the Latin word pater, patris, father—one's country is, in a sense, one's fatherland.

Let us see what other interesting words are built on this same root.

1. patrimony(PAT′-rə-mō-nee)—an inheritance from one's father. The -mony comes from the same root that gives us money, namely Juno Moneta, the Roman goddess who guarded the temples of finance.

The adjective is patrimonial(pat´-rə-MŌ´-nee-əl).

2. patronymic(pat´-rə-NIM´-ik)—a name formed on the father's name, like Johnson (son of John), Martinson, Aaronson, etc. The word combines pater, patris with Greek onyma, name. Onyma plus the Greek prefix syn-, with or together, forms synonym(SIN´-ə-nim), a word of the same name (or meaning), etymologically "a together name." Onyma plus the prefix anti-, against, forms antonym(AN´-tə-nim), a word of opposite meaning, etymologically "an against name." Onyma plus Greek homos, the same, forms homonym(HOM´-ə-nim), a word that sounds like another but has a different meaning and spelling, like bare—bear, way—weight, to—too—two, etc., etymologically "a same name." A homonym is more accurately called a homophone(HOM´-ə-fōn´), a combination of homos, the same, and phone, sound. The adjective form of synonym is synonymous(sə-NON´-ə-məs). Can you write, and pronounce, the adjective derived from:

antonym? _____

homonym? _____

homophone? _____

3. paternity(pə-TUR´-nə-tee)—fatherhood, as to question someone's paternity, to file a paternity suit in order to collect child support from the assumed, accused, or self-acknowledged father. The adjective is paternal(pə-TUR´-nəl), fatherly. Paternalism(pə-TUR´-nə-liz-əm) is the philosophy or system of governing a country, or of managing a business or institution, so that the citizens, employees, or staff are treated in a manner suggesting a father-children relationship. (Such a system sounds and often is, benign and protective, but plays havoc with the initiative, independence,

and creativity of those in subordinate roles.) The adjective is patern alistic(pə-turn´-ə-LIS´-tik).

4. patriarch(PAY´-tree-ark´)—a venerable, fatherlike old man; an old man in a ruling, fatherlike position. Here pater, patris is combined with the Greek root archein, to rule. The adjective is patriarchal (pay´-tree-AHR´-kəl), the system is a patriarchy(PAY´-tree-ahr´-kee).

5. patricide(PAT´-rə-sīd´)—the killing of one's father. Pater, patris combines with -cide, a suffix derived from the Latin verb caedo, to kill. The adjective is patricidal(pat-rə-SĪ´-dəl).

This list does not exhaust the number of words built on pater, father, but is sufficient to give you an idea of how closely related many English words are. In your reading you will come across other words containing the letters pater or patr—you will be able to figure them out once you realize that the base is the word father. You might, if you feel ambitious, puzzle out the relationship to the "father idea" in the following words, checking with a dictionary to see how good your linguistic intuition is:

1. patrician	4. patronizing(adj.)
2. patron	5. paterfamilias
3. patronize	6. padre

● the old lady

Pater, patris is father. Mater, matris is mother.

For example:

1. matriarch(MAY´-tree-ahrk´)—the mother-ruler; the "mother person" that controls a large household, tribe, or country. This word, like patriarch, is built on root archein, to rule. During the reign of Queen Elizabeth or Queen Victoria, England was a

matriarchy(MAY´-tree-ahr´-kee). Can you figure out the adjective f orm? _____.

2. maternity(mə-TUR´-nə-tee)—motherhood

3. maternal(mə-TURN´-əl)—motherly

4. matron(MAY´-trən)—an older woman, one sufficiently mature to be a mother. The adjective matronly(MAY´-trən-lee) conjures up for many people a picture of a woman no longer in the glow of youth and possibly with a bit of added weight in the wrong places, so this word should be used with caution; it may be hazardous to your health if the lady you are so describing is of a tempestous nature, or is a virago.

5. alma mater(AL´-mə MAY´-tər or AHL´-mə MAH´-tər)—etymologically, "soul mother"; actually, the school or college from which one has graduated, and which in a sense is one's intellectual mother.

6. matrimony(MAT´-rə-mō-nee)—marriage. Though this word is similar to patrimony in spelling, it does not refer to money, as patrimony does; unless, that is, you are cynical enough to believe that people marry for money. As the language was growing, marriage and children went hand in hand—it is therefore not surprising that the word for marriage should be built on the Latin root for mother. Of course, times have changed, but the sexist nature of the English language has not. The noun suffix -mony indicates state, condition, or result, as in sanctimony, parsimony, etc. The adjective is matrimonial(mat´-rə-MŌ´-nee-əl).

7. matricide(MAT´-rə-sīd´)—the killing of one's mother. The adjective?

_____.

☻ murder most foul. . .

Murder unfortunately is an integral part of human life, so there is a word for almost every kind of killing you can think of. Let's look at some of them.

1. suicide($\overline{SOO}'$-ə-sīd′)—killing oneself (intentionally); -cide plus sui, of oneself. This is both the act and the person who has been completely successful in performing the act (partially doesn't count); also, in colloquial usage, suicide is a verb. The adjective?

   _____.

2. fratricide(FRAT′-rə-sīd′)—the killing of one's brother; -cide plus frater, fratris, brother. The adjective? _____.

3. sororicide(sə-RAWR′-ə-sīd′)—the killing of one's sister; -cide plus soror, sister. The adjective? _____.

4. homicide(HOM′-ə-sīd′)—the killing of a human being; -cide plus homo, person. In law, homicide is the general term for any slaying. If intent and premeditation can be proved, the act is murder and punishable as such. If no such intent is present, the act is called manslaughter and receives a lighter punishment. Thus, if your mate/lover/spouse makes your life unbearable and you slip some arsenic into his/her coffee one bright morning, you are committing murder—that is, if he/she succumbs. On the other hand, if you run your victim down—quite accidentally—with your car, bicycle, or wheelchair, with no intent to kill, you will be accused of manslaughter—that is, if death results and if you can prove you didn't really mean it. It's all rather delicate, however, and you might do best to put thoughts of justifiable homicide out of your mind. The adjective? _____.

5. regicide(REJ′-ə-sīd′)—the killing of one's king, president, or other

governing official. Booth committed regicide when he assassinated Abraham Lincoln. Adjective? _____. Derivation: Latin rex, regis, king, plus -cide.

6. uxoricide(uk-SAWR´-ə-sīd´)—the killing of one's wife. Adjective? _____. Derivation: Latin uxor, wife, plus -cide.

7. mariticide(mə-RIT´-ə-sīd´)—the killing of one's husband. Adjective? _____. Derivation: Latin maritus, husband, plus -cide.

8. infanticide(in-FAN´-tə-sīd´)—the killing of a newborn child. Adjective? _____. Derivation: Latin infans, infantis, baby, plus -cide.

9. genocide(JEN´-ə-sīd´)—the killing of a whole race or nation. This is a comparatively new word, coined in 1944 by a UN official named Raphael Lemkin, to refer to the mass murder of the Jews, Poles, etc. ordered by Hitler. Adjective? _____. Derivation: Greek genos, race, kind, plus -cide.

10. parricide(PAIR´-ə-sīd´)—the killing of either or both parents. Adjective? _____. Lizzie Borden was accused of, and tried for, parricide in the 1890s, but was not convicted. A bit of doggerel that was popular at the time, and, so I have been told, little girls jumped rope to, went somewhat as follows:

> Lizzie Borden took an ax
> And gave her mother forty whacks—
> And when she saw what she had done,
> She gave her father forty-one.

ORIGIN

◉ brothers and sisters, wives and husbands

Frater, brother; soror, sister; uxor, wife; and maritus, husband—these roots are the source of a number of additional English words:

1. to fraternize(FRAT´-ər-nīz´)—etymologically, to have a brotherly relationship (with). This verb may be used to indicate social intercourse between people, irrespective of sex, as in, "Members of the faculty often fraternized after school hours."

   Additionally, and perhaps more commonly, there may be the implication of having a social relationship with one's subordinates in an organization, or even with one's so-called inferiors, as in, "The president of the college was reluctant to fraternize with faculty members, preferring to keep all her contacts with them on an exclusively professional basis"; or as in, "The artist enjoyed fraternizing with thieves, drug addicts, prostitutes, and pimps, partly out of social perversity, partly to find interesting faces to put in his paintings."

   The verb also gained a new meaning during and after World war II, when soldiers of occupying armies had sexual relations with the women of conquered countries, as in, "Military personnel were strictly forbidden to fraternize with the enemy." (How euphemistic can you get?)

   Can you write the noun form of fraternize? _____.

2. fraternal(frə-TUR´-nəl)—brotherly. The word also designates non-

identical (twins).

3. fraternity(frə-TUR´-nə-tee)—a men's organization in a high school or college, often labeled with Greek letters (the Gamma Delta Epsilon Fraternity); or any group of people of similar interests or profession (the medical fraternity, the financial fraternity).

4. sorority(sə-RAWR´-ə-tee)—a women's organization in high school or college, again usually Greek-lettered; or any women's social club.

5. uxorious(uk-SAWR´-ee-əs)—an adjective describing a man who excessively, even absurdly, caters to, dotes on, worships and submits to the most outlandish or outrageous demands of, his wife. This word is not synonymous with henpecked, as the henpecked husband is dominated by his wife, perhaps because of his own fear or weakness, while the uxorious husband is dominated only by his neurosis, and quite likely the wife finds his uxoriousness(uk-SAW R´-ee-əs-nəs) comical or a pain in the neck. (There can, indeed, be too much of a good thing!)

6. uxorial—pertaining to, characteristic of, or befitting, a wife, as uxorial duties, privileges, attitudes, etc.

7. marital(MAIR´-ə-təl)—etymologically, pertaining or referring to, or characteristic of, a husband; but the meaning has changed to include the marriage relationship of both husband and wife (don't ever let anyone tell you that our language is not sexist!), as marital duties, obligations, privileges, arguments, etc. Hence extramarital is literally outside the marriage, as in extramarital affairs (hanky-panky- with someone other than one's spouse). And premarital (Latin prefix pre-, before) describes events that occur before a planned marriage, as premarital sex, a premarital agreement as to the division of property, etc.

⊜ of cabbages and kings (without the cabbage)

Rex, regis is Latin for king. Tyrannosaurus rex was the king (i.e., the largest) of the dinosaurs (etymologically, "king of the tyrant lizards"). Dogs are often named Rex to fool them into thinking they are kings rather than slaves. And regal(REE´-gəl) is royal, or fi for a king, hence magnificent, stately, imperious, splendid, etc., as in regal bearing or manner, a regal mansion, a regal reception, etc. The noun is regality(rə-GAL´-ə-tee).

Regalia(rə-GAYL´-yə), a plural noun, designated the emblems or insignia or dress of a king, and now refers to any impressively formal clothes; or, more commonly, to the decorations, insignia, or uniform of a rank, position, office, social club, etc. "The Shriners were dressed in full regalia," "The five-star general appeared in full regalia," etc.

⊜ "madness" of all sorts

The monomaniac develops an abnormal obsession in respect to one particular thing(Greek monos, one), but is otherwise normal. The obsession itself, or the obsessiveness, is monomania(mon´-ə-MAY´-nee-ə), the adjective is monomaniacal(mon´-ə-mə-NĪ´-ə-kəl). Monomaniacal, like the adjective forms of various other manias, is tricky to pronounce—practice carefully to make sure you can say it correctly without stuttering.

Psychology recognizes other abnormal states, all designating obsessions, and built on Greek mania, madness.

1. dipsomania(dip´-sə-MAY´-nee-ə)—morbid compulsion to keep on absorbing alcoholic beverages (Greek dipsa, thirst). The dipsomaniac has been defined as the person for whom one drink is too many, a thousand not enough. Recent investigations

suggest that dipsomania, or alcoholism, may not necessarily be caused by anxieties or frustrations, but possibly by a metabolic or physiological disorder. Adjective: dipsomaniacal(dip´-sə-mə-NĪ´-ə-kəl).

2. kleptomania(klep´-tə-MAY´-nee-ə)—morbid compulsion to steal, not from any economic motive, but simply because the urge to take another's possessions is irresistible. The kleptomaniac (Greek klepte, thief) may be wealthy, and yet be an obsessive shoplifter. The kleptomaniac, for reasons that psychologists are still arguing about, is more often a female than a male, and may pinch her best friend's valueless trinket, or a cheap ashtray or salt shaker from a restaurant, not because she wants, let alone needs, the article, but because she apparently can't help herself; she gets carried away. (When she arrives home, she may toss it in a drawer with other loot, and never look at it again.) Can you write (and correctly pronounce) the adjective? _____.

3. pyromania(pī´-rə-MAY´-nee-ə)—morbid compulsion to set fired. Pyromania should not be confused with incendiarism(in-SEN´-dee-ə-riz-əm), which is the malicious and deliberate burning of another's property, and is not a compulsive need to see the flames and enjoy the thrill of the heat and the smoke. Some pyromaniacs join volunteer fire companies, often heroically putting out the very blazes they themselves have set. An incendiary(in-SEN´-dee-air-ee) is antisocial, and usually sets fired revenge. Either of these two dangerous character is called, colloquially, a "firebug."

In law, setting fired to another's, or to one's own, property for the purpose of economic gain (such as the collection of the proceeds of an insurance policy) is called arson(AHR´-sən) and is a felony.

The pyromaniac sets fire for the thrill; the incendiary for revenge; the arsonist(AHR´-sə-nist) for money. Pyromania is built on Greek pyros, fire; incendiarism on Latin incendo, incensus, to set fire; arson on Latin ardo, arsus, to burn. Can you write, and pronounce, the adjective form of pyromaniac?_____.

4. megalomania(meg´-ə-lə-MAY´-nee-ə)—morbid delusions of grandeur, power, importance, godliness, etc. Jokes accusing the heads of governments of megalomania are common. Here's an old chestnut from the forties:

> Churchill, Roosevelt, and Stalin were talking about their dreams.
>
> Churchill: I dreamed last night that God had made me Prime Minister of the whole world.
>
> Roosevelt: I dreamed that God had made me President of the whole world.
>
> Stalin: How could you gentlemen have such dreams? I didn't dream of offering you those positions!

Hitler, Napoleon, and Alexander the Great have been called megalomaniacs—all three certainly had delusions about their invincibility.

Can you write (and pronounce correctly!) the adjective derived from megalomaniac? _____.

Megalomania is built on Greek megas, great, big, large, plus mania. Can you think of the word for what someone speaks through to make the sound (phone) of his voice greater? _____.

5. nymphomania(nim´-fə-MAY´-nee-ə)—morbid, incessant, uncontrollable, and intense desire, on the part of a female, for sexual intercourse (from Greek nymphe, bride, plus mania).

The person? _____.

The adjective? _____.

6. satyromania(sə-teer´-ə-MAY´-nee-ə)—the same morbid, incessant, etc. desire on the part of a male (from Greek *satyros*, satyr, plus *mania*).

The person? _____.

The adjective? _____.

A satyr(SAY´-tər) was a mythological Greek god, notorious for lechery. He had horns, pointed ears, and the legs of a goat; the rest of him was in human form. Satyromania is also called satyriasis(sat´-ə-RĪ´-ə-sis).

☻ and now phobias

So much for maniacs. There is another side to the coin. Just as personality disorders can cause morbid attraction toward certain things or acts (stealing, fire, power, sex, etc.), so also other emotional ills can cause violent or morbid repulsions to certain conditions, thing, or situations. There are people who have irrational and deep-seated dread of cats, dogs, fire, the number thirteen, snakes, thunder or lightning, carious colors, and so on almost without end: Such morbid dread of fear is called, in the language of psychology, a phobia, and we might pause to investigate the three most common ones. These are:

1. claustrophobia(klaw´-strə-FŌ´-bee-ə)—morbid dread of being physically hemmed in, of enclosed spaces, of crowds, etc. From Latin *claustrum*, enclosed place, plus Greek *phobia*, morbid fear. The person: claustrophobe(KLAW´-strə-fōb´). Adjective claustroph obic(klaw´-strə-FŌ´-bik).

2. agoraphobia(ag´-ə-rə-FŌ´-bee-ə)—morbid dread of open space, the reverse of claustrophobia. People suffering from agoraphobia prefer to stay shut in their homes as much as possible, and become panic-stricken in such places as open fields, large public buildings, airport terminals, etc. From Greek agora, market place, plus phobia.

The person? _____.

The adjective? _____.

3. acrophobia(ak´-rə-FŌ´-bee-ə)—morbid dread of high places. The victims of this fear will not climb ladders or trees, or stand on tops of furniture. They refuse to go onto the roof of a building or look out the window of one of the higher floors. From Greek akros, highest, plus phobia.

The person? _____.

The adjective? _____.

⟨Word Power⟩ p.338

ORIGIN

◉ no reverence

The iconoclast sneer at convention and tradition, attempts to expose our cherished beliefs, our revered traditions, or our stereotypical thinking as shams and myths. H. L. Mencken was the great iconoclast of the 1920s; Tom Wolfe (The Kandy-Kolored Tangerine-Flake Streamline Baby), of the 1960s. Adolescence is that confused and rebellious time of life in which iconoclasm(ī-KON′-ə-klaz′-əm) is quite normal—indeed the adolescent who is not iconoclastic(ī-kon′-ə-KLAS′-tik) to some degree might be considered either immature or maladjusted. The words are from eikon, a religious image, plus klaein, to break. Iconoclasm is not of course restricted to religion.

∞ is there a God?

Atheist combines the Greek negative prefix a- with theos, God. Do not confuse atheism(AY′-thee-iz-əm) with agnosticism(ag-NOS′-tə-siz-əm), the philosophy that claims that God in unknowable, that He may or may not exist, and that human beings can never come to a final conclusion about Him The agnostic(ag-NOS′-tik) does not deny the existence of a deity, as does the atheist, but simply holds that no proof can be adduced one way or the other.

∞ how to know

Agnostic (which is also an adjective) is built on the Greek root gnostos, known, and the negative prefix a-. An agnostic claims that all but material phenomena is unknown, and, indeed, unknowable.

A diagnosis(dī′-əg-NŌ′-sis), constructed on the allied Greek root gnosis, knowledge, plus dia-, through, is a knowing through examination or testing. A prognosis(prog-NŌ′-sis), on the other hand, is etymologically a knowing beforehand, hence a prediction, generally, but not solely, as to the course of a disease. (The Greek prefix pro-, before, plus gnosis.)

Thus, you may say to a doctor: "What's the diagnosis, Doc?"

"Diabetes."

Then you say, "And what's the prognosis?"

"If you take insulin and watch your diet, you'll soon be as good as new."

The doctor's prognosis, then, is a forecast of the development or trend of a disease. The doctor knows beforehand, from previous similar cases, what to expect.

The verb form of diagnosis is diagnose(dī´-əg-NŌS´); the verb form of prognosis is prognosticate(prog-NOS´-tə-kayt´). To use the verb prognosticate correctly, be sure that your meaning involves the forecasting of developments from a consideration of symptoms or conditions—whether the problem is physical, mental, political, economic, psychological, or what have you.

In school, you doubtless recall taking diagnostic(dī´-əg-NOS´-tik) tests; these measured not what you were supposed to have learned during the semester, but your general knowledge in a field, so that your teachers would know what remedial steps to take, just as doctors rely on their diagnosis to decide what drugs or treatments to prescribe.

In a reading center, various diagnostic machines and tests are used—these tell the clinician what is wrong with a student's reading and what measures will probably increase such a student's reading efficiency.

The medical specialist in diagnosis is a diagnostician(dī´-əg-nos-TISH´-ən). The noun form of the verb prognosticate is prognostication(prog-nos´-tə-KAY´-shən)

● getting back to God

Theos, God, is also found in:

1. Monotheism(MON´-ə-thee-iz-əm)—belief in one God. (Monos,

one, plus theos, God.) Using atheism, atheist, and atheistic as a model, write the word for the person who believes in one God: _____. The adjective? _____.

2. Polytheism(POL´-ee-thee-iz-əm)—belief in many gods, as in ancient Greece or Rome. (Polys, many, plus theos.) The person with such a belief? _____. The adjective? _____.

3. Pantheism(PAN´-thee-iz-əm)—belief that God is not in man's image, but is a combination of all forces of the universe. (Pan, all, plus theos.) The person? _____. The adjective? _____.

4. Theology(thee-OL´-ə-jee)—the study of God and religion. (Theos plus logos, science or study.) The student is a theologian (thee´-ə-LŌ´-jən), the adjective is theological(thee´-ə-LOJ´-ə-kəl).

☻ of sex and the tongue

A lecher practices lechery(LECH´-ər-ee). The derivation is Old French lechier, to lick. The adjective lecherous(LECH´-ə-rəs) has many close or not-so-close synonyms, most of them also, and significantly, starting with the letter l, a sound formed with the tongue, supposedly the seat of sensation.

1. libidinous(lə-BID´-ə-nəs)—from libido, pleasure.

2. lascivious(lə-SIV´-ee-əs)—from lascivia, wantonness.

3. lubricious(loo-BRISH´-əs)—from lubicus, slippery, the same root found in lubricate. The noun is lubricity(loo-BRISH´-ə-tee).

4. licentious(lī-SEN´-shəs)—from licere, to be permitted, the root from which we get license, etymologically, "permission,: and illicit, etymologically, "not permitted."

5. lewd—the previous four words derive from Latin, but this one is from Anglo-Saxon lewed, vile.

6. lustful—from an Anglo-Saxon word meaning pleasure, desire. Noun: lust.

Libidinous, lascivious, lubricious, licentious, lewd, lecherous, lustful are seven adjectives that indicate sexual desire and/or activity. The implication of all seven words is more or less derogatory.

Each adjective become a noun with the addition of the noun suffix -ness; lubricity and lust are alternate noun forms of two of the adjectives.

☻ of sex and the itch

Prurient(PROO'-ee-ənt), from Latin prurio, to itch, to long for, describes someone who is filled with great sexual curiosity, desire, longing, etc. Can you form the noun? _____.

Pruritis(proo-Ī'-tis), from the same root, is a medical condition in which the skin is very itchy, but without a rash or eruptions. (Scratch enough, of course, as you will be irresistibly tempted to do, and something like a rash will soon appear.) The adjective is pruritic(proo-IT'-ik).

☻ under and over

Hypochondria(hī-pə-KON'-dree-ə) is built on two Greek roots: hypos, under, and chondros, the cartilage of the breastbone. This may sound farfetched until you realize that under the breastbone is the abdomen; the ancient Greeks believed that morbid anxiety about one's health arose in the abdomen—and no one is more morbidly, unceasingly, and unhappily anxious about health than the hypochondriac.

Hypochondriac is also an adjective—an alternate and more commonly used adjective form is hypochondriacal(hī′-pə-kən-DRĪ′-ə-kəl).

Hypos, under, is a useful root to know. The hypodermic needle penetrates under the skin; a hypothyroid person has an under-working thyroid gland; hypotension is abnormally low blood pressure.

On the other hand, hyper is the Greek root meaning over. The hypercritical person is excessively fault-finding; hyperthyroidism is an overworking of the thyroid gland; hypertension is high blood pressure; and you can easily figure out the meanings of hyperacidity, hyperactive, hypersensitive, etc. The adjective forms of hypotension and hypertension are hypotensive and hypertensive.

MAGAZINES THAT WILL HELP YOU

When a pregnant woman takes calcium pills, she must make sure also that her diet is rich in vitamin D, since this vitamin makes the absorption of the calcium possible. In building your vocabulary by learning great quantities of new words, you too must take a certain vitamin, metaphorically speaking, to help you absorb, understand, and remember these words. This vitamin is reading—for it is in books and magazines that you will find the words that we have been discussing in these pages. To learn new words without seeing them applied in the context of your reading is to do only half the job and to run the risk of gradually forgetting the additions to your vocabulary. To combine your vocabulary-building with increased reading is to make assurance doubly sure.

You are now so alert to the words and roots we have discussed that you will find that most of your reading will be full of the new words you have learned—and every time you do see one of the words used in context in a book or magazine, you will understand it more fully and will b e taking long steps toward using it yourself.

Among magazines, I would like particularly to recommend the following, which will act both to keep you mentally alert and to set the new words you are learning:

1. Harper's Magazine

These periodicals are aimed at the alert, verbally sophisticated, educated reader; you will see in them, without fail, most of the words you have been studying in this book—not to mention hosts of other valuable words you will want to add to your vocabulary, many of which you will be able to figure out once you recognize their etymological structure.

SOME INTERESTING DERIVATIONS

PEOPLE WHO MADE OUR LANGUAGE

Bloomers

Mrs. Elizabeth Smith Miller invented them in 1849, and showed a working model to a famous women's rights advocate, Amelia J. Bloomer. Amelia was fascinated by the idea of garments that were both modest (they then reached right down to the ankles) and convenient— and promptly sponsored them. . .

Boycott

Charles C. Boycott was an English land agent whose difficult duty it was to collect high rents from Irish farmers. In protest, the farmers ostracized him, not even allowing him to make purchases in town or hire workers to harvest his crops.

Marcel

Marcel was an ingenious Parisian hairdresser who felt he could improve on the button curls popular in 1875. He did, and made a fortune.

Silhouette

Finance Minister of France just before the Revolution, Etienne de Silhouette advocated the simple life, so that excess money could go into the treasury instead of into luxurious living. And the profile is the simplest form of portraiture, if you get the connection.

Derrick

A seventeenth-century English hangman, Derrick by name, hoisted to their death some of the most notorious criminals of the day.

Sadist

Because Count de Sade, an eighteenth-century Frenchman, found his greatest delight in torturing friends and mistresses, the term sadist was derived from his name. His works shocked his nation and the world by the alarming frankness with which he described his morbid and bloodthirsty cruelty.

Galvanism

Luigi Galvani, the Italian physiologist, found by accident that an electrically charged scalpel could send a frog's corpse into muscular convulsions. Expressing further, he eventually discovered the principles of chemically produced electricity. His name is responsible not only for the technical expressions galvanism, galvanized iron, and galvanometer, but also for that highly graphic phrase, "galvanized into action."

Guppies

In 1868, R. J. Lechmere Guppy, president of the Scientific Association of Trinidad, sent some specimens of a tiny tropical fish to the British Museum. Ever since, fish of this species have been called guppies.

Nicotine

Four hundred years ago, Jean Nicot, a French ambassador, bought some tobacco seeds from a Flemish trader. Nicot's successful efforts to popularize the plant in Europe brought him linguistic immortality.

PLACE THAT MADE OUR LANGUAGE

Bayonne, France

Where first was manufactured the daggerlike weapon that fits over the muzzle end of a rifle—the bayonet.

Cantalupo, Italy

The first place in Europe to grow those luscious melons we now call cantaloupes.

Calicut, India

The city from which we first imported a kind of cotton cloth now known as calico.

Tuxedo Park, New York

In the country club of his exclusive and wealthy community, the short (no tails) dinner coat for men, or tuxedo, was popularized.

Egypt

It was once supposed that the colorful, fortunetelling wanderers, or Gypsies, hailed from this ancient land.

Damascus, Syria

Where an elaborately patterned silk, damask, was first made.

Tzu-t'ing, China

Once a great seaport in Fukien Province. Marco Polo called it Zaitun, and in time a silk fabric made there was called satin.

Frankfurt, Germany

Where the burghers once greatly enjoyed their smoked beef and pork sausages, which we now ask for in delicatessen stores and supermarkets by the name of frankfurters, franks, or hot dogs.

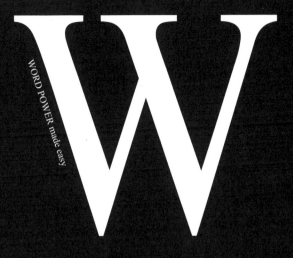

CHAPTER
9

HOW TO FLATTER YOUR FRIENDS

Terms for describing friendliness, energy, honesty, mental keenness,
bravery, charm, sophistication, etc. Excursions into expressive words that
refer to ways of eating and drinking, believing and disbelieving, looking and
seeing, facing the present, past, and future, and living in the city and country.
How the new words you are learning have begun to influence your thinking.

ORIGIN

⊛ eat, drink, and be merry

The Latin verb vivo, to live, and the noun vita, life, are the source of a number of important English words.

Convivo is the Latin verb to live together; from this, in Latin, was formed the noun convivium (don't get impatient; we'll be back to English directly), which meant a feast or banquet; and from convivium we get our English word convivial, an adjective that describes the kind of person who likes to attend feasts and banquets, enjoying (and supplying) the jovial good fellowship characteristic of such gatherings.

Using the suffix -ity can you write the noun form of the adjective convivial? _____. (Can you pronounce it?)

⊛ living it up

Among many others, the following English words derive from Latin vivo, to live:

1. vivacious(vī-VAY´-shəs)—full of the joy of living; animated; peppy—a vivacious personality. Noun: vivacity(vī-VAS´-ə-tee). You can, as you know, also add -ness to any adjective to form a noun. Write the alternate noun form of vivacious: _____.

2. vivid—possessing the freshness of life; strong; sharp—a vivid imagination; a vivid color. Add -ness to form the noun: _____.

3. revive(rə-VĪV´)—bring back to life. In the 1960s, men's fashions of the twenties were revived. Noun: revival(rə-VĪ´-vəl).

4. vivisection(viv´-ə-SEK´-shən)—operating on a live animal. Sect-
is from a Latin verb meaning to cut. Vivisection is the process
of experimenting on live animals to discover causes and cures of
disease. Antivivisectionists object to the procedure, though many
of our most important medical discoveries were made through
vivisection.

5. Viviparous(vī-VIP´-ər-əs)—producing live babies. Human beings
and most other mammals are viviparous. Viviparous is contrasted
to oviparous(ō-VIP´-ər-əs), producing young from eggs. Most fish,
fowl, and other lower forms of life are oviparous.

The combining root in both these adjectives is Latin pareo, to give
birth (parent comes from the same root). In oviparous, the first two
syllables derive from Latin ovum, egg.

Ovum, egg, is the source of oval and ovoid, egg-shaped;
ovulate(Ō´-vyə-layt´), to release an egg from the ovary:
ovum(Ō-vəm), the female germ cell which, when fertilized by a
sperm, develops into an embyro, then into a fetus(FEE´-təs), and
finally, in about 280 days in the case of humans, is born as an
infant. The adjective form of ovary is ovarian(ō-VAIR´-ee-ən); of
fetus, fetal(FEE´-təl). Can you write the noun form of the verb ovul
ate? _____.

Love, you may or may not be surprised to hear, also comes from
ovum.

No, not the kind of love you're thinking of. Latin ovum became
oeuf in French, or with "the" preceding the noun (the egg), l'ouef,
pronounced something like LO͡OF. Zero (picture it for a moment) is
shaped like an egg(0), so if your score in tennis is fifteen, and your
opponent's is zero, you shout triumphantly, fifteen love! Let's go!"

☯ more about life

Latin vita, life, is the origin of:

1. vital(VĪ´-təl)—essential to life; of crucial importance—a vital matter; also full of life, strength, vigor, etc. Add the suffix -ity to form the noun : _____. Add a verb suffix to construct the verb: _____ (meaning: to give life to). Finally, write the noun derived from the verb you have constructed: _____.

2. Revitalize(ree-VĪ´-tə-līz´) is constructed from the prefix re-, again, back, the root vita, and the verb suffix. Meaning? _____. Can you write the noun formed from this verb? _____.

3. The prefix de- has a number of meanings, one of which is essentially negative, as in defrost, decompose, declassify, etc. Using this prefix, can you write a verb meaning to rob of life, to take life from? _____. Now writhe the noun form of this verb: _____.

4. Vitamin—one of the many nutritional elements on which life is dependent. Good eyesight requires vitamin A (found, for example, in carrots); strong bones need vitamin D (found in sunlight and cod-liver oil); etc.

Vitalize, revitalize, and devitalize are used figuratively—for example, a program or plan is vitalized, revitalized, or devitalized, according to how it's handled.

☯ French life

Sometimes, instead of getting our English words directly from Latin, we work through one of the Latin-derived or Romance languages. (As you will recall, the Romance languages—French, Spanish, Italian,

Portuguese, and Romanian—are so called because they were originally dialects of the old Roman tongue. English, by the way, is not a Romance language, but a Teutonic one. Our tongue is a development of a German dialect imposed on the natives of Britain by the Angles, Saxons, and Jutes of early English history. Though we have taken over into English more than 50 per cent of the Latin vocabulary and almost 30 per cent of the classical Greek vocabulary as roots and prefixes, our basic language is nevertheless German).

The French, using the same Latin root vivo, to live, formed two expressive phrases much used in English. French pronunciation is, of course, tricky, and if you are not at least superficially acquainted with that language, your pronunciation may sound a bit awkward to the sophisticated ear—but try it anyway. These phrases are:

1. joie de vivre—pronounced something like zhwahd´-VEEV´(zh is identical in sound to the s of pleasure).

   Literally joy of living, this phrase describes an immense delight in being alive, an effervescent keenness for all the daily activities that human beings indulge in. People who possess joie de vivre are never moody, depressed, bored, or apathetic—on the contrary, they are full of sparkle, eager to engage in all group activities, and, most important, always seem to be having a good time, no matter what they are doing. Joie de vivre is precisely the opposite of ennui (this is also a word of French origin, but is easy to pronounce: AHN´-wee), which is a feeling of boredom, discontent, or weariness resulting sometimes from having a jaded, oversophisticated appetite, sometimes from just finding all of life tedious and unappetizing, and sometimes implying in addition physical lassitude and general inactivity. Young children and simple people rarely experience ennui—to them life is always exciting, always new.

2. bon vivant, pronounced something like BŌNG´-vee-VAHNG´—the -NG a muted nasal sound similar to the -ng in sing.

A bon vivant is a person who lives luxuriously, especially in respect to rich food, good liquor, expensive theater parties, operas, and other accouterments of upper-class life. Bon vivant means, literally, a good liver; actually, a high liver, one who lives a luxurious life. When you think of a bon vivant (usually, language being sexist, a male), you get the picture of someone attired in top hat, "soup and fish" or tuxedo, raising his cane to call a taxi while a beautiful, evening-gowned and sophisticated-looking woman, sparkling in diamonds and furs, waits at his side. They're going to a champagne and partridge supper at an outrageously expensive restajrant, etc.— fill in your own details of the high life.

The bon vivant is of course a convivial person—and also likely to be a gourmet(gōor-MAY´), another word from French.

☻ food and how to enjoy it

The gourmand(GOOR´-mənd) enjoys food with a sensual pleasure. To gourmands the high spots of the day are the times for breakfast, lunch, dinner, and midnight supper; in short, they like to eat, but the eating must be good. The verb form, gormandize(GAWR´-mən-dīz´), however, has suffered a degeneration in meaning—it signifies to stuff oneself like a pig.

A gourmand is significantly different from a gourmet, who has also a keen interest in food and liquor, but is much more fastidious, is more of a connoisseur, has a most discerning palate for delicate tastes, flavors, and differences; goes in for rare delicacies (like hummingbirds' tongues and other such absurdities); and approaches the whole business from a scientific, as well as a sensual, viewpoint. Gourmet is always a complimentary term, gourmand somewhat less so.

The person who eats voraciously, with no discernment whatever, but merely for the purpose of stuffing himself ("I know I haven't had enough to eat till I feel sick"), is called a glutton(GLUT′-ən)—obviously a highly derogatory term. The verb gluttonize is stronger than gormandize; the adjective gluttonous(GLUT′-ə-nəs) is about the strongest epithet you can apply to someone whose voracious eating habits you find repulsive. Someone who has a voracious, insatiable appetite for money, sex, punishment, etc. is also called a glutton.

⟨Word Power⟩ p.378

ORIGIN

☯ no fatigue

Indefatigable is a derived form of fatigue—in- is a negative prefix, the suffix -able means able to be; hence, literally, indefatigable means unable to be fatigued. The noun is indefatigability(in′-də-fat′-ə-gə-BIL′-ə-tee).

☯ how simple can one be?

Ingenuous is a complimentary term, though hits synonyms naive, gullible, and credulous are faintly derogatory.

To call people ingenuous implies that they are frank, open, artless—in other words, not likely to try to put anything over on you, nor apt to hide feelings or thoughts that more sophisticated persons would consider it wise, tactful, or expedient to conceal.

Ingenuous should not be confused with ingenious(in-JEEN′-yəs)—note the slight difference in spelling—which on the contrary means shrewd, clever, inventive. The noun form of ingenuous is ingenuousness; of ingenious, ingenuity(in′-jə-NOO′-ə-tee) or ingeniousness.

To call people naive(nah-EEV′) is to imply that they have not learned they ways of the world, and are therefore idealistic and trusting beyond the point of safety; such idealism and trust have probably come from ignorance or inexperience. The noun is naiveté(nah-eev-TAY′).

Credulous(KREJ′-ə-ləs) implies a willingness to believe almost anything, no matter how fantastic. Credulity(krə-JOO′-lə-tee), like naiveté, usually results, again, from ignorance or inexperience, or perhaps from an inability to believe that human beings are capable of lying.

Gullible(GUL′-ə-bəl) means easily tricked, easily fooled, easily imposed on. It is a stronger word than credulous and is more derogatory. Gullibility(gul′-ə-BIL′-ə-tee) results more from stupidity than from ignorance or inexperience.

These four synonyms, ingenuous, naive, credulous, and gullible, are fairly close, but they contain areas of distinction worth remembering. Let's review them:

1. ingenuous—frank, not given to concealment

2. naive—inexperienced, unsophisticated, trusting

3. credulous—willing to believe; not suspicious or skeptical

4. gullible—easily tricked

🏵 belief and disbelief

Credulous comes from Latin credo, to believe, the same root found in credit (if people believe in your honesty, they will extend credit to you; they will credit what you say). -Ous, is an adjective suffix that usually signifies full of. So, strictly, credulous means full of believingness.

Do not confuse credulous with credible(KRED′-ə-bəl). In the latter word we see combined the root credo, believe, with -ible, a suffix meaning can be. Something credible can be believed.

Let's chart some differences:

Credulous listeners—those who fully believe what they hear

A credible story—one that can be believed

An incredulous(in-KREJ′-ə-ləs) attitude—an attitude of skepticism, of non-belief

An incredible(in-KRED′-ə-bəl) story—one that cannot be believed

Incredible characters—persons who are so unique that you can scarcely believe they exist.

Nouns are formed as follows:

credulous-credulity (krə-JOO′-lə-tee)

incredulous-incredulity (in-krə-JOO′-lə-tee)

credible-credibility (kred'-ə-BIL′-ə-tee)

incredible-incredibility (in-kred′-ə-BIL′-ə-tee)

To check your understanding of these distinctions, try the next test.

CAN YOU USE THESE WORDS CORRECTLY?

Use credulous, credible or corresponding negative or noun forms in the following sentences:

1. She listened _____ly to her husband's confession of his frequent infidelity, for she had always considered him a paragon of moral uprightness.

2. He told his audience an _____ and fantastic story of his narrow escapes.

3. He'll believe you—he's very _____.

4. Make your characters more _____ if you want your readers to believe in them.

5. We listened dumb-struck, full of _____, to the shocking details of corruption and vice.

6. He has the most _____ good luck.

7. The _____ of it! How can such things happen?

8. Naive people accept with complete _____, whatever anyone tells them.

9. "Do you believe me?" "Sure—your story is _____ enough."

10. I'm not objecting to the total _____ of your story, but only to your thinking that I'm   enough to believe it!

☻ what people believe in

Credo, to believe, is the origin of four other useful English words.

1. Credo(KREE´-do)—personal belief, code of ethics; the principles by which people guide their actions.

2. Creed—a close synonym of credo; in addition, a religious belief, such as Catholicism, Judaism, Protestantism, Hinduism, etc.

3. Credence(KREE´-dəns)—belief, as in, "I place no credence in his stories." or "Why should I give any credence to what you say?"

4. Credentials(krə-DEN′-shəls)—a document or documents proving a person's right to a title or privilege (i.e., a right to be believed), as in, "The new ambassador presented his credentials to the State Department."

🔗 heads and tails

We can hardly close our book on the words suggested by ingenuous without looking at the other side of the coin. If ingenuous means frank, open, then disingenuous(dis-in-JEN′-yoo-əs) should mean not frank or open. But disingenuous people are far more than simply not ingenuous. They are crafty, cunning, dishonest, artful, insincere, untrustworthy—and they are all of these while making a pretense of being simple, frank, and aboveboard. You are thinking of a wolf in sheep's clothing? It's a good analogy. Similarly, a remark may be disingenuous, as may also a statement, an attitude, a confession, etc. Add -ness to form the noun derived from disingenuous: _____.

⚛️

〈Word Power〉p.386

ORIGIN

🔗 how to look

The Latin root specto, to look, is the source of a host of common English words: spectacle, spectator, inspect, retrospect (a looking back), prospect (a looking ahead), etc. In a variant spelling, spic-, the root is found in conspicuous (easily seen or looked at), perspicacious, and perspicuous.

A perspicacious(pur´-spə-KAY´-shəs) person is keen-minded, mentally sharp, astute. Per- is a prefix meaning through; so the word etymologically means looking through (matters, etc.) keenly, intelligently. The noun: perspicacity(pur´-spə-KAS´-ə-tee). Write an alternate noun ending in -ness: _____. Perspicacity is a synonym of acumen(ə-KYOO´-mən), mental keenness, sharpness, quickness; keen insight. The root is Latin acuo, to sharpen.

☺ sharpness

From acuo, to sharpen, come such words as acute, sharp, sudden, as acute pain, an acute attack of appendicitis, acute reasoning, etc; and acupuncture(AK´-yoo-punk´-chər), the insertion of a (sharp) needle into the body for medical purposes. The noun form of acute, referring to the mind or thinking, is acuteness or acuity(ə-KYOO´-ə-tee); in other contexts, acuteness only.

Acupuncture combines acuo, to sharpen, with punctus, point. When you punctuate a sentence, you put various points (periods, commas, etc.) where needed; when lightning punctuates the storm, or when the silence is punctuated by the wailing of police sirens, again points, etymologically speaking, interrupt the atmosphere, the quiet, etc.

If you are punctual, you're right on the point of time(noun: punctuality); if you're punctilious(punk-TIL´-ee-əs), you are exact, scrupulous, very careful to observe the proper points of behavior, procedure, etc. (noun: punctiliousness). And to puncture something, of course, is to make a hole in it with a sharp point—as to puncture someone's tire, or figuratively, illusions, fantasies, or ego. Pungent(PUN´-jənt) comes from another form of the root punctus (pungo, to pierce sharply), so a pungent smell or taste is sharp, spicy, pricking the nose or taste buds, so to speak; and a pungent wit sharply pierces one's sense of humor. Can you write the noun forms of this adjective? _____ or _____.

☻ some more looking

Perspicacious should not be confused with perspicuous(pər-SPIK´-yōō-əs). Here is the important distinction:

Perspicacious means smart, sharp, able to look through and understand quickly. This adjective applies to persons, their reasoning, minds, etc.

Perspicuous is the obverse side of the coin—it means easily understood from one look, and applies to writing, style, books, and like things that have to be understood. Hence it is a synonym of clear, simple, lucid. If you write with perspicuous style, your language is clear, easy to understand. If you are perspicacious, you understand quickly, easily.

The noun form of perspicuous is perspicuity(pur´-spə-KYOO´-ə-tee), or, of course, perspicuousness.

A spectacle is something to look at; spectacles(eyeglasses) are the means by which you get a comfortable and accurate look at the world. Anything spectacular is, etymologically, worth looking at. A spectator is one who looks at what's happening. To inspect is to look into something.

Retrospect(RET´-rə-spekt´) is a backward look—generally the word is preceded by the preposition in, for instance, "His life in retrospect seemed dreary and dull," or "Most experiences seem more enjoyable in retrospect than in actuality" (retro-, backward).

Prospect(PROS´-pekt´) is a forward look; prospective(prə-SPEK´-tiv) is the adjective. What's the prospect for inflation, for world peace, for the domestic energy supply? Your prospective mother-in-law is the one you can look forward to if you marry a certain person; similarly, your prospective bridge, groom, child, job, vacation, etc. is the person, thing, or activity in the future that you look forward to. (The prefix is pro-, forward, ahead, before.)

If you enjoy looking at yourself, figuratively speaking, then you like to examine your mental processes and emotional reactions, in the intense way characteristic of the introvert. Your mind's eye turns inward, and you spend a good deal of time analyzing yourself, your character, your personality, your actions. Hence, since you look inward, you are introspective(in´-trə-SPEK´-tiv)—the prefix is intro-, inside, within. If you introspect(in´-trə-SPEKT´), you look inward and examine your inner reactions. Too much introspection(in´-trə-SPEK´-shən) or introspectiveness may lead to unhappiness or to depressing thoughts or feelings of anxiety—few people have the courage to see themselves as they really are.

There are times when you have to look around most carefully; you must then be circumspect(SUR´-kəm-spekt´)—watchful, cautious, alert(circum-, around). The noun is circumspection(sur´-kəm-SPEK´-shə n) or circumspectness. If something looks good or sensible, but actually is not, we call is specious(SPEE´-shəs). A specious argument sounds plausible, but in reality is based on an error, a fallacy, or an untruth. The noun is speciousness.

ORIGIN

❀ the great and the small

You are familiar with Latin animus, mind. Animus and a related root, anima, life principle, soul, spirit (in a sense, these meanings are all very similar), are the source of such words as animal, animate and inanimate, animated, and animation; knowing the meaning of the roots, you have a better understanding of any word built on them.

Magnanimous contains, in addition to animus, mind, the root magnus, large, great, which you recall from magniloquent. Magnanimous people have such great, noble minds or souls that they are beyond seeking pretty revenge. The noun is magnanimity(mag´-nə-NIM´-ə-tee).

On the other hand, people who have tiny, tiny minds or souls are pusillanimous(py$\overline{oo}$´-sə-LAN´-ə-məs)—Latin pusillus, tiny. Hence, they are contemptibly petty and mean. The noun is pusillanimity(py$\overline{oo}$´-sə-lə-NIM´-ə-tee).

Other words built on animus, mind:

1. unanimous(y$\overline{oo}$-NAN´-ə-məs)—of one mind. If the Supreme Court hands down a unanimous opinion, all the judges are of one mind (Latin unus, one). The noun is unanimity(y$\overline{oo}$-nə-NIM´-ə-tee).

2. equanimity(eek´-wə-NIM´-ə-tee or ek´-wə-NIM´-ə-tee)—etymologically, "equal (or balanced) mind." Hence, evenness or clamness of mind; composure. If you preserve your equanimity under trying ircumstances, you keep your temper, you do not get confused, you remain calm(Latin aequus, equal).

3. animus(AN´-ə-məs)—hostility, ill will, malevolence. Etymologically, animus is simply mind, but has degenerated, as words often do, to mean unfriendly mind. The word is most often used in a pattern like, "I bear you no animus, even though you have tried to destroy me." (Such a statement shows real magnanimity!)

4. animosity(an´-ə-MOS´-ə-tee)—ill will, hostility. An exact synonym of animus, and a more common word. It is used in patterns like, "You feel a good deal of animosity, don't you?", "There is real animosity between Bill and Ernie," "If you bear me no animosity, why do you treat me so badly?"

⊛ turning

Vesatile comes from verto, versus, to turn—versatile people can turn their hand to many things successfully. The noun is versatility(vur´-sə-TIL´-ə-tee).

⊛ Zero and the front porch

Centuries ago, in ancient Greece, the philosopher Zeno lectured on a topic that still piques the human mind, to wit: "How to Live a Happy Life." Zeno would stand on a porch (the Greek word for which is stoa) and hold forth somewhat as follows: people should free themselves from intense emotion, be unmoved by both joy and sorrow, and submit without complaint to unavoidable necessity.

Today, psychologists suggest pretty much the exact opposite—let your emotions flow freely, express your love or animosity, don't bottle up your feelings. But in the fourth century B.C., when Zeno was expounding his credo, his philosophy of control of the passions fell on receptive ears. His followers were called Stoics, after the stoa, or porch, from which the master lectured.

If we call people stoical, we mean that they bear their pain or sorrow without complaint, they meet adversity with unflinching fortitude. This sounds very noble, you will admit—actually, according to modern psychological belief, it is healthier not to be so stoical. Stoicism(STŌ´-ə-siz-əm) may be an admirable virtue (mainly because we do not then have to listen to the stoic's troubles), but it can be overdone.

☻ fear and trembling

Intrepid is from Latin trepido, to tremble. Intrepid people exhibit courage and fearlessness (and not a single tremble!) when confronted by dangers from which you and I would run like the cowards we are. (You recognize the negative prefix in-.)

The noun: intrepidity(in´-trə-PID´-ə-tee), or, of course, intrepidness.

Trepido is the source also of trepidation(trep´-ə-DAY´-shən)—great fear, trembling, or alarm.

☻ quick flash

Scintilla, in Latin, is a quick, bright spark; in English the word scintilla(sin-TIL´-ə) may also a spark, but more commonly refers to a very small particle (which, in a sense, a spark is), as in, "There was not a scintilla of evidence against him."

In the verb scintillate(SIN´-tə-layt´), the idea of the spark remains; someone who scintillates sparkles with charm and wit, flashes brightly with humor. The noun is scintillation(sin´-tə-LAY´-shən).

⊕ city and country

People who live in the big city go to theaters, attend the opera, visit museums and picture galleries, browse in bookstores, and shop at Robinson's, Bloomingdale's, Marshall Field, or other large department stores. These activities fill them with culture and sophistication.

Also, they crowd into jammed subway trains or buses, squeeze into packed elevators, cross the street in competition with high-powered motorcars, patiently stand in line outside of movie houses, and then wait again in the lobby for seats to be vacated. Also, they have the privilege of spending two hours a day going to and coming from work. As a result, city-dwellers are refined, polished, courteous—or so the etymology of urbane (from Latin urbs, city) tells us. (And you must be absurdly credulous, if not downright gullible, to believe it.) The noun is urbanity(ur-BAN´-ə-tee). So urbane people are gracious, affable, cultivated, suave, tactful—add any similar adjectives you can think of.

Urban(UR´-bən) as an adjective simply refers to cities—urban affairs, urban areas, urban populations, urban life, urban development, etc.

Consider some prefixes: sub-, near; inter-, between; intra-, inside, within; ex-, out.

Add each prefix to the root urbs, using the adjective suffix -an:

sub_____ : near the city (Sub- has a number of meanings; under, near, close to, etc.)

inter_____ : between cities

intra_____ : within a city

ex_____ : out of the city

The suburbs are residential sections, or small communities, close to a large city; Larchmont is a suburb of New York City, Whittier a suburb of Los Angeles. Suburbia(sə-BUR´-bee-ə) may designate suburbs as a group; suburban residents, or suburbanites(sə-BUR´-bə-nīts´), as a group; or the typical manners, modes of living, customs, etc. of suburban residents. An interurban bus travels between cities, an intraurban bus within a single city.

An exurb(EKS´-urb) lies well beyond, way outside, a large city, and generally refers to a region inhabited by well-to-do families. Exurb has derived forms corresponding to those of suburb. Can you construct them?

Plural noun: _____.

Adjective: _____.

Resident: _____.

As a group; manners, customs, etc.: _____.

Urbs is the city; Latin rus, ruris is the country, I.e., farmland, fields, etc. So rural(ROŌR´-əl), refers to country or farm regions, agriculture, etc.—a wealthy rural area.

Rustic(RUS´-tik) as an adjective may describe furniture or dwellings made of roughhewn wood, or furnishings suitable to a farmhouse; or, when applied to a person, is an antonym of urbane— unsophisticated, boorish, lacking in social graces, uncultured. Noun: rusticity(rus-TIS´-ə-tee). Rustic is also a noun designating a person with such characteristics, as in, "He was considered a rustic by his classmates, all of whom came from cultured and wealthy backgrounds."

Urbane and rustic, when applied to people, are emotionally charged words. Urbane is complimentary, rustic derogatory.*

To rusticate(RUS´-tə-kayt´) is to spend time in the country, away from the turmoil and tensions of big-city life. Can you construct the noun?

_____.

* Incidentally, a word with a derogatory connotation (bitch, piggish, glutton, idiot, etc.) is called a pejorative(pə-JAWR´-ə-tiv). Pejorative is also an adjective, as in, "She spoke in pejorative terms about her ex-husband." The derivation is Latin pejor, worse.

WORDS INFLUENCE YOUR THINKING

By now, you have thoroughly explored hundreds upon hundreds of valuable words and scores upon scores of important Greek and Latin roots.

As you went along you stopped at frequent intervals to say aloud, think about, work with, and recall the words you were adding to your vocabulary.

By now, therefore, the words you have been learning are probably old friends of yours; they have started to influence your thinking, have perhaps begun to appear in your conversation, and have certainly become conspicuous in your reading. In hosrt, they have been effective in making changes in your intellectual climate.

Let us pause now for another checkup of the success of your study. Take the test cold if you feel that all the material is at your fingertips.

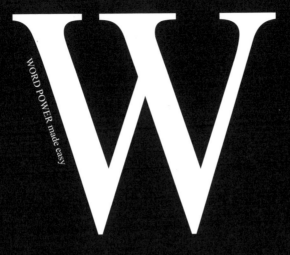

CHAPTER
10

HOW TO TALK ABOUT COMMON PHENOMENA
AND OCCURRENCES

Words for poverty and wealth, direct and indirect emotions not calling
a spade a spade, banter and other light talk, animal-like contentment,
homesickness, meat-eating, and different kinds of secrecy. Excursions into
terms expressive of goodness, of hackneyed phraseology, of human similarity
to various animals, of kinds of sound, etc. How to react to the new words you
meet in your reading.

ORIGIN

⊜ money, and what it will buy

The modern world operates largely by means of a price structure—wealth and poverty are therefore words that indicate the possession, on the one hand, or the lack, on the other, of money. Penury, from Latin penuria, need, neediness, is dire, abject poverty, complete lack of financial resources. It is one of the two strongest English words there are to denote absence of money. The adjective form, penurious(pə-NYŌŌr′-ee-əs or pə-NŌŌR′-ee-əs), strangely enough, may mean poverty-stricken, but more commonly signifies stingy, close-fisted, niggardly; so sparing in the use of money as to give the appearance of penury.

Penurious is a synonym of parsimonious(pahr′-sə-MŌ′-nee-əs), but is much stronger in implication. A parsimonious person is stingy; a penurious person is twice as stingy. Penury for poverty (if you can imagine a mild degree of poverty) is indigence(IN′-də-jəns). Indigent (IN′-də-jənt) people are not absolutely penniless—they are simply living in reduced circumstances, forgoing many creature comforts, forced to undergo the type of hardships that may accompany a lack of sufficient funds. On the other hand, a close synonym of penury, and one of equal strength, is destitution(des′-tə-TŌŌ′-shən). Destitute(DES′-tə-tōōt) people do not even have the means for mere subsistence—as such, they are perhaps on the verge of starvation. Penury and destitution are not merely straitened circumstances—they are downright desperate circumstances.

To turn now to the brighter side of the picture, the possession of money, especially in increasing amounts, is expressed by affluence(AF´-lōō-əns). Affluent(AF´-lōō-ənt) people, people of affluence, or those living in affluent circumstances, are more than comfortable; in addition, there is the implication that their wealth is increasing. People who live in affluence probably own large and costly homes, run big, new cars, belong to expensive golf or country clubs, etc.

A much stronger term is opulence(OP´-yə-ləns), which not only implies much greater wealth than affluence, but in addition suggests lavish expenditures and ostentatiously luxurious surroundings. People of opulence own estates; drive only outrageously expensive and specially equipped cars (Rolls-Royces, Mercedes-Benzes, Porsches, etc.); have a crops of servants, including a major-domo; belong to golf and yacht and country clubs, etc., etc. Embroider the fantasy as much as you with to. Opulent(OP´-yə-lənt) may describe people, surroundings, styles of life, or the like.

Affluent is a combination of the prefix ad-, to, toward (changing to af- before a root beginning with f), plus the Latin verb fluo, to flow-affluence is that delightful condition in which money keeps flowing to us, and no one ever turns off the spigot. Other words from the same root, fluo, to flow, are fluid, influence, confluence (a "flowing together"), fluent (the words flow smoothly), etc. Opulent is from Latin opulentus, wealthy. No other English words derive from this root.

◕ doing and feeling

If you watch a furious athletic event, and you get tired, though the athletes expend all the energy—that's vicarious fatigue. If your friend goes on a bender, and as you watch him absorb one drink after another, you begin to feel giddy and stimulated, that's vicarious intoxication. If you watch a mother in a motion picture or dramatic play suffer horribly at the death of her child, and you go through the same agony, that's vicarious torment.

You can experience an emotion, then, in two ways: firsthand, through actual participation; or vicariously, by becoming empathetically involved in another person's feelings.

Some people, for example, lead essentially dull and colorless lives. Through their children, through reading or attending the theater, however, they can experience all the emotions felt by others whose lives move along at a swift, exciting pace. These people live at second hand; they live vicariously.

● time is relative

Elephants and turtles live almost forever; human beings in the United States have a life expectancy in general of sixty-eight to seventy-six years (though the gradual conquest of disease is constantly lengthening our span); dogs live from seven to ten years; and some insects exist for only a few hours or days.

One such short-lived creature is the dayfly, which in Greek was called ephemera. Hence anything so short-lived, so unenduring that it scarcely seems to outlast the day, may be called ephemeral.

A synonym of ephemeral is evanescent(ev-ə-NES´-ənt), fleeting, staying for a remarkably short time, vanishing. Something intangible, like a feeling, may be called evanescent; it's here, and before you can quite comprehend it, it's gone—vanished.

The noun is evanescence(ev′-ə-NES′-əns); the verb is to evanesce(ev-ə-NES′).

Evanescent is built on the prefix e-(ex-), out, the root vanesco, to vanish, and the adjective suffix -ent.

The suffix -esce often, but not always, means begin to. -Escent may mean becoming or beginning to. Thus:

> adolescent—beginning to grow up; beginning to become an adult
>
> evanesce—begin to vanish
>
> convalesce—begin to get well after illness
>
> putrescent—beginning to rot; beginning to become putrid
>
> obsolescent—becoming obsolete

∞ an exploration of various good things

A euphemism is a word or expression that has been substituted for another that is likely to offend—it is built on the Greek prefix eu-, good, the root pheme, voice, and the noun suffix -ism. (Etymologically, "something said in a good voice!") Adjective: euphemistic(yōō′-fə-MIS′-tik)

Other English words constructed from the prefix eu-:

1. euphony(YOO′-fə-nee)—good sound; pleasant lilt or rhythm (phone, sound)

    Adjective: euphonic(yōō-FON′-ik) or euphonious(yōō-FŌ′-nee-əs)

2. eulogy(YOO′-lə-jee)—etymologically, "good speech"; a formal speech of praise, usually delivered as a funeral oration. logos in this term means word or speech, as it did in philology. logos more commonly means science or study, but has the alternate meaning

in eulogy, philology, monologue, dialogue, epilogue(words upon the other words, or "after-words"), and prologue(words before the main part, "before-words," or introduction).

Adjective: eulogistic(y$\overline{oo}$-lə-JIS´-tik); verb: eulogize(Y$\overline{OO}$-lə-jīz´); person who delivers a eulogy: eulogist(Y$\overline{OO}$-lə-jĭst)

3. euphoria(y$\overline{oo}$-FAWR´-ee-ə)—good feeling, a sense of mental buoyancy and physical well-being

Adjective: euphoric(y$\overline{oo}$-FAWR´-ik)

4. euthanasia(y$\overline{oo}$´-thə-NAY´-zhə)—etymologically, "good death"; method of painless death inflicted on people suffering from incurable diseases—not legal at the present time, but advocated by many people. The word derives from eu- plus Greek thanatos, death.

❦ exploration of modes of expression

Badinage is a half-teasing, non-malicious, frivolous banter, intended to amuse rather than wound. Badinage has a close synonym, persiflage(PUR´-sə-flahzh´), which is a little more derisive, a trifle more indicative of contempt or mockery—but still totally unmalicious.

In line with badinage and persiflage, there are four other forms of expression you should be familiar with: cliché(klee-SHAY´), bromide(BRŌ´-mīd´), platitude(PLAT´-ə-t$\overline{oo}$d), platitude (PLAT´-ə-t$\overline{oo}$d), and anodyne(AN´-ə-dīn´).

A cliché is a pattern of words which was once new and fresh, but which now is so old, worn, and threadbare that only banal, unimaginative speakers and writers ever use it. Examples are: fast and furious; unsung heroes; by leaps and bounds; conspicuous by its absence; green with envy; etc. The most devastating criticism you can make of a piece of writing is to say, "It is full of clichés"; the most pointed insult to a person's way of talking is, "You speak in clichés."

A bromide is any trite, dull, and probably fallacious remark that shows little evidence of original thinking, and that therefore convinces a listener of the total absence of perspicacity on the part of the speaker.

For instance, some cautious, dull-minded individual might warn you not to take a chance in these words: "Remember it's better to be safe than sorry!"

Your sneering response might be: "Oh, that old bromide!"

A platitude is similar to a cliché or bromide, in that it is a dull, trite, hackneyed, unimaginative pattern of words—but, to add insult to injury (cliché), the speaker uses it with an air of novelty—as if he just made it up, and isn't he the brilliant fellow!

An anodyne, in the medical sense, is a drug that allays pain without curing an illness, like aspirin or morphine. Figuratively, an anodyne is a statement made to allay someone's fears or anxieties, not believed by the speaker, but intended to be believed by the listener. "Prosperity is just around the corner" was a popular anodyne of the 1930s.

A bromide is also a drug, formerly used as a sedative. Sedatives dull the senses—the statement labeled a bromide comes from a speaker of dull wit and has a sedative effect on the listener. The adjective is bromidic(brō-MID´-ik), as in :his bromidic way of expressing himself."

Platitude derives from Greek platys, broad or flat, plus the noun suffix -tude. Words like plateau (flat land), plate and platter (flat dishes), and platypus (flat foot) all derive from the same root as platitude, a flat statement, i.e., one that falls flat, despite the speaker's high hopes for it. The adjective is platitudinous(plat´-ə-TOO-də-nəs), as in, "What a platitudinous remark."

Anodyne is a combination of the negative prefix an- with Greek odyne, pain. Anodynes, as drugs, lessen pain; as statements, they are intended to reduce or eliminate emotional pain or anxiety.

⟨Word Power⟩ p.444

ORIGIN

⊛ people are the craziest animals

Bovine, placid like a cow, stolid, patient, unexcitable, is built on the Latin word for ox or cow, bovis, plus the suffix -ine, like, similar to, or characteristic of. To call someone bovine is of course far from complimentary, for this adjective is considerably stronger than phlegmatic, and implies a certain mild contempt on the part of the speaker. A bovine person is somewhat like a vegetable: eats and grows and lives, but apparently is lacking in any strong feelings.

Humans are sometimes compared to animals, as in the following adjectives:

1. leonine(LEE´-ə-nīn´)—like a lion in appearance or temperament.

2. canine(KAY´-nīn´)—like a dog. As a noun, the word refers to the species to which dogs belong. Our canine teeth are similar to those of a dog.

3. feline(FEE´-līn´)—catlike. We may speak of feline grace; or (insultingly) of feline temperament when we mean that a person is "catty."

4. porcine(PAWR′-sīn′)—piglike.

5. vulpine(VUL′-pīn′)—foxlike in appearance or temperament. When applied to people, this adjective usually indicates the shrewdness of a fox.

6. ursine(UR′-sīn′)—bearlike.

7. lupine(LOO′-pīn′)—wolflike.

8. equine(EE′-kwīn′)—horselike; "horsy."

9. piscine(PIS′-in′)—fishlike.

All these adjectives come from the corresponding Latin words for the animals; and, of course, each adjective also describes, or refers to, the specific animal as well as to the person likened to the animal.

1. leo	lion	6. ursus	bear
2. canis	dog	7. lupus	wolf
3. felis	cat	8. equus	horse
4. porcus	pig	9. piscis	fish
5. vulpus	fox		

The word for mear from a pig—pork—derives, obviously, from porcus. Ursa Major and Ursa Minor, the Great Bear and the Little Bear, the two conspicuous groups of stars in the northern sky (conspicuous, of course, only on a clear night), are so labeled because in formation they resemble the outlines of bears. The feminine name Ursula is, by etymology, "a little bear," which, perhaps, is a strange name to burden a child with. The skin disease lupus was so named because it eats into the flesh, as a wolf might.

☻ you can't go home again

Nostalgia, built on two Greek rots, nostos, a return, and algos, pain (as in neuralgia, cardialgia, etc.), is a feeling you can't ever understand until you've experience it—and you have probably experienced it whenever some external stimulus has crowded your mind with scenes from an earlier day.

You know how life often seems much pleasanter in retrospect?

Your conscious memory tends to store up the pleasant experiences of the past (the trauma and unpleasant experiences may bet buried in the unconscious), and when you are lonely or unhappy you may begin to relive these pleasant occurrences. It is then that you feel the emotional pain and longing that we call nostalgia.

The adjective is nostalgic(nos-TAL´-jik), as in "motion pictures that are nostalgic of the fifties," or as in, "He feels nostalgic whenever he passes 138th Street and sees the house in which he grew up."

∞ soundings

Cacophony is itself a harsh-sounding word—and is the only one that exactly describes the unmusical, grating, ear-offending noises you are likely to hear in man-made surroundings: the New York subway trains thundering through their tunnels (they are also, these days in the late 1970s, eye-offending, for which we might coin the term cacopsis, noun, and cacoptic, adjective), the traffic bedlam of rush hours in a big city, a steel mill, an automobile factory, a blast furnace, etc. Adjective: cacophonous(kə-KOF´-ə-nəs).

These words are built on the Greek roots kakos, bad, harsh, or ugly, and phone, sound. Phone, sound, is found also in:

1. telephone—etymologically, "sound from afar"

2. euphony—pleasant sound

3. phonograph—etymologically, "writer of sound"

4. saxophone—a musical instrument (hence sound) invented by

Adolphe Sax

5. xylophone—a musical instrument; etymologically, "sounds through wood" (Greek xylon, wood)

6. phonetics(fə-NET´-iks)—the science of the sounds of language; the adjective is phonetic(fə-NET´-ik), the expert a phonetician (fō´-nə-TISH´-ən)

7. phonics—the science of sound; also the method of teaching reading by drilling the sounds of letters and syllables

∞ the flesh and all

Carnivorous combines carnis, flesh, and voro, to devour. A carnivorous animal, or carnivore(KAHR´-nə-vawr´), is one whose main diet is meat.

Voro, to devour, is the origin of other words referring to eating habits:

1. herbivorous(hur-BIV´-ər-əs)—subsisting on grains, grasses, and other vegetation, as cows, deer, horses, etc. The animal is herbivore(HUR´-bə-vawr´). Derivation: Latin herba, herb, plus voro, to devour

2. omnivorous(om-NIV´-ər-əs)—eating everything: meat, grains, grasses, fish, insects, and anything else digestible. The only species so indiscriminate in their diet are humans and rats, plus, of course, some cats and dogs that live with people (in contrast to felines and canines—lions, tigers, bobcats, wolves, etc.—that are not domesticated). Omnivorous (combining Latin omnis, all, with voro, plus the adjective suffix -ous) refers not only to food. An omnivorous reader reads everything in great quantities (that is, devours all kinds of reading matter).

3. voracious(vaw-RAY´-shəs)—devouring; hence, greedy or gluttonous; may refer either to food or to any other habits. One may be a voracious eater, voracious reader, voracious in one's pursuit of money, pleasure, etc. Think of the two noun forms of loquacious. Can you write two nouns derived from voracious? (1) _____,

(2) _____

❦ "allness"

Latin omnis, all, is the origin of:

1. omnipotent(om-NIP´-ə-tənt)—all-powerful, an adjective usually applied to God; also, to any ruler whose governing powers are unlimited, which allows for some exaggeration, as King Canute the Great proved to his sycophantic countries when he ordered the tide to come so far up the beach and no further. He got soaking wet! (Omnis plus Latin potens, potentis, powerful, as in potentate, a powerful ruler; impotent(IM´-pə-tənt), powerless; potent, powerful; and potential, possessing power or ability not yet exercised). Can you write the noun form of omnipotent? _____.

2. omniscient(om-NISH´-ənt)—all-knowing; hence, infinitely wise. (Omnis plus sciens, knowing.) We have discussed this adjective in a previous chapter, so you will have no problem writing the noun:_____.

3. omnipresent(om´-nə-PREZ´-ənt)—present in all places at once. Fear was omnipresent in Europe during 1939 just before World War II. A synonym of omnipresent is ubiquitous(yoo-BIK´-wə-təs), from Latin ubique, everywhere. The ubiquitous ice cream vendor seems to be everywhere at the same time, tinkling those little bells, once spring arrives. The ubiquitous little red wagon

rides around everywhere in airports to refuel departing planes. "Ubiquitous laughter greeted the press secretary's remark," i.e., laughter was heard everywhere in the room. The noun forms are ubiquity(yoo-BIK´-wə-tee) or _____. (Can you think of the alternate form?)

4. omnibus(OM´-nə-bəs)—etymologically, "for all, including all." In the shortened form bus we have a public vehicle for all who can pay; in a John Galsworthy omnibus we have a book containing all of Galsworthy's works; in an omnibus legislative bill we have a bill containing all the miscellaneous provisions and appropriations left out of other bills.

⊜ more flesh

Note how carnis, flesh, is the building block of:

1. carnelian(kahr-NEEL´-yən)—a reddish color, the color of red flesh.
2. carnival(KAHR´-nə-vəl)—originally the season of merry-making just before Lent, when people took a last fling before saying "Carne vale!" "Oh flesh, farewell!" (Latin verb, farewell, goodbye). Today a carnival is a kind of outdoor entertainment with games, rides, side shows, and, of course, lots of food—also any exuberant or riotous merrymaking or festivities.
3. carnal(KAHR´-nəl)—most often found in phrases like "carnal pleasures" or "carnal appetites," and signifying pleasures or appetites of the flesh rather than of the spirit—hence, sensual, lecherous, lascivious, lubricious, etc. The noun is carnality(kahr-NAL´-ə-tee).
4. carnage(KAHR´-nəj)—great destruction of life (that is, of human flesh), as in war or mass murders.

5. reincarnation(ree´-in-kahr-NAY´-shən)—a rebirth or reappearance. Believers in reincarnation maintain that one's soul persists after it has fled the flesh, and eventually reappears in the body of a newborn infant or animal, or in another form. Some of us, according to this interesting philosophy, were once Napoleon, Alexander the Great, Cleopatra, etc. The verb is to reincarnate(ree-in-KAHR´-nayt), to bring (a soul) back in another bodily form.

6. incarnate(in-KAHR´-nət)—in the flesh. If we use this adjective to call someone "the devil incarnate," we mean that here is the devil in the flesh. Or we may say that someone is evil incarnate, that is, the personificaion of evil, evil invested with human or bodily form. The verb to incarnate(in-KAHR´-nayt) is to embody, give bodily form to, or make real.

✿ dark secrets

Clandestine comes from Latin clam, secretly, and implies secrecy or concealment in the working out of a plan that is dangerous or illegal. Clandestine is a close synonym of surreptitious(sur´-əp-TISH´-əs), which means stealthy, sneaky, furtive, generally because of fear of detection.

The two words cannot always, however, be used interchangeably. We may speak of either clandestine or surreptitious meetings or arrangements; but usually only of clandestine plans and only of surreptitious movements or actions. Can you write the noun form of surreptitious? _____.

ADVICE

GETTING USED TO NEW WORDS

Reference has been made, in previous chapters, to the intimate relationship between reading and vocabulary building. Good books and the better magazines will not only acquaint you with a host of new ideas (and, therefore, new words, since every word is the verbalization of an idea), but also will help you gain a more complete and a richer understanding of the hundreds of words you are learning through your work in this book. If you have been doing sufficient amount of stimulating reading—and that means, at minimum, several magazines a week and at least three books of nonfiction a month—you have been meeting, constantly, over and over again, the new words you have been learning in these pages. Every such encounter is like seeing an old friend in a new place. You know how much better you understand your friends when you have a chance to see them react to new situations; similarly, you will gain a much deeper understanding of the friends you have been making among words as you see them in different contexts and in different places.

My recommendations in the past have been of non-fiction titles, but novels too are a rich source of additions to your vocabulary—provided you stay alert to the new words you will inevitably meet in reading novels.

The natural temptation, when you encounter a brand-new word in a novel, is to ignore it—the lines of the plot are perfectly clear even if many of the author's words are not.

I want to counsel strongly that you resist the temptation to ignore the unfamiliar words you may meet in your novel reading: resist it with every ounce of your energy, for only by such resistance can you keep building your vocabulary as you read.

What should you do? Don't rush to a dictionary, don't bother underlining the word, don't keep long lists of words that you will eventually look up en masse—these activities are likely to become painful and you will not continue them for any great length of time.

Instead, do something quite simple—and very effective.

When you meet a new word, underline it with a mental pencil. That is, pause for a second and attempt to figure out its meaning from its use in the sentence or from its etymological root or prefix, if it contains one you have studied. Make a mental note of it, say it aloud once or twice—and then go on reading.

That's all there is to it. What you are doing, of course, is developing the same type of mind-set toward the new words that you have developed toward words you have studied in this book. And the results, of course, will be the same—you will begin to notice the word occurring again and again in other reading you do, and finally, having seen it in a number of varying contexts, you will begin to get enough of its connotation and flavor to come to a fairly accurate understanding of its meaning. In this way you will be developing alertness not only to the words you have studied in this book, but to all expressive and meaningful words. And your vocabulary will keep growing.

But of course that will happen only if you keep reading.

I do not wish to recommend any particular novels or novelists, since the type of fiction one enjoys is a very personal matter. You doubtless know the kind of story you like—mystery, science fiction, spy, adventure, historical, political, romantic, Western, biographical, one or all of the above. Or you may be entranced by novels of ideas, of sexual prowess, of fantasy, of life in different segments of society from your own. No matter. Find the kind of novel or novelist you enjoy by browsing in the public library or among the thousands of titles in bookstores that have a rich assortment of paperbacks as well as hardbacks.

And then read! And keep on the alert for new words! You will find them by the hundreds and thousands. Bear in mind: people with rich vocabularies have been reading omnivorously, voraciously, since childhood—including the ingredients listed in small print on bread wrappers and cereal boxes.

HOW TO SPELL A WORD

The spelling of English words is archaic, it's confusing, it's needlessly complicated, and, if you have a sense of humor, it's down-right comical. In fact, any insulting epithet you might wish to level against our weird methods of putting letters together to form words would probably be justified—but it's our spelling, and we're stuck with it.

How completely stuck we are is illustrated by a somewhat ludicrous event that goes back to 1906, and that cost philanthropist Andrew Carnegie $75,000.

Working under a five-year grant of funds from Carnegie, and headed by the esteemed scholar Brander Matthews, the Simplified Spelling Board published in that year a number of recommendations for bringing some small semblance of order out of the great chaos of English spelling. Their suggestions affected a mere three hundred words out of the half million then in the language. Here are a few examples, to give you a general idea:

SPELLING THEN CURRENT	SIMPLIFIED SPELLING
mediaeval	medieval
doubt	dout
debtor	dettor

head	hed
though	tho
through	thru
laugh	laf
tough	tuf
knife	nife
theatre	theater
centre	center
phantom	fantom

These revisions seemed eminently sensible to no less a personage than the then President of the United States, Theodore Roosevelt. So delighted was he with the new grab in which these three hundred words could be clothed that he immediately ordered that all government documents be printed in simplified spelling. And the result? Such a howl went up from the good citizens of the republic, from the nation's editors and schoolteachers and businessmen, that the issue was finally debated in the halls of Congress. Almost to a man, senators and representatives stood opposed to the plan. Teddy Roosevelt, as you have doubtless heard, was a stubborn fellow—but when Congress threatened to hold up the White House stationery appropriation unless the President backed down, Teddy rescinded the order. Roosevelt ran for re-election some time later, and lost. That his attitude toward spelling contributed to his defeat is of course highly doubtful—nevertheless an opposition New York newspaper, the day the returns were in, maliciously commented on the outgoing incumbent in a one-word simplified-spelling editorial: "THRU!"

Roosevelt was not the first President to be justifiably outraged by our ridiculous orthography. Over a hundred years ago, when Andrew Jackson was twitted on his poor spelling, he is supposed to have made this characteristic reply, "Well, sir, it is a damned poor mind that cannot think of more than one way to spell a world!" And according to one apocryphal version, it was Jackson's odd spelling that gave birth to the expression "okay." Jackson thought, so goes the story, that "all correct" was spelled "orl korrect," and he used O.K. as the abbreviation for these words when he approved state papers.

Many years ago, the British playwright George Bernard Shaw offered a dramatic proposal for reducing England's taxes. Just eliminate unnecessary letters from our unwieldy spelling, he said, and you'll save enough money in paper and printing to cut everyone's tax rate in half. Maybe it would work, but it's never been put to the test—and the way things look now, it never will be. Current practice more and more holds spelling exactly where it is, bad though it may be. It is a scientific law of language that if enough people make a "mistake," the "mistake" becomes acceptable usage. That law applies to pronunciation, to grammar, to word meanings, but not to spelling. Maybe it's because of our misbegotten faith in, and worship of, the printed word—maybe it's because written language tends to be static, while spoken language constantly changes. Whatever the cause, spelling today successfully resists every logical effort at reform. "English spelling," said Thorstein Veblen, "satisfies all the requirements of the canons of reputability under the law of conspicuous waste. It is archaic, cumbrous, and ineffective." Perfectly true. Notwithstanding, it's here to stay.

Your most erudite friend doubtless misspells the name of the Hawaiian guitar. I asked half a dozen members of the English department of a large college to spell the word—without exception they responded with ukelele. Yet the only accepted form is ukulele.

Judging from my experience with my classes at Rio Hondo College, half the population of the country must think the word is spelled alright. Seventy-five per cent of the members of my classes can't spell embarrassing or coolly. People will go on misspelling these four words, but the authorized spellings will remain impervious to change.

Well, you know the one about Mohammed and the mountain. Though it's true that we have modernized spelling to a microscopic extent in the last eighty years(traveler, center, theater, medieval, labor, and honor, for example, have pretty much replaced traveller, centre, theatre, mediaeval, labour, and honour), still the resistance to change has not observably weakened. If spelling won't change, as it probably won't, those of us who consider ourselves poor spellers will have to. We'll just have to get up and go to the mountain.

Is it hard to become a good speller? I have demonstrated over and over again in my classes that anyone of normal intelligence and average educational background can become a good speller in very little time.

What makes the task so easy?

First—investigations have proved that 95 per cent of the spelling errors that educated people make occur in just one hundred words. Not only do we all misspell the same words—but we misspell them in about the same way.

Second—correct spelling relies exclusively on memory, and the most effective way to train memory is by means of association or, to use the technical term, mnemonics.

If you fancy yourself an imperfect or even a terrible speller, the chances are very great that you've developed a complex solely because you misspell some or all of the hundred words with which this Intermission deals. When you have conquered this single list, and I shall immediately proceed to demonstrate how easy it is, by means of mnemonics, to do so, 95 per cent of your spelling difficulties will in all likelihood vanish.

Let us start with twenty-five words from the list. In the first column you will find the correct spelling of each, and in the second column the simple mnemonic that will forevermore fix that correct spelling in you memory.

CORRECT SPELLING	MEANING
1. all right	Two words, no matter what it means. Keep in mind that it's the opposite of all wrong.
2. coolly	Of course you can spell cool-simply add the adverbial ending -ly.
3. supersede	This is the only word in the language ending in -sede (the only one, mind you—there isn't a single other one so spelled).
4. succeed 5. proceed 6. exceed	The only three words in the entire language ending in -ceed. When you think of the three words in the order given here, the initial letters from the beginning of SPEED.
7. cede, precede, recede, etc.	All other words with a similar-sounding final syllable end in -cede.
8. procedure	One of the double e's of proceed moves to the end in the noun form, procedure.
9. stationery	This is the word that means paper, and notice the -er in paper.
10. stationary	In this spelling, the words means standing, and notice the -a in stand.
11. recommend	Commend, which we all spell correctly, plus the prefix re-.

| 12. separate | Look for a rat in both words. |
| 13. comparative | |

| 14. ecstasy | to sy(sigh) with ecstasy |

| 15. analyze | The only two non-technical words in the whole |
| 16. paralyze | language ending in -yze. |

| 17. repetition | First four letters identical with those in the allied form repeat. |

| 18. irritable | Think of allied forms irritate and imitate. |
| 19. inimitable | |

| 20. absence | Think of the allied form absent, and you will not be tempted to misspell it absence. |

| 21. superintendent | The superintendent in an apartment house collects the rent—thus you avoid superintendant. |

| 22. conscience | Science plus prefix con-. |

| 23. anoint | Think of an ointment, hence no double n. |

| 24. ridiculous | Think of the allied form ridicule, which we usually spell correctly, thus avoiding rediculous. |

| 25. despair | Again, think of another form—desperate—and so avoid dispair. |

Whether or not you have much faith in your spelling ability, you will need very little time to conquer the preceding twenty-five demons. Spend a few minutes, now, on each of those words in the list that you're doubtful of, and then test your success by means of the exercise below. Perhaps to your astonishment, you will find it easy to make a high score.

A TEST OF YOUR LEARNING

Instructions: After studying the preceding list of words, fill in the missing letters correctly.

    1. a_____right   14. ecsta_____y

2. coo_____y

3. super_____

4. suc_____

5. pro_____

6. ex_____

7. pre_____

8. proc_____dure

9. station_____ry (paper)

10. station_____ry (still)

11. sep_____rate

12. compar_____tive

13. re_____o_____end

15. anal_____e

16. paral_____e

17. rep_____tition

18. irrit_____ble

19. inimit_____ble

20. ab_____ence

21. superintend_____nt

22. con_____nce

23. a_____oint

24. r_____diculous

25. d_____spair

Mere repetitious drill is of no value in learning to spell a word correctly. You've probably heard the one about the youngster who was kept after school because he was in the habit of using the ungrammatical expression "I have went." Miss X was going to cure her pupil, even it if required drastic measures. So she ordered him to write "I have gone" one thousand times. "Just leave your work on my desk before you go home," she said, "and I'll find it when I come in tomorrow morning." Well, there were twenty pages of neat script on her desk next morning, one thousand lines of "I have gone's," and on the last sheet was a note from the child. "Dear Teacher," it read, "I have done the work and I have went home." If this didn't actually happen, it logically could have, for in any drill, if the mind is not actively engaged, no learning will result. If you drive a car, or sew, or do any familiar and repetitious manual work, you know how your hands can carry on an accustomed task while your mind if far away. And if you hope to learn to spell by filling pages with a word, stop wasting your time. All you'll get for your trouble is writer's cramp.

The only way to learn to spell those words that now plague you is to devise a mnemonic for each one.

If you are never quite sure whether it's indispensible or indispensable, you can spell it out one hundred, one thousand, or one million times—and the next time you have occasion to write it in a sentence, you'll still wonder whether to end it with -ible or -able. But if you say to yourself just once that able people are generally indispensable, that thought will come to you whenever you need to spell the word; in a few seconds you've conquered another spelling demon. By engineering your own mnemonic through a study of the architecture of a troublesome word, you will become so quickly and completely involved with the correct spelling of that word that it will be impossible for you ever to be stumped again.

Let us start at once. Below you will find another twenty-five words from the list of one hundred demons, each offered to you in both the correct form and in the popular misspelling. Go through the test quickly, checking off what you consider a proper choice in each case. In that way you will discover which of the twenty-five you would be likely to get caught on. Then devise a personal mnemonic for each word you flunked, writing your ingenious result out in the margin of the page. And don't be alarmed if some of your mnemonics turn out kind of silly—the sillier they are the more likely you are to recall them in an emergency. One of my pupils, who could not remember how many l's to put into tranquillity (or is it tranquility?), shifted his mind into high gear and came up with this: "In the old days life was more tranquil than today, and people wrote with quills instead of fountain pens. Hence—tranquillity!" Another pupil, a girl who always chewed her nails over irresistible before she could decide whether to end it with -ible or -able, suddenly realized that a certain brand of lipstick was called irresistible, the point being of course that the only vowel in lipstick is i—hence, -ible! Silly, aren't they? But they work. Go ahead to the test now; and see how clever—or silly—you can be.

SPELLING TEST

1. a. supprise   b. surprise
2. a. inoculate   b. innoculate
3. a. definitely   b. definately
4. a. priviledge   b. privilege
5. a. incidently   b. incidentally
6. a. predictible   b. predictable
7. a. dissipate   b. disippate
8. a. descriminate   b. discriminate
9. a. description   b. discription
10. a. baloon   b. balloon
11. a. occurence   b. occurrence
12. a. truely   b. truly
13. a. arguement   b. argument
14. a. assistant   b. asisstant
15. a. grammer   b. grammar
16. a. parallel   b. paralell
17. a. drunkeness   b. drunkenness
18. a. suddeness   b. suddenness
19. a. embarassment   b. embarrassment
20. a. weird   b. wierd
21. a. pronounciation   b. pronunciation

22. a. noticeable   b. noticable

23. a. developement   b. development

24. a. vicious   b. viscious

25. a. insistent   b. insistant

By now you're well on the way toward developing a definite superiority complex about your spelling—which isn't a half-bad thing, for I've learned, working with my students, that many people think they're awful spellers, and have completely lost faith in their ability, solely because they get befuddled over no more than two dozen or so common words that they use over and over again and always misspell. Every other word they spell perfectly, but they still think they're prize boobs in spelling until their self-confidence is restored. So if you're beginning to gain more assurance, you're on the right track. The conquest of the one hundred common words most frequently misspelled is not going to assure you that you will always come out top man in a spelling bee, but it's certain to clean up your writing and bolster your ego.

So far you have worked with fifty of the one hundred spelling demons. Here, now, is the remainder of the list. Test yourself, or have someone who can keep a secret test you, and discover which ones are your Waterloo. Study each one you miss as if it were a problem in engineering. Observe how it's put together and devise whatever association pattern will fix the correct form in your mind. Happy spelling!

SPELLING DEMONS

These fifty words complete the list of one hundred words that most frequently stump the inexpert spellers:

1. embarrassing   26. panicky

2. judgement   27. seize

3. indispensable
4. disappear
5. disappoint
6. corroborate
7. sacrilegious
8. tranquility
9. exhilaration
10. newsstand
11. license
12. irresistible
13. persistent
14. dilemma
15. perseverance
16. until (but till)
17. tyrannize
18. vacillate
19. oscillate
20. accommodate
21. dilettante
22. changeable
23. accessible
24. forty
25. desirable

28. leisure
29. receive
30. achieve
31. holiday
32. existence
33. pursue
34. pastime
35. possesses
36. professor
37. category
38. rhythmical
39. vacuum
40. benefited
41. committee
42. grievous
43. conscious
44. plebeian
45. tariff
46. sheriff
47. connoisseur
48. necessary
49. sergeant
50. misspelling

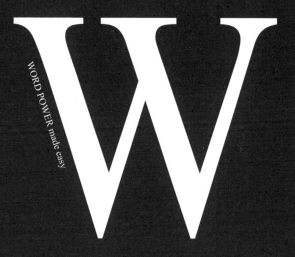

W

CHAPTER
11

HOW TO TALK ABOUT WHAT GOES ON

Verbs that show exhaustion, criticism, self-sacrifice, repetition, mental stagnation, pretense, hinting, soothing, sympathizing, indecision, etc. How you can increase your vocabulary by picking your friends' brains.

ORIGIN

☻ more than fatigue

When you are enervated, you feel as if your nerves have been ripped out—or so the etymology of the word indicates.

Enervate is derived from e-(ex-), out, and Latin nervus, nerve. Enervation (en´-ər-VAY´-shən) is not just fatigue, but complete devitalization—physical, emotional, mental—as if every ounce of the life force has been sapped out, as if the last particle of energy has been drained away.

Despite its similar appearance to the word energy, enervation is almost a direct antonym. Energy is derived from the Greek prefix en-, in, plus the root ergon, work; erg is the term used in physics for a unit of work or energy. Synergism(SIN´-ər-jiz-əm)—the prefix syn-, together or with, plus ergon—is the process by which two more substances or drugs, by working together, produce a greater effect in combination than the sun total of their individual effects.

Alcohol, for example, is a depressant. So are barbiturates and other soporifics. Alcohol and barbiturates work synergistically(sin´-ər-JIS´-tik´-lee)—the effect of each is increased by the other if the two are taken together.

So if you're drinking, don't take a sleeping pill—or if you must take a pill for your insomnia, don't drink—the combination, if not lethal, will do more to you than you may want done!

Synergy(SIN´-ər-jee), by the way, is an alternate form of synergism.

☻ verbal punishment

Castigate is derived from a Latin verb meaning to punish; in present-day usage, the verb generally refers to verbal punishment, usually harsh and severe. It is somewhat synonymous with scold, criticize, rebuke, censure, reprimand, or berate, but much stronger than any of these—rail at, rant at, slash at, lash out at, or tongue-lash is a much closer synonym. When candidates for office castigate their opponents, they do not mince words.

Can you construct the noun form of castigate? _____.

☻ saying "NO!" to oneself

Abnegate is derived from Latin ab-, away (as in absent), plus nego, to deny—self-abnegation(ab´-nə-GAY´-shən), then, is self-denial. Nego itself is a contraction of Latin neg-, not, no, and aio, I say; to be self-abnegating is to say "NO!" to what you want, as if some inner censor were at work whispering, "No, you can't have that, you can't do that, you don't deserve that, you're not good enough for that. . ."

To negate(nə-GAYT´) is to deny the truth or existence of, as in "The atheist negates God"; or, by extension, to destroy by working against, as in, "His indulgence in expensive hobbies negates all his wife's attempts to keep the family solvent." Can you writhe the noun form of the verb ne gate? _____.

Negative and negativity obviously spring from the same source as negate.

☻ heads and headings

Latin caput, capitis means head. The captain is the head of any group; the capital is the "head city" of a state or nation; and to decapitate(dee-KAP'-ə-tayt') is to chop off someone's head, a popular activity during the French Revolution after the guillotine was invented. Write the noun form of decapitate: _____.

Latin capitulum is a little head, or, by extension, the heading, or title, of a chapter. So when you recapitulate, you go through the chapter headings again(re-), etymologically speaking, or you summarize or review the main points.

Remembering how the noun and adjective forms are derived from adulate, can you write the required forms of recapitulate?

Noun: _____

Adjective: _____

When you capitulate(kə-PICH'-ə-layt'), etymologically you arrange in headings, or, as the meaning of the verb naturally evolved, you arrange conditions of surrender, as when an army capitulates to the enemy forces under prearranged conditions; or, by further natural extension, you stop resisting and give up, as in, "He realized there was no longer any point in resisting her advances, so he reluctantly capitulated." Can you write the noun form of capitulate? _____.

☻ mere vegetables

Vegetable is from Latin vegeto, to live and grow, which is what vegetables do—but that's all they do, so to vegetate, is, by implication, to do no more than stay alive, stuck in a rut, leading an inactive, unstimulating, emotionally and intellectually stagnant existence. Vegetation(veg'-ə-TAY'-shən) is and dull, passive, stagnant existence; also any plant life, as the thick vegetation of a jungle.

ORIGIN

🙂 not the real McCoy

Simulate is from Latin simulo, to copy; and simulo itself derives from the Latin adjectives similis, like or similar.

Simulation(sim´-yə-LAY´-shən), then, is copying the real thing, pretending to be the genuine article by taking on a similar appearance. The simulation of joy is quite a feat when you really feel depressed.

Genuine pearls grow inside oysters; simulated pearls are synthetic, but look like the ones from oysters. (Rub a pearl against your teeth to teel the difference—the natural pearl feels gritty.) So the frequent advertisement of an inexpensive necklace made of "genuine simulated pearls" can fool you if you don't know the word—you're being offered a genuine fake.

Dissimulation(də-sim´-yə-LAY´-shən) is something else! When you dissimulate(də-SIM´-yə-layt´), you hide your true feelings by making a pretense of opposite feelings. (Then again, maybe it's not something completely else!)

Sycophants are great dissimulators—they may feel contempt, but show admiration; they may feel negative, but express absolutely positive agreement.

A close synonym of dissimulate is dissemble(də-SEM´-bəl), which also is to hide true feelings by pretending the opposite; or additionally, to conceal facts, or one's true intentions, by deception; or, still further additionally, to pretend ignorance of facts you'd rather not admit, when, indeed, you're fully aware of them.

The noun is dissemblance(də-SEM´-bləns).

In dissimulate and dissemble, the negative prefix dis- acts largely to make both words pejorative.

● hints and helps

The verb intimate is from Latin intimus, innermost, the same root from which the adjective intimate(IN´-tə-mət) and its noun intimacy(IN´-tə-mə-see) are derived; but the relationship is only in etymology, not in meaning. An intimation(in´-tə-MAY´-shən) contains a significance buried deep in the innermost core, only a hint showing. As you grow older, you begin to have intimations that you are mortal; when someone aims a .45 at you, or when a truck comes roaring down at you as you drive absent-mindedly against a red light through an intersection, you are suddenly very sure that you are mortal.

Alleviate is a combination of Latin levis, light (not heavy), the prefix ad-, to, and the verb suffix. (Ad- changes to al- before a root starting with l-.)

If something alleviates your pain, it makes your pain lighter for you; if I alleviate your sadness, I make it lighter to bear; and if you need some alleviation(ə-lee´-vee-AY´-shən) of your problems, you need them made lighter and less burdensome. To alleviate is to relieve only temporarily, not to cure or do away with. (Relieve is also from levis, plus re-, again—to make light or easy again.) The adjective form of alleviate is alleviative(ə-LEE´-vee-ay´-tiv)—aspirin is an alleviative drug.

Anything light will rise—so from the prefix e-(ex-), out, plus levis, we can construct the verb elevate, etymologically, to raise out, or, actually, raise up, as to elevate one's spirits, raise them up, make them lighter; or elevate someone to a higher position, which is what an elevator does.

Have you ever seen a performance of magic in which a person or an object apparently rises in the air as if floating? That's levitation (lev′-ə-TAY′-shən)—rising through no visible means. (I've watched it a dozen times and never could figure it out!) The verb, to so rise, is levitate (LEV′-ə-tayt′).

And how about levity(LEV′-ə-tee)? That's lightness too, but of a different sort—lightness in the sense of frivolity, flippancy, joking, or lack of seriousness, especially when solemnity, dignity, or formality is required or more appropriate, as in "tones of levity," or as in, "Levity is out of place at a funeral, in a house of worship, at the swearing-in ceremonies of a President or Supreme Court Justice," or as in, "Okay, enough levity—now let's get down to business!"

⊕ sharing someone's misery

Latin mister, wretched, the prefix con- (which, as you know, becomes com- before a root beginning with m-), together or with, and the verb suffix -ate are the building blocks from which commiserate is constructed. "I commiserate with you," then, means, "I am wretched together with you—I share your misery." The noun form? _____.

Miser, miserly, miserable, misery all come from the same root.

⊕ swing and sway

Vacillate—note the single c, double l—derives from Latin vacillo, to swing back and forth. The noun form? _____.

People who swing back and forth in indecision, who are irresolute, who can, unfortunately, see both, or even three or four, sides of every question, and so have difficulty making up their minds, are vacillatory(VAS´-ə-lə-t awr´-ee). They are also, usually, ambivalent(am-BIV´-ə-lənt)—they have conflicting and simultaneous emotions about the same person or thing; or they want to go but they also want to stay; or they love something, but they hate it too. The noun is ambivalence(am-BIV´-ə-ləns)—from ambi both.

Ambivalence has best been defined (perhaps by Henny Youngman—if he didn't say it first, he should have) as watching your mother-in-law drive over a cliff in your new Cadillac.

To vacillate is to swing mentally or emotionally. To sway back and forth physically is oscillate—again note the double l—(OS´-ə-layt´), from Latin oscillum, a swing. A pendulum oscillates, the arm of a metronome oscillates, and people who's had much too much to drink oscillate when they try to walk. The noun? _____.

ADVICE

PICKING YOUR FRIENDS' BRAINS

You can build your vocabulary, I have said, by increasing your familiarity with new ideas and by becoming alert to the new words you meet in your reading of magazines and books.

There is still another productive method, one that will be particularly applicable in view of all the new words you are learning from your study of these pages.

That method is picking your friends' brains.

Intelligent people are interested in words because words are symbols of ideas, and the person with an alert mind is always interested in ideas.

You may be amazed, if you have never tried it, to find that you can stir up an animated discussion by asking, in a social group that you attend, "What does _____ mean?" (Use any word that particularly fascinates you.) Someone in the group is likely to know, and almost everyone will be willing to make a guess. From the point on, others in the group will ask questions about their own favorite words (most people do have favorites), or about words that they themselves have in some manner recently learned. As the discussion continues along these lines, you will be introduced to new words yourself, and if your friends have fairly good vocabularies you may strike a rich vein of pay dirt and come away with a large number of words to add to your vocabulary.

This method of picking your friends' brains is particularly fruitful because you will be learning not from a page of print (as in this book or as in your other reading) but from real live persons—the same sources that children use to increase their vocabularies at such prodigious rates. No learning is quite as effective as the learning that comes from other people—no information in print can ever be as vivid as information that comes from another human being. And so the words you pick up from you friends will have an amazingly strong appeal, will make a lasting impression on your mind.

Needless to say, your own rich vocabulary, now that you have come this far in the book, will make it possible for you to contribute to your friends' vocabulary as much as, if not more than, you take away—but since giving to others is one of the greatest sources of a feeling of self-worth, you can hardly complain about this extra dividend.